MW01600716

THE
DEVIL
WE KNOW

MERCYANN SUMMERS

Copyright © 2024 by MercyAnn Summers

All rights reserved. No part of this publication may be reproduced, distributed, or transmitted in any form or by any means, including photocopying, recording, or other electronic or mechanical methods, without the prior written permission of the publisher, except as permitted by U.S. copyright law. For permission requests, contact MercyAnnSummersAuthor@gmail.com

Without limiting the author's exclusive rights, any unauthorized use of this publication to train generative artificial intelligence (AI) technologies is expressly prohibited.

The story, all names, characters, and incidents portrayed in this production are fictitious. No identification with actual persons (living or deceased), places, buildings, and products is intended or should be inferred.

Image: © WANDER AGUIAR PHOTOGRAPHY

Model: Travis S.

Cover Designer: Jay Aheer, @ Simply Defined Art

Edited by: Kirsty McQuarrie, @ Let's Get Proofed

Formatted by: Kayla L. PA, aka Kayreereads

(Updated 8-23-25) Dear Reader:

Welcome to Book 4 of the Ends World.

While The Devil We Know (TDWK) is considered an interconnected standalone within the Ends World, there is an underlying story line that weaves its way from the Ends Duet through A Fine Line to this book. As a pantser I literally had no idea until I got to the end of the series, hence this unsolicited update.

Jessica, the FMC in TDWK, is first introduced in Declan (my golden retriever stalker rock star). You will find her initial POV of chapter one of this book in chapter 26 of Declan.

TDWK is classified as romantic suspense with dark themes and...tons of jokes. Still me showing up with all the jokes. And yes, I remain unapologetically not funny. And just for good measure I added a new song to this one. You're quite welcome.

If you have no triggers and have zero issues reading any kind of questionable content, please skip ahead to the prologue to not risk any type of spoilers. Even if you are seldom triggered, please read this note in its entirety, and make a conscious decision on whether this book will be a good choice for you. Your mental health is important. Always choose wisely for your own personal well-being.

TW/CW: Mafia, death of loved one, death of parent, choking, mentions of sexual assault, submissive play, depression, grief, kidnapping, pregnancy of minor (not FMC), attempted rape (not between FMC/MMC), forced exhibitionism, organized crime, vigilante fuckery and more naughty words and graphic depictions of sexual acts and violence than I would care to count. (706 fucks, 44 cocks, 40 dicks, 21 pussies, and just for good measure, 7 cunts). **This book is not suitable for persons under the age of 18.**

Thank you for reading. It's fuck around time.

—Mercy

A therapist's take on the unhinged and healing world of MercyAnn Summers...

When you love your fictional men murdery with a tsunami of spice...

Welcome to The Devil We Know. Relax, you're home.

When you want to throw back double shots of chaotic mayhem and wake up without the hangover, keep reading.

When you want to sip on this tall glass of flirty goodness with that splash of twisty, wholesome mischief on the side, drink up.

When you want to submerge yourself in the healing waters of BIG LOVE, friendship, and found family, keep reading.

When you want to deep dive into what it means to love, how to survive in the craziest of circumstances while grappling with grief and loss... only to suddenly be washed ashore refreshed and healed in unexpected ways, keep reading.

When you want to snuggle up and feel something beautiful and real, keep reading. The Devil We Know is a wild and epic love story that is infused with redemption, healing and laughter that we all need more of in our books and in our lives.

Keep reading.

M. Losinski, LCSW

To the suffering. The haunted.
The rejected. The betrayed.
I see you.
Take my hand.

1

The Aftermath

Matt

SIX MONTHS AGO

When I first arrived at Declan's estate to find it empty, I was somewhat relieved. I don't have time to decompress very often, so I was going to take the reprieve for what it was; a gift.

That is until I saw his phone light up on the table.

Answer Me.

I blink at the screen a couple of times, then shrug, scooping it up and accepting the call before putting the phone to my ear. "Who is this?"

"Declan?" a feminine voice whispers, and I frown, momentarily startled that Declan's "Answer Me" is female.

After a moment, I reply, "No, this isn't Declan. His phone is here, but he must have stepped out because no one was home when I got here."

She curses, annoyance in her voice as she replies, "Oh. Sorry to have bothered you."

"Wait," I interject hurriedly. "Why are you calling Declan?"

"N-n-no reason," she stutters. "I'll try again."

"Maybe I can help?"

"Who are you?" she asks hesitantly.

"Mathias Shields," I answer. "But you can call me Matt. I'm a good friend of Declan's."

She falls quiet, and I wait patiently, straining for some indication that she hasn't disconnected the call. Then I say, "Hello? Are you still there?"

"Y-yes," she stutters again, then clears her throat and adds, "I'm here."

"Are you in trouble?"

She laughs, the sound coming off slightly crazy. "I'll take that as a yes."

She says nothing, and after a few minutes, I add, "Tell me where you are."

She rattles off an address, and then I hear the distinctive chatter of her teeth indicating she's shivering.

"I'm going to stay on the phone with you," I say clearly. "What's your name?"

"Jessica," she whispers, as I put the call on speaker, exiting Declan's house and making my way to my rental car. I get behind the wheel, starting the ignition and switching the call to Bluetooth. "Okay, Jessica. Are you in immediate danger?"

"No."

"Good," I respond evenly. "That's good. Do you have a sofa or a comfortable chair nearby?"

"Yes."

"Great, that's perfect," I reply, maneuvering the car onto the free-way and flooring it. "First, I need you to find a blanket, and then I need you to wrap yourself in the it and curl up on the sofa or in the chair, facing the back of it. Can you do that for me, Jessica?"

"Yes," she says through her chattering teeth.

"Are you able to bring this phone with you?"

"No, but there's another phone beside the sofa."

"Do you need to disconnect this call and call again from the other phone?"

"No. I'll put you on hold and then pick the call back up."

"Okay," I respond calmly, doing my best to keep my tone level. "You do that now. Put this call on hold, then focus on the steps I gave you. I'll be right here waiting. Are you ready?"

"Yes."

"Good," I whisper. "Then, go."

The call cuts to silence, and I wait patiently, keeping an eye on the road and the clock as time seems to drag on. What feels like hours later, the line clicks and I hear her shivering breaths on the other line.

"I'll be there soon," I whisper.

She makes an affirmative noise but says nothing, and by the time I make it to her office, she's borderline unresponsive, the shock taking its toll on her.

She manages to give me access to the building, and from where she falls short, I manage to get myself access to the floor her office is on.

I walk into her office to find her lying on the sofa just as instruct-ed, a bloody, motionless body a few short feet away from her. She's curled inward, appearing small beneath the large blanket she wrapped around herself, her hair gleaming a burnt copper even in the dim light.

At first, she doesn't move or acknowledge I'd entered the room but then after a beat, her upper body twists, bright green eyes locking with mine, as a choked sob falls from her lips.

I raise my hands in front of me, my voice calm and even as I say, "It's me. It's Matt."

She flinches ever-so-slightly, the corner of her eyes wrinkling minutely as she squints. Her lips then press together tightly, and she swallows slowly.

She says nothing, so I slowly move closer until I'm standing next to her, and then I kneel in front of her. "Are you okay?"

At first, she stares at me, then frowns and shakes her head. I nod in acknowledgment of what she's not saying and then reply, "You stay here. I'll be right back."

Not waiting for a response, I rise and walk over to the obviously dead body, pulling out my phone and texting my clean-up crew. Their reply is instantaneous, confirming the vague orders and the quick turnaround for completion.

I retrieve the man's phone, wallet, and other personal effects, securing them in the inside pocket of my jacket to be disposed of secondary to the body.

If I had more time, I'd remove his head and hands, but since I'm leaving the disposal of the body to a third party, I'll just have to let them do whatever they think is best.

I walk back across the room to where Jessica is still lying on the sofa, kneeling in front of her and catching her eyes as I say, "We need to get out of here."

She blinks at me a few times and opens her mouth to speak, but nothing comes out. I pull the blanket off of her, wadding it into a ball and tossing it over onto the body.

Grasping both of her hands in mine, I grimace at the blood stains on them. I grab a bottle of water from the table next to the sofa, snagging the small bar towel, pouring the cool liquid onto it before turning back to her. I gently pick up one of her hands, resting it on the wet towel and dribbling water from the bottle onto her palm.

She doesn't move, doesn't even blink; she just lies there, staring off into the void as I work methodically to rid her of as much blood spatter as I can. When I'm satisfied she's as clean as she's going to get, I toss the bottle of water and soiled towel toward the body, knowing the cleanup crew will take care of it.

I kneel in front of her again, grasping her hands and giving a little tug, but she doesn't move. She just stares at me with a decidedly pained expression on her face and then she shivers.

I move my hands up to her forearms, pulling on her firmly to urge her into an upright position, and eventually, she manages to sit up on her own.

"I'm going to remove your top," I whisper. "There's blood on it."

She nods, and I remove my jacket, unbuttoning the necessary buttons on my dress shirt and then pulling that and my undershirt over my head. I put my button-down and jacket back on and then quickly unbutton her blouse, helping her free her arms, then tossing it away.

I pull my undershirt over her head, and she manages to push her arms through the sleeves as I pull it down her torso. She just sits there stonily, but when she blinks at me, she appears to focus a bit more. Then she says, "I want to go home."

"Good," I reply softly. "Can you tell me where that is?"

She blinks a few more times and swallows before she gasps out, "Yes."

"Can you walk?"

She's trembling, and I know we're on borrowed time before the shock wipes her out completely, so I pull out my phone, open the GPS app, and hand it to her. "Put in your address."

She takes it from me with shaking hands. It takes her a few attempts before she's happy with the coordinates that pop up, then she hands it back to me.

Still, she says nothing, so I stoop down, wrapping my arms around her upper body and pulling her to her feet. She comes willingly, though the tension in her body is evident. I drop my head and whisper near her ear, "I'm going to need you to walk. I'll wipe the cameras, but just in case I miss one and it shows me carrying you out of here, people might ask questions."

She leans into me suddenly, her face pressed into my neck, as a deep, guttural sob wrenches from deep inside her chest. I tighten my arms around her, pulling her in for a moment until she lets out a shuddering exhalation, and then I release her, my arms moving to her biceps as I step back and look into her face. "It's okay. I've got you."

She nods and then steps back, straightening to her full height. I turn to walk out the door, reaching back with my hand, which she takes in both of hers. I lead her from the room and down the hall, grateful the elevator is still there.

As I step onto the elevator, I watch her facial expressions in the mirror, noting how calm she appears on the outside. It only takes us a few minutes to reach my car. I help her into the passenger side, shutting the door and going around to get behind the wheel.

Luckily, she's only a short drive from the office. Thankfully, when we arrive, she tells me where to park.

I shut off the ignition, exit the vehicle, and walk around to the passenger door, but when I open it, she doesn't even look at me. She's staring at the dash, visibly shaking and teeth chattering, so I stoop down, gather her up into my arms, and ease her out of the car. I heft her up, swinging around and using my ass to shut the door, and then

I ask, "I'm a little late asking you this, but do you have your keys?"

She continues to shake as she rests her head against my shoulder and whispers, "Don't need them."

I frown, heading toward the entrance to the building. "What do you mean? How are you going to get in?"

She laughs, short and bitter, as she mutters, "I'm the key."

It takes me a moment to understand what she's referring to, and then I laugh to myself as I recall Declan asking me to set up security at an apartment downtown. I'm sure she doesn't know that that's how it came about—not the owners of the building—but I suppose I'll keep his cover for now.

But this also means I could easily gain access to her apartment.

"What number?"

She doesn't answer, and as I approach the doors, the doorman comes out and nods to me, so I turn so he can see who I'm carrying as I say, "I'm afraid she's fallen ill while we were out. Are you able to let us up?"

He steps in close so he can get a look at her face and then asks, "Are you okay, Jessica?"

She peeks an eye open, the corner of her lips turning up slightly as she nods.

The man steps back, opening the door and motioning for me to enter, and then I follow him through the lobby to the set of elevators. The elevator doors open, and he motions for me to enter first. As I turn to face the doors again, he reaches in and presses number ten, looks at me, and says, "There's only two apartments up there. She's apartment A. If you have any problems getting in, buzz me."

"Thank you," I respond politely. It isn't that I'm not grateful for the assistance; I was just leery of any witnesses surrounding criminal deeds.

Not wanting to put her down, it takes some maneuvering to get us into her apartment.

I close the door behind us, jostling her to get her attention as I ask, "Where's your bedroom?"

"End of the hall," she replies.

I walk in the direction she indicated, the door at the end of the hallway being open. I enter the room, heading directly to the bed and setting her down on it gently. "I'll be right back."

I walk back down the hallway, quickly locating the kitchen, where I grab a bottle of juice and a bottle of water from the refrigerator. Returning to the bedroom, I find she hasn't moved at all, so I set the two bottles on the nightstand and then adjust her on the bed, so her head's on the pillow.

Though I managed to remove a lot of the blood from her previously, I know if she wakes up to any evidence of what happened, it could set her back.

So, I remove her shoes, walk into the ensuite bathroom, and turn on the shower.

Back in the bedroom, I see she still hasn't moved, so I walk over to her, putting an arm beneath her and forcing her to sit up. She still looks somewhat vacant, although some of the color is back in her cheeks.

"You need to get cleaned up." She nods but says nothing, so I ask, "Do you think you can do it?"

At first, she nods again and then moves like she's going to stand but immediately gives up on the idea. Then she shakes her head and whispers, "No. I don't think I can."

"Do you want me to help you?"

She frowns, uncertainty clear in her eyes, and then shrugs. Understanding that there's no way she's going to manage even the quickest shower on her own, I sigh in resignation.

Not that I'm at all opposed to showering with a woman, but the current circumstances are less than ideal, and I have to be careful not to do anything that might panic her.

I lean down, pressing both my palms into the mattress on either side of her so my face is level with hers as I say, "I'll help you, Jess. You just need to focus on remaining calm, and remember I won't do anything to hurt you."

She searches my eyes momentarily, her lips pressing together again. Finally, she nods, so I straighten, pulling my jacket off and tossing it in the chair that's beside the nightstand. I strip down methodically until I'm standing there in my underwear, and I chuckle internally at the fact that she's not even looking at me. I don't want to sound egotistical, but that is a sure indication that she is completely fucked in the head right now.

Walking back over to her, I quickly remove my shirt and then help her stand. Her arms on my shoulders are heavy as I pull her pants over her hips and down her legs, where they pool on the floor. She steps out of them and stands before me in her bra and underwear. I was going to leave her undergarments on, but I can see where blood had soaked through her shirt and stained the lace of her bra, so I pull back and ask, "Do you want to leave it on?"

She gives me a questioning look and then glances down at the front of herself, her frown deepening as she shakes her head erratically. Her hands leave my shoulders, and she jumps back, clawing at the fabric in an attempt to be rid of it.

I reach for her, intent on helping her, but she slaps me away, her hands frantic as she manages to unhook the bra and yank it free, throwing it away. She looks down at her underwear, frantic again as she struggles to push them down. After a couple of failed attempts, she manages to coordinate herself enough to push them down to her ankles, where she steps out of them, kicking them away.

Her earlier vacant expression is gone, her eyes burning now with anger and disgust. Her chest heaves, and I do my damndest not to focus on her breasts and hard nipples.

She stares at me, unflinching, as she lifts her chin at me almost defiantly. I keep my eyes locked with hers as I ask, "Do you think you can do it now?"

She deflates a little bit, then she glances around the room as if she forgot where we are. She looks down at her nude body, her hands coming up to cover her chest, but then she looks down further, and one arm drops down in front of her, and the other one crosses over her breasts as she groans, "I'm sorry."

I chuckle, shaking my head as I reply, "No reason to be sorry, but you're going to have to tell me what you need me to do."

She stares at me, contemplating the question before answering, "It's probably safer if you help me. If you don't mind."

"Don't worry about me, Jess" I respond. "I'm here to help you. Anything you need, all you have to do is ask."

Indecision crosses her features again, quickly replaced by sadness, and then she says quietly, "Just help me. I don't even know what that means, but please help me."

I do have an idea of what she means. Having grown up in less-than-desirable circumstances, I certainly didn't take my first kill to heart, but that doesn't mean it didn't bother me.

Even killing in self-defense. It's all the same torment.

I say nothing further, instead extending my hand to her which she takes it without hesitation. Turning, I lead her to the bathroom, walking directly to the running shower and opening the door, motioning for her to enter. I step in behind her, close the door then turn back to find her standing on the edge, just outside of the spray of the water. I smile, urging her under the warm spray with my hands on her upper arms.

She stands there motionless and emotionless, water pouring down on her as she stares at the ground, her hands now grasped in front of her.

I turn her until the spray of the water hits her in the chest, so she has to tilt her head back to avoid getting hit in the face. For some reason, I prefer her looking at the ceiling than the ground, and I laugh to myself at the lack of sense it makes.

I stand just outside of the spray of the water, trying to give her some space to get her bearings. Her eyes close, then her hand comes up, fingers outstretched, reaching. Every nerve ending in my body tells me to ignore it, to step back where she can't touch me, but I don't. Instead, I extend my hand and grasp hers, allowing her to pull me closer.

I stand there with the front of my body pressed into her side, and her lips twitch, the corners turning up slightly. If nothing else, I'm glad that the natural instincts of my body has worked to at least cut some of the tension in the air.

I press my hips forward, bumping her side with the obvious erection in my underwear, and she giggles. I shake my head as I say, "Don't judge me. Dicks don't have brains."

She giggles again, one of her hands coming up and covering her mouth as she attempts not to laugh, and I add, "Go ahead and laugh. Dicks don't get offended."

She drops her hand and gives up all semblance of not being amused by the betrayal of my own body. Then, she parrots, "Dicks don't have brains."

Now, I laugh as I reply, "It really is that simple. Some men like to pretend that it's not, but they're also usually fucking stupid."

She laughs for a moment longer and then sighs, some of the tension leaves her body, but I can sense she's still on edge, hovering over the precipice of being fine and complete lunacy.

"Hand me that washcloth," I say evenly. "And whatever soap you want to use."

She does as I ask without comment, handing them both to me and then standing there, waiting.

I soap up the washcloth and hand her back the bar of soap that she puts back on the shelf, and then I step back and turn her so she's facing me. "Put your head back into the water, we'll wash your hair next."

Again, she does what I ask without comment, and I slide the washcloth along her neck, down around one shoulder, and back across the top of her chest to the other shoulder, swooping back down, quickly washing across her breasts and circling down around beneath them. I follow this path, over and down, over and down, until I have to kneel to wash her legs.

I slide the washcloth along her outer thigh, behind her knee, along her calf, and then start my way back up the inside. At mid-thigh, her breath catches, and I stop, intent on going to the other leg and doing the same path, but her voice stops me. "Don't stop."

I freeze with the washcloth pressed against her inner thigh. I look up and see her watching me. My eyes meet hers, and she says louder, "Please don't stop."

I give her an assessing look, unsure how to proceed, given the trauma she has suffered and what she is asking me. I don't get the impression Jessica is the type of woman who jumps into bed with a man without proper consideration, and the last thing I want to do is cause her more harm, even if I'm only doing what she's asking.

I ignore her request, moving the washcloth to the outside of her other leg and following the same path down, around, and back up, where once again, I pause at the inside of her thigh. She adjusts her stance, giving me better access as she says more firmly, "Fucking Christ, don't stop."

I clench my jaw, my cock throbbing at the sound of her voice making demands of me, but again, I ignore her request, rising to my feet and turning her so she's facing the spray of the water.

The tension rolls off of her and I see that she's starting to tremble, though I have no idea if it's from shock, hunger, or anger.

I grab the soap off the shelf, sudsing up the cloth and then putting the soap back again.

This time, I use the same cross-wards sweeping motions down her back, kneeling and doing the backs of her legs before wiping the slick cloth along her ass cheeks. She pushes her ass back against me, agitation evident in her voice as she croaks, "Please, Matt. Please."

I grit my teeth again, reaching in front of her and rinsing the cloth off before squeezing the excess water out of it and hanging it on the bar.

I grab the shampoo, dump some in my hand, put the bottle back, and quickly work it into her scalp as she leans her head back, moaning softly at the press of my fingers.

I move around her, turning her so I'm still behind her. I help her rinse the soap out of her hair, turn the water off, and walk back in front of her, intent on finding a towel, and that's when I see it's not just water on her face but also tears.

I stop, my hand extended to the shower door as a sob breaks free, and I reach for her just as she falls forward, collapsing into me.

I wrap my arms around her, one hand pressing into her back, the other coming up to tangle in the hair at the back of her head as I whisper, "It's okay. Just let it out."

She stiffens in my embrace, her hands coming between us as she pushes against my chest almost violently, and I stumble backward. Her eyes are wild as she screams, "Give me what I want."

My heart gallops in my chest, stupidly caught off-guard by the volatility of her emotions, even knowing that this is the stuff that will happen.

I keep some distance between us, bringing my hands up so she'll know I'll hold my ground for as long as she needs me to, and I say, "You're okay, Jess. I'm still right here."

She launches herself at me, knocking me backward into the wall, and she comes with me. I all but have the wind knocked out of me by the force, and then her fists are connecting with my chest as she's shouting, "Please. Just do it. Make me forget. Take it away. Please."

I barely manage to grasp hold of both of her wrists to put a stop to her assault on me. I manage to take her feet out from under her, and then we slide to the floor, my body taking the brunt of the fall. I get my legs around her lower body, one arm wrapping around her front, pinning her forearms so she can no longer flail at me. But now, she's crying—more like sobbing, gasping, begging—and that dark part of me wants to give in.

I push it down, refusing to take the excuse, refusing that lifelong calling to cause harm to a person who clearly does not deserve it.

We sit there, long minutes going by, as she continues her anguished crying. I ignore her begging words until finally, she calms enough that I say, "It's okay. I'm still here. I'm not going anywhere."

After a few more moments, she manages a shuddering inhalation and a steadier exhalation, and then she quiets and whispers, "Why won't you just give me what I want?"

I hesitate to answer, and then she must take my hesitation as a cue because she starts to squirm. I tightened my hold on her and then respond, "I can't. Not after all you've been through."

She chokes out a bitter laugh and struggles as she says, "It's okay. I get how it wouldn't be an appealing idea."

Now, I laugh bitterly as I spit out, "Seriously?"

I push my hard dick against her, where she's sitting in my lap, and then add, "I don't think not being interested is the problem."

She presses back against me, and I repress the moan that builds in my throat at the pressure and friction.

Ignoring her teasing, I manage to get my feet beneath me and use the leverage against the wall to bring us both to our feet. I step away from her, moving over to open the shower door, where I reach out and grab two towels that are hanging there.

Wrapping one around my waist, I then motion for her to step out of the shower. She's standing there, glaring at me, so I glare back and grab a second towel, stepping into her. I lean in close so my nose is only an inch from hers, our eyes locked as I say clearly, "You, listen to me. Obviously, I'd like nothing more than to fuck the shit out of you right now, but given everything you've just been through, I'm not going to do that."

She glares daggers as she retorts, "You know, I think I've heard stories about you."

I raise a brow at her and say blandly, "Oh, yeah?"

The corner of her lip turns up as she sneers, "Yep. Always the fucking boy scout."

My fucking blood boils in my veins, and my hands fist in the towel, my urge to throttle her skyrocketing. It takes every ounce of self-control in my body to refrain from bending her over my knee and slapping her ass.

I lean in a little closer, sure my breath is painting her lips as I say, "Don't be getting any grand ideas that I'm a fucking boy scout, a gentleman, or even a good man. At some point, you're going to find out exactly how fucking false that is, but that day isn't going to be today."

She jerks back as if slapped, her mouth snapping shut, and so I add, "I'll make a deal with you."

I pause, my eyes searching hers until she finally nods and asks, "What kind of deal?"

I step back, moving around behind her and using the extra towel I'd grabbed to dry her hair. I lean in so I'm speaking right near her ear, "Let's get you taken care of tonight. Calmed down to the point where you're no longer volatile, where you can think objectively and process what has happened. And after that, if you still feel this urge to find pleasure, then we'll take care of it."

She twists her body, so she's looking me in the face, and she says, "Really?"

I nod, my eyes locked with hers. "Yes, but there's a catch."

She frowns. "And what might that be?"

"That you take what you want from me."

Her frown deepens and she steps back abruptly as she says, "What do you mean?"

I close the distance between us again, forcing her to look at me as I reply, "You can use me for anything you want. But you're not in any condition for me to be taking anything from you."

Her breath catches, and then she shudders, her eyes squeezing shut, and I use this moment of silence to finish drying her hair.

I move to walk toward her closet. Her hand on my arm stops me, and I turn back, and she answers clearly, "You have a deal."

I nod in acknowledgment and continue toward the closet.

But then I hear her whispered words behind me.

"Thank you."

2

Taking Control

Jessica

I WAKE IN STAGES, my eyes blinking into the darkness as I try to pinpoint what woke me.

The eery silence echoes gently. I stretch my legs out, my hands reaching forward as I realign myself, then tuck my hands in and roll toward the center of the bed. Only to stop mid-roll, a gasp of surprise caught in my throat to find that I'm not alone.

He stayed.

I swallow the sudden lump in my throat, my heart pounding in my chest as the events of the past twelve hours flood back.

Bobby attacking me.

Bobby is dead.

The wrong man answered the phone of the person I called for help.

The wrong man turned out to be the right man.

He is now lying on his back, his head turned slightly toward me. I take a moment to look at him, this man I barely know but who already knows more about me than people I've known for decades.

His sandy blond hair gleams in the dim light. Long overdue for a trim, the silky-looking locks fall onto his forehead, accentuating the fall of his lashes on his cheeks as he sleeps. High cheekbones, full lips, and a strong neck, my eyes scan down his body until my view is disrupted by the sheet covering him from his midsection down.

He's kind of hot in a boring Midwest kind of way.

Sighing, I adjust my position on the mattress so I'm turned to face him, my bottom leg bent at the knee to keep me from rolling into him completely.

He sighs, his hand closest to me slowly moving until it settles on my bent leg, his hand warm on the skin of my inner thigh.

Emotion builds in my chest with such sudden ferocity that it barrels up my throat and out of my mouth before I have a chance to temper it. The sob is violent and guttural, and I choke as I roll onto my back, fully intent on rolling to the floor to make an escape.

A hand on my shoulder stops me, and I look over just as Matt sits up. His hands hook in my armpits, and then he's lying back in his original position, using his momentum to yank me over on top of him.

I struggle halfheartedly, and he wraps his arms around my torso, trapping my arms to my sides and pulling me into him so my breasts are pressed firmly against his chest.

He holds me steady, waiting patiently for me to stop fighting, and once I do, he lifts his head, forcing me to meet his eyes as he whispers, "I've got you, Jess."

Another sob breaks free, but this one is quieter and more controlled. Slowly, I allow my body to relax until I'm lying limply on top of him, my face pressed into his neck.

Shivering, I work to control my breathing, taking deep inhalations followed by slow shuddering exhalations until, finally, my heart rate slows, and the only sound in the room is our mingled breathing and that eery silence.

Shivering again, I burrow closer, and he sits up slightly, jostling me around as he reaches down and yanks the sheet free from where it was stuck, pulling it over us.

Matt settles back down, his arms around me firm and comforting, and I squirm, my legs bracketing him snugly as I get as close as possible to him.

And that's when I realize I'm naked.

Naked and straddling the hips of an obviously interested man.

An obviously interested man, who is also obviously naked.

I giggle, watery as it may be, and he shakes his head as he mutters, "Ignore that. It doesn't mean anything."

I giggle again and then reply against his neck, "So, you're saying it doesn't mean your dick is happy to see me?"

Chuckling, he replies quietly, "Well, no. But he's not the boss, so ignoring it is always an option. He'll live."

I lie there for a few long moments, enjoying the easy silence, but then I whimper, frustration quickly building inside me as I struggle to manage the quietness I seek.

Matt's hands move to my upper arms, then to my shoulders, and he pushes me gently until I sit up. His eyes remain on mine, even as his hands glide across my collarbone, down my arms, finally settling on my hips. "What is it? What do you need?"

I shake my head, my words stuck in my throat as I attempt to answer and fail. He waits patiently and then adds, "You can tell me. It's okay."

"Please," I manage to whisper brokenly. "Please help me forget."

He smiles softly, his gaze warm as his hands gently stroke my hips. "Take what you need, sugar. Take it all."

I frown, unsure how I'm supposed to know what I need, but then he presses his hips up, and the slide of his dick against my slippery pussy awakens a new kind of tension.

White-hot arousal.

Rocking my hips, I slide my cunt along his hard length, enjoying the contrast of hard and slippery against my aching clit. He remains passive beneath me, watching me calmly as I try to decide how much I want to take from him.

How much I'm willing to give of myself in the process.

Matt moans softly, lying completely still on the mattress, but heat burns in his eyes as his gaze flits from my face to my breasts to the spot where I'm rubbing against him shamelessly.

I stroke my hands down his chest, fluttering over his toned stomach as I say, "Touch me. Put your hands on me."

Without hesitation, his hands tighten on my hips, his touch a tad less gentle, his eyes on mine questioning, and I slowly raise my hands, gliding my fingers up my stomach to my breasts. He's watching me, his eyes now intent on my breasts, and I cup them, my fingers playing with my nipples as I rub my clit against his cock.

His groan is guttural, his tongue peeking out and wetting his lips. I lean forward, my hands pressed into the mattress on both sides of his head, and put my breasts right in his face, silently begging for him to lick, suck, and bite my nipples.

His wet lips brush the very tip of my sensitive flesh. I gasp with pleasure and lean closer. "Please. Please."

That's all it takes. He opens his lips, closing them around my tight peak and sucking hard. Pulling back, his firm lips are replaced by the sharp edge of his teeth, and my gasp turns into a moan as my hips move urgently, my clit rubbing against his cock with intent.

He provides the same treatment to my other breast, using his lips, teeth, and tongue to tease me mercilessly. When I straighten, he attempts to sit up, his seeking mouth still intent on torturing me. My hand on his chest keeps him away, and he lies there, chest heaving, his eyes feral as he watches me.

I stroke my hands up his chest, my fingers touching along his collarbone. His breath catches, a low moan falling from his lips, so I do it again, my touch harder this time, more intent. His breath catches, his moan louder, and he shudders beneath me.

"Put your hands on my neck," he gasps, his hands moving from my hips to my wrists, pulling my hands up until I'm bracketing his neck. He sighs, his eyes closing as I squeeze tentatively, then he smiles and adds, "Harder. You won't hurt me."

I tighten my hold, and he bucks his hips in response, the head of his dick sliding partway inside me. I gasp in response to the sudden intrusion.

But I fucking love it.

And I want more.

He attempts to pull back, but I lean into my hands, keeping him in place with the pressure on his neck. I rotate my hips, taking more of him inside me.

His eyes open, meeting mine, and I slide down, inch-by-inch, and we watch each other, unblinking, unflinching as I sit astride him, his cock speared all the way inside me.

I lean forward, my hands still encircling his throat, using the press of my forearms on his chest to balance as I brush my lips against his tentatively. He doesn't move, allowing me a moment of exploration, but then my tongue brushes against his bottom lip, and he opens for me, his tongue flicking against mine teasingly.

A short laugh bursts out of me so suddenly I'm briefly frozen, and then he laughs, the sweet vibration sending a jolt of pleasure right to my pussy. I clench around him, his laugh quickly becoming a moan, so I press my lips firmly against his, my tongue sweeping in, drinking his sounds of pleasure like the lifeline it is.

He stops playing, his arms wrapping around me, holding me in place as he kisses me ravenously. I rock my hips, reveling in the slick stretch of him inside me. I press down firmly, grinding against him, stimulating my aching clit.

I set a fast rhythm, sliding up and down, my clit rubbing against him with each rotation of my hips. I'm panting, my hands still gripping his neck, ignoring the burn in my arms and lower back from the awkward angle as I feel the tension building rapidly.

I move faster, a sheen of sweat coating both of us, and his expression turns almost pained. His eyes squeeze shut as he gasps, "Oh, fuck, Jess. What are you doing?"

"Taking what I want," I reply breathlessly.

A whimper falls from his lips, and I answer with a whimper of my own, my pussy clenching tighter in response, and then he ask, "Birth control? Are you safe?"

Recklessly, I ignore his words, wanting to forget anything and everything other than this moment. He stills beneath me, his eyes pleading as he waits for my response, so finally, I nod. Relief shines in his eyes, and then he growls, "Choke me harder."

I tighten my grip, unsure exactly how best to do it and nervous I'm going to hurt him, but then his hands are over mine, and he's turning my hands so I'm gripping the sides of his neck, my thumbs pressed in firmly. "Like this. Restrict the blood flow without injuring the windpipe."

I nod, doing exactly as instructed, and his hips buck up sharply. His eyes are half-closed in pleasure, and suddenly, a sense of power rushes over me, fueling my need even further.

"Come inside me," I command, my pace increasing until I'm undulating wildly. "Mark me. Mark all of me."

"Fuck, fuck, fuck," he responds, his hands gripping my hips tightly as he pumps up into me, hitting just right inside me, over and over, my clit rubbing against his pubic bone, just so. Then, he adds, "I'm gonna fucking come. Oh, yeah. I'm gonna come."

The pleasure pulses inside me, cresting and overflowing.

Matt curses, and I squeeze his neck, my fingers digging into his carotid on both sides. His words cut off incoherently as he tenses beneath me, his cock pulsing rhythmically, the sounds of our pleasure echoing around us.

Slowing my movements, I release my grip on his neck, watching in awe as the white marks quickly redden. I smile, warmth rushing over me at the sign of ownership.

His throat clearing jars me from my thoughts, and I glance up at his face to see he's smiling knowingly. I return his smile, though it's likely a tad sheepishly.

I clear my throat, suddenly feeling a bit awkward. Fidgeting, my hands stroke where I was just squeezing, then he swallows, and I grin again, swallowing my own bubble of nervous laughter.

"Do you feel better?" His words are quiet, almost hesitant, and then I do laugh.

"Yes. I mean, obviously, I'm not back to normal, but I don't feel so chaotic now."

He sighs, some of the tension leaving his body, and I move to ease off him, the mess between us now more than evident between my legs.

His hands on my hips stop me, and I look back at him questioningly.

"Leave it," he replies firmly. "Just stay."

I smile softly, straightening over him, my eyes locking with his. His brow furrows, the amused glint in his eyes darkening slightly. So, I ask, "What is it?"

He shakes his head, his features softening as he continues to stare up at me. "Do you feel that?"

"Feel what?"

"The magnetic pull. The tangle of electricity."

I laugh, sliding my pussy along the slick mess between us. "Do you mean that?"

With his breath catching in his throat, his fingers flex on my hips. "Well, that, too. But no."

"Then, what do you mean?"

His hand slides from my hip, up over my waist, coming to rest between my breasts. "Right here. It's all right here."

My heart skips in my chest, and my breath is suddenly stuck in my throat. He doesn't blink; he just lies beneath me, his hand pressed firmly against my chest. I glance down at his hand, his fingertips digging in ever-so-slightly, and after a long moment, I manage to drag in a ragged breath. "What does it mean?"

"I have no fucking idea."

"Should we be worried?"

His lips curve up in a sexy smirk. "Probably."

"Would that stop you?"

"Fuck, no."

I smile again, content we both feel the same about what appears to be our whirlwind courtship. I grip his hand between both of mine, pulling it away from my chest and lifting it to my mouth. Placing a soft kiss on his knuckles, I smile, allowing myself to relax back into my original position, sprawled on top of him. Tucking my arms into my sides, his arms come back around me, squeezing tightly.

And for the first time in a long time, I breathe.

3

A Fork in the Road

Matt

What the actual fuck?

It seems this is basically the tagline of my life.

When I first received the news my life was unraveling, I didn't think too much of it. It was no great surprise that things were coming to a head, and though I would have preferred to have done it on my own terms, I wasn't surprised the end turned out to be a shitshow.

When I made the decision to live my life constantly dancing between good and bad, I knew at some point, the bad would take over, and I would have to give up the good—at least, on the outside.

Hindsight being what it is, I should have planned an exit strategy far sooner, and then maybe, I wouldn't have felt forced into it because the whole early retirement option obviously wasn't my first choice.

The fact the alleged charges against me were entirely bogus is irrelevant. The people who set me up did a bang-up job because the only way I'd be able to prove my innocence and clear my name would've been to reveal my whereabouts during the times when I was supposedly seen conducting criminal deeds. And since my actual whereabouts was likely conducting criminal deeds of another sort, it all seemed recklessly pointless.

That being said, I'm fortunate that I was given the option at all. In most cases, people in my position would have been fired outright, dragged through the coals in the papers and turned into the classic lesson to my peers.

The only reason they didn't choose this path was because they were scared.

And they should be.

This is also just another example of the path to hell being paved with good intentions.

Not that my good intentions negate the fact that I'm a cold-blooded killer. Some people would try to argue that cold-blooded is a bit of a stretch, given how closely I have edged between good and bad, but at the end of the day, when push comes to shove, I have no qualms about shooting somebody between the eyes to save my own skin.

I suppose that's probably a little simpler than the actual truth, but since we're talking simplistically, that's what I'm going with.

It's going to take me some time to adjust to my new life. No longer having to toe the line, I can basically do whatever I want.

It's amusing for me, considering I've always been labeled the geek of the group. Tony would even go so far as to call me soft, accusing me of being in love with all of my tech stuff and being incapable of the same atrocities that he is.

The fact of the matter is that he has no clue who I am. At least, not truly.

Darius, on the other hand, has a rather accurate idea of who I am. He's a giant pain in the ass, but he's incredibly observant, most often when you think he's not paying attention.

He's also likely to recognize himself in me, something a lot of people wouldn't be able to see at all.

That's because I'm more of a high-functioning psychopath than anything else. I didn't even realize this was a thing until later in life when I started to do more research on my own personality traits. I didn't think it was possible to be clinically insane and also have a conscience. It isn't even so much that I'm driven by my conscience as the fact that I've always chosen to lead with it.

But now, here I am, sitting on the cusp of a new beginning, trying to decide which path I want to go down.

The path of the straight-laced family man is lost to me. I'm not saying I ever considered that path as a real option or that I would even want to do it, but when sitting here contemplating what I like to think are my many choices for the future, I have to put it on the list. Only to immediately strike it out, which kind of annoys me.

After signing my resignation paperwork, or my early retirement package as they like to refer to it, I had to acknowledge there were still things going on in the background that had to be tended to.

There were still people within the force who would like nothing more than to see me punished. People who know I know they're not truly on the right side of the law.

And then there are the many people in the criminal world who would most definitely like to take me out permanently.

Which leaves me with one choice: Kill them all first.

When I first broached this subject with Darius and Tony, they rolled their eyes a bit. Tony mostly because he probably thought I was just talking, and Darius because he may have thought I was overreacting, but after a thorough discussion, they both recognized I had valid points, and my plans suited an ending that we'd been looking for most of our lives.

But what they wouldn't sign off on was me going about it alone. Because we've always been a team and going it alone is dangerous.

Which means they're going to be furious when they realize what I've done.

They were the ones who reminded me I had one loose end that could pose a serious problem, given they would likely become a target if my enemies found out about her.

Jessica.

We met under such unusual circumstances and somehow forged an untenable bond I never dreamed was possible, making it unlikely I could ever forget her.

Then there's the fact that I'm obsessed with everything about her.

I'm not one to give too much merit to Antoinette's fascination with romance novel tropes, but I'm certain she would have a field day with our relationship if ever given the chance.

We've enjoyed several months of secrecy, sneaking off whenever possible and losing ourselves in each other. When we're not together, we're basically in each other's pockets, calls, texts, and the kind of constant dialogue that would have Tony rolling his eyes and gagging at how gross we are.

Like two young people in love.

The thought of having to stop makes my chest hurt. The thought of having to hurt her without explanation makes me inexplicably furious. The thought of her inevitably getting over it and moving on makes me tremble with emotions I'd rather not even address right now.

So, knowing Darius is correct, I realize I have no other option but to cut her loose, even knowing this could mean she'll just move on and no longer be available to me once the dust settles.

I pull out my phone, bring up our chat, and scroll back, smiling as I read over our previous conversations. Some are serious, some comical, some sexy.

I skip over the sexy ones, knowing my body will respond immediately, and jump to the very end, where I type out a quick message.

> **Me**: You need to forget about me.

I hit send.

I wait for the message to be delivered, then jump to my contacts, pull her up, scroll to the bottom, and block her, knowing my message will go through, but I won't receive anything else from her number.

Then I go one step further, powering the phone off and walking to the far end of the room, tossing it into the incinerator.

I know this seems extreme, but I can't take any chances that she'll come up in the world that I'm about to head into.

There are some things I need to take care of—things she cannot be a part of—things I don't want anybody I know to be a part of.

I take special care to wipe everyone I love from my existence, hoping it will be enough to protect them from what I'm about to do.

Then I step into the darkness.

4

A Semi-Familiar Road

Jessica

> **Matt:** You need to forget about me.

Once again, I find myself sitting at my desk, staring at this now-months-old message on my phone.

Then, of course, the subsequent messages thereafter that are undelivered, one after another, into oblivion.

I have no idea why he sent this message to me, and I certainly have no idea why I was immediately blocked afterward, but I won't lie and say it doesn't sting.

I'm also certain something must have happened. I have no idea why he wouldn't tell me what that something was unless he felt it was for my own good, which is also incredibly infuriating because fuck him.

Frankly, it seems completely out of character for him, but maybe I just don't know him as well as I thought I did.

It's not like I've never been ghosted before. I just honestly never thought it would happen with Mathias Shields, a man who I thought to be an unassuming, stand-up guy who always does the right thing.

Which is a clear indication to me that something is horribly wrong.

A voice pipes up from the door, and I glance up to see Issa standing there with her hands on her hips. I raise a brow at her and ask, "What?"

She frowns, walking further into the room, stopping in front of my desk with her arms crossed over her chest. "I've been saying your name for like a full minute. What the fuck are you doing on your phone?"

I glare at her. "That's none of your fucking business." Her eyes narrow further, and then she lunges across the desk, snatching my phone from my hands, and I screech, "Give that back."

She scurries out of the way as I come around the desk to chase her, but I already know it's too late. She would have seen the screen almost immediately and realized what I've been hiding from her.

She stops trying to get away from me, her eyes meeting mine as she asks, "What happened?"

I shrug, shaking my head sadly as I reply, "I have no idea. I have no fucking idea."

"Why didn't you say anything to me?"

I shrug again. "Say what, exactly? That a guy who helped me manage my murderous episode has decided he doesn't want to talk to me anymore?"

She rolls her eyes. "Really, Jess? It's more than that, and you fucking know it."

We've never really spoken of the circumstances in which I first met Matt, but she knows me very well. She may even know me better than

I know myself some days, and she certainly has a long history of calling me out on my bullshit, so I suppose this is going to be that same exact scenario.

"Bullshit," she replies, and I snort, earning a glare from her as she continues, "Seriously. This is fucking weird, and the fact that you haven't mentioned it to me before now is idiotic."

I bristle, annoyed that she's correct. "And what the hell are you going to do about it?"

She sighs again, fiddling around with my phone before she hands it back to me. I glance at the open messages and see that she has taken a screenshot of my last conversation with Matt and then texted it to herself. "What the fuck, Issa. Why would you do that?"

She glares at me even harder for a moment before going back to her phone, and then, suddenly, a new message pops up on my end.

> **Issa**: Anyone know why Matt is being a douchebag to my friend?

I gasp in horror and then hiss, "Oh my God. What have you done?" She smiles at me, putting her hand in my face. "You just wait."

> **Unknown number**: What the fuck did he do?

> **Another unknown number**: Have you seen him?

> **Issa**: Jessica is in this group, too. This is the last message she got from him, which appears to be a little out of character. You tell me.

The screenshot pops through, and that first unknown number immediately replies.

> **Unknown number**: Absolutely not. Nope. That's not Matt.

> **Another unknown number**: Yeah, that seems a little suspicious. He's not the type to do that without an explanation, even if that explanation makes no sense. It'd still be some form of an explanation.

I look up at Issa and ask, "Who the fuck are these people? All I have are unknown numbers."

She snags my phone from me and then, a few moments later, hands it back, and when I look, the unknown numbers now have names. Antoinette and Carolina.

I look up at Issa again and ask, "Who are these people?"

"Declan's sisters-in-law," she explains. "I guess technically, my sisters-in-law."

I had forgotten about them. I've only met them once or twice, and I've never had to make real conversation with them, but I remember Issa telling me how fucking crazy they are, which makes sense considering Declan and his brother are also fucking crazy.

My phone pings again.

> **Antoinette**: When did this happen?

> **Jessica**: A few months ago. He sent that to me, and I replied immediately, and it remains undelivered.

> **Carolina**: Yeah, that's fucking dumb. There's no way that's something he does without a very good reason.

> **Issa**: Can you ask him?

There's no reply for almost a minute, and we stand in the middle of the office, staring at our phones, until finally, a message pops up.

> **Antoinette**: We don't know where he is.

My heart stops in my chest, and my stomach bottoms out as panic bubbles up inside me. I look over at Issa, who's frowning at her phone, and then her eyes rise to meet mine, and she says, "Was everything fine up until that point? Like normal?"

I nod. "Nothing unusual. Certainly nothing that raised any flags for me." Issa looks back at her phone, and then another message pops up.

> **Issa**: Obviously, something is wrong. What can we do?

> **Antoinette**: #FAAFO.

I frown at the screen. "What the fuck does that mean?"

She laughs and responds, "Fuck around and find out."

I sigh again, then continue to shake my head because these fucking people.

My phone pings again, and this time, more people have been added to the conversation. I look over at Issa questioningly, and she snags my phone, obviously inputting more names. When she hands it back to me, I see someone has added Tony and Dare to the conversation.

Tony: Another group chat?

Darius: Oh, for fuck's sake.

Antoinette: It's all for a good cause, baby.

Antoinette: Issa, send the screenshot again.

The screenshot pops up again, and new messages appear almost immediately afterward.

Tony: Well, that's fucked up.

Darius: What the fuck?

Antoinette: So, it appears that our good buddy Matt isn't just taking a short sabbatical between jobs.

Tony: I told you fuckers this didn't feel right.

Darius: I didn't disagree with you. I just said there wasn't much we could fucking do about it.

Tony: Don't try to pretend like you didn't poo poo it, Dare.

Jessica: What the fuck does any of this mean?

Darius: Who the fuck are you?

Issa: It's Jessica. That was her conversation I sent.

Darius: Oh, yes. Issa's murderous friend. Welcome to the chat.

Tony: Are you going to tell us what Matt was doing chatting you up?

Jessica: I don't think that's any of your fucking business.

Tony: *laugh emoji*. I will take from that whatever I may.

The chat falls silent, and I stare at it expectantly, annoyed that no one is saying anything. Issa steps close, her arm coming up around my shoulder, and when I look over at her, she says, "Just give them a minute. They'll do something."

A few moments later, the phone pings again.

Darius: There isn't any chatter right now, but I'll put some feelers out and see what we can get going.

Tony: I'll go grab my gloves and do some finding out of my own.

Jessica: What the fuck should I do, then?

Darius: If you want to help, get your ass to New York.

Issa's phone pings, and I stare at my phone in confusion when no message pops up for me. She spends a few minutes texting someone back and forth and then hands me her phone, and I look down to see she sent Declan a message.

Issa: I need your plane.

Declan: Dare I ask what for?

Issa: Well, Jessica needs your plane.

Declan: Okay. It can be ready within an hour. Where's she going?

Issa: NYC.

Declan: Does she need an escort?

Isa: As much as it pains me to say this, yes.

Declan: Done.

I hand the phone back to Issa and ask, "Who's going to be my escort?"

Issa replies, "Declan will go with you. I will sacrifice him for a few days to at least get you over there and get you acclimated to the very colorful characters you're about to come in contact with. You have obviously met Darius and Tony, and Antoinette is super cool; however, she is also somewhat crazy. You'll like her."

I sigh again, moving over behind my desk and putting all my papers back neatly before turning off my laptop, disconnecting it, and stuffing it in a bag. I put the strap over my shoulder and walk back around my desk, falling in step beside Issa as we walk out of the room and down the hallway.

Issa stops a few feet from the elevator, turns to me, and grabs me by my forearms, her eyes meeting mine as she whispers, "You'll find him."

I swallow the lump in my throat and then ask, "At what cost?"

She lifts a shoulder dismissively and responds, "It doesn't fucking matter. You'll pay it."

And she's right.

5

Decisions, Decisions

Jessica

We make it to New York in record time.

Working in the same industry, I've known Declan for many years, but I haven't spent a lot of time with him. It's actually a bit annoying how intuitively charming he is in this stressful situation, though I suppose I shouldn't be surprised, given that seems to be how most of these men are.

Back when I had my altercation with Bobby, I learned firsthand how intuitively charming some men can be. When Matt showed up to help me manage the situation, he was also like that, though in a much more matter-of-fact manner. Declan is, at baseline, a bit more of a showboater, always the entertainer, and it comes through in a lot of his conversations when he's trying to distract me.

It's a short drive from the airport, and thinking we're going to someone's home, I'm a bit taken aback when we arrive at what appears to be a giant warehouse.

Upon entering the building, it becomes clear that it is much more than a warehouse, and I find myself gaping when we first walk into the entryway.

I stand there for so long that Declan's voice startles me, and I glance over at him and say, "What?"

He laughs as he replies, "Impressive, isn't it?"

I raise my brows and nod. "That's putting it lightly. This is certainly the nicest warehouse I've ever been in."

Declan motions for me to follow him, and as we're walking, he adds, "Yeah. These guys have a long history with nasty warehouses, and Darius insisted that this one would be different. Common consensus is that he's gone completely overboard, but you can't reason with him."

"Does everyone live here?"

"No," he replies as he leads me down a hallway. "They all have separate residences, but they can all live here if they want to. They probably spend more time here than they thought they would, but since Darius has made it so comfortable, they're probably not mad about that."

We walk to the end of the hallway where there are two large doors, one of which is propped open, and we stop in the doorway as Declan turns back to me and says, "I did let them know that we're coming. I figured Darius would want to have a chance to make other plans, do some reconnaissance, and try to get to the bottom of things before we got here."

"And has he learned anything?" I ask.

Declan shakes his head. "Not last I spoke to him, but they're usually pretty quick, especially if Tony's put on the case."

"Who all is here, then?"

"As far as I know, it's just Dare, Tony, and Antoinette. Maybe Carolina. I'm sure Lilith will pop in eventually if she's not already here. There's also a chance that Carolina's brother, Jayme, will make an appearance, and maybe even Antoinette's sister, Agatha."

My eyes widen, and I laugh as I say, "Well, they got a whole ass posse or something?"

Declan laughs as he says, "You could say that. They tend to be spread across the world at different points in time, but as soon as there's a problem, they all congregate quickly."

"Then, why did no one know there was a problem before now?"

Declan continues walking into the next room, and I follow along as he replies, "Matt had been going through some stuff. I'm not sure how much you know about the situation or how much you've spoken to him otherwise, but having to leave his job with the police was a real slap in the face for him. Honestly, we all just thought he was going to go out and lick his wounds for a while and then come back with some big new plan on how to take over the universe."

I nod and respond, "Yeah, I knew about that. I knew he took it to heart, and I also figured he was going to go out and get some R and R. That's why that text he sent me was so jarring."

"Yeah, that fucking text makes no sense at all coming from him," Declan replies seriously. "Even if Matt genuinely wanted you to leave him alone, he's the type of guy who'd literally fly across the country and sit down and have a conversation with you and give you a spreadsheet and a play-by-play on why this is the best plan that there is, and have a rebuttal for any kind of reasoning you may have of why he's full of shit."

I smile, nodding in agreement. "Yes, that sounds like Matt."

"We're glad you said something because if you hadn't, who knows how much more time would have gone by before any of us caught on."

"I wonder how long it'll take for them to find him," I say quietly.

Declan stops walking and turns back to me, his gaze serious. "They *will* find him, Jessica."

"What if it's too late?"

Declan's lips press together, and his gaze flits away momentarily before coming back to me. "That's not possible. Don't even think about it."

I inhale sharply through my nose, expelling the breath just as quickly out of my mouth, and I nod a bit more aggressively than necessary as I attempt to shake the negative thoughts from my brain.

I can't imagine Matt being gone, but there's always a little part of me that thinks worst-case scenarios in an attempt to prepare myself to deal with it.

We stop beside the next set of doors, these being closed, and Declan turns to me and says, "I gotta use the facilities. I'll be right back. Just wait here."

I nod in agreement, and he walks off, disappearing through the door on the other side of the hallway.

This room is small and nondescript, but I suddenly hear voices sounding through the doorway, so I lean closer to try to listen. I can't quite make out what the voices are saying, so I slowly ease the door open an inch and listen more intently.

"We're going to get made within seconds. They all know us."

I don't recognize the voice, and without context, it's impossible for me to know what they're talking about, but I feel, given the current circumstances, it's safe to assume it has to do with Matt.

Someone mentions Antoinette. I can't make out exactly what they're saying, but then a female voice says clearly, "We can't leave him there, so what are we going to do?"

I clench my jaw, annoyed when the voice becomes too faint for me to understand, and I'm tempted to open the door fully and step inside but also fearful my sudden appearance will stop the conversation dead, and I won't be able to determine what's going on.

Then, an impatient male voice pipes up, "There has to be someone who can get the job done without us having to worry about them turning on us."

There's a pause in the conversation, and I strain to hear more of what's being said, to no avail. Easing the door open a few more inches, I peer through the crack, catching a glimpse of Darius and Tony still speaking to each other, but I can no longer make out their words.

I attempt to move closer quietly but lose my footing and fall heavily into the door, a loud squeak punctuating my clumsiness.

Knowing I'm caught, I give up any semblance of sneakiness, pushing the door open fully and stepping into the room.

6

Deciphering the Unknown

Darius

> **Lilith:** I found him.

THE TEXT DROPS INTO our group chat, and we all clammer to respond, the succession of pings reverberating throughout the room.

> **Tony:** Where?

> **Antoinette:** Where the fuck is he?

> **Darius:** Tell us.

The dots show up, and we're all holding our breath as we wait, and wait, and wait. Finally, after what feels like hours, the message pings through.

> **Lilith**: I was actually en route to you when I got the information. Be there in less than an hour.

Tony curses loudly, and another message pings through.

> **Tony**: Cut the fucking shit, Lils. Just tell us.

> **Lilith**: Calm the fuck down. There's nothing we can do about it right this second, so just wait.

> **Antoinette**: Is he alive?

> **Lilith**: Yes.

That's all I need to hear. I toss my phone down on the table, heaving a long sigh of relief at the knowledge that if nothing else, the man lives. Tony curses some more, obviously intent on being angry, even knowing that isn't going to get us anywhere.

Antoinette looks down at her phone again, typing out a message. Nothing pings on my end, so I give her a look, which she returns with a short nod that means she sent a message to Carolina to come rein in her man.

We haven't been looking for Matt for long, but it feels like a lifetime. When things first went south with his job, he went a little berserk, and we gave him some space to handle issues as needed, but somewhere along the way, things got fucked.

We're not even sure exactly when he disappeared. We all figured he was out sowing some wild oats, living it up for once, and taking a much-needed break from us and our bullshit.

It wasn't until Jessica reached out to us, asking what his fucking problem was, that we realized something was fucked up, and then we spent way too much time scurrying around like fucking idiots.

Tony and I had a conversation with Matt back when his career in law enforcement ended, and he had alluded to the fact that he felt there were many loose ends he needed to follow up on in terms of who may have aided in shortening his career and who may still be out there waiting to strike.

At first, his concerns were brushed off, but after a thorough briefing, PowerPoint presentation and extensive spreadsheets included, Tony and I agreed that he may be onto something.

What he failed to do was circle back and update us about his plans, which quite obviously took a turn deep behind enemy lines or, worse, ended up with him being taken prisoner.

I feel that same anger, that helpless rage that bubbles under the surface at the thought that anything could have happened to him while we had our damn pants down, all because he couldn't be bothered to share his fucking plans.

We knew Matt and Jessica had become friendly since everything went down with Declan and Issa. We all assumed that was going somewhere, and I'm thankful she thought to reach out to us rather than just believing that he was a stupid, fucking ghoster.

Even though we were aware that something was going on between them, Matt never really divulged any secrets to us. We would joke around with him about it, and for the most part, he deflected it, but you can tell when a man is enamored with someone else.

Once we realized something was wrong, we threw everything we had at finding him, only to run into a dead end and a cold trail. The amount of blood that was shed in only a few hours was a bit extreme, but, of course, Tony didn't give a fuck, and I don't think any of us really did, but having it be all for nothing was like twisting the knife in the wound.

Luckily, Lilith makes good time, and before too long, she strolls in the doorway to be met by a rabid Tony. She gives him a bland look, putting a hand up when he rushes toward her. "Don't even fucking try me, Tony. I'm not in the fucking mood."

He stops short, glaring at her, but says nothing. Antoinette steps around him, enfolding her mother into a hug. Lilith returns her embrace, relaxing into her momentarily before pulling back and then walking further into the room to stop before me. We all gather around, and she finally says, "According to my sources, he's basically been under our nose the whole time."

"What do you mean?"

"Are you saying he's in the city?" Antoinette asks.

Lilith shakes her head and replies, "No, but he's in the state. Not too far from here, really."

"How is that fucking possible?" Tony snarls.

Lilith gives him a patient look and then turns her gaze back to mine, and I can tell she's contemplating her next words. I prod, "What is it, Lils? Just spit it out."

"Matt isn't who you think he is."

I'm sure my eyebrows are in my hairline as I snort. "You're going to have to elaborate because that makes no fucking sense."

Tony scoffs, "Yeah, we've basically known him his entire fucking life."

Lilith presses her lips together for a moment, sighs, and then says, "Yes and no. There was a short amount of time when you didn't know him at all, and you guys were young enough that you probably didn't know he just showed up one day."

Antoinette steps closer to Lilith, her hand coming out to rest on her arm as she asks, "If that's the case, why haven't you said anything sooner?"

Lilith rolls her eyes at her, her shoulders shrugging and one of her hands waving dismissively, all at the same time as she mutters, "Not everything needs to be told."

Tony glares at her, his fists clenching, and I can tell he's contemplating doing something he might regret. Then he says, "You and your fucking secrets. I'm so sick of your fucking secrets."

She rolls her eyes at him again and then says, "Some secrets are necessary, you imbecile."

"Necessary, how?"

"Some secrets are more trouble than they're worth. Some secrets are safer being secrets."

I can't exactly argue with this, given the lifestyle we lead. Sometimes, things are safer if you don't know everyone's secrets, which could be one of the reasons Matt has always been in trouble. He's the keeper of everyone's secrets.

"Is Matt aware?" I ask quietly.

"Yes," Lilith responds. "I had to tell him when his job went to shit because I believed there may be a correlation."

"And is this the reason he's missing?" Antoinette asks.

Lilith nods. "That is highly possible, though I'm uncertain on the circumstances of his being where he is."

Tony steps closer to Lilith until he's mere inches from her, leans down until his face is directly in front of hers, and says, "And you don't think that maybe if we had known this secret, we could have done something to prevent this from happening?"

"No, Tony," she replies snippily. "I don't."

Antoinette interjects, "Well, maybe being prepared would have made us more aware of possible complications such as where we currently are, but arguing about it is entirely pointless now."

Lilith shrugs and responds, "I didn't know for certain it was going to be an issue, but I know just as soon as we think all the fucking dirtbags are gone, they just keep springing up like rats."

Tony opens his mouth to say something further, and I interject, "Well, are you going to tell us what the story is or not?"

She gives me a dirty look, though I'm not really sure why, but then says, "Not to sound like Matt or anything, but it's not my story to tell."

I frown, shaking my head with a sigh, and then say, "Fine. But don't think we're not going to revisit this at some point."

She nods, walks over to the desk where Matt's laptop is, and opens the top. She types in the password, and it starts up, and Tony says, "What the fuck, Lilith? You know Matt's password?"

"Of course, I know a bunch of his passwords. Matt and I worked together pretty closely over the last little bit, especially when I wasn't dead-dead, so take from it what you will."

She opens a mapping program Matt had created for himself years ago, putting in coordinates and then zooming in to a wooded area a few miles outside the city. Then she turns to us and says, "This is where he is."

"Well, let's go in and get him out," Tony replies stonily.

She shakes her head, her fingers tapping on the desk. "It's not that simple."

"How can it not be simple? You know where he is. We go fucking get him."

Lilith sighs, her head falling forward briefly as she stares at the desk blankly. After a few moments, she looks over at me as she says, "We can't go in there."

I reply, "Why not?"

"We're going to get made within seconds. They all know us."

"Even Antoinette?" I ask.

Lilith nods and then adds, "Antoinette, Agatha, me, you, Tony, everyone. It will be nearly impossible for us to sneak in there."

Tony's jaw clenches, and I can tell he's getting pretty close to breaking shit. Then, Antoinette asks, "Well what are we gonna do? We can't leave him there, not even knowing if he's there of his own accord, so what are we gonna do?"

We continue to look at each other for a few moments, everyone contemplating our options, and finally, Lilith responds, "We're gonna have to find someone who can do it. I'm not sure who, considering the majority of the people I trust would be known to everybody involved."

Tony raises his hands in the air helplessly, shaking his head as he says, "There has to be someone who can get the job done without us having to worry about them turning on us."

We all fall silent, each of us considering our limited options. Lilith and Antoinette turn back to the computer, but Tony moves closer to me, his voice low as he mutters, "Do you really think we'd be made that easily?"

"Sadly, she's probably not exaggerating. We've used up all of our inconspicuous cards at this point in the game."

"That fucking blows," Tony snipes grumpily. "I wonder if we—"

Tony's words are interrupted by a ruckus in the doorway, a loud squeak of the door punctuating we have a new arrival.

7

A New Recruit

Jessica

I STOP JUST INSIDE the doorway, eyes wide, to find they've all turned to gawk at me.

The room is quiet for a moment, and then Antoinette smiles broadly, walking toward me excitedly. "Oh, it's the Bobby killer!"

I frown, a bit taken aback by her excited statement, but then, from what I've heard about Antoinette from Issa, it isn't overly surprising. Apparently, it's a well-known fact that Antoinette is a *little out there*.

My brain registers that she's not going to stop within a reasonable distance of me right before she wraps her arms around me. That's another thing I learned from Issa. Antoinette is a hugger.

I stand there rather stiffly, mostly because I can't do anything with my arms pinned to my sides. A voice pipes up from across the room,

"Come now, Antoinette. Release the poor woman."

She does the opposite of that and instead squeezes me a bit tighter, and then her voice is in my ear, "Super jealous that you got to take out that douchebag. But good job."

A choked laugh falls from my mouth, and I shrug as I reply, "Thank you?"

Antoinette laughs, and I'm immediately enveloped in this warmth that has no real definition. I suppose that's just Antoinette.

After another moment, Antoinette releases me and steps back. She grabs my hand and gives me a yank, so I follow her across the room, none too gracefully. We stop in front of the two men, and Darius shakes his head at her, but Tony just grins, obviously entertained by her antics.

The blonde woman walks toward me, stops in front of me and asks, "Who the fuck are you?"

I stand up straight, reaching my hand out in offering as I reply, "Jessica."

She stares at my hand warily and looks back up at my face with her eyebrows raised as she says, "That doesn't fucking tell me anything."

Darius interrupts, "Lilith, give her a fucking break."

Lilith turns and looks at Darius over her shoulder as she says, "Give who a break? Why give her a break?"

"Jessica is Issa's manager and long-time friend," he explains. "She's the one who notified us that something was wrong. She's one of the good guys."

Lilith turns, eying me again, and finally, she asks, "Like, what kind of good? Like, goody two shoes, gonna fuck with our shit, good? Or will fuck some shit up if put into a corner, good?"

I smirk, a small laugh escaping. "I'll smash some skulls if I have to, though I prefer not to."

"Ever got your hands dirty?"

I snort. "My hands, my arms, pretty much all of me that blood spatter can reach when you're bashing somebody's head in with a giant doorstopper."

Her eyebrows raise again, but this time, her eyes light up excitedly, and then she turns back to Dare and retorts, "Oh, yes. I like her."

Another blonde woman enters the room, Declan right behind her. Declan heads toward his brother, not giving me a glance or even attempting to make an introduction.

Smiling rather sheepishly, the woman walks directly to me and holds her hand out, which I take easily. She steps close and places a kiss against my cheek, a move I've always considered to be quite posh. I just manage to hide my smile when she pulls back and says, "Carolina Andersen. It's nice to finally meet you."

Now I do smile, gripping her hand firmly in both of mine as I say, "Likewise. I've heard quite a bit about all of you."

A snort comes from Tony as he says, "Well, depending on who that's from, it's not necessarily a good thing."

Shrugging, I laugh and reply, "A little good, a little bad. Depends on your perspective."

Tony nods in agreement. "I already know you know how to fuck around, so I have a feeling you'll fit in just fine here."

Heat rushes up my neck into my cheeks, and I feel a bit uncomfortable at the second reminder of the man I killed.

I never considered myself to be the murdering kind until I was put into a situation where it was kill or be killed. Most of the time, I don't think anything of it, and half of the time that I do, I still think, '*fuck that guy.*'

But there's always that tiny part of me that wonders who I would be if that had never happened. If I'd never been forced to get blood on my hands and was still going about my days, pretending to be innocent of the darker sides of the world.

Innocent. That's laughable, considering the industry I've been in for more than half of my life. Sometimes, those who don't shed blood are even worse than those that do.

"That was a one-off," I answer dismissively. "I don't think I have any type of long-term career in the mercenary business."

The look Tony gives me can only be described as assessing. He stares at my face, his eyes boring into mine, and I'm just bordering on squirming under his gaze when he says matter-of-factly, "If I'm betting against you or the snake, I'm going to pick the snake. I have a feeling you'll do what you have to do."

I cock my head at him, squinting, then lift a shoulder dismissively. "I have no qualms about doing what needs to be done when it shows up on my doorstep, but that doesn't mean I'm keen on going out looking for it."

"She can do it," Lilith interrupts almost happily.

Tony gives her a bland look. "Do what?"

"She can be the one to go find Matt."

I scowl, shaking my head in denial. "I don't think that would work out very well for Matt."

Lilith frowns at me. "Why the hell not? No one knows you. You're perfect!"

"No, I'm not at all perfect. I'm exceedingly uncomfortable with the idea of inserting myself into possible danger with Matt's life on the line."

"Oh, it's not 'possible' danger. It's most definitely danger danger."

"Exactly my point. I don't want to bring more danger down on Matt since we have no idea what he's doing there in the first place."

"I don't know, Lils," Tony retorts flippantly. "She may not have what it takes to get the job done, and right now, we need someone with guts."

I bristle, turning my scowl on Tony as I mutter, "I've got guts."

He raises his brows, his look a touch condescending as he shrugs. "No, it's okay. We totally understand if you're scared to walk into the lion's den. It's not for everyone."

My scowl turns into a glare, knowing he's baiting me yet unable to stop myself from rising to meet his challenge. So, I cross my arms over my chest, lifting my chin obstinately. "I'll fucking do it."

Tony quirks a brow at me mockingly. "I don't know if that's a good idea."

That fucking bastard.

I take a step toward him, jabbing him in the chest with my index finger. "Let me be clear here, bucko. I do what I want, and if you don't like it, you can get the fuck out of my way and go fuck yourself."

I open my mouth with another biting retort, but Antoinette clears her throat, effectively interrupting our exchange. I turn my gaze to her amused one as she says, "If you really want to find Matt, you're going to have to be prepared to do anything."

I straighten, taking a calming breath and then exhaling it before saying firmly, "I'll do what has to be done. Matt would do the same for me."

"Yes," Darius interjects. "But Matt has been in this life for a long time. He's been trained and conditioned to do what has to be done."

I lift a shoulder dismissively as I reply, "Then teach me. Condition whatever you gotta condition in the short time we have available. Because I'm going to go get him."

Darius gives me the same assessing look Tony did a few moments ago, and somehow, I manage not to squirm under his stern assessment. After a few moments, he says, "You won't be able to go in with any weapons."

I snort and roll my eyes a bit as I snark, "Didn't have one last time, either."

Antoinette laughs, moving closer to me and putting an arm over my shoulder as she says, "That's right. Bludgeoned that motherfucker to death. It must have been beautiful."

Carolina joins in with her giggles and adds, "That must have been a sight to see. I bet you he was still running his fucking mouth, too, and then you shut it up."

I can't help but laugh a bit, though I'm sure it comes out rather awkward. If anybody deserved the violent end they got, it was Bobby Schmidt. I know without a doubt that I'd do it again if I had to.

"We don't have a lot of time to prepare, so we better get our shit together. We don't really have any idea what's going on. He may be there of his own free will, he may be there under duress, he may be a prisoner. We won't have any of those answers until you set eyes on him."

"And what do I do when I find him?"

Now, Tony shrugs. "That will depend on how you find him. If he's a prisoner, you'll have to try to find a way to get him out."

I nod but then ask, "And if he's not a prisoner? If he's in that place of his own volition?"

They all look between each other for a few moments, uncertainty written on all their faces, and then finally, Darius looks at me and replies, "I guess you'll have to cross that path when you get to it."

I frown as I say, "And if he's turned into the enemy? Is that a possibility?"

Again, they all look at each other, the uncertainty even sharper on their features, and then Tony walks closer to me and stops in front of me, stooping over a bit so he can meet my eyes. "Then you get the fuck out of there, and you leave it to me."

He doesn't wait for me to answer; he just turns on his heel and stalks across the room, slamming the door on the other side of the room.

Carolina sighs, giving me a reassuring smile. She pats me on the arm and then follows him out of the room.

I look at Dare and then Antoinette nervously, and it's Darius who replies, "If you get in there and you find out that Matt has switched teams—if he truly is the enemy—we will have to deal with it."

Antoinette smiles sadly, walking over to Darius and resting her hand on his arm as she says, "You know that isn't going to happen. Matt wouldn't do that."

Dare sighs and shakes his head as he says quietly, "I don't know fucking anything anymore."

She steps in even closer to him, forcing him to meet her gaze as she says firmly, "No. *No.*"

Declan, who has remained silent this entire time, interjects, "If somehow hell has frozen over and Matt has switched sides, then we will all come together and deal with it. But I'm with Antoinette on this. There's no way."

Dare gives a curt nod, and then Antoinette steps back, turns to me, and asks, "Are you ready to do this?"

I nod. It's not like I really have any choice otherwise.

She smiles, and I know what she's going to say before it even leaves her mouth. "Fuck around time."

8

A Pep Talk, Of Sorts

Jessica

"You one hundred percent sure you want to do this?"

The question comes out of nowhere, and I turn my head to see Tony standing over me.

I've been lying on this sofa for a spell, attempting to get my bearings from all the "training" that have been going on the last couple of days. We've done weapons training, speed training, lingo training—so many seemingly pointless exercises I wondered a few times if they were fucking with me. Tony even led a very brief stint in torture training, something I am not ashamed to admit I did not withstand at all.

Needless to say, this entire endeavor has been a lot, but since I know there's no way around it, I've been doing my best to take it all in stride.

I say nothing in response to a question I've been asked a dozen times before, and after a beat, Tony adds, "I know I razzed you hard over it, but you still have time to get out of it."

I sigh, then frown as I sit up, placing my feet on the floor. I give him an assessing look, much like the one he gives me most of the time, and then snort as I reply, "It's too late for that."

Raising his brows, the corner of his mouth twitches as he says, "It's never too late. You can walk out of here right now and never have to think another thing about it."

"But I would know," I reply firmly. "I would know I walked out and turned my back on someone when they needed me. That's not something I can live with."

He lifts his shoulder dismissively, his lip turning up as he scoffs, "Who fucking cares? It's not really your problem."

Now, I'm annoyed. I glare at him, then shake my head. "I didn't rearrange my entire life to come here to then not follow through, so whether you agree with it or not, I'm gonna do it."

"But why?"

"Why not?"

He cocks his head at me, presses his lips together before replying, "It's really worth risking your life for?"

"Yes."

"That doesn't make sense," he says flippantly. "You choosing violence to protect yourself or your closest friend is one thing. But sneaking into a secure facility of some seriously dangerous people is ludicrous."

"You don't have to understand it."

"But I want to understand it. I want to know what would possess you to put your own life on the line for the likes of Matt."

"Matt was there for me when I needed him, and that was when he didn't even know me."

"Sounds like Matt," Tony responds with a laugh. "Always the Boy Scout."

Rolling my eyes a bit, I laugh humorlessly. "Yeah, that's what I've been told. But I know without a doubt if our situation was reversed, he would go in there and get me. Blindly or not."

"That's different. Matt knows the life. Matt knows the risks, and he has the training and experience that makes the odds in favor of his success."

"Is that why you're giving me a hard time right now? Because I lack the expertise and the experience, and you're worried I'm going to end up dead?"

Tony sighs. His shoulders relax a bit, and then he steps closer and plops down on the sofa beside me. I turn my body so my back is pressed against the side armrest and pull my feet up, hugging my knees to my chest as I watch him.

After a few moments, he turns and looks at me and says, "I just don't want something to happen to you and then have Matt destroyed."

"Destroyed? That sounds kind of extreme."

"Let's not pretend he won't be upset if he comes out of whatever bullshit he's part of and finds you no longer exist."

I shrug as I reply, "And if I don't do this? I'm supposed to be okay with doing nothing, then having *him* not come out of it alive?"

"Yeah, this could easily be a lose-lose situation, no matter how you cut it."

I nod, hugging my legs a little tighter as I try not to think about losing anything. Then I say, "I think he'd be fine. He might be a little annoyed to start with and curse me a bit, but at the end of the day, he'd be fine."

Tony turns wide eyes on me, his jaw a little slack, and then he mutters, "Are you out of your fucking mind?"

"What do you mean?"

"Matt would not be okay. Why would you think he would be okay?"

"Why wouldn't he be okay? We're friendly and all, but it's not like we have any grand romance from which he'd have to recover."

The laugh that comes out of Tony's mouth is almost bitter. He looks around the room for a few minutes before turning his gaze back to me. "You don't know Matt as well as the rest of us, but you should at least know him well enough to know that he's not just 'friends' with people. You're either an acquaintance, an enemy, or family."

"So, I'm an acquaintance then. Even better."

"If you were an acquaintance, you wouldn't fucking be here. Stop lying to yourself."

My lips curve up in a small smile. I know I'm more than an acquaintance, but I'm not so sure I really want to talk to Tony about it. Though, from this entire interrogation, I'm getting the idea I'm going to have to spill something to make him satisfied enough to allow me to continue with this mission.

"Do you think of Matt as an acquaintance?" he asks seriously.

I don't answer for a moment, and it must be a moment too long because he adds, "You'd go risk your life in a den of vipers for an acquaintance?"

Finally, I shake my head, but I don't say anything.

"You're going to have to tell me, Jessica. If you can't tell me why, then I can't let you go in."

I sigh, shaking my head and releasing my grip on my legs as I shift back around, placing my feet on the floor. I sit beside him, nearing his position. We sit there in silence as he waits for me to answer.

Finally, I say the only thing I can think of. "He's mine."

Tony looks over at me, his eyes searching mine intensely for a few long moments. Then he gives a nod, reaches his hand out, and grips mine to the point it's borderline painful.

I don't flinch or pull away.

I grip him back just as tightly, and he leans in and whispers, "Then let's go get him."

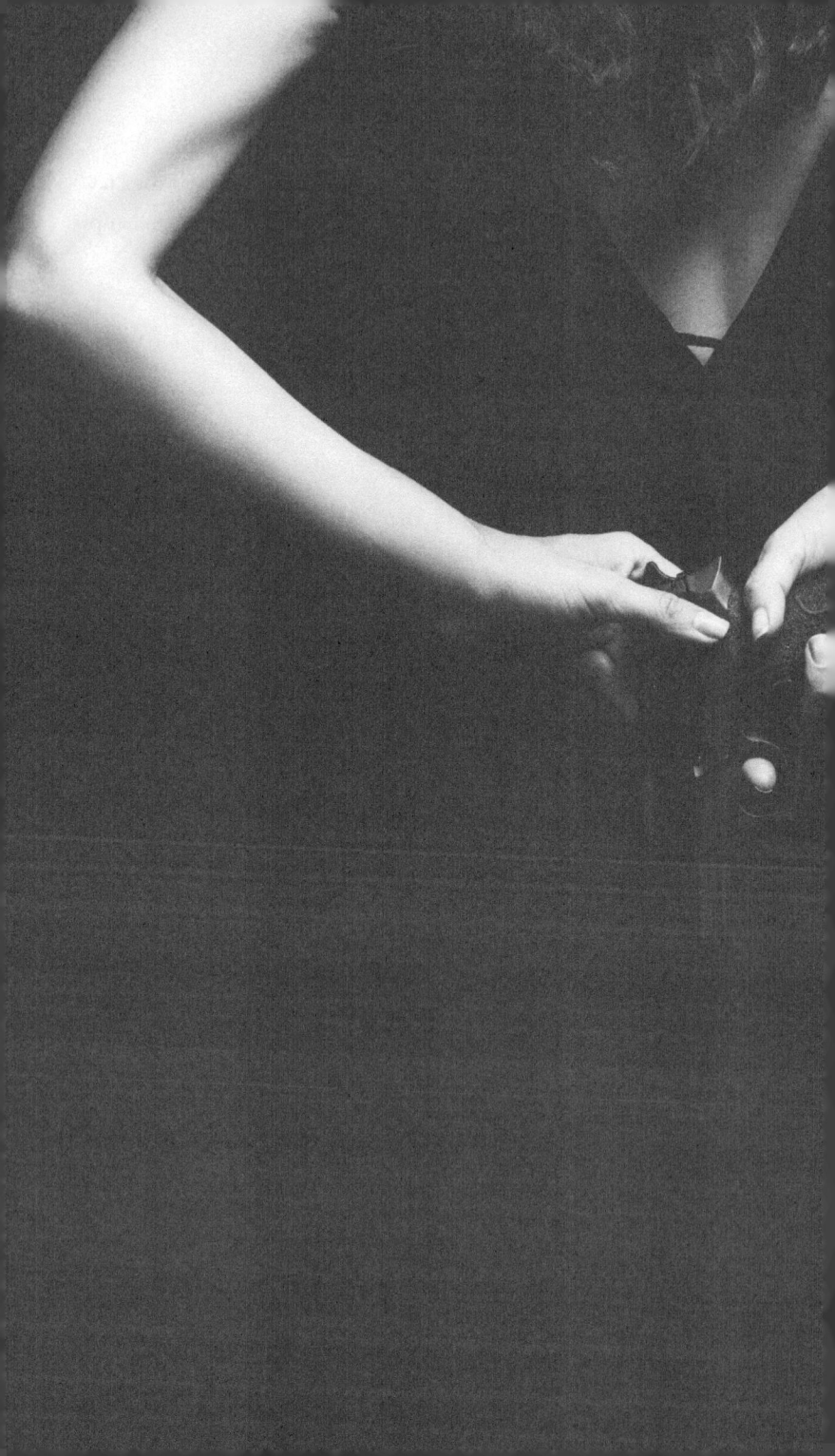

9

Playing Dumb

Jessica

WELL, I AM OFFICIALLY fucked.

It seems our training time was short-lived, and now, here I am, on my way down into what appears to be a viper's nest.

Yes, I'm being overly dramatic, but in my defense, the whole idea that I accidentally found myself in the facility of the enemy is rather preposterous, given the lengths we had to go to get me in here.

This means I'll have to try playing the ditzy trick until what could possibly be my dying breath.

The odds of me not being found out before finding Matt are slim to none, given the amount of activity in this shit hole.

Of course, calling it a shit hole seems even more preposterous, given how lavish this fucking place is. The original structure is obviously old;

the large black stone blocks that make up the floors, walls, and ceiling are shiny with polish. There are few windows; instead, faux windows have been added down the hallways, and heavy draperies surround the glow of light emitting from them.

It reeks of money and power and I know exactly what kind of chaos can be reaped from money and power.

I already had to do a quick turnabout when I accidentally entered what appeared to be a large functional room overflowing with people, and luckily, they were just busy enough that they didn't notice me in the brief second that I was in the doorway. As it turns out, the blueprints of this building they had me study were complete bullshit because so far, none of these rooms existed. Which means I'm fucking lost.

I appeared to be rather put together when I burst out on this venture, but I now fear that I look a little worse for wear. I'm sure my hair is in tatters, and I'm sweating profusely. It's going to be rather difficult for me to sell any type of nonchalance when I'm finally found out because I am feeling anything but nonchalant.

This brings to mind all of Antoinette and Carolina's teachings on vague idiocy.

It's basically as simple as being intentionally confusing to throw them off.

Of course, then Carolina worries that if you act too stupid, they're going to think that you're a plaything, and that's not something you want, either.

Though as Antoinette further explained, being a plaything is better than being a dead thing.

Not wanting to be a plaything or a dead thing, my heart is racing in my chest. I take a moment to lean back against the wall in this darkened hallway to get my bearings.

I'm slowly realizing that this was a bad fucking idea. Just because you bludgeon one poor bastard to death doesn't a secret agent make.

Needing to get my heart rate under control, I take a few calming breaths, and remember what all of them repeated over and over again. Worry about right now. Worry about this moment.

I remain in place until my pulse begins to slow, and then I take one more cleansing breath and push myself off the wall, heading down the hallway with some purpose. I stupidly go around a corner with zero caution and run directly into a hard, tall person.

I attempt to push away and jump backward, but strong hands grip my biceps. I struggle for a moment, but the grip on me tightens painfully, so I freeze, staring at a chest, and then a voice grits out, "Who the fuck are you?"

Words are stuck in my mouth; though I open it, nothing comes out. And then I choke and cough on my own saliva, and the man releases me but steps in closer so I'm crowded against the wall while I continue to sputter and gag.

This is fucking embarrassing.

After a few painful moments, I compose myself and stand up straight, pressing my back against the wall, finally looking up at the man who's standing there, giving me a disgusted look.

"I'm sorry. What did you ask?" I finally manage to say.

The man glares at me, and I do my best not to laugh because, honestly, that's my first inclination.

He steps close to me, and I attempt to move backward. I just end up pressing myself more firmly against the wall as he says levelly, "I asked who the fuck you are. How the fuck did you get in here?"

I blink at him, opening my mouth to reply and then snapping it shut as I try to decide how best to answer. Finally, I decide to play dumb.

"You know, I'm not quite sure how I got here, either."

His frown deepens, his arms coming up and crossing over his chest as he replies dryly, "Really? You're going to play dumb?"

I gasp, my hand coming up and pressing against my chest as I say, "Dumb? Why, I never."

His frown deepens again, and now he's glaring at me as his hands drop down to his sides, fisting in aggravation. "I don't think now is an appropriate time for you to pull this shit. Tell me what the fuck you're doing here and how you got here."

I rest my hands on my hips and lift my chin defiantly as I say, "Well, there's no reason to be rude."

Shockingly, his frown manages to deepen even further and a little zing of glee zaps through me. I'm totally understanding where Antoinette comes from with this type of strategy.

He moves quickly. I hardly see his hand moving until the next thing I know it's in front of me with a blade stuck under my nose. Now, my mouth snaps shut for other reasons. He leans in until his face is only a few inches from mine, his eyes on the blade as he whispers, "I suggest you fucking tell me."

I'm also staring at the blade, going over every bit of advice given to me over the last few days.

Finally, I say, "I was sent for Matt."

The man freezes, his eyes moving from the blade to mine. He cocks his head at me and says, "Really?"

I nod as I finally manage to reply, "Yes. They sent me over for Matt. That's all I know. They told me to go into the building and find Matt."

He raises his brows, backing away an inch or two as he asks, "Then why didn't you say so?"

I shrug, shaking my head as I mutter, "I have anxiety. Okay?"

He steps back from me, putting the knife back into his pocket where I'm assuming there must be some kind of sheath for it. He says sternly, "I'll take you to him. But no funny business, or I'll fucking break your neck."

I nod in agreement, my hands waving around dismissively, or crazily, or however he's probably going to take it. "You got it. No funny business."

We walk along a maze of corridors until, eventually, he stops short in front of me, and I have to pull up quickly to avoid running into the back of him. He turns around, glowers at me, and says, "Stay here. Don't fucking move."

I give him a short nod and say nothing, and then he walks a few feet away and stops in front of a door, pounding his fist on it a few times before standing there, waiting. After a few beats, the door opens a crack, and the man whispers something incoherent. After a short exchange, the door closes, and he comes back over to me and says, "He's in there. Knock on the door and wait until you're let in. Don't try anything fucking stupid, or you'll think I was a nice guy."

Again, I nod but say nothing. He steps to the side, so I walk over to the door, slamming my fist on it a few times the same way he did. I look over at him. He simply glares at me, spins on his heel, and stalks away.

I swallow the lump in my throat, turning my focus back to this nondescript door, and then I wait.

10

A Complicated Conundrum

Matt

I'VE HAD THE LONGEST fucking week of my life, and given my history, that's saying something.

I've been out dealing with endless bullshit for the last few days. I've only been back for maybe an hour, and I can already tell something fucking stupid is brewing.

All I wanted was a hot shower and one hot meal, but from the knocking on my door, I have a feeling I'm not going to get either of them.

I know that I could take my time answering, and whoever is knocking would still be there in five minutes, twenty minutes, or even two hours because that's just how these people operate.

Not wanting to listen to incessant knocking while I'm trying to wash the filth off myself, I figure it's best if I just pause my initial shower plan and go answer the fucking door.

Muttering expletives to myself, I yank my filthy jeans back up my legs, zipping them but leaving them unbuttoned. Storming over to the door, I yank it open as I bark, "What the fuck do you want?"

There's a startled, feminine gasp, and then I quickly lose my mad as I see the woman standing on the other side.

I sigh and shake my head as I say, in a calmer tone, "Marieka, what are you doing here?"

She shrugs, her hands twisting in front of her as she replies, "Looking for you."

I step back and open the door all the way so she can enter, closing it behind her and moving a few feet away. She steps back, leaning against the door, uncertainty written over her features.

"Give me a minute," I say hurriedly, and then rush back over to the bathroom where I grab my shirt and pull it on over my head as I return to the main room.

There's nothing fancy about my accommodations, but they're some of the larger ones I've had, and at least they're clean. She's still standing against the door, looking even more unsure than when she first arrived. My annoyance eases as I stand a few feet from her and ask, "Did you need something?"

Her brow furrows, and she hesitates for a moment, so I add, "Just spit it out, Marie."

She swallows, clears her throat, and then whispers, "I needed to see you. To make sure you're alright."

"I'm perfectly fine, but you shouldn't be here."

Her eyes drop to the floor, and I wait as she works to collect her thoughts. After a few moments, her eyes finally lift to meet mine, and she says, "I overheard the men talking about what would happen here if you were to end up injured or worse."

I close the short distance between us, my hands reaching out and gripping hers tightly before holding them loosely as I stoop over so I'm looking into her eyes as I say softly, "I'm fine. That's not going to happen."

Her jaw clenches, and her nostrils flare. She chokes out, "But it could. And then what?"

"Then you immediately go to plan B. Honestly, you'd probably be better off if something did happen to me because plan B is probably your safest bet."

Her eyes narrow, and she shakes her hands free of my own as she snorts, "I have a hard time believing that."

I smile, relieved that her unease is shifting back to her underlying sass.

I can always tell when I've been gone for a longer period of time because she starts to resort back to her earlier demeanor of being more of a wilted flower, a quiet little mouse destined to hang out on the outskirts and be overlooked by the masses. Of course, learning how to go under the radar being the safest bet, I can't say I really blame her.

She clears her throat again, nodding to what seems to be mostly herself, and then she turns, putting a hand on the doorknob where she pauses and turns back to me and says, "You stay alive."

I laugh and reply, "I'll certainly do my best, Marie. You need to stay out of trouble. And don't get caught down here, or you're going to be in a whole heap of trouble."

She nods in agreement and then opens the door, moving as if she's going to step out into the hallway, but I pull her back. I lean out, looking in both directions before reaching back and taking her hand, maneuvering her into the hallway.

She goes easily, but when she turns back to look at me, I still see that shadow of fear across her face, so I touch her shoulder, lean down, and whisper, "Everything will be all right. You'll see."

She huffs and then nods more firmly before spinning on her heel and taking off down the hallway with her head down.

There's a knocking down the hall in the other direction, so I lean out in the hallway and peer down just in time to see a woman disappear into a room.

A shiver runs down my spine, and I squint and shake my head, forcing the apprehension down as I step back into my room and shut the door.

I'm almost to the bathroom and the shower that's been waiting for me when the door to my room bursts open behind me. I whirl around, ready to fuck up some shit, and then immediately relax when I see who it is.

Kaian stands in the doorway, looking proud to have startled me.

I glare at him and say, "Stop fucking doing that."

He grins at me, lifting his shoulder nonchalantly as he shuts the door behind him and then replies, "Well, remember to lock your fucking door, then."

"Maybe you should just stay in your own room and quit fucking bothering me."

He walks further into the room, dropping into the large armchair I have in the corner, sprawling out as if he owns the place.

Which technically is kind of true, given he's one of the princes of the underworld, taking a pit stop down here with us common folk as part of his mission to earn the job.

Frankly, I'm not sure he's entirely cut out for it, given he doesn't take anything seriously, but I suppose like most people, he'll be serious when the time comes.

"We're going to need to tighten up security around this place," he says randomly.

"Security?" I ask incredulously. "The security in this place is top-notch."

He raises his brows at me, gives me a serious look, and then says, "Well, that's what I thought, but I found somebody just wandering around here today."

Now I frown, my arms crossing over my chest as I respond, "Wandering around?"

He nods, then sighs, his head falling back to rest on the back of the seat, his eyes closed as he relaxes. "That's what I said. Some woman, just wandering around here."

"And you believed that she's just randomly wandering around here?"

He peeks an eye open at me and says, "Yeah, that's what I said. I mean, I scared the shit out of her, and I'm pretty certain that she couldn't have been up to much, considering how easily she practically pissed her pants. She wasn't too bright, either."

"And what did she say she was doing here?"

"She said she was dropped off for Matteo."

I cock my head at him, confused why anyone would be dropped off for Matteo, given the fact that he is a huge piece of shit. Now I sigh, my hands coming up and rubbing over my face tiredly, and then I ask, "And did she say why she was here for Matteo?"

"She just said she was a gift or whatever. I don't know. I kind of feel bad for her now."

"And so, you just blindly brought her to him?"

He shrugs. "I just did what the lady told me. She's not my problem."

"Is anyone your problem?"

He grins, opens his eyes, and looks at me. "Nope. I am my only problem. And I like to keep it that way."

"It's a damn fucking shame, too, Kai. You're in a position to do a lot of good in this world if you chose to."

"Attempting to do good in the world is what gets us killed in our world."

He's not wrong. All too often, good intentions lead to pain, suffering, and death. All we can hope in those circumstances is that death comes swiftly, though in most cases, the person who thought they were going to do some good has to be an example to anyone else who ever thought they wanted to do the same.

I go to say something further, but Kai takes out his phone and says, "If you want that shower, you better make it quick."

I groan, already stripping down as I head back to the bathroom, thoroughly annoyed that I now have time for the most basic military shower instead of the thorough lathering I more than need.

11

A Case of the Wrongs

Jessica

A NOISE DRAWS MY attention away from the door in front of me, and I glance to my right to see a woman leaving another room.

I quickly face forward, not wanting to draw attention to myself by gawking, and when I step into the doorway further, hoping to avoid attention, the door in front of me suddenly pops open, and I fall forward.

I yelp, my hands coming up to stop my forward momentum, and I run right into a body.

I attempt to step backward as solid arms wrap around me, preventing me from doing so.

My eyes move to the face, and I blink a few times as I realize this is not Matt.

Fuck my life.

"You're not Matt."

The words fall out of my mouth before I can get control of my response. I immediately press my lips together, cursing myself for saying something so stupid. I watch as dark eyes harden, dark eyebrows lifting as he says, "Were you expecting a different Matt?"

I laugh. It's brittle and a little crazy, the perfect kind of crazy laugh that was taught to me by Antoinette, and his eyebrows raise even higher. He cocks his head at me as he says, "What could possibly be funny right now?"

I shrug, an exceedingly awkward endeavor given he's still embracing me, and every instinct in me tells me to shake him off, run screaming, and never look back. I manage to squash it down, forcing myself to be just one step shy of stone, and laugh again.

His brows lower, and he narrows his eyes at me, his hands gripping my biceps as he pushes me away from him and gives me a little shake. "Fucking stop that."

My breath hitches as my laughter immediately ceases, and I hold my breath, doing my best not to choke on the mania brewing inside me.

Perhaps I'm not cut out for this. Well, too fucking late, but I can't help but think this as he stares down at me like I'm some disease that needs to be eradicated.

He steps back from me fully, his hands crossing over his chest as he looks me up and down and asks, "Are you going to fucking tell me who you are or not?"

I can't move. I can't breathe. The pressure in my chest is excruciating as I clear my throat a few times, and he continues to stare at me like I'm completely insane. Which I fucking am. I inhale deeply through my nose, shaking my head as I attempt to sort my jumbled thoughts.

He rolls his eyes, muttering to himself under his breath, and he reaches down and grips the bottom of his shirt, yanking it over his head as he says, "Well, if you're not going to fucking talk, we may as well get it over with, then."

I'm pretty sure my eyes are bugging right out of my head at his words.

Fuck. Fuck. Fuck.

He grabs for my arm, yanking me over to a table where he pushes me against it face-first, his hand on my back, pushing my upper body down flat on it.

I expel a breath forcefully and then choke out, "Wait! What the fuck are you doing?"

The metal from his belt buckle jingles, and he replies, "Should be pretty fucking obvious."

I attempt to stand, but he pushes me back down, his hands on my hips, yanking my pants. I push back against him, but his hand keeps me anchored in place.

I stop struggling, crane my head around and look at him as I exclaim, "I wouldn't fucking do that if I were you."

He doesn't remove his hand from my back, but he stops pulling at my clothing, his narrowed eyes locking with mine as he snarls, "Or fucking what?"

"Or my fucking father will have your head."

He's obviously taken aback for a moment, and then he chuckles quietly as he asks, "And who the fuck might that be?"

I never speak of my father. He's one of my best-kept secrets and the reason I've changed my name and pretended to be an orphan for my entire adult life.

And I'm fortunate that he allowed this. I mean, it's only because it was my mother's dying wish, and if nothing else, he loved her, but I've always been grateful that she gave me the out that I deserved.

I swallow the lump in my throat, bracing myself to say his name for the first time in decades, and it takes me a moment to center myself.

The man waits impatiently, and I can tell my borrowed time is almost up when he rolls his eyes, then once again starts messing with my clothes. I finally spit out, "Seamus Killeen."

He freezes behind me, the hand against my back easing slightly as he says, "Fucking Irish? Are you serious?"

I nod almost frantically, continuing to swallow the giant lump in my throat. And then he adds, "And what's your name?"

"Jessica."

He steps back from me, and I slowly straighten and then step away from the table, adjusting my rumpled clothing as I turn to face him. He looks me up and down again and then says, "You do realize if your daddy gave you to me, I'm still going to fuck you, right?"

I nod, knowing how this all works. I'm just trying to roll with the punches as best I can. "Yes, but I'm pretty sure if it's not legal, he will be very upset. And you know what happens when my daddy's upset."

"I don't see why he would care if I got a taste beforehand."

"He didn't protect his baby girl's virginity this long to have some-one take it before the wedding."

"Wedding?" he asks incredulously. "Who said anything about a fucking wedding?"

"Don't fucking ask me," I say seriously. "I was just told to come here and find Matt. And here I fucking am."

He sighs heavily. He steps into me, his hand coming up and grip-ping my jaw as he says softly, "And what's stopping me from just taking what I want and then disposing of you?"

A chill runs down my spine, but somehow, I manage to meet his eyes without flinching as I whisper, "That's certainly your right if that's what you choose. But you also know you'll be choosing war."

"What if I don't care about war? What if I yearn for it?"

I laugh again. This one isn't quite as maniacal as my earlier laughing fit, but the more he talks, the more likely it is that I'm going to go completely insane. "Well, maybe you better be asking other people if they give a shit about war or not. Before you start making that decision for everyone."

Annoyance crosses over his features, and his grip on my jaw tightens painfully. He pushes me away forcefully, and I fall back on the table.

I quickly stand again, not wanting to leave myself in a position that leaves me too vulnerable, which is laughable, considering I'm basically at the mercy of a man I don't know and have given personal information to that could help me or hinder me.

He pulls his phone out, tapping the screen and then putting it to his ear. After a moment, he says, "Get everyone together. We have a situation."

He ends the call and returns the phone to his pocket, saying, "We're gonna get their opinion right now."

I give a short nod, checking my clothes to make sure everything is back to rights, but when I go to step toward the door, he steps right in front of me, his hand squeezing my neck mercilessly. I grab onto his wrist with both my hands, attempting to ease the pressure on my throat as he lifts me so I'm on my toes, and then he's right in my face as he says menacingly, "But just know that I am no one's pet. I'll listen, and then I'll fucking decide what I do with you."

I nod in his grasp, and after one final extended squeeze, he releases me. I fall to the ground, choking and coughing. I can only think about Antoinette's long lecture on never letting the enemy speak.

I've only ever given into violence on one occasion where it was literally kill or be killed. I didn't react overly well to that, but I managed to sort it out and come out of it generally unscathed. But I can see how living in a murderous rage could have you turning a blind eye to right and wrong more regularly. How living your life not knowing what may happen one moment to the next would have you in fight mode twenty-four-seven.

I push myself up onto my hands and knees, coughing, and for a brief moment, I wish I had a weapon within easy reach so I could eliminate this fucking prick. I also recognize that this would be premature on my part and most likely get me killed without question, but that urge is still there.

After a few moments, I manage to stand on my feet, and he looks at me with disdain, most likely because finding out who I am has made him have to have a discussion rather than just doing what he wants.

He walks over to the door and then motions for me to follow him as he says, "Don't get me into any fucking trouble, or else."

I remain quiet as I step out into the hallway, and wait for him to follow and then lead me down to our destination.

It doesn't take too long for us to enter what looks like a large meeting hall. I could see how someone—someone being me—would get lost in this place, given it appears to be somewhat of a maze, and the blueprints we had were completely inaccurate. Or it could be that that's only showing one level, but it's really fucking annoying.

A group of people are congregating at the far end, and we walk in that direction without pause.

There are four men standing on what appears to be a makeshift stage, and it's all I can do to choke back my snort of laughter at the ridiculousness of the situation I'm finding myself in.

An older man finally speaks up and asks, "What is the meaning of this, Matteo?"

He inclines his head toward me and replies, "Someone sent me a gift."

All eyes turn towards me, and I squirm from the attention. Finally, that same man who spoke previously says, "And who the fuck is she?"

They all look at me expectantly, and once again, I find I'm incapable of speech, so Matteo rolls his eyes and replies, "This is Jessica Killeen, Seamus's daughter."

There are a few gasps from the men standing around and widening of eyes as they are obviously surprised at this news.

One of the younger guys standing on the stage says, "You're fucking kidding me, right?"

"Well, that's what she says," Matteo responds. "Of course, we'll have to verify this is true. If any of you even care?"

The man who spoke initially speaks up, "Unfortunately, we have to care."

Matteo frowns and mutters, "That's what I was afraid of."

One of the other younger men asks, "Why do we have to fucking care? They dropped their bitch off here. Can't we do what we want with her?"

The older man laughs almost bitterly as he replies, "Sure, if we want to start the war of all wars with the Irish."

The younger guy pipes up again, "We're not afraid of the fucking Irish."

The older man turns his eyes toward him and glares as he says, "It would be one thing if it was just the Irish. But you would be better served to remember that most times, if you piss off one family, you piss off everyone associated with that family."

The younger guy looks a little bit sheepish for a moment and then nods. The older guy turns back to Matteo and says, "I'll verify her identity. If she is who she says she is, we need to proceed cautiously."

"And if she's not?"

The man shrugs. "Then you can do whatever the fuck you want

with her."

A commotion on the other side of the room draws everyone's attention, so I turn to look, my heart stopping in my chest as my eyes clash with the eyes of one Mathias Shields.

He mostly looks through me, though I'm sure he must recognize me.

I move to take a step toward him, but the minuscule shake of his head stops me, and I look away.

He walks further into the room, the same tall, dark-haired man who brought me to Matteo following with him. He stops a few feet from us as he asks, "What the fuck's going on now?"

The older gentleman answers, "It appears the Irish have sent a gift for Matteo."

He looks at me briefly, those dead eyes flat as he then looks over at Matteo and responds, "Is that right?"

Matteo's expression turns decidedly smug, and I see Matt's hand twitching in response. And then Matteo says, "That's right. Sent me a virgin bride."

Matt's lips twitch minutely, and I feel that laughter bubbling up in me again. I choke it down, my eyes on the floor, knowing if I look him in the face, I'm going to lose it. I don't know if that means laughter, tears, or rage, but whatever's going to come out of me next isn't going to be good for my self-preservation.

And then Matteo says, "See, Mathias? Maybe you could have been so lucky if you weren't stuck with Kaian's fucking sister."

My entire body freezes, and my jaw clenches as the insinuation behind his words sinks in, and now I do look at him, but suddenly, he won't meet my eyes.

I'm saved from any kind of response that I'm dying to come out with when the older man says, "Jessica, consider yourself a guest for the time being. I'll have one of the women set you up with your own quarters while we get this sorted."

I turn and focus on him as I nod and reply, "Thank you. That is appreciated."

The man nods and motions to someone on the outskirts. Then, the next thing I know, a middle-aged woman is beside me, and she motions for me to proceed with her back across the room. I do as I'm told, suddenly desperate to be out of this room and away from these fucking people.

We pause at the doorway as one of the men opens the door for us, and then we walk through. I pause for a moment, glancing over my shoulder, hoping to catch a glimpse of Matt.

But he's gone.

12

An Answer, Of Sorts

Matt

WHEN WE GOT THE call to report for a situation briefing, never in my wildest dreams would I have considered that I would end up face-to-face with Jessica.

I'll admit it was only my lifetime experience of controlling my outward emotions that kept me from completely giving away our relationship.

And to say that would have been a disaster is a serious understatement.

I also realized that she likely said she was here for Matt and intended to find me rather than Matteo. And of course, Kaian would naturally assume she was for Matteo because no one is gonna send anyone for me.

What an absolute fucking clusterfuck.

My first instinct is to reach out to Darius and find out why Jessica is here. There's not a chance in hell she would be here if she wasn't somehow involved with those fucking assholes, and why any of them would think it was a good idea to send her into this hellhole is beyond me.

And I'm fucking pissed.

I barely manage to temper my anger as the men around me discuss the pertinent details of how we're supposed to handle this new situation.

I'm still reeling as I finally manage to exit the room, and Kaian, being the observant person that he is, is right on my heels, and I know I only have a matter of moments before he's all up in my ass, trying to figure out what the fuck my problem is.

No sooner are we through the doorway and the door is shut behind us than he asks, "What the fuck's going on, Matt?"

I don't bother looking at him as I reply, "I don't know what you're talking about."

"Don't give me that shit, man," he responds. "Maybe you can pull one over on those other assholes, but I'm not that stupid."

I ignore him, hoping that he'll drop it though also knowing that he won't. So it's no great surprise to me when he adds, "Seriously. If you don't tell me what's going on, I can't help you."

I turn to him then and say, "You can't help me."

He glares at me, his arms crossing over his chest as he says, "Like fuck I can't."

I don't know what it is about this guy, but I'm not entirely sure I trust his mission to possibly help me. Typically, when people consistently go out of their way to help you, it's because they have an agenda that would be detrimental to your overall well-being.

He stares at me, waiting for me to say something, so finally, I shrug, and shake my head. "I'm not saying that you're not capable of helping me, Kai. But helping me would only put you at risk, and I'm not willing to do that."

This time, his eye-roll is obnoxious, and he snorts and then replies, "Give me a fucking break. You don't get to decide where and when I put my life at risk."

"Well, that may be so, but right now, I don't really see how you can help. That doesn't mean there won't be something that comes up in the near future, though, so consider your offer noted."

"See that you do."

He stares me down until I nod in agreement, and then he nods as well before turning and exiting the room.

I stand there in the middle of the room for a moment, unsure what the fuck I should do next. And then I curse, pushing down my urge to destroy something.

I honestly had no idea that Jessica has ties to a criminal organization. I'm more annoyed that we missed it, though I understand that unless we have good reason to suspect someone, we tend to only do a very basic background check.

Something we'll be making some changes on going forward, given the fact this isn't the first time that we've fucked ourselves over by not being thorough.

Of all the people she could possibly end up shackled to, Matteo is the worst of the worst. The man's a fucking sadist, and he would think nothing of using her, abusing her, and then tossing her to the side, regardless of who her father is. It's only dumb luck that he thought to bring her appearance to the attention of people that actually have a fucking brain.

I quickly change my clothes, pull on workout gear, and head toward the gym. I know they'll have her housed in the guest quarters, which are on the same level as the gym, so hopefully, I'll be able to find her without drawing any attention to myself.

The entire floor is quiet, which is typical for this time of day. The majority of people don't bother working out, and the ones that do tend to do it in the morning. They reserve the evening and nighttime hours for fucking, fighting, or just generally partying.

I pretend to be doing a circuit around the gym, and after about thirty minutes or so, I head toward the locker rooms, quietly veering off in the direction of the guest quarters.

The empty rooms have the doors left open, so it doesn't take me long to pinpoint where she's being kept. She probably wasn't very happy when she realized she was locked in, but hopefully, she's smart enough not to raise too much of a ruckus about it.

I enter the room soundlessly, closing the door behind me and then scanning the dimly lit room, but coming up empty. A rustling comes from the bathroom, so I walk in that direction, and then she's there in the doorway, a yelp of surprise echoing through the room.

"What the fuck, Matt?"

I can't help but smirk, a small laugh escaping as I reply, "I think I'm the one that should be saying that, Jess."

She glares at me, pushing past me and walking toward the bed as she says, "I think you gave up the right to ask questions when you ghosted me."

"I didn't ghost you. Ghosting you would have been not responding without giving you an explanation."

She whirls on me, her hands resting on her hips as she says, "Explanation?" She pauses and then says quite sarcastically, "You need to forget about me." She pauses again, glaring at me, and then laughs bitterly as she adds, "Quite the fucking explanation, you asshole."

I grit my teeth, rushing toward her and stopping only a few inches from her as I snarl, "That was the only explanation I could give you without putting you in danger."

She scoffs, her tone still mocking as she says, "Well, maybe if you'd been a little clearer, I wouldn't be in the situation I'm currently in."

"Explanation or no explanation, why in the fuck would you come here?"

"Because we were worried about you."

"Who is we?" I ask incredulously.

"Your friends, you moron."

My fucking friends. I'm completely appalled that my idiotic friends would do something so shortsighted as to send her here. "Why would they choose you?"

"Because I'm the only one no one would recognize," she replies calmly. "Anyone else would be recognized too quickly to actually locate you."

"And then you end up literally stuck with the biggest asshole here."

"Well, I didn't do it intentionally. And then, once I was there, what the fuck was I supposed to do?"

I take a deep breath, still shaking my head as I put a little space between us. "Why didn't you tell me who your father is?"

She raises her brows at me and then replies, "Because it's irrelevant."

"How can it be irrelevant?"

"I haven't seen the man in decades. I intended to never see the man again, so that seems irrelevant."

"Well, it's not fucking irrelevant now," I spit out. "Is he going to corroborate your story, or is this going to be a bigger problem?"

She gives me a blank look for a moment and then grimaces. "I really don't know. My mother's dying wish was that I be released from the family duties to live my own life. I got a new name, background, and life, and I never looked back."

My anger and frustration leave my body, and I back away, sitting in the chair against the wall. I lean forward and brace my forearms on the tops of my thighs as I stare over at her and say, "This is really fucking bad."

"I kind of gathered that."

I shake my head as I reply, "No, really. If he tells them that you're full of shit, you're a goner. And it won't be an easy end, either."

"And if his story matches mine?"

I groan, sitting back in the chair; my hands come up as I shrug with my entire body. "I honestly don't know if you're better off being dead or married to Matteo."

She sighs, sitting on the edge of the bed as she says, "Well, it's not really your problem, Matt."

"Not my problem?"

"Yep," she says shortly. "I came here to make sure you were all right, and clearly you are. So, I'll just have to take whatever comes and hope for the best."

My eyes practically bug out of my head as I parrot, "Hope for the best?"

She nods, and I can see she believes her bullshit lines as best as she can, given the circumstances. "The ship has sailed, and I'm doubtful I'll be able to get off, so it is what it is."

"It is what it is," I parrot again.

She looks over at me, quirking a brow as she asks, "Are you all right?"

The fury that had left me only a few minutes ago suddenly rushes back, and I jump to my feet, crossing the room in a few long strides. I stop in front of her and grasp her by her upper arms as I lean in close and say forcefully, "No, I'm not fucking okay."

She glares up at me, pushing against me and shaking me off. When I step back, she jumps to her feet and shouts, "Well, too fucking bad. If you think you can go gallivanting off without giving anyone any information until they worry about you, then you're a moron. But now that we know you're okay, I guess I'll just have to pay my penance for giving a shit."

I deflate a bit, wishing there was a way for me to explain without giving her information that will just put her more at risk. I've always been a straight shooter, and the last couple of years of having to toe the line at every turn has become exhausting. I'm sure the expression on my face is pained as I say softly, "I don't know if I can save you from this."

She gives me a bland look and says clearly, "It's not your job to save me."

My first instinct is to call bullshit on her statement, but I do know what she means. Sometimes, we have no choice but to save ourselves.

I nod, and she steps back and resumes her previous seat on the bed and then mutters, "So you can just go and get yourself hitched to somebody's sister without fucking worrying about me."

Shit. I forgot about that.

"Jessica," I begin as I take a short step toward her. She puts her hand up, and I stop my forward momentum, but then I add, "It's not what you think."

She puts both her hands up. I snap my mouth shut, and then she says, "Just save it. It's just something else that's irrelevant, given our current circumstances. Though I do find it amusing that we're technically both betrothed to other people."

I wince at the word *betrothed*. I also can't give her a proper explanation, and since I do my best not to blatantly lie, I just keep my mouth shut.

She's quiet for a few moments, and I stand there rather awkwardly, and then she says, "So I guess we just wait?"

I nod. "It's all we can do. I'll try to get as much information as I can ahead of time in the hope it can be fixed, but I don't have the control here that I have in the outside world."

"What the fuck are you doing here, Matt?"

I just look at her, hoping she can see in my eyes all the things I want to say to her—that I'm just not allowed to. And maybe she can, but I'm sure that doesn't take the sting out of my silence.

Finally, I say, "I assume Antoinette and Carolina gave you a full briefing before sending you in here?"

She nods. "Yes. Right down to the tiniest, most violent detail."

"So, they've told you how to react and how not to in most situations?"

She nods again. "Yes. I think I have it under control now, though, for a few minutes in the beginning there, I almost fucked it up royally."

"Maniacal laughter?" I ask.

She giggles and nods some more. "Yeah, Carolina was right. That playing daft worked like a charm, but it only works so far before you have to dial it in and actually act like you have one fucking brain cell in your head. It's a fine line."

I smile, wanting nothing more than to whisk her out of here, being entirely frustrated that I can't.

We laugh together quietly for a few moments, and eventually, silence settles around us. She rises from where she was seated on the bed and walks over to me, stopping a few inches from me. She reaches up and strokes her fingertips along my cheek as she whispers, "You should go."

I close my eyes, wanting to sink into her touch for as long as I possibly can, but knowing that our moment is over just as quickly as it had begun.

I swallow the lump in my throat, incapable of finding any words, even with everything that I want to say in the moment, and then her touch is gone. I open my eyes, and she says a little louder, "Get the fuck out of here before you get us both killed."

I sigh heavily, moving to walk away, but then I pause, turning back to look at her. "If I get an opportunity to fix this, just remember that I'm going to have to say and do some things you're not going to like."

"I have a feeling I'm going to have to get used to a lot of things I'm not going to like, regardless of who they're coming from."

"Yes," I reply seriously. "But these things will be more difficult for you to swallow, coming from me. It will seem completely out of character from the Matt that you know, and I won't be able to sway, no matter what you say or do in response to my words and actions. I will have to stay the course. And if you fight me, I will have to hurt you."

She frowns and steps back from me, almost unconsciously as she asks, "Hurt me how?"

"That I don't know. But I need you to remember that when it comes down to it, I will literally do anything to save you."

She shivers visibly, and I know that she understands exactly what I'm saying.

And I mean every word of it.

The hierarchy of the criminal underworld is quite literally kill or be killed. And in most cases, if you attempt to usurp the current order, bloodshed is imminent, and the kill or be killed mentally becomes imperative.

I stare at her intently, unblinking. "Do you understand what I'm saying, Jessica?"

She takes a deep breath, slowly exhales it, and then nods as she replies, "I understand. Don't worry."

I turn to leave the room, but her voice draws my attention back to her when she says, "Matt."

I meet her eyes again, noting the yearning there, the desperation, and I take a step back toward her, extending my hand, which she takes. I stand there for a moment, stroking my thumb along the back of her hand. We watch each other silently, communicating wordlessly what we're feeling.

I wait another moment and then slowly release her hand as I say, "I got you."

And then I spin on my heel and walk away.

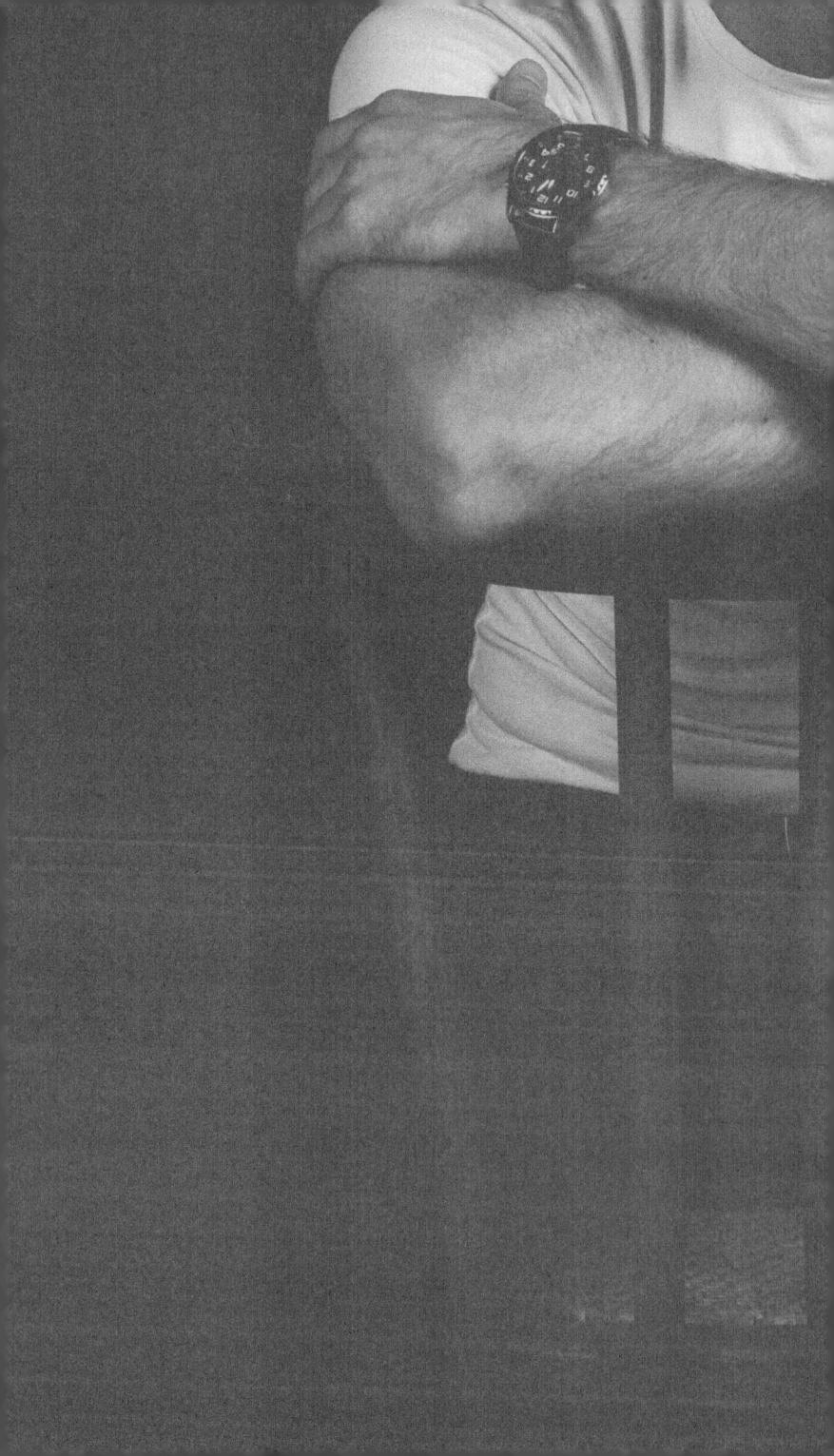

13

The Messenger, of Sorts

Matt

I MANAGE TO MAKE it back to my room without being seen.

I burst into the room, immediately startled by Kaian sitting in the goddamn chair in the corner, obviously waiting for me.

"And where have you been, Matt?" he asks sarcastically.

I ignore him and immediately start removing my clothes as I make my way into the bathroom. I'm completely bare-assed by the time I get to the shower, and I flip the taps on, not waiting for the water to warm before I step under the spray.

Of course, ignoring him doesn't deter Kaian one bit, and I hear him from the doorway say, "You know ignoring me won't work, Shields. Fucking spill already."

"There's nothing to say, Kai," I reply impatiently. "I went to the gym and now I'm back."

I'm met by a long moment of silence until, finally, curiosity has me peeking out to see that he's no longer in the doorway. I take my moment of reprieve, even knowing he won't have actually left the room. He won't be that easily deterred.

I wash myself quickly, turning off the water and grabbing a towel, and I'm half-dry as I walk back into the bedroom. Sure enough, Kai is back in the chair, waiting patiently.

I throw my wet towel at him and then walk to the chest of drawers, pulling out clean clothes and dressing myself quickly.

I go and sit on the bed across from the chair he's sitting in and look at him intently, but I say nothing. I stare at him long enough that he starts to squirm, and after another few moments, he mutters, "What the fuck are you looking at?"

"Shut up. I'm trying to see something."

He frowns, sitting up straighter in the chair but closing his mouth as I asked. I continue to stare at him, not entirely certain what I'm looking for, but if nothing else, I enjoy making him uncomfortable.

After a few more moments go by, I finally respond, "I'm trying to decide if I can trust you."

He snorts and shakes his head. "Can we really trust anyone?"

I incline my head in agreement. "My point exactly. The other part of it is that I don't want to cause trouble for you."

He shrugs as he responds, "Nothing but trouble in this business. Sometimes, it's nice to make my own trouble rather than accepting everyone else's."

I stare at him again, and finally, I sigh, realizing I don't really have a choice but to hope that he won't fuck me over. "I need you to do me a favor."

His eyes narrow and he leans forward in the chair as he says, "Well, what is it, then?"

"I need you to deliver a message for me to someone in the city."

He frowns, giving me an incredulous look. "You can't just go and do it yourself?"

"I have other things to attend to right now. And I can't be seen anywhere near these people."

"And I can?"

"Yes," I reply. "You have no ties to these people, and I'm sure you have ways to make it either look like an accident, a coincidence, or just something that's funny."

He sits back in his chair and says, "Okay. Who am I delivering the message to?"

I pause, knowing that this will be the moment where he either gives himself away as being a problem or confirms that he's going to be helpful. I clear my throat, not really wanting to say it but knowing I have no choice, and it comes out as more of a croak than anything else. "The Beast."

His eyes bug out of his head quite comically, and then he shakes his head and says, "Nope. Not a fucking chance."

"Why the fuck not?"

He gives me a bland look. "You know why not." I shrug, unsure what he's insinuating and not wanting to give my hand away too much. After a few moments, he adds, "You don't just go looking for the Beast, man. You actually spend most of your days hoping to never have to see that guy."

I hide my smile behind my hand, always amused when other people talk about Darius with such horror and awe. "Oh, come on. He can't be that bad."

"Can't be that bad?" Kai exclaims. "Even the tamest stories of the Beast will make your blood run cold."

"You really believe all that shit?"

He nods emphatically, and so I continue, "You know that 90% of that shit has got to be made up. There's no way someone that infamous hasn't been taken down just out of principle."

He laughs. "They've tried, and eventually, everyone gave up."

I don't bother hiding my smile this time when I say, "Well, I can tell you the best place to find him and what to say so you won't get yourself killed before you get in the door."

He looks at me thoughtfully, and then, after a few moments, he responds, "So it's true, then?"

"What's true?"

"You are friends with the Beast."

I shrug, one hand coming up and waving in the air. "Yes and no."

"There is no yes and no, Matt. Either you're in good with the Beast, you don't exist to the Beast, or you're dead by the hand of the Beast."

"I may have seen him a time or two."

Kaian laughs boisterously, and he leans forward in his chair and slaps his thigh with his hand a couple of times as he crows, "I fucking knew it. People told me I was crazy, but I fucking knew it."

"Knew what?"

"That you two were thick as thieves."

"Well, I don't know about thick as thieves," I reply dryly.

"And frankly, I don't know who is more frightening?"

I give him a questioning look, shaking my head, and then he says, "The Beast or Mrs. Beast?"

Now I laugh loudly, truly going to enjoy the day when I get to tell Antoinette that she's known as "Mrs. Beast" because that's going to piss her off. "I wouldn't call her that to her face."

Kai puts his hands up defensively as he quips, "Don't look at me."

I sigh. For a moment, I don't feel as out of control as I have for the last few hours, and I say, "So, you'll do it?"

He doesn't answer at first, and I eye him speculatively, as I watch the wheels in his head turning. But then he nods. "Well, fuck it. I may as well."

"You'll have to remember the location and what you have to say. I don't want anything in writing, no text strings, nothing."

He nods and then stands and states, "Make sure you keep the message short then because my memory isn't what it once was."

"Oh, don't worry," I reply with a snort. "It will be short and sweet."

He raises his brows as he asks, "Well, what is it then?"

I smile. "Fuck around time."

14

Busted Chops

Antoinette

FOR THE LAST THIRTY minutes, I've been watching this guy on the outside cameras wander along, feigning nonchalance.

For the last five minutes, I've been trying to decide which door I want to have miraculously be unlocked, while also hoping someone else might come along in the meantime and ask him what he's doing.

Because I can't figure out what he thinks he's doing, given the fact he's not even dressed stealthily. Actually, there's nothing stealthy about him, considering he's been lumbering around out there blatantly looking for a way in.

Part of me wants to allow him into the building so I can play a few games with him, but I know if anyone finds out I did such a thing, I'll be in deep trouble. Not that I'm entirely opposed to trouble, but I prefer to stay out of the type of trouble that could get anybody I care about killed.

Sighing, I switch to the cameras to my phone and then slowly make my way out the far side of the building so I can circle around and play with him out of doors.

I send off a quick message, letting everyone know that trouble may be about and I'm going to investigate.

I then immediately mute my phone so I don't have to hear the incessant pinging of a bunch of people telling me to cool my jets and wait.

They should know by now that cooling my jets isn't really something I do. While I won't intentionally throw myself into danger, the idea that I can't handle one lone man in the darkness is ludicrous.

Of course, I'm sure there could be a whole slew of men out there waiting to ambush me, and if that's the case, then I am a dumb shit.

I hoist myself up on the edge of the large stone planter I insisted we put in various places around the warehouse, and that's where I'm sitting when the man strolls around the corner, still looking for a way in.

He's so focused on his mission that he foolishly doesn't notice me sitting there. As soon as he gets just beyond me, I ask playfully, "Whatcha doin'?"

He freezes, his body stiff as his slowly turns, so he's looking at me. He grimaces and then laughs nervously as he replies, "Nothing?"

Definitely sounds like a question, which makes me smile. I laugh, and he visibly tenses even further until he's standing there like a wide-eyed statue, which makes me laugh even louder.

After a few moments of listening to me laugh, he turns his body toward me, crosses his arms over his chest, and says, "I was sent for the Beast."

Abruptly, I stop laughing.

I slowly slide forward until my feet are touching the ground and then I stand, all humor gone from my tone as I ask, "Are you now?"

He frowns, indecision crossing his face, and after a moment, he adds, "Oh, not like that."

I take a step toward him and then another and another until I'm standing naught more than a foot from him. I look up into his face and respond quietly, "Then, by all means, explain yourself."

He swallows, and I watch his Adam's apple bob in his neck before looking back into his face again. He answers, "I just need to talk to him."

"What could you possibly have to talk to him about?"

"Matt sent me," he rushes out. "He asked me to send a message."

I narrow my eyes, leaning in slightly as I say, "A message?"

He gives me a humorless, toothy grin as he winces and stutters, "To-to deliver him a message, to-to tell him something."

"What's the message?"

Now, he narrows his eyes at me and replies, "I'm supposed to tell him, not you."

I roll my eyes, my hands settling on my hips as I respond, "Well, you're not going to get to him until you tell me, so you decide."

His lips press together, and he looks me over, obviously unsure how he wants to proceed, so I ask, "What's your name?"

"Kaian," he answers easily. "Kaian Volkov."

I tilt my head, squinting at the ground as I say, "Kind of an odd mix of names."

He laughs as he replies, "Yeah, let's just say my mother was the only person the great Vladimir Volkov ever allowed to have an opinion."

I raise my brows, now understanding why he looks vaguely familiar. "Another prince of the underworld."

He barks out a short laugh, drawing my attention back to his face as he says, "Please don't judge me for that."

"I won't judge you, but you're still gonna have to give me the message."

He nods and swallows again before saying, "Matt says it's fuck around time."

Well, that gets my attention. It's like music to my ears.

I do my best to squash my outward excitement as I reply, "And how do I know Matt sent you?"

He gives me an incredulous look as he sputters, "How else would I have known where to find you if Matt hadn't told me in great detail?"

"You're not very good at this sneaking around stuff. I would think that at your age, you'd at least know the basics by now."

He frowns as he says, "Believe me, I'm well-versed in clandestine tactics. Just in this particular case, I needed you to see me because I needed you to find me so I can speak to the Beast."

I sigh and incline my head at him in acknowledgment of the validity behind his statement. "Were you going to tap dance out here if I'd waited any longer to come out?"

"Whatever it takes to draw some attention, apparently."

"Who the fuck are you?" Tony asks from behind him.

He jumps, obviously startled, and I laugh. "You didn't notice we weren't alone for the last two minutes, either. Was that part of your plan, too?"

Kaian's gaze swings back to me, and he glares at me. "Well, you don't have to be mean about it."

Tony laughs as he walks closer, stopping when he's standing next to Kaian. "You obviously don't know Antoinette very well."

His eyes light up as he says, "Mrs. Beast? What a pleasure."

Tony's laughter increases, and he slaps his hand against his thigh as he jokes, "Mrs. Beast. That's great."

I mean, I've been called far worse things than "Mrs. Beast.". Unlike Darius, nicknames in general don't bother me much. So, I smile as I reply, "Mrs. Beast in the flesh."

After a few moments, Tony finally stops laughing. "Kaian Volkov. Now, I heard a fair amount about you in passing, so your behavior so far tonight seems kind of odd."

"Did you catch our previous conversation?"

Tony nods, an excited gleam in his eye as he says, "You know I like me some fuck around time."

I raise my brows at Tony as I ask, "What are you doing here?"

He gives me a bored look as he responds, "You said there was a possible intruder, and you're going to go investigate. Did you think we would just sit back and wait for you to report back as to what happened?"

I shrug. "Didn't really think one way or another about any of it."

He shakes his head, looks at Kaian, and says, "Women."

My hand shoots out, and I grip his earlobe between my thumb and index finger knuckle, squeezing viciously before he can yank himself away as I say, "What was that? What did you say?"

He yelps, and Kaian jumps back as Tony laughs and yells, "Nothing. I didn't say anything."

I yank my hand away without releasing my grip on his earlobe to get one last dig in. "That's what I thought."

I look over at Kaian, who is staring at us wide-eyed, likely uncertain what the hell is going on as I ask, "How about you? You got something you want to say?"

He puts both his hands up in front of him and shakes his head. "Nope. I'm good."

Tony straightens, throwing me a crooked grin as he responds, "You know I'm only messing with you, Nettie."

I snort, resisting my urge to give him another slap, and then Kaian mutters, "Are you guys always like this?"

"Like what?"

"I don't know," he replies. "Just seems like an inappropriate time for jokes?"

Tony rolls his eyes, and I snort dismissively. "No such thing as an inappropriate time for jokes. Sometimes, you gotta do whatever it takes to get through the day."

Kaian gives me a confused look, and Tony adds, "If you don't like our jokes, you can fuck off."

I laugh again, and Kaian puts his hands up again as he retorts, "I'm sure they'll grow on me over time."

"Sure they will," Tony scoffs. "We may as well go in. Everyone else should be here soon, and we can try to figure out what we're going to do next."

We turn and walk toward the door into the building, and then I realize Kaian isn't following behind, so I turn back to him and ask, "What are you doing?"

"Aren't we done here?"

Tony walks back, swinging his arm over Kaian's shoulder, his fingers gripping on as he jerks him in close and says, "I have a feeling that we're only just beginning."

I smile, opening the door and then holding it for them as Tony maneuvers an obviously reluctant Kaian through the doorway, and then I follow behind, relishing the sound of the heavy door as it slams shut behind us.

15

A Family Reunion

Jessica

I T'S BEEN AN INTERESTING couple of days since Matt showed up to my room asking questions.

For the most part, I've stayed in my room, though at least once a day, I'm summoned down to the equivalent of the great hall, where a bunch of old, crusty men talk about me as if I'm not actually there.

Luckily, given my career in entertainment as well as my previous experience living amongst these types of people, I'm entirely accustomed to the dealings of old, crusty men. I was barely sixteen when I was finally released from my life sentence of misery. I'd been working on getting an out for myself when my mother passed, securing me a future outside what was going to be expected of me as the daughter of a criminal overlord.

This means I know the best way to handle these types of men is by pretending they're not there.

I'm not sure if this knowledge is making it easier or more difficult, considering the urge to roll my eyes is high most of the time. I only got caught one time so far, which earned me a pretty good slap, and then choking down maniacal laughter just about sent me into a tizzy.

I haven't seen Matt at all, and I wish I could say the same thing about Matteo.

One thing I learned about him is that he's vile. He's come sniffing around here a few times, and I've managed to maneuver him back out the door relatively unscathed, but I feel it's only a matter of time before he stops playing nice.

I'm contemplating whether or not a person can die of boredom when one of the women shows up, stating my presence is required. If she has any actual information, she's not sharing it with me, and I don't bother prodding too much, knowing it would be pointless.

The room isn't nearly as full as normal—maybe two dozen men—half of whom I don't recognize. I scan the faces of each person, taking a mental note of the ones who appear to be new, and then I look at the end of the room where the old men who typically call the shots are all congregating.

And that's when I see him.

I frown, swallowing the suddenly painful lump in my throat, and then I sigh, putting my shoulders back and straightening my spine as I walk toward him.

My father has arrived.

I'm annoyed yet not surprised that they wouldn't provide me with a private word with him before making a spectacle. I'm sure they decided to do that so we wouldn't be able to come up with any kind of story together, but knowing my father, he has it all in hand anyway.

My general feeling as I look at him is ambivalence.

I recognize that his allowing me to go out on my own wasn't something he had to do. It's also something that would be frowned upon by basically everyone.

So for that, I'm grateful.

But it also leaves me vulnerable because I have no idea what's happened since I've been gone. I'm sure he hasn't suddenly shifted into a good person, but that doesn't necessarily mean he would want to cause me harm, especially knowing how my mother would've felt about it.

If there was ever anyone he loved more than himself, it was her.

I stop when I'm a few feet in front of him, and he looks me over quickly, his eyes briefly meeting mine. The coldness emanating from him sends a shiver down my spine.

No one says anything for a few moments, and I grip my hands together in front of me and do my best not to fidget nervously as I wait for someone to say something.

After a few long, awkward moments, my father nods shortly and says, "I see you've finally managed to do one thing correctly."

I frown and then quickly shift my features back to neutral as I nod, knowing I'm not meant to say anything. If nothing else, I do remember my place is to be seen and not heard, and even if I'm heard, it's only to say what I've been told to say.

My father turns back to the men in charge and says, "I'm glad my gift made it to you unharmed. Shall I assume that it is well received?"

The men look amongst themselves for a moment before the older one, who typically does the talking, says, "Very well. Once the shock wore off, of course."

My father smiles as he replies, "Well, I would think Matteo would be pleased. If nothing else, she's not bad to look at."

The men laugh, and my lip curls minutely before I'm able to school myself, now completely understanding what Antoinette was talking about when she said they will make your blood boil.

I remain quiet, my eyes downcast to not draw attention to myself. The less I have to say, the better because nothing I say at this point is going to help me see the light of day outside of this shithole.

The older man laughs as he says, "Well, he's certainly pleased with her pure status. Imagine our surprise to find there's still a virgin left."

My father's eyes dart to mine, and one of his brows lifts in such an out-of-character move that I have to suppress the urge to giggle. He immediately goes back to his typical, aloof coldness as he responds smoothly, "That's right. Some of us still know how to keep our daughters in hand."

The urge to snort is overwhelming.

Of all the ridiculous and insulting statements one could make about me, this one really takes the cake.

I grit my teeth and stare hard at the floor, so lost in my suddenly murderous thoughts that it takes me a moment to register that my father is saying my name.

My eyes jump to his, hopefully wide-eyed and innocent and not at all reminiscent of my inner feelings, as I respond demurely, "Yes, Father? My apologies. I'm so overwhelmed with the events of the last few days that I got lost in thoughts of the future."

He presses his lips together, and the look on his face can only be described as incredulous, and once again, I have to suppress my urge to giggle.

"We just decided that you and Matteo will be married in two days' time," he replies coldly. "Everything will be taken care of for you, so all you have to do is put on a dress and show up and do your job. Do you understand?"

I nod. "Yes, sir. I understand."

His hand comes out and makes a shooing motion that has me biting the inside of my cheek, and I quickly turn on my heel and head to the door for fear I will say something I will instantly regret.

The same woman leads me back to my room, and as soon as I get there, I slam the door shut and lean back against it, my heart galloping in my chest.

Two days is a lot of time when you fear you'll die of boredom, but it's a very short amount of time to figure out how you're going to dodge the biggest bullet of your life.

And after Bobby, that's saying something.

I know if it comes down to it and I find myself standing across from Matteo at a marriage ceremony, there's nothing I can do to stop it.

I think back on all the conversations I've had with Carolina and Antoinette about how to survive in this kind of life. Then, I think back on the common theme that all women fall back on time and time again. When you're stuck in an impossible, kill-or-be-killed situation, you always go for the jugular.

And there's no rule saying you can't become a widow on your wedding night.

16

An Irish in the Shadows

Matt

I'VE BEEN GONE FOR two days, trying to pinpoint how I ended up in my current position.

Kaian, through his brief conversation with my people, established that Jessica being here is purely a coincidence fueled by her own curiosity and annoyance that I might have ghosted her.

It's true that that wasn't my typical behavior, but desperate times called for desperate measures, and I was hopeful she would just do what I said and move on with her life.

Hindsight being what it is, it was clearly a stupid idea and reaffirms my stance on clear and concise communication always being the best bet.

I enter my room, so desperate for my bed that I don't even turn the light on. I drop my stuff at the end of my bed and walk through the dark room into the bathroom where I strip down and then proceed to take a quick, cold shower, exhaustion almost overwhelming me.

I pull on a pair of sleep pants as I exit the bathroom. When I step back into the bedroom, a movement in the corner catches my eye.

I groan, annoyance bubbling up as I reach for the light switch and say, "Really, Kaian? How many times do I have to tell you to sto—"

I stop talking abruptly as the light blinks on, and instead of being face to face with Kaian sprawled in the chair, as is his norm, I'm met by the piercing green eyes of an Irish mobster.

I don't bother attempting to make a move for a weapon, or even a shirt. At this point, if the man wants to kill me, he's got me, and there's nothing I can do about it. I'm relatively sure if he wanted to finish me off, he would have done so at any time between me entering the room and now, but you never know if someone's just waiting to get some info before finishing the job.

I sigh, leaning a shoulder against the doorjamb as I cross my arms over my chest and ask, "And to what do I owe the honor?"

Jessica's father, Seamus Killeen, doesn't spare me any emotion as he replies, "Are you looking to be dead?"

I snort as I respond, "People have tried numerous times, yet here I stand."

He raises his brows at me, the corner of his mouth twitching as he says, "Are you really trying to tell me that I couldn't have knocked you off at least a dozen times in the last ten minutes?"

I lift a shoulder dismissively. "I'm not saying shit."

"Why is my daughter here?"

I lift my chin, squinting in concentration as I answer, "How the hell would I know?"

The man stands so abruptly that I have to stop myself from flinching. I'm not generally intimidated by men of any size, but this Irish mobster is a formidable figure on a bad day. He's tall and broad and has a reputation of being lethal under any circumstances, but he's also smart, clever, and not afraid to make the hard choices. He's probably the reason no one's made a move on the Irish in a generation.

He steps close to me, and I don't move. I just meet him face to face as he says, "Don't play stupid with me. You don't think I haven't had eyes on her every second of her life since she went off on her own?"

"If that's the case," I reply stonily. "How come she ended up needing my help when she was in trouble?"

He squints at me, giving me a small nod as he says, "That issue has been dealt with. And I owe you a debt for stepping up when I was unable to, but that doesn't change the fact that she's here in this situation because of you."

My hands fall to my sides, and I push off the doorjamb so I'm standing in front of him, unable to deny it at this point. Because I know it's true. If I hadn't tried to use the path of least resistance to push her away, she wouldn't be here right now, potentially tied to a devil man.

Seamus is still standing there staring at me, waiting for me to answer, and I know if I decide I want to play a waiting game with him, we'll be waiting a long damn time. So, after a moment, I step back into the bathroom, pulling a shirt off the counter and yanking it over my head.

When I walk back into the bedroom, he backs off, giving me room to move freely. I stop in the middle of the room, turn back to him, and say, "This is not what I wanted. I told her to stay away."

He laughs and then sighs as he replies, "Sounds familiar."

He moves back across the room, falling into the chair haphazardly. I smile at how out of character it appears to his reputation. I sit across from him on the edge of the bed, leaning forward and resting my forearms on the tops of my thighs as my eyes meet his. "I'm going to fix it."

He snorts loudly, one of his hands coming up and waving around as he says, "And how the fuck do you expect to do that?"

"Hopefully some fancy footwork."

"And if that doesn't work?"

I pause, not sure how best to respond, but then I say, "If that doesn't work, then we resort to bloodshed. Isn't that how it works?"

He quirks an eyebrow at me, and I'm briefly taken aback, but then he asks, "You'd do that?"

"Yes," I answer without hesitation. "Wouldn't you?" He shrugs, and it's not lost on me that I'm seeing a side of this man that most people don't get to see. When he remains silent, I ask, "You wouldn't go to any lengths to save your daughter?"

"It's not that simple. I have far too many people depending on me to throw it all away over one person, blood-related or not."

I frown, anger bubbling up inside me, even though I know what he's saying is valid. When you're in charge of a widespread organization, you can't think of things in terms of one person versus another. That's not always how it is, given a lot of the people in charge tend to think of themselves and their own power and greed, so I can't fault him for his thinking, even if that means Jessica is at risk.

Then he says, "There is no love lost between me and my daughter. We've basically had no relationship for the majority of her life, and I know right now, her mother, God rest her soul, is rolling over in her grave at the idea that I didn't prevent this."

He stops talking, staring off into space, and just when I'm about to speak, he continues, "I don't know that I'm the type of man that knows how to love. The only person I've ever loved was my wife, and I loved her enough to grant her dying wish, which was to have her daughter free from the constraints of our lifestyle. I've bent and broken every rule there is to ensure that she would be kept far away from any of this, and then the next thing I know, I'm getting a message thanking me for the gift. I fear my initial response was not great."

"Well, that seems reasonable. Just the fact you were taken off-guard, I can't believe anyone would react reasonably under the circumstances."

"It came as quite a surprise to a few people that I even had a daughter, never mind an adult daughter that I could hand off to some sadistic fucking prick. There are a few people who think it's a great business strategy to try to merge families, as they say. But even if I had a child to use as a pawn, that is not a move I would make."

We fall silent, both of us lost in our own thoughts, and then I say, "I won't let them have her. That's a promise."

He nods and sits up straight in his chair, and the shift between the haphazard and the figurehead is quite abrupt. Shocking, even.

He rises to his feet, and I do the same. He closes the distance between us, extending his hand as he says, "I guess I will be indebted to you twice."

I take his hand, grasping it firmly in mine. "That's completely unnecessary. In my family, we take care of what's ours. We don't leave anyone to the wolves."

"I've heard that about you. So, tell me what I can do behind the scenes to help you succeed."

I know at some point I'm going to need assistance to get us out of here. Kaian already got the process moving by delivering my message, but this is about to get far more complicated.

"We don't have much time to lose since now they want to get this marriage sorted in two days."

My heart stops in my chest. "Two days?"

He nods and sighs heavily. "That's what they said. So, whatever you're going to do, you'll have to do it fast."

"I guess I'm going to need you to deliver some messages for me, then."

He nods and then replies, "Tell me who, what, and where, and I'll get it done."

"You'll have to deliver it yourself."

"Done," he replies firmly.

"Have you ever met the Beast?"

He rolls his eyes, and I laugh as he says, "Yes, and I know he hates that stupid name."

I smile, nodding in agreement. "That's one reason we use it. But obviously, you're going to have to go to them and let them know they'll have to try to get us out of here at some point."

"There's no way they'll be able to come in here without somebody noticing," he replies. "They may have to recruit some other people."

"I'm not sure we have anyone left who's inconspicuous."

He looks over at me thoughtfully, then his eyes light up, and he says, "I think I can help with that."

I raise my brows, falling behind him as he walks toward the door. Pausing with his hand on the doorknob, he turns back to me and says, "I know a person who can make anyone blend in anywhere. I'll take care of it."

Without another word, he opens the door and disappears through it, shutting it silently behind him. I stand there in the middle of the room, even more exhausted than I was before.

I flip the light switch, and the room falls into darkness. Then I walk over to the bed and flop onto it.

I can't imagine how he thinks any of my people are going to be able to come here without ending up dead within minutes.

I also know that my people will stop at nothing until they find a way.

17

An Irish Comes Calling

Tony

Tony: Someone wanna tell me why I'm getting word that some Irish mad man is looking for me?

Darius: Well, I don't know. Is there something you need to tell us?

Antoinette: That definitely sounds like a you problem.

Carolina: What the hell did you do now?

> **Tony**: I didn't do anything.

> **Carolina**: That's what you always say.

> **Darius**: Have you considered just asking why he's looking for you?

> **Tony**: Admitting I don't know what's going on would be a mistake.

> **Antoinette**: That may still be better than not knowing.

> **Tony**: I hate you.

> **Antoinette**: Liar.

I CLOSE OUT OF my texting app and pick up my burner phone, calling my Irish contact. The call connects, and no one says anything, so I say, "What does he want?"

"To meet."

"Why?"

My question is met with silence, which I suspected would happen, but it doesn't make it any less annoying. I let the silence drag on until I can't take it anymore, and then I sputter, "Fine. When?"

"He'll see you in three minutes. Don't move."

The line goes dead, and I curse under my breath because I should have known this would happen. These people have no use for boundaries or notice, so it's no great surprise that they've got a tail on me, and the man himself is likely within spitting distance of me. This also proves that I'm slacking because I didn't even notice that I was being followed.

Realizing I have no other option, I do as I'm told and don't move from my current seat. Happy I already ordered myself a coffee, I take a sip and enjoy the last few moments of silence I'm probably going to get for a while.

Sure enough, within moments, that Irish motherfucker is pulling out the chair across from me and having a seat like we're old friends.

I don't waste time with niceties or any of that fake bullshit. I just ask, "What do you want?"

"Matt sent me."

Well, this gets my attention. I almost drop my coffee halfway to my mouth, but I catch myself in time and set it on the table hard enough that some of the hot liquid splashes onto the table. "You've seen Matt?"

He nods and then says, "I got word that somehow my daughter ended up in the same building he's in. Apparently, engaged to a truly horrific man under the guise that we're going to unite the families."

I frown, shaking my head as I ask, "Your daughter? What the fuck does this have to do with Matt?"

He raises his brows at me, and for a moment, it feels like I'm going to be reprimanded for being a moron, but I raise my brows back and then wait until he finally answers, "Jessica. Is it safe for me to assume she's in that building because of you?"

Now, I squirm a bit under his intense stare, which isn't something I do very often, but I'm not going to bother lying to the man. "That would be a group effort, actually. But entirely her choice."

He lifts his arms and rests his hands on the table, palms down flat, and I get the impression he's repressing his urge to snatch up the butter knife in front of him and stab it through my neck. I mean, I wouldn't let him, but it would definitely be a fight for the ages. So, I add, "Jessica being your daughter is news to me. It's news to all of us. I'm relatively sure Matt didn't even know that."

I pull my phone back out, bring up my group text, and ignore the slew of messages I missed as I send a new one.

> **Tony**: Did any of you know that Jessica is linked to the Irish?

Darius: Excuse me?

Antoinette: Well, that would explain her murderous tendencies.

Darius: It's becoming increasingly obvious that we're missing more things than we're catching lately, and that perhaps once we get Matt back, we should fine-tune our processes so we can stop looking like assholes.

> **Tony**: Well, since you're the boss, you're the only one that actually looks like an asshole.

Carolina: *skull emoji*

Darius: *middle finger emoji*

I close out of my messages again, setting it on the table as I say, "No, we didn't know. Kind of annoyed that we didn't know, but it is what it is at this point."

"It's irrelevant," he says tiredly. "Now we just have to work on getting her out. Matt said he'll do whatever he can to prevent her from marrying that snake, but it's highly likely he won't be able to manage that without significant bloodshed. At some point, it will likely require an extraction, something that I can't be linked to."

I narrow my eyes at him, my arms crossing over my chest as I lean back in my chair. "Why can't it be linked to you?"

"I have far too many people depending on me to end up in a war over one life."

I smile and reply, "How about the war of all wars?"

He cocks his head at me and asks, "Explain."

"If we go in there on an extraction mission, it usually ends up being more of an extermination," I explain. "We're not going to go in there and just remove the two people we need. We're going to eliminate every last motherfucking one of them while completing the mission."

"So, you're saying if I don't want to be part of the extermination, I had better leave?"

"That depends on which side you're on," I answer honestly. "If you're with us, you're safe. If you're against us, you're dead." He gives me a rather arrogant look and chuckles under his breath. He says nothing, and eventually, I ask, "What's so funny?"

"I don't think I've ever been threatened so nonchalantly before."

"What can I say," I reply affably. "I'm a nonchalant kind of guy."

"Now, I know that's a fuckin' lie."

I can't help but smile, and then I change the subject. "So, how does Matt suggest we do this? Everyone knows us, and I can't say I'd pass for a very pretty woman."

"I have that handled. I'll be sending someone over to the warehouse this evening with everything you need to go deep undercover."

"How deep?"

He stands and looks down at me as he replies, "You won't even recognize yourself."

Stuffing my phone into my pocket, I rise from my chair, pick up my cold coffee, and throw it in the bin as I follow him out the door. I stop on the street, and he extends his hand to me as he says, "We don't necessarily want to be part of a war, but rest assured that the Irish won't stand in your way."

I take his hand, giving it a good shake before releasing it, and I nod. "Rest assured that we'll go in there and get it taken care of."

He says nothing further, just turns and walks away, quickly disappearing into the crowd. I reach into my pocket to pull out my phone only to come out with a rectangular business card.

I flip it over, and written on it is: *Camilla McDonough - Illusionist*. There's no phone number, email address, or anything else, but I know he must have slipped it into my pocket at some point.

I shake my head, annoyed that everyone seems to be quicker than me lately.

Shrugging off my brief moment of inferiority, I head off in the direction of the warehouse, whistling.

18

An Irish Canoodle

Tony

Camilla McDonough showed up later that same evening.

And when I say showed up, I mean she managed to infiltrate our warehouse, the spitting image of Carolina.

To say I was a little confused is an understatement.

Also, seriously perturbed.

Disgruntled.

And also not at all surprised, given the reputation of the Irish.

Of course, Carolina thought it was hilarious and even started joking around about how easy it would be for her to get away without me even knowing she's gone.

And Antoinette just fueled this with her own laughter and teasing.

With Camilla's point being made, she went on to explain exactly how she was going to get us in under the enemy's nose, and then it was decided that we would attend the upcoming wedding as guests of Seamus Killeen.

Since we know how we're going to get in, we just have to decide what we're going to do once we're there. Are we going to allow this wedding to take place? Do we sit back and wait for a sign from Matt that it's our turn to step in and fuck around? Or do we just do what we always do: wing it and see what happens?

We decide that Darius, Antoinette, and I will go under Camilla's magic and that we'll take point on the extraction mission. Mostly because we need someone on the outside who can take charge if things go to shit.

Being near the end of his US tour, Declan had to return to LA to keep his shows on track. So, Anton and Agatha came to assist Lilith and Carolina with managing the behind-the-scenes maneuvering. They'll wait on the outskirts of the property, out of sight, so if things go well, they can just pick us up, and if things go shit, they can come in and light the place on fire.

After hours of sitting in the chair, the reflection that blinks back at me is unrecognizable. It's amazing but also disconcerting, and then two strangers pop up in the mirror behind me, and I jump, staring in shock at who must be Darius and Antoinette.

"Isn't it amazing?" Antoinette asks. "Like, I could get used to this."

Darius laughs, turning his head from side to side, getting all of the angles of his new face as he replies, "It is amazing. Also disturbing."

She smiles brightly. "Disturbing how? We can be anyone we want to be."

He raises his brows, his eyes meeting hers in the mirror as he says, "Yes, and so can anyone else."

The smile drops from her face, and she frowns as his words sink in, and then she replies quietly, "Oh, shit. You're right."

Carolina appears behind me, one of her hands coming up over my shoulder, sliding across my chest. She whispers into my ear, "Well, do you think you might have some time for your wife before you go?"

I shake her off, sputtering, "You stop that."

She laughs, and Darius and Antoinette join her. Antoinette eyes Darius in the mirror again as she says, "I totally get it."

He gives her a decidedly smug look as he replies, "Likewise. We can literally be two strangers in a bar right now."

Carolina straightens, her hand moving to my shoulder as she says excitedly, "You could be three strangers in a bar right now."

I bristle, narrowing my eyes as I grit out, "All of you fucking cut it out."

"Oh, this could be fun," Antoinette exclaims.

Carolina steps closer to Antoinette, her hand coming up, her fingers tangling in Antoinette's now-blonde hair, the smile on her face coy as she leans in and whispers, "Fancy meeting you here."

I jump up from my chair, whirling around on them as I say, "Really? Do you really think this is the time for joking?"

Darius turns and leans against the desk in front of the mirror as he says nonchalantly, "Like you're one to talk about when it's appropriate to joke."

I cross my arms over my chest, grinding my teeth together, and then Carolina says, "Of all the bars in all the world, you had to walk into this one."

Antoinette throws her head back, laughs, and then steps closer to Carolina. She wraps an arm around her shoulder, leaning in so she can whisper words into her ear that I can't make out. Carolina giggles in response, and Darius chuckles beside me, throwing his elbow into my side. "You really need to lighten up, Tony."

I turn and glare at him. "If you ever get into the baby-making stage of your relationship, maybe you would understand."

Antoinette gasps beside me and then asks, "Really? Baby making?"

Carolina rolls her eyes at me, then gives me a middle finger and explains, "Well, we're not *not* trying to avoid pregnancy. But we're not necessarily actively trying to make a baby, either."

Antoinette cocks her head at her as she says slowly, "That sounds to me an awful lot like trying to make a baby."

Darius snorts beside me as he retorts, "Regardless of if you are or are not, it's not like she's going to get pregnant canoodling with Antoinette."

Antoinette and Carolina both nod in agreement, and I groan, realizing that nothing I say will stop these assholes once they get started.

I'm torn between shutting down their nonsense and teaching them a lesson.

I glance over at Dare, who's eyeing me quizzically. I roll my eyes and say, "Don't fucking tempt me, man."

He laughs as he says affably, "Temptation is the spice of life. I thought you knew that."

I shake my head, unsure of the best way to proceed, given I'm well aware of how Carolina and Antoinette get when they get together and have an idea in their heads.

I look over at the two women, still standing exceedingly close together, giggling naughtily. I finally look back at Darius and say, "Well, if there was ever gonna be a time, I suppose it would be when you look like a complete fucking stranger."

He barks out a laugh that draws the attention of both women, and Antoinette asks suspiciously, "What's so funny over there?"

Darius shrugs and answers easily, "Oh, nothing. Just a conversation amongst strangers."

Antoinette's lips twist, and she squints but says nothing. Carolina crosses her arms over her chest and says, "I get the feeling the boys are up to something."

Antoinette nods. "Quite obviously."

It's my turn to smirk at them as I retort, "Maybe we are. And what are you going to do about it?"

I know these words are a mistake as soon as they're out of my mouth, but it's too fucking late for regret. They look at each other, and I grimace, and Dare laughs, elbowing me again as he whispers, "Way to go, buddy."

The two women step closer together, and they're about an inch and a few seconds away from fully embracing when I panic. We really don't have time for this shit right now.

Out of time and out of options, I say loudly, "You two want to see something?"

Startled, the two women step away from each other and turn to look at me questioningly, and for a moment, I freeze, fully unsure of where the fuck I thought I was going with this. And then I do the only thing that I can think of.

I close the distance between Darius and me, my hands reaching, grabbing him on both sides of his head. I yank him closer to me, and all he can do is give a small grunt before I press my lips against his forcefully.

He freezes, momentarily stunned, and I grip his head harder, my eyes meeting his questioning ones intently. I give him a little shake, hoping he'll get the point to go along with it.

There's never been any hidden agenda between the two of us throughout our friendship. It's not like we have any unrequited sexual feelings toward each other, but we've known each other long enough and been in enough questionable situations to know when you just kind of roll with it. And so, after a brief hesitation, that's what he does.

Darius shifts closer, his entire demeanor changing as one of his hands moves to the back of my head, and he steps into me fully. Our eyes are still locked, and I see the humor glimmering in his, even as their typical golden hue is now more of a green to try to blend in with the Irish crowd.

We both do our part to play our roles convincingly, our lifelong friendship and complete dedication to our partners fueling the show.

Antoinette whisper-shouts behind me, "It's happening. Carolina, it's happening."

I recognize the whimper being hers, and then she replies, "I know. And it's so weird because it doesn't look like them. Should we like it or not? I'm so confused."

Antoinette cries, "I know. I don't know what to think."

Darius and I continue our show for a few moments more before pulling back at the same time. He grins at me, and I laugh because he looks so different that it *is* almost like kissing a stranger.

It's not like Dare's the first man I've kissed before, and though I can honestly say I'm not typically sexually attracted to men, I'm not opposed to some canoodling for the enjoyment of others. I'm well aware he feels the same way, especially with the concessions he's made throughout his relationship with Antoinette to accommodate her flair for the wild.

I turn around and face Carolina and Antoinette, and they're grinning stupidly, occasionally giggling. I give them a stern look and then say, "That will have to tide you over for now."

They both nod, continuing to giggle, and I turn my attention back to Darius, who's now leaning back against the table as if nothing happened.

He sighs and then says, "I guess we better get back to business."

I nod and ask, "Do you think that took care of their curiosity?"

"Not a fucking chance," he answers without hesitation.

"That's what I thought," I respond. "What do you think they'll do next?"

"I think you know the answer to that."

"I do. But I'm sure that will be a story for another day."

I walk around Carolina, snagging her hand and pulling her along with me as I say over my shoulder, "Come along, kids. We got fuckin' work to do."

19

A Friendly Explanation

Jessica

I'M STARTLED BY A soft knock on my door.

For a brief moment, excitement rushes through me, thinking it might be Matt, but I quickly squash any type of excitement at the thought because there's no way in hell he'd be knocking on my door right now. It's too risky, and this is not the point in the game where it would be okay for his connection to me to be known.

I also find it amusing that anyone would knock, so I know it must be someone who doesn't typically come down here.

I wait, and then the knock sounds again, and I say, "Hello?"

A small feminine voice replies, "May I come in?"

I snort, shrug, and then laugh at the fact that they can't see me. "Sure."

The door cracks open and then swings inward barely a foot, and a small figure squeezes in, quickly closing the door behind.

She turns to face me, and I cock my head, trying to place why she seems familiar, and then it occurs to me where I've seen her before.

Sneaking out a doorway when I was waiting outside what turned out to be Matteo's door.

This must be her.

Matt's betrothed.

I grind my teeth together, incredibly annoyed at the rush of jealousy that eats at me.

She gives me a tentative smile that I don't return. I squint at her, having no idea why she would bother coming to see me, of all people. Finally, I ask, "What do you want?"

The smile falls from her face, and she looks at the floor as she says, "I need to speak with you."

"I can't imagine why," I respond rather pissily.

I know whatever has gone on with her and Matt isn't anything personal against me. I'm sure this woman knew nothing about me, and most likely, she still knows nothing about me. But that doesn't make me feel any better about it.

She moves to walk toward me, and I put my hand up. "Stay over there."

She nods and then swallows, watching me thoughtfully. "You have nothing to fear from me."

"Not the first time I've heard that."

She laughs softly, her eyebrows lift slightly. "I get that."

She's quiet, so after a brief pause, I say, "Well, you may as well spit it out, then."

"I just want you to know that this thing between Matt and me is nothing."

Well, I wasn't expecting that.

I frown, unsure what to say, and when I remain silent, she says, "Matt's a great guy." She pauses and laughs, bobbing her head around as she adds, "Like I need to tell you that."

I stare at her in puzzlement, unsure where she's going with this conversation, though certainly curious to find out why she decided to come all this way to explain herself. Then she says, "We have no plans ever to be married. Frankly, he's too old for me and sometimes kind of a bore."

Now, I laugh. Most people mistake Matt for being a bore, but once you get to know him, that idea just becomes laughable. She does look quite young, though, so considering him to be too old seems reasonable.

"You don't need to explain anything to me," I say tiredly. "It's really none of my business."

Her eyes widen, and she rushes toward me so quickly that I take a step back. She stops when she's a couple of feet from me as she says, with great feeling, "Oh, but it is. Of course it is."

"I don't see how it's any of my business. Given my current circumstances, I don't really have a lot of leeway to be upset."

She shakes her head vigorously and then exclaims, "Oh, don't you worry about that. Matt will fix it. He's going to fix everything."

I laugh humorlessly, my arms crossing over my chest as I retort, "Well, I wish him a lot of fucking luck with that. Because from where I'm standing, this seems kind of final."

She looks at me thoughtfully for a moment and then says, "He told me about you."

Startled, I scoff, "Seriously? Try again."

She smiles brightly and nods. "He told me he has a girl, and he hoped she'd still be there when all this shit was over."

Now, I'm annoyed that her statement has warmth flaring inside me. Because I really don't have time for warm tingles and butterflies.

"That's all good and well, but that doesn't change the fact that he's an idiot."

She snorts, and for some reason, such an indelicate sound coming from such a delicate-appearing person makes me a giggle. And then she says, "Well, that goes without saying."

I like her. And now I'm annoyed that I like her.

She glances around the room, and I scan her while she's distracted. She's not as delicate as I thought she was when she first entered the room. While she's on the petite side and certainly smaller than me, I can tell she's strong.

I motion to the chairs in the corner, and we walk over, and both take a seat. I look over at her and ask, "What's your name?"

"Marieka," she answers easily. I must have another puzzled look because she smiles and adds, "My father allowed my mother to name me anything she wanted. That's how come I ended up with a name that didn't line up with my heritage. Same thing happened with my brother, Kaian."

"Oh, that was the man with Matt when I first got here?"

She nods. "Yes, that's my older brother. He's the one who set up the situation between us."

"But why do that if you don't plan on going through with it?"

"It's all a ruse," she explains. "Just a cover to keep me out of harm's way until we can make other arrangements. Being connected to Matt will at least keep most of the undesirables away from me and prevent my father from accidentally making a deal with someone else."

"Accidentally?"

"I know it sounds stupid, but when those assholes get drinking and then start running their mouths, anything can happen."

I'm sure more bad deals have been made over a bottle of booze than anything else, so I can't really argue with her logic.

"So, what would you do if you found yourself forced down the aisle?"

She waves her hand dismissively as she replies, "That wouldn't happen. This is just a short-term Band-Aid until we can get me out of here."

"But how can you know that?" I ask incredulously. "You can't control anything with these people."

"This is true, but my brother wouldn't have allowed it. Even if we made it to the altar, none of it would have been real. And even if it had been real, it could have just been annulled."

"I can't decide if you are delusional or not."

She frowns and asks, "What do you mean?"

"Are you so sheltered that you haven't been privy to the disgusting bullshit that goes on around marriages here?"

Her eyes widen, and she swallows visibly before whispering, "Probably."

"I don't know about your specific family, but a lot of these families require proof of the legitimacy of a union."

"What do you mean proof?"

I stare at her, and she stares back at me wide-eyed, and then I say, "Like, actual, visual proof of consummation of the vows. And I don't mean just the bloody sheets after the fact. A lot of times, they're going to watch."

She gasps, her hand moving over her chest, and she grimaces. "Are you serious?"

"Yeah," I reply. "I thought maybe it was just some overly fictionalized craziness, too. But I know people who have told me some of the horror stories of what goes on. And frankly, Matt already told me that at some point, he's going to have to do some nasty shit that I'm not going to like, and I'm going to have to pretend not to care. He was very clear on that."

Her brows pinch together, sadness falling over her features. She grasps her hands together on her lap as she says softly, "And that is probably true. He's going to fix this, but God only knows what lengths he'll have to go in order to do so."

I nod, sitting back in my chair with a sigh, and then I say, "Luckily, I had an extensive briefing by some women who knew exactly what could go on here. They didn't sugarcoat anything. I'd even say they went so far as to smash any type of rose-colored glasses I could possibly have just to make sure I understood how bad it could get."

She goes to reply, but a ruckus on the other side of the door cuts her short. She whirls around and then turns back to me and whispers, "I can't be caught here."

I groan, rising from my chair, reaching for her hand, and pulling her to her feet. "Hide under the bed. The odds of them thinking someone is here is basically nil, so there's a high likelihood you'll be safe there."

The ruckus turns into pounding on the door, and it's obvious that it's more than one set of fists, and then boisterous voices sound through the thick wood, and my heart rate increases. She squeezes my hand. I meet her eyes, and she says, "This can't be good."

I nod, shooing her with my hands as I say, "Hide, quick."

She drops down on the floor, looking up at me and saying quietly, "What about you?"

"If things get fucked, you wait until the coast is clear, and you go find Matt and your brother."

She meets my eyes again, staring intently as she nods, and then she drops to the floor and rolls under the bed.

I move back to the chair, and I've just sat myself back down when they finally realize the door is unlocked, and then the door bursts open, and a whole group of men flood in, led by a wild-eyed Matteo.

My stomach bottoms out, and my heart races in my chest as I try to keep the bile down, knowing that things just got fucked.

20

I Do or Die

Matt

WHATEVER REASON THEY HAVE to move this marriage up is lost on me.

I can only assume it's because they're concerned something will happen to change the Irish's stance on it. That and Matteo's inability to control his own bullshit and the people in charge being rightfully worried that he's going to do something to piss off the Irish. That seems to be the most likely scenario, but it doesn't leave me much time to get my shit together.

Jessica's father let me know that he fulfilled his part of the agreement, and Kaian was able to confirm that plans are in place to stop this before it starts.

Kaian and I are just going over the official timeline for the big event when loud pounding and shouting sound at my door. I yank it open, and Marieka is standing there. She all but falls into the room, her eyes panicked as she gasps and stutters, "J-Jessica. Ma-Matteo. Cr-crazy. H-hall. H-help."

I don't wait for further explanation, and Kaian is right on my heels as I sprint toward the hall in the hopes I can stop whatever craziness Matteo has put into action.

We burst into the room as Jessica shouts, "We must wait for my father."

"I don't have to wait for shit," Matteo spits out angrily. "You've been given to me, and you'll do whatever the fuck I tell you to."

I rush to the bottom of the altar where they're standing, a dozen of Matteo's cronies milling around on the other side.

Kaian pulls on my arm, drawing my attention to him, and then he gives me a hard look as he whispers, "Get it together, man."

I slow my steps and take a deep breath as I walk toward them and then stop a few feet away as I ask, "What the fuck is going on here?"

Matteo looks over at me and sneers, "None of your fucking business."

I raise my brows, crossing my arms over my chest as I retort, "I'm making it my fucking business."

Jessica presses her lips together. I see the panic in her eyes and also the pain. At a glance down her body, I note where he's gripping her arm, his fingers digging into her flesh. "Take your fucking hands off of her."

He snorts, his whole face twisting as he says, "I'll do whatever the fuck I want with her. There's nothing you can fucking do about it, Mathias."

I grind my teeth together, and Kaian steps closer to me until he's almost pressing against my back and whispers, "You gotta keep your cool, man."

I inhale sharply through my nose, doing my best to temper the rage that's burning inside me, and then I say more calmly, "She may be yours, but that doesn't mean you can just do what you want without her father present."

The priest is standing on the other side of them, fidgeting nervously, his eyes wide as he glances from Matteo to me and back to Matteo. He may be a man of God, but that doesn't mean he doesn't fear for his own life when it comes to the whims of an obviously unhinged man.

What he doesn't know is there are two unhinged men in this room right now, and getting between us would be a mistake.

I take a step closer, my eyes locked with Matteo's as I say, "Think about it. If you go through with this, there could be hell to pay. And not just from her father, but from your own people."

He keeps his eyes locked with mine for a moment, but then he blinks, and that vacant coldness is there, so I add, "Are you on something? Are you fucking high or something?"

I look behind him, where all of his cronies are congregated, appearing nervous and on edge. I look back at Kaian, who's shaking his head, and he whispers, "They're all fucking gone. There's no talking to them."

He pauses, scanning the room before turning back to me and shrugging as he adds, "I got your back, man. Do what you gotta do."

I don't get a chance to reply when Jessica's pained exclamation draws my attention back to her, and I see Matteo gripping her by the hair as he snarls at the priest, "Get the fuck on with it."

The priest opens his mouth to speak, and I interrupt, "This is your last fucking chance, Matteo. Fucking let her go."

Matteo laughs humorlessly, and it's obvious that Kaian is correct; there's no reasoning with him at this point. Again, I try one last time,

"I'm not fucking around right now. Let her go, or you're a fucking dead man."

Matteo's friends squirm nervously, but he laughs, which cues them all to laugh with him, and my blood fucking boils. Matteo lurches forward, his hand in Jessica's hair yanking viciously as he forces his mouth against hers. Her hands come up between them, and she punches at his chest, a scream of outrage bubbling from her mouth, as he shrieks, "You fucking bitch!"

He steps away from her, one hand moving to his now-bleeding mouth, and Kaian's hand touches my side, then the hard press of steel in my hand. I close my fingers around it, the familiar coolness heating almost immediately as he whispers, "Fuck around time."

Matteo is still screaming, his furious gaze directed at Jessica, his hand coming up to attack, but I jump between them. I step into him, and his scream quickly turns to a gurgle as my blade slices cleanly through his windpipe. Blood sprays everywhere, and Jessica lets out a scream as I push her out of the way, stepping into Matteo in the hopes I can save her some of the gore.

Kaian uses the few moments of surprise to initiate an attack against the buffoons standing there watching as the man gurgles his last breath and falls to the ground. Kaian takes out the first one, similarly to how Matteo met his end, and he's already on the second guy before he even realizes that he's about to die.

Everyone scurries like rats, pandemonium ensues, and I turn to Marieka, who's standing in the doorway, and shout, "Secure the door."

She nods, pulling the door with all her strength, and it slams shut, the locks engaging with a click.

Kaian faces off with another man just as the rest of them realize they're trapped. They turn on us, realizing their only chance is to fight their way out.

I turn to the priest, snarling, "Stay with her." I don't wait for him to respond. I turn back to the swarm of people closing in on me, and I dive in.

Ready to destroy.

21

A Forceful Bride

Jessica

I'M FROZEN.

Normally, I wouldn't find myself standing in the same spot, completely incapable of voice or thought.

Normally, my fight response is instantaneous, my refusal to just stand there and be killed prevalent in my mind.

Normally, my brain is operating on all cylinders, and I'm capable of making decisions in high-stress situations.

Normally.

What a funny fucking word.

A hand on my arm startles me from my ridiculous thought process, and I see the priest standing beside me, urging me out of the way. I go with him, mostly because I'm incapable of doing anything else, and with the room sealed, there's not exactly a flight option.

Matt and Kaian are making their way through the room, obviously fighting for their lives, and I'm torn.

Torn between jumping out into the middle of the fray and helping someone I care about and running screaming from my first glimpse of the devil I never knew existed.

Even thinking this, I know it's not a fair assessment. Previously, I've witnessed the type of chaos Matt and his friends are capable of. I'm not sure why I thought that maybe he was a little different than the others, but that naïve thought process has now been squashed.

He's a fucking blood-thirsty psycho.

I turn to the priest and whisper-shout, "We should get out of here."

He raises his brows at me, seeming to be entirely unaffected by the chaos around us, as he replies calmly, "That is not an option, my dear."

I frown, bristling at the idea that I'm a prisoner, still. "And why not?"

"Do you value your life?"

"Matt won't hurt me," I scoff.

The man gives me an almost pitying look, but then he says, "That may be true, but I cannot say the same thing. And I value my life."

More shouting across the room draws my attention, and I see three men surrounding a fallen figure. Glancing around, I locate Kaian on the other side of the room, fighting his way out of the fray.

The sounds of laughter draw my attention back to the previous group, a shiver zapping down my spine as I realize who is on the ground, attempting to rise above the men forcing him to stay down.

My heart jackhammers in my chest, fury and agony fueling me as I jump up and yank my arm from the grasp of the priest. I run toward the small group, rushing them blindly, numbness enveloping me as I manage to bend down and, without breaking stride, scoop up a fallen blade. Three lunging steps, and I launch myself through the air, weightless and merciless, as I leap onto the back of the laughing man.

Kill or be killed.

My left hand grabs him by the hair. I yank viciously as my right hand comes around, impaling the blade into the side of his neck. He screams, his hands coming back and knocking me in the head. I don't budge. I twist and twist and twist, realizing that I'm screaming like a banshee.

The two other men stare at me, wide-eyed, and Matt uses the few seconds' distraction to gain his footing, taking them both out with a few swipes of his knife.

The man I'm still clutching falls to the ground with me on top of him, and only then do I release him, panting for breath. I scramble to my feet, attempting to rise, but I stagger. The priest is there again, assisting me to my feet and helping me back to the edge of the room. He pushes me into a chair and kneels in front of me, a bottle of water in one hand and a square of cloth in the other. He pours water on the cloth, and then the coolness is against my face.

His eyes meet mine, and he says grimly, "Apparently, you can take care of yourself."

I laugh. That maniacal sense of self that was locked in my gut erupts, and I laugh even more loudly. His eyes widen, and then he shakes his head as he continues to rub the wet cloth against my face.

He hands the water bottle over to me. "Drink some of this."

I take the bottle, pour some into my mouth, and immediately choke through my laughter. He winces as water sprays against his face, and he steps back, taking the bottle from me and muttering, "Get control of yourself."

I snap my mouth shut, holding my breath, glancing around at the now-quiet room. Matt and Kaian are standing in the middle of it, chests heaving, what I can only assume are trickles of sweat leaving rivulets in the blood staining their skin.

I can't make out their words, but they're speaking forcefully to each other, and then they both nod and walk toward me. Kaian is still looking at Matt, but Matt is focused on me.

He stops a few feet from me and motions to the priest, who walks over and stops in front of him. They put their heads together, and the priest nods, speaking incoherently. Not being able to understand is starting to piss me off.

Matt turns to Kaian and says, "See if Marie is still out there."

Kaian takes off across the room, opens the door, and peeks out. Then, the younger woman steps back into the room and shuts the door behind them.

I force myself to stand, my entire body feeling like lead, and then I walk over to the group and ask, "What's going on?"

The priest hands another cloth and bottle of water to Matt. He dumps the water on the cloth, swiping at himself, dumping some of the water straight onto his face and using the cloth to scrub. He does the same with his hands and grabs onto my right hand which I didn't even realize was still bloody, and does the same to it.

"Someone answer me," I growl.

Matt swallows and clears his throat, his gaze focused on cleaning the blood off my hands as he whispers, "You need to get out of here."

"Wait. What?"

He doesn't say anything for a moment, and then the priest responds, "The marriage pact has been broken. That's the only way to protect you."

I frown, shaking my head. "You've got to be fucking kidding me."

Matt raises angry eyes to mine, and he spits out, "Nothing about this is a fucking joke. And you're going to fucking do what you're told."

I bristle, not at all accustomed to being dictated to and certainly not accustomed to having those types of words come out of his mouth.

I go to speak, but Marieka steps over to me. Resting her hand on my forearm, she leans in and says, "He's right, Jessica. You must do it."

I look at her and ask, "But what about you all? Won't that put you in danger?"

She shrugs and then answers, "That is not our main concern right now."

Kaian speaks up, "We have several different plans on ways to protect ourselves. We'll figure it out, but right now, we don't have any time to waste."

Matt drops the bloody cloth and the water bottle on the floor. His hand grips my wrist painfully, and he yanks me closer to him, his eyes boring into mine, pleading. "Please. You have to go."

The priest doesn't spare me a glance, and I frown at him and then glare at Matt and glare down at myself, covered in blood. I can't say this is how I ever saw myself once I managed to get out of this shithole.

I lean closer to Matt and whisper-shout, "There has to be another way."

"There isn't. If you're not here, then they can't touch you."

I don't say anything for a moment, panic rising in my throat. Not because I have any concerns about leaving, as frustrating as it would be to be once again shoved out, but I can only imagine what's going to happen to Matt and Kaian once the slaughter is found out.

Matt leans close, his hands gripping the sides of my head, and he leans in, staring into my eyes as he says, "This should be the easy part, Jess. Any other option will be hell. You have to go before it's too late."

A sob catches in my throat. I raise my hands, gripping his wrists as I contemplate my answer. Not that my answer even matters at this point because it's too fucking late for any of it. So, after a moment, I shake my head, letting a little of that maniacal laughter trickle out as I say, "No. I'm not fucking leaving."

His eyes widen, his brow furrowing as my words sink in. Then he glares down at me, his hands tightening painfully on my head. "You must. I swear to fucking Christ, Jess, I can't have something happen to you."

"Then you'll do what has to be done for me stay."

"What the hell are you talking about?"

"You know me leaving won't be the end of it. You know there will always be someone looking for a reason to be mad, demanding restitution for some wrong done to them."

"No," he sputters. "Not this time, they won't."

I laugh bitterly, shoving his hands away from me angrily. "Yes, they will, and you know it."

Matt's hands drop to his side, his shoulders dropping slightly as he stands before me helplessly. But he says nothing, so I continue, "They will hunt me down like a fucking dog and drag me back here to pay for my sins."

"But you didn't fucking do anything," he barks.

"That won't matter. No one cares about what women did and didn't do when it comes to a man feeling disrespected. No one cares about the truth when they're out to gain so much more from their duplicity."

"She's right," Marieka whispers beside me, her voice sad yet firm. "That's exactly what will happen. And leaving would insinuate to anyone looking for culpability that she has something to hide."

Matt turns to Kaian, his hands in front of him as he says, "Help me out, man. There has to be a way."

Kaian looks at me and then back to Matt, but he says nothing.

He just shakes his head. Matt deflates, his eyes going to the ceiling, muttering curses before turning back to me. "So, you stay here and what? Tell the truth and get punished for my sins?"

"No," I reply hesitantly. "There's only one way this won't blow up in our faces."

Matt stands there staring at me expectantly, and after a few beats, I turn my gaze to the ground, muttering, "I have to marry someone else."

I could hear a pin drop in the room if someone dropped it.

Holding my breath, I chance a glance at Matt.

His expression, at first, is unreadable. But then, he frowns slightly and shakes his head. "What? No."

I jerk back as if he has physically slapped me, for a moment, stunned into silence. He's scowling at me now, his jaw set in a stubborn line I know quite well. I narrow my eyes, my hands moving to my hips as I retort, "If you find the idea of being married to me so reprehensible you'd rather see me punished by a bunch of crusty old men, then forget it."

"Forget it?"

"Yeah," I snarl. "You can just forget it. I'll find someone else to take the old marriage bullet in your stead."

Matt's expression turns thunderous, but his words are eerily calm as he asks, "Oh, really? And who are you gonna even ask at this point?"

I grit my teeth, my eyes flitting around the room wildly as if there's suddenly going to be a horde of eligible men for me to choose from. Realizing I'm out of options, I point at Kaian. "Him. He'll have to do it."

Kaian's eyes widen comically, and Marieka giggles briefly before slapping her hands over her mouth. Then Kaian's lips twitch, and he steps forward with a swagger. "I mean, this is kind of sudden, but I'm not one to leave a lady in distress."

"Over my dead fucking body."

"If you don't get your shit together, then that can be arranged," I spit out through gritted teeth. "Lord knows I'd rather not drag you to the altar kicking and screaming."

His expression changes instantly, his eyes softening as he whispers, "I'm not kicking and screaming."

I purse my lips, tilting my head as I reply sulkily, "Could've fooled me."

He steps into me, wraps his arms around me, and pulls me close. Then he drops his head, pressing his face into my neck. "This is gonna sound fucking stupid, but I'm gonna say it anyway." He pauses, lifting his head as his hands move to my cheeks, and he looks me in the eyes. "I'd marry you a thousand times over for no other reason than the fact I fucking want you. But I don't want *you* to marry *me* just because you have no other choice."

I smile sheepishly, poking him in the gut. "I do have another choice. Kaian said he'd do it, remember."

His eyes narrow at the mention of Kaian, and I laugh, enjoying his annoyance.

The corners of his lips twitch, and I see that familiar sparkle in his eyes that has me breathing a touch easier. Then he nods, releasing his grip on my head, his hands sliding down my shoulders and along my arms until he's holding my hands. He turns to the priest and says, "Make it quick. We're out of time."

"Dearly beloved…"

22

A Moment, Please

Matt

FIGURING HE'S THE BEST first responder we can get at this point, we send Marieka to fetch Jessica's father with instructions to give him the cliff notes on what happened.

When he first enters the room, he stops just inside the doorway, scanning around wide-eyed. He says nothing at first, his eyes jumping from one body to another before finally settling on me. He raises his brows and asks, "This was your plan?"

I give him a dirty look and retort, "Not exactly. We could call this, like, plan M."

Jessica rises from the chair she was seated in, stepping between us, and says, "He didn't have a choice. They'd all lost their fucking minds."

He turns his gaze to her, cocking his head as he says, "What do you mean?"

Marieka speaks up from behind him, "They showed up at her room like animals. There was no reasoning with any of them, especially Matteo."

"What was his intention?"

Jessica crosses her arms over her chest in a defensive manner and then answers, "My understanding is that he wanted to marry me, so then he could make me do whatever he wanted."

Marieka nods, and then she says, "The things he said were disgusting. The things he was going to make her do."

Seamus frowns. "He admitted that he was going to abuse my daughter?"

Marieka nods emphatically, and Jessica responds, "Yes. Let's just say I was going to have a lot of company on my wedding night."

My hands tighten into fists at the thought. Suddenly, I wish I could kill him again, but this time, I'd take my time with it.

Seamus sighs, shaking his head as he mutters, "Well, this is a problem."

Jessica glares at him. "So, you think we should have just let him do it?"

He turns his frown on her and spits out, "I didn't fucking say that."

Jessica walks toward him, stopping a foot in front of him where she says quietly, "Sometimes, it's what you don't say that matters."

He looks at her impatiently, his jaw tense as he contemplates his answer. Then, after a beat, he responds, "You think I would willfully allow something horrible to happen to you?"

"Yes, if the alternative would interfere with your fucking job."

He narrows his eyes. One of his hands comes up, and I instinctively lunge for him, gripping his wrists tightly as I say, "I wouldn't fucking do that if I were you."

He raises his brows at me, his look sheepish as he says, "I would never hit her, Mathias."

I yank his hand down and then release his wrist. "Don't even touch her."

He's quiet for a moment, then inclines his head at me, stepping back a few inches before looking back to Jessica. "Regardless of how you think I feel about you; your mother would roll over in her grave, and you know I couldn't have that."

Sadness shadows her features. "How could I forget your undying love for a dead woman."

He flinches at her words, his gaze moving to a spot just behind her, and then Kaian speaks up. "We don't have time for your fucking family feud right now. Someone could show up here at any moment, and we're all going to be fucked."

Seamus sighs and then nods. "I'll go break the news of the change in plans. I'll explain what happened and why and make sure that I'm threatening in regard to what almost happened to Jessica." He pauses, glancing at her before looking at me as he continues, "You better prepare her for what's next. I don't know my daughter very well, but I know her well enough to know she's not going to fucking like it."

She turns to me and asks, "What's next?"

"I'll explain in a minute," I reply firmly. I turn to Kaian and Marieka and say, "You two get cleaned up and be prepared to make a statement. Marieka, your statement needs to be something that does not include you being in her room."

She nods, and Kaian slaps me on the back as he says, "I'm on it."

They both exit the room, Seamus right behind them, leaving me and Jessica alone for the first time in an age.

I extend my hand to her, and she takes it without hesitation. I lead her from the room and down the hallway, keeping her close as we head toward my room. "Those old men will not be happy that the plans changed without their permission. There's not much they can do about it at this point, and since they're going to need to save face with Seamus, they're probably going to begrudgingly allow it. But that doesn't mean we're off the hook."

"What do you mean off the hook?"

I say nothing as we continue down the hallway, and I feel her gaze burning a hole in the back of my skull.

Frankly, I don't want to answer her. I want to have this short walk back to my quarters, pretending that nothing horrible is going to go on. That I'm not going to have to do anything to her that might make her question me as a person. That she won't be put into a situation where she may question herself and everything she's ever known.

I increase my pace until I'm practically dragging her down the hallway behind me. She still comes willingly, but I feel a bit of resistance, and just as soon as we reach my door. I waste no time kicking it open, pulling her inside and pushing her into the middle of the room as I slam the door behind me, locking it.

I turn back to her, and I haven't taken more than two steps toward her before she puts her hands up defensively as she asks, "What are you doing?"

I continue walking toward her even as she's backing up slowly and then more quickly, looking behind her so as not to run her into a wall, but the only place for her to go is the bathroom door, which is exactly where I want her to go anyway.

She backs up hurriedly, and I follow closely until she finds herself pressed up against the bathroom wall. I press myself against her.

She's panting, and there's a tremble in her bottom lip. Her eyes are wide as she stares at me and whispers, "What are you doing, Matt?"

I lean in close so I'm pressed against her from hip to chest, not even a hair's breadth away from her lips, as I reply, "Shut your fucking mouth."

Her breath catches, and I pull back a bit and see her frown, which makes me smile.

I move in closer, pressing my face into her neck, and then I just lean there, breathing slowly. And then I chuckle.

She rests her hands on my shoulders, most likely because she is unsure what to do with them, and after a moment, she asks, "What could possibly be funny right now?"

I shake my head, my words muffled against her neck as I reply, "Everything."

She sighs, and her hands on my shoulders become heavier. She clutches at me.

I ease away from her, standing up straight, my hands circling her upper arms, yanking her off the wall. She yelps but doesn't attempt to extricate herself from my arms, and I turn and hustle her toward the shower door.

I release her and say, "Don't move."

I walk over to the shower door, open it, and turn the water on before returning to her and stripping my shirt off my body. I quickly rid myself of my shoes and socks, my pants and underwear, until I'm standing there completely naked.

She's eyeing me suspiciously, but she makes no move to escape, so I step into her again, this time pulling on her shirt until she allows me to remove it from her body.

I stoop to remove her shoes, and she rests her hands on my head, tangling her fingers in my hair, and then I'm pulling her pants down her hips, and she's wiggling to assist me.

I rise to my feet, staring into her eyes as I say, "Can we just pretend none of this happened?"

She frowns as she says, "Pretend what didn't happen?"

I laugh bitterly and then sigh, my hands coming up to my face and rubbing vigorously. I motion for her to enter the shower before me, quickly following behind and closing the door behind us. I push her into the hot spray of the water, saying nothing as I grab for the soap and a washcloth, quickly ridding her of the blood spatter I'm sure she doesn't even realize is still on her person.

She giggles, and I stop the soapy path of the washcloth. I look up at her face and ask, "What's so funny?"

She giggles again and then shrugs as she replies, "We keep meeting here like this."

I frown, squinting at her until I remember the first time we met, and then I laugh. "Apparently, you like to get me naked and wet," I reply dryly.

She laughs, sending a jolt of warmth down my spine.

I quickly finish cleaning her up and then make short work of cleaning myself. I move to turn the water off, but her hand on my arm stops me, and when I look at her, I see the naked need in her eyes.

She moves closer to me, and this time, I retreat, backing up one step and then two until I'm pressed against the cool shower wall.

She presses into me from hip to chest, and my breath catches in my throat. She rises up on her toes and brushes her lips against mine.

I don't return her soft kiss. I just ask against her lips, "What are you doing?"

She pulls back the tiniest of a fraction as she replies, "You shut your fucking mouth."

I frown, her words completely throwing me off, but before I can reply, she presses into me fully, rotating her hips so she's rubbing firmly against my hard cock that's pressed against her stomach.

I moan, feeling a slight tremble in my legs, and when I say nothing, her eyes meet mine, and her hand strokes up from my belly, along my chest to my neck, where she brackets my throat, squeezing firmly. I whimper, a soft choking moan.

I shouldn't be surprised at her actions. After all, Jessica knows my most intimate secrets, but I am surprised at the timing. "You don't know what's going to happen."

Her laugh is bitter and hollow, and I see the determined look in her eye as she sneers, "Oh, I fucking know."

"What do you mean you know?"

Her hand on my throat tightens, and what little blood I had left in my brain shoots south, and my cock twitches. Then she replies, "You seem to forget I spent a good number of years in this bullshit. All impressionable years where I listened when I wasn't supposed to. And my mother, God rest her soul, was always very transparent with me on expectations and the atrocities of the life."

She's right. I had forgotten. Her being a part of all this being so new to me that it's not something I would immediately think about.

So, I don't hedge my words when I say, "So you know what they're going to make me do to you?"

She nods, her free hand coming around and squeezing my ass, and she rubs against me with purpose. She says nothing, so I add, "And you're okay with that? You're going to be okay being a spectacle while I fuck you?"

She shrugs. "I'll do what I have to do, just like I've always done."

Her hand moves from my ass around to my front, gripping onto my dick, squeezing. I thrust into her grip, my hands gliding up her back and over her shoulders, gripping each side of her head. I force her to look at me. "No matter what happens, you know I'd never hurt you."

She nods and whispers, "I know that. But let's use what little time we have left to create a good memory."

I frown, understanding what she means but uncertain if that's even a good idea.

She doesn't wait for me to reply, moving away and yanking me over to the wide bench that sits right outside the reach of the water. She pushes me down, and I ask again, "What are you doing?"

She pushes me back, so I'm sprawled across the bench, where she straddles my hips, rubbing her slick pussy along the hard length of my dick. She leans her upper body over, bracing herself on my shoulders as she says, "Taking what I want."

I attempt to sit up, but her hands on my shoulders keep me down, so I say, "Wait. Let me—"

"No," she interrupts. "I've been 'letting people' my whole life, and now, it's my turn." I frown up at her, and she smiles and then adds, "You told me months ago, don't you remember?"

I certainly remember me and my big fucking mouth. But I just nod and then ask, "Tell me what you want."

"Just be here with me. Let's have this moment."

Nodding, I relax beneath her, my hands moving to her hips as I whisper, "Anything. Anything you want."

Her soft smile is back, and then she licks her fingers, raising her hips up and wiping her saliva between her legs and along my dick. She grasps me with the same hand, raising me up and rubbing the tip of me against her clit rhythmically before shifting so the head of my cock is pressed against her quivering cunt.

My fingers flex on her hips, and I'm trembling as I allow her to take what she wants at whatever pace she chooses.

It takes every ounce of self-control I have not to shove up inside, to wrap my arm around her hips and fuck her into oblivion. To flip us over so she's pressed into the floor with me rutting into her like the feral beast I am.

I shake that image from my head, refocusing on her as she takes me inside slowly, inch by inch until I'm pushed up inside of her as far as I can go.

She pauses like that, fully seated, taking every inch of me, her eyes boring into mine, and then she whispers, "Touch me."

I stroke my hands from her hips up her sides and around the front of her to her breasts. I glide my fingertips along the underside before cupping them in my palms, feeling the full, heavy weight of them as my thumb and forefingers twist and tease her nipples.

The height of the bench is a perfect level for her to have her feet planted on the floor, and she uses this leverage to rhythmically bounce up and down, each downward motion grinding against my pubic bone, as she gasps and moans.

I release her breasts, sitting up and bracing an arm behind me as I ask, "What do you need? Tell me what you need."

She doesn't answer me in words, and I see the tension in her body. Her brow is furrowed, and her eyes are now squeezed shut in concentration as she rides me.

I wrap my free arm around her hips, leaning more of my weight back on my outstretched hand as I move one foot to the floor, pulling her in close as I thrust upward. Her breath catches in her throat, and her eyes open. She stares at me and gasps, "Yes. Right there."

My dick throbs at her words, and I already feel the heat in my pelvis and at the base of my spine. I clench my teeth as I force myself to maintain control and not just empty inside her right now.

"Touch yourself, sugar. Rub that clit. Come on my cock."

Her hand immediately moves between us, her fingers rubbing against her clit rhythmically, putting more pressure into my groin, and I groan, "That's right. That's my good girl."

Her free hand moves around my shoulders, her hands sliding up until her fingers are tangled in the hair at the back of my head. She pulls, and I go willingly. My face pressed is between her breasts, and then I lick and suck a path to her nipple.

I suck urgently on one and then lick and bite a path to the other side, where I bite her nipple until she sobs, and then I lick and suck as she gasps. Her fingers stroke, rub, and pinch her clit, and I feel every movement against my pelvis as I continue to thrust up into her in long, hard pulses.

She's chanting brokenly, begging and pleading for me not to stop, the sound of her voice sending sparks of lightning down my spine and directly into my balls.

I pull back, my arm around her hips firm as I continue to jackhammer up into her. My eyes scan up her body, reveling in the sight of her riding me with abandon. Her head is thrown back, her eyes once again squeezed shut, and the ball of emotion that erupts in my chest almost chokes me, but I manage to grit out, "Open your eyes. You open your fucking eyes and look at me."

She immediately does what she's told, her eyes opening, her head coming forward so she's staring directly into my eyes as I whisper, "I love you."

She blinks at me, confusion, surprise, and then awe showing along her features, and then she smiles and sobs, her hand on the back of my head tightening as she forces my head up, and then she's kissing me feverishly, riding my cock and her hand as she gasps over and over and over again, "I love you. I love you. I love you."

And then she comes.

She sobs into my mouth, earning an answering, guttural reply as my body tightens. Her body twitches, her pussy spasming as I thrust up into her forcefully.

She sobs and moans through her release, grinding down, her fingers on her clit extending her pleasure, as she says against my lips, "Come, baby. Come inside me. Mark me. Please."

And I fucking come.

She sucks my pleasure from my mouth and my balls as I empty inside her, allowing myself this one last moment of pure bliss before we both step out into the complete unknown.

I thrust up inside her a few more times before finally, I still, and then we rest there with my dick still inside her, both of us trembling.

She wraps both arms around me, pressing my face into her neck, her breath hot on my ear as she repeats over and over, "Don't let go. Don't let go."

I sit up, wrapping both of my arms around her back and pulling her as tightly to me as possible as I answer her plea.

"I'll never let go."

23

The Calm Before the Storm

Jessica

Just as quickly as our moment began, it's over.

And no sooner do we exit the bathroom than there's a loud knock at the door.

Matt walks across the room, opens it a few inches, and speaks in a hushed tone to whoever is on the other side. A bundle of items is shoved through the crack, and he takes it and then shuts the door without further comment.

He walks back toward me, tossing the items on the bed and then stopping in front of me, his gaze intent as he says, "Are you ready for this?"

I frown, swallowing the lump in my throat before saying, "Don't really have any other choice, do I?"

He cocks his head at me, a faint smile on his lips as he responds, "You always have a choice, sugar. But if you can manage it, if you can push through, then we get to see what's on the other side of all the bullshit."

He pauses, his lips pressing together, and then he steps in closer, so the front of his body is just brushing the front of mine. He stoops down so he's looking directly into my eyes as he adds, "But if you can't. I won't judge you. I won't take it personally, I won't hold it against you, and I won't punish you. Instead, we'll find a way to get you out of it. I'll make a call right now and have you out of here before they even realize what's happening."

"And what about you?"

Now, his smile is sad, and he shakes his head. "There's no way out for me yet."

"Yet?"

His lips curve up a little more, and there is a sparkle in his eye as he says, "Someday. But I don't know when that someday is, and it's not fair of me to expect you to take part in what's going to happen. So, if you change your mind and want to go, I'll make that work."

"But you didn't answer me when I said what about you?"

"Then I take the hit," he replies calmly. "There will be hell to pay, but it won't be the first time I've had to pay it and likely won't be the last."

I stare back at him, sure the indecision is evident on my face, but I'm able to keep my true feelings hidden as I think about Antoinette. Carolina. Even Issa.

Antoinette grew up in this life. She knows the ins and outs more clearly than anyone.

Carolina had it shoved down her throat from the time she could even be considered an adult.

And Issa. Lord knows we've had our trials, but I know at the end of the day, if she had to choose between her own well-being and her husband's, she would choose Declan every time.

I take a hard look at him, staring directly into his eyes, and even though I have no idea what exactly I'm looking for, I see everything he wants me to see and likely even the things he doesn't.

Matt has always come across as easygoing—or the boy scout, as the guys like to call him. And I probably fell into this thought process as well, always assuming he was a stand-up guy who managed to toe the line between good and evil while always coming out on the side of good.

But my experiences in the entertainment industry, never mind my previous life as the daughter of a criminal overlord, taught me that sometimes, the fine line between good and evil is so blurred that people lose sight of the so-called bad deeds that must be done for the greater good.

I raise my hands, cupping both sides of his face as I whisper, "I can do it."

His eyes snap shut, and he expels a shuddering breath so forcefully that I laugh. Emotion wells in my chest, my eyes burn, and I know when he looks at me again, he'll see the glassiness, even as I attempt to blink it away.

I rise up on my toes, pressing my lips against his softly and then a bit more firmly as he returns my kiss.

Then I drop my hands and step back as I ask, "Now what?"

He inhales deeply through his nose and exhales out his mouth and then motions to the bed as he replies, "Now, we get dressed and get ready for the shitshow."

"Shitshow? Any chance whatsoever that it could end up not being a shitshow?"

"No," he replies, shaking his head. "Given the circumstances, it will definitely be a huge shitshow. They're going to pull out all the stops. They will demand a full show as proof that we're not trying to pull one over on them."

He reaches for a tiny plastic item on the bed and holds it out to me. I take it from him, examining it as I ask, "What is this?"

He rummages through the rest of the items on the bed, turning back to me with a needle in his hand. I frown, and then he replies, "That's for your blood."

My eyebrows rise practically into my hairline as I parrot, "My blood?"

He nods and then shrugs, "You're the one that lied about being a virgin."

"What the fuck does that have to do with anything?"

He gives me an incredulous look and then says, "I thought you said you knew how this worked."

"Knew how what worked?"

"The ceremonies? The idiotic, ritualistic bullshit hoops they can insist on."

I frown, my arms crossing over my chest defensively as I whisper, "Well, I knew about a lot of them, but really, some of them seem a bit over the top."

"There's a high likelihood they wouldn't demand it if you hadn't said you're a virgin, but Matteo's family is definitely going to require proof of it because if he could kill you over anything right now, he would totally do it."

"You're saying that proof of virginity shit is still enforced?"

And now he's looking at me like I'm a complete fucking moron, which is fine with me because I feel like a complete fucking moron. So, I sputter, "I was kind of hoping that was just a bunch of outrageous folklore parents used to keep their daughters from sleeping around."

He laughs bitterly as he says, "Well, quite often, there's a little truth in folklore."

I grimace and hand him back the little plastic ball, then I move and sit on the side of the bed. "Do what you gotta do."

He doesn't waste any time making quick work of drawing blood from my arm and then inserting it into the little plastic ball. "You're pretty good at that. Is that one of your side gigs?"

"What do you mean, side gig?"

"Phlebotomist," I reply seriously. "I've heard a good phlebotomist is worth their weight in gold."

He stares at me and shakes his head as he mutters, "I fear you've lost the plot."

I laugh, becoming comfortable with the overwhelming urge for the maniacal laughter.

Matt shakes his head again and sighs as I continue to laugh. "I fear you're starting to act like the rest of us."

I shrug and then reply, "Inappropriate humor certainly has its place in uncomfortable situations."

He snorts but says nothing, and then a wad of fabric hits me in the face. I grab at it as Matt laughs and says, "Put that on."

I stop laughing but I'm still smiling as I drop the towel and pull on what appears to be a white dress of some sort. It's rather shapeless, but at least it covers most of me.

Matt pulls on a pair of cotton pants and a shirt in the same fabric as my dress and then we stand there and look at each other and I feel that maniacal laughter coming back.

He moves close to me, the back of his hand stroking down my cheek softly as he says, "Don't forget what I said."

I frown and ask, "Which part?"

"The part about me having to do shit you're not going to like. Just remember when it gets really bad, and it's going to get bad, it's all just a game. It's a bullshit show for some bullshit people, and once this is all said and done, every single one of those motherfuckers will pay."

I nod. "I'll remember. Don't worry. I'll be okay."

He nods, leaning down and pressing a soft kiss against my lips, and then there's a knock at the door.

"We gotta go."

I say nothing. I just take his hand, turn, and lead him to the door.

24

The Storm

Matt

WHEN JESSICA REACHES FOR my hand, I grab onto hers tightly, like the lifeline that it is.

We walk like that down the hallway with her just ahead of me, leading the way. The closer we get to our destination, the subtle shift of her being ahead of me to beside me to behind me takes place.

By the time we reach the door, she has let go of my hand and is walking several feet behind with her head bowed and her eyes on the floor. My heart pounds in my chest, rage building inside me at the idea that she's to remain unseen and unheard.

Kaian is waiting for me, and his presence helps me find the cold place inside me I'll have to live in to get through this next event.

I move to enter the room, and his hand on my shoulder stops me.

My eyes meet his as he says, "Stay the course."

I nod, my hand coming up and slapping him on the shoulder before returning my focus ahead of me.

I step into the room. The din of voices immediately falls flat, and I'm enshrouded by the echo of silence.

Jessica's father walks toward me, and I use that opportunity to glance back, relief flooding me as I see Jessica still playing the part of a docile submissive.

If I was further along in my extermination mission, I would take this opportunity to light up every last motherfucker in this room. But knowing the timing isn't right has me biting my tongue and, instead, smiling smugly at Seamus and taking his hand when he extends his.

He grips my hand firmly, leaning in and whispering, "Everything is set."

I return his handshake, leaning in and asking, "No way out of it?"

He shakes his head, turning us so my back is to the men in the room, and his face is hidden from their view. "No. Matteo's father is looking for proof that they have been wronged. He will use the virginity claim to seek retribution if it's not proven with blood."

I press my lips together, my jaw clenching in agitation at the implication that harm may come to Jessica. "It's taken care of."

He glances back at Jessica, who's still looking at the ground, and then turns back to me and asks, "Can she do this?"

I glance at her fleetingly and then turn to him and reply, "She's good. She'll do what she has to do."

"We have no backup plan here, Mathias," he replies seriously. "If you fuck this up, we're all fucked."

"I won't fuck it up. It's just a steppingstone to the end game."

He says nothing further, simply turning and walking back to the men standing there looking furious. "We can proceed."

Old man Matteo speaks up, "Yes, let's get on with it."

Jessica makes an almost inaudible gasp, and I have to force myself not to turn to her. I chance a look and see her standing awkwardly with her hands grasped in front of her tightly. Once again, I force down my urge to go to her and, instead, walk toward the group of men. They make a path for me, and I swagger up onto a staging area where a rudimentary bed is set up.

Normally, they would do this in the bigger hall, but given they wouldn't have time to clean up the blood bath in there, they've opted for this one. I'm surprised they didn't do it there surrounded by the dead bodies, but at least this is one reprieve for Jessica.

I strip my shirt over my head, turning back to Jessica and motioning for her to step up beside me. She does so silently, her eyes remaining downcast, and when she stops next to me at the foot of the bed, I ease fractionally closer so if nothing else, she may feel the heat of my body, and I say quietly yet authoritatively, "Strip."

She freezes, and for a moment, I think I'll have to repeat myself, but then shaking hands come up, and she strips the dress from her body in one movement, letting it drop to the floor at her feet. She stands there like a statue, the tremble in her body increasing as I'm sure she can feel all the eyes on her naked back and ass, and once again, fury builds up inside me.

A throat clears, and I look over and see Seamus staring at me pointedly with a little shake of his head. I nod in response, and then he turns and says, "I will leave my man here in my stead. I will be right outside in case anyone gets any bright ideas."

Old Matteo grunts and replies, "There will only be ideas if she turns out to be a fucking lying whore."

Seamus' eyes narrow, but he says nothing in response as he turns and swiftly exits the room.

Kaian steps up, his eyes locked with mine as he says, "Get on with it, Matt."

I nod again, take a deep breath, and center myself down into that darkness.

I turn back to Jessica and say, "Get on the bed."

She does as she's told without hesitation or comment, and when she pauses on her hands and knees, my lips twitch as I add, "On your back, legs spread."

She glances back at me briefly, and her lips also twitch, and for a moment I fear the maniacal laughter may be boiling up inside her again. She manages to control herself, and I move onto the bed, kneeling between her legs. I reach into my pocket, pulling out a small tube of lube, half-expecting someone to tell me I can't use it, and breathing a sigh of relief when they don't.

I open the cap, smearing some on my fingers while at the same time removing the tiny plastic ball I had hidden in there. I drop the bottle neatly, taking my lube-smeared fingers and shoving them between her legs. She gasps but manages not to cry out as I scissor my fingers inside her cunt, making sure the little plastic ball bursts, counting on the lube and the fluids to dissolve the evidence. I shove my fingers into her hard and fast, taking some reassurance from the fact I'm not actually hurting her while applauding the show she's putting on of being uncomfortable.

If nothing else, knowing a bunch of dirty old men are gawking at you is enough to make you uncomfortable, but I temper my movements enough not to draw her any real pleasure.

A soft curse draws my attention to her face, and I see her glaring at me, and my urge to laugh grows. Finally, she whispers, "Quit fucking around."

I withdraw my fingers from inside her, then yank the front of my pants down, moving closer and positioning myself between her legs. Rubbing the head of my dick in the mixture of blood, lube, and semen from our earlier encounter, I push inside, and she tenses. Her legs squeeze me, and I slap the inside of her thighs until she spreads them for me.

I slide in about halfway and then allow my upper body to fall over hers, so I'm bracing myself on my elbows, with my forearms up under her shoulders, my hands bracketing her head.

I press my cheek against hers and whisper, "Are you okay?"

She makes a choking noise in her throat and manages a slight nod, and I feel her jaw clenching against my cheek. I slowly push the length of my cock inside her until my pelvis is pushing into her clit. She gasps again, a low moan in her throat, and her hips buck up. I pull back slightly as I say, "Oh, you fucking like that? You like having my dick inside you?"

Her response is a quiet sob, her hands clutching at my shoulders.

I adjust my arm so I grip her head more firmly, one hand delving into her hair and pulling her head to the side so I can lick and nibble her ear as I say, "Do you like knowing those dirty fuckers are watching?"

She shakes her head, and I pull back, shoving back inside with more force, and another sob falls from her lips. I do it again and again, enjoying her sounds and the slap of our body together. She clutches at me, her nails digging into my skin, and then she shifts so her heels are digging into my lower back as she tries to pull me deeper.

"None of that now," I tsk, adjusting myself over her so I'm no longer stimulating her clit with each inward thrust. "This is all just for show. There will be no coming for you. No one else gets to see your pleasure."

I raise myself up on my arms so I can see her face, her eyes scrunched closed as she frowns.

I move myself up even more and then sit back on my haunches so just the tip of my dick is still inside her. Blood and my own cum glistens along my length. I scan back up her body, now racked with tiny shivers, until once again, I'm staring at her face, but now she's looking at me through the slits of her eyes.

I see determination there, but her bottom lip quivers, and a shadow of sadness crosses her features. I can handle her anger and even her disgust, but sadness. No.

"Fuck this," I spit out.

I slide back to the end of the bed, standing as I turn, wiping my hand along my dick as I step down from the altar. I yank my pants up with my free hand as I walk toward Matteo's father with my blood-smeared hand outstretched. "Is this fucking proof enough for you?"

He glares at me and snarls, "You didn't finish it."

"I don't have to finish shit."

The older man looks around as if he's waiting for someone to also demand that I get up there and keep going. Everyone remains quiet, and finally, Kaian speaks up, "There are no rules on how far it goes. All he has to do is show proof, and you can see that on his hand."

I hold it up even higher so it's right under the old man's nose as I ask, "Would you like me to make you a fucking painting with it?"

The man says nothing. He just continues to glare at me, his jaw clenching and unclenching in time with his fists.

Kaian hands me a towel, and I wipe my hand on it, and then take it and put it in my pocket before turning and scooping up Jessica's dress.

I walk back to the bed, moving to the side and kneeling beside her. "Sit up," I mutter.

She raises her head, and I slide the dress over, helping her put her arms through the holes and then sliding it down her body as she sits upright. I help her to the side of the bed, and she puts her feet on the floor. I kneel so I can watch her face and ask, "Can you stand?"

She nods, but she's shivering, so I rise to my feet, gripping her hands and helping her stand on shaky legs.

She takes one wobbly step before I stop her, stooping down and lifting her into my arms, careful to scoop the dress beneath her ass. She doesn't struggle or attempt to get away. She just leans into me, much like she did long ago when we first met.

I heft her up higher up my chest, and her head settles on my shoulder. I feel puffs of her breath against my neck as I walk off the altar and head to the door.

One of the old men shouts, "Where the fuck do you think you're going?"

I stop, turning and glaring as I reply, "Any business you all have with me will be addressed tomorrow. If anyone wants to challenge me, that's your time."

Without another word, I turn and walk out the door.

25

A Devil's Reflection

Jessica

I'M WEIGHTLESS.

Suspended in the air, my physical body is held aloft by strong bands as I float along haphazardly.

Pain blooms in my chest. A hard knot of anguish unfurls in my guts, and then warm breath fans my cheek as Matt whispers, "Breathe, sugar. You've gotta breathe."

I open my mouth to respond, but nothing comes out, and then I'm briefly suspended in the air as he jostles me violently. He does it again, this time tossing me bodily so I land back against his chest sharply, forcing the oxygen from my lungs on a sob.

He stiffens in preparation to do it again, and I manage to drag in a short breath, spitting it back out almost immediately and dragging in a deep, ragged, and painful one.

He walks swiftly now, and I work on controlling my breathing and heart, ignoring the din of voices as they slowly get quieter, eventually fading into nothing.

And then all that remains is footfalls on concrete, Matt's breaths of exertion from carrying me, and my own shuddering breaths.

Matt's gait falters, and I glance up to see Marieka standing in the hallway, a worried expression on her face. She asks, "Is she okay?"

Matt says nothing as he continues to rush down the hallway. Marieka falls in beside him, and I manage to croak. "I'm okay. I'm okay."

Matt stops in front of his door, turns to Marieka, and says, "You need to get back to your rooms and lock yourself in. Barricade the door. Don't open it for anyone other than me or Kaian."

She nods, turning to go when I ask, "Is she in danger?"

"Probably," Matt replies tersely.

"Then she can't go," I exclaim, suddenly struggling in his arms until he releases me. I stand there on shaky legs, calling for her, "Marieka, wait."

She turns back, her eyes questioning, and then Matt says, "Are you sure?"

I nod, motioning for her to come back, and after a moment's hesitation, she does. I take her hand, pulling her into the room, and then Matt follows, shutting the door behind us.

"She shouldn't be left alone to fend for herself," I say. "I would never forgive myself if something happened to her."

Matt squints at me, then at her, and back to me as he says, "Did I miss something?"

There's that maniacal laughter again.

I slap my hands over my mouth, and the bubble of laughter turns into more of a strangled gurgle. He shakes his head at me, and Marieka giggles as she responds, "We had a heart-to-heart."

Matt sighs, glances up at the ceiling briefly, and mutters, "Just what the team needs: more girls."

Now I do laugh, allowing the heat of hysteria to run up my spine as I bend at the waist, my hands braced on my thighs as I howl.

Marieka joins me. Matt stands there, staring at us both, completely dumbfounded, only fueling our hysterics.

Finally, he says, "I'm just going to give you two a minute to collect yourselves." Then he walks away, headed toward the bathroom, where he leaves the door open. Water rushes in the sink, and Marieka and I continue to giggle for a few more moments before, finally, we manage to straighten, wiping tears from our eyes.

Marieka walks over to the chair in the corner and falls back into it. I back up against the edge of the bed, sitting down and shaking my head at how incredibly fucked up this entire mission has gone.

Matt exits the bathroom wearing a new pair of sweatpants, water droplets still on his cheeks as he moves to the dresser where he opens a drawer and pulls out a shirt before closing it.

Pulling the shirt over his head, he adjusts his clothes and says, "Do you need help getting cleaned up?"

I think for a moment, making a mental checklist of how I'm feeling, and then I shake my head and say, "I think I can do it."

I stand slowly, getting my bearings before walking to the bathroom. He says from behind me, "Just yell if you need me."

I turn back in the doorway, nod, and then close the door, making my way to the sink, where I lean my hands against it, staring at my reflection in the mirror.

I reach down and grasp the hem of the makeshift dress, and there's a knock on the door, and then Matt says, "It's me."

"Come in," I reply, yanking the dress up over my body, crumbling it into a ball, and tossing it toward the garbage can. The door opens, and Matt appears, a pile of clothes in his hands, which he places on the counter. He looks me up and down, but he says nothing. I cock my head at him, and he just shrugs and then walks back out of the room, closing the door behind him.

I sigh, grabbing a clean towel from the pile and putting it on the hook by the large shower. I open the shower door, turn the water on, and then step inside, just outside the spray's reach, as I wait for the water to warm. I glance at the bench, warmth rushing over me as I think about our brief interlude before the nastiness that followed.

I shiver and then shake my head to rid myself of the grossness of that entire experience. I step under the spray of the water, allowing it to hit me fully in the face before turning and wiping the water from my eyes as I wet my hair. I'm probably not even dirty since Matt helped clean me up a little while ago. But it feels like it.

I wash my hair quickly, sudsing it up and rinsing it clean before grabbing the washcloth hanging on the rack.

I pick up Matt's soap, inhaling its scent, before rubbing it along the wet cloth until there's a lather.

Placing the bar on the shelf, I step out of the water and then methodically rub the soapy cloth on every inch of my skin until I start to feel clean again.

I step back under the water, watching the soap bubbles slide down my body until they pool in the drain. I stand there until the water runs clear, and then I reach out and turn off the spray.

I open the shower door and grab the towel, quickly drying myself and then wrapping the towel around my torso. The mirror is foggy, and I'm unable to see my reflection, so I grab the hand towel, pressing it against the glass and sliding it across until I appear.

I look different.

I feel different.

Perhaps I am different.

Sighing, I continue to study my reflection, the woman staring back at me almost seeming foreign. Just a few days ago, I lived a completely different existence. A life where I could completely forget my origins, where I came from, and who I came from.

A few short days ago, Matt was still the boy scout, the good guy who only ever stepped over the line into evil when forced.

And now, here we both are.

Sullied. Our previously rounded edges now jagged and sharp, neither of us able to sit back and pretend to be someone we're not.

Because at the heart of it all, it has always been there, lurking beneath the surface.

It has always been the devil we know.

26

A Promise

Jessica

I EXIT THE BATHROOM to find Matt alone, lying prone in the center of the mattress.

I walk to the edge of the bed and ask, "Where's Marieka?"

"Kaian came for her. He'll keep her safe."

I nod but say nothing, staring down at him a bit awkwardly until finally, he extends his hand to me and says, "Come here."

I grip his hand in mine, allowing him to pull me across the bed, and then I tuck myself into his side, my head on his shoulder. His arm is a comforting weight around me. I slide my top leg over his thighs, my foot hooking around his calf, and after a fair amount of squirming I settle, sighing deeply at the familiarity around me.

We're both quiet, lost in our own thoughts. The eerie, echoing silence is once again playing in time with the beating of his heart in my ear.

I let the silence drag out, and then, after a few long minutes, I ask, "What are you thinking about?" He says nothing. I crane my head around so I can see his face, squinting at his smiling lips and his closed eyes and mutter, "You better not say my fucking sweet pussy."

He laughs, a deep belly one that vibrates in his chest, and I'm suddenly enveloped by a comforting warmth that has me laughing with him.

Slowly, our laughter dies, but the warm feeling remains, and then he says, "I mean, always your sweet pussy. But this time, I was literally thinking about nothing."

I nod as I reply, "Same. Nothing seems good right now."

We fall back into that comfortable silence. I close my eyes as his fingers stroke lightly over my forehead, giving myself this reprieve to slip into the nothing where the dark can't touch me.

I doze a bit, but then I'm roused by his movement jostling me, and I'm unceremoniously dumped onto the mattress as he suddenly rolls toward me.

"What the fuck are you doing?" I sputter, annoyed that he took away my comfortable pillow.

He settles on his side facing me, his expression serious as he says, "Sorry, sugar. But our time to think about nothing is over. It was either I make a move right then or we continue to sit here, wasting valuable time."

I frown, knowing he's right but also wanting to sulk.

He moves closer so mere inches separate us, and then he reaches down, pulling my leg back up over him and yanking me so there's no space between us. He wedges his bottom arm under my head so I'm pillowed on his bicep, but he's still able to look me in the eyes. I pull my hands in, tucking myself into the cocoon as his free hand gently pushes the hair back from my face. His eyes search mine, the silence dragging out until finally, I whisper, "What are you looking for?"

"The answers."

I snort, rolling my eyes a bit as I respond, "Good fucking luck finding any answers there."

He smiles, his eyes warming as he says, "You are the answer." I swat at his chest, rolling my eyes a bit more forcefully as I snort a little more loudly. He chuckles but remains unflinching as he says, "You're *my* answer."

Suddenly, my eyes burn, and I squeeze them shut, a sudden well of emotion burning in my chest and rising up my throat. I cough as I attempt to keep it down. I've never considered myself to be much of a crybaby, but the events of the last six months have proven I tend to leak under long periods of stress and anxiety.

"Look at me."

I shake my head, squeezing my eyes tighter. I push at his chest in an attempt to escape, but he uses both arms to pull me tighter, his forehead pressed against mine. I open my eyes, and he's so close that his two eyes blend into one, the pale green burning with every emotion I could ever fathom.

Finally, I ask, "How much time do we have?"

He eases his grip on me, putting a bit more distance between us, and his one eye becomes two as he replies, "If I had to guess, probably tomorrow evening."

"And there's no chance they won't come for you?"

He shakes his head. "Given the circumstances, the odds of them just walking away are pretty much nil. So, the real question is whether or not other people will show up."

"Who else has a stake in it?"

He laughs bitterly and then answers, "That list is long. Matteo was a pretty big shit in the game. He was also the eldest heir in that family, and his younger brother is more of a party animal than murderous animal, so they really have no choice. There were some other lower-level players who were fodder in the slaughter, but that doesn't mean they're just going to go quietly, either."

"Are you saying you're going to die?"

He stiffens, frowning as he says firmly, "No. At least, I fucking hope not."

"But it's a possibility."

"Dying is a possibility regardless of multiple people wanting me dead."

"That doesn't make me feel any better," I say sullenly.

He sighs, shrugging and then shaking his head. "I don't think there's anything I can say to make you feel better. I'm not going to lie to you, and I'm not going to sugarcoat anything."

"I know."

"Do you?"

I glare at him and then spit out, "Yes, I fucking know."

"We have help coming," he whispers. "I won't be in there entirely alone, but I need you to promise me something."

"Anything," I say easily. "You know I'll do anything you ask."

"You're not going to like it."

Now I laugh as I say, "Nothing new there, but I promise, nonetheless."

"When the time comes where you're able to escape," he says. "I need you to promise me that you'll go."

I frown, all laughter leaving me as I shake my head and whisper, "I can't."

"You must. You must get out of there so I'll know you're safe."

I shake my head almost violently, that low sob once again stuck in my throat as I whimper, unable to just do what he wants.

He pulls away from me, his hands gripping my head, forcing me to look at him. In a commanding voice I've never heard before, he says, "You will. You will promise me, and you will do it. Do you hear me?"

I close my mouth, pressing my lips together tightly, shaking my head in his hands. He gives me a little shake as he whisper-shouts, "Yes. Promise me."

The sob breaks free, and I gasp, "And leave you behind?"

"Yes," he replies more calmly. "I can take care of myself."

"And how is it you suggest I escape?"

"I don't know for sure, but you'll know when the time is upon us and you *will* turn and you *will* leave without even looking back."

Tears stream from my eyes now, running along my nose into my hairline, onto his arm, and I know that the fuss I'm putting up is all for naught because there really isn't any other choice. But I don't want to. I don't want to take the chance that I leave him behind only for him to die when I'd sooner stay behind and die with him.

He's quiet now, and I take a shuddering breath in, nodding and swallowing the lump in my throat as I meet his eyes again.

"You have to say the words, sugar. I need to hear them."

I let loose one final sob and a shaky inhalation through my nose, and then I exhale. "I promise."

27

Seek Forgiveness, Not Permission

Matt

WE MANAGE TO HAVE the shortest, most basic honeymoon in the history of honeymoons. Food is delivered to our door, courtesy of Kaian, and fresh clothes for Jessica are delivered to the door, courtesy of Marieka.

But just as suspected, not even twenty-four hours later, there's a louder knock on the door, this one much more authoritative and foreboding.

I open the door to find Seamus on the other side, and though I'm a bit relieved to have it be him instead of any number of the other assholes who it could have been, I'm still annoyed he showed up so soon.

He steps inside the room, closing the door behind him. He makes no move to sit or get comfortable. He just looks at me, then at Jessica, and then back at me and says, "Time's up."

Jessica interjects from across the room, "Surely, there's another way."

He raises his brows at her and says, "Come now, daughter. I know you're smarter than that."

She rolls her eyes and snorts as she says a touch belligerently, "Like you fucking know anything about me."

His lips twitch, and for a moment, I wonder if he's going to smile. But then his lips turn down, and he frowns at her as he says, "Regardless, you know certain restitutions will need to be made."

She glares back at him but says nothing, so I cross the room, grab onto her biceps and pull her close as I say, "It'll be fine, Jess. You'll see."

She raises her chin at me obstinately, and I sigh. Knowing there's nothing I can say to make her feel better about the situation, I release her, turning back to Seamus and asking, "How many?"

"I haven't the foggiest."

"Not even a guesstimate?"

He shakes his head, his hands coming out and waving around as he replies, "I attempted to count at first, but then there were just too many people, and I couldn't figure out who was regular pissed at you and who was pissed at you enough to kill you. So, I gave up."

"That's fair," I reply seriously. After a couple of decades working with the likes of Darius and Tony, I'm sure the list of people out for my blood is rather extensive.

"Is everything in place?" I ask.

"Yes," he answers, his arms crossing over his chest as he adds, "Good luck recognizing anyone."

I walk toward the dresser, rummaging through the drawers and pulling out clothes to dress appropriately as I ask, "What do you mean?"

"I had an associate of mine pay your friends a visit."

"Yes, I remember that," I answer with a nod.

"Well, let's just say she's a master of disguises."

I pause with one leg in my pants and look over at him with my eyebrows raised as I say, "Then how the fuck am I supposed to know who I'm not supposed to kill?"

He smiles at me broadly and shrugs, and I shake my head, cursing under my breath as I finish putting my pants on.

My boots appear in front of my face as Jessica hands them to me. I take them with a smile and sit in the chair to pull my socks on. Then, she says, "Is it safe for me to assume that these friends are my ticket out of here?" Seamus nods, and then she asks, "And how am I supposed to know that I'm leaving with the right person?"

Seamus smiles even more broadly as he says, "Oh, they have a password."

She quirks a brow at him, her lips twisting as she asks exasperatedly, "A password?"

He nods, looking quite proud of himself, and finally, I ask, "And what might the password be?"

He laughs and then says, "Fucklicker."

I chuckle, nodding appreciatively at one of Tony's clever insults. And then Jessica parrots, "Fucklicker?"

I laugh again, tying my boots and then rising to my feet. I walk over to her, stooping down to look her in the face when I say, "That's right. Fucklicker."

Seamus laughs again, and then she looks between us and says, "You all keep proving the rumors about you to be true."

I incline my head at her and ask rhetorically because it amuses me, "And which rumor might that be?"

"Your penchant for acting inappropriately in high-stress situations."

"Oh, yeah," I reply. "That's definitely true."

Seamus speaks up. "Sometimes, you gotta do what you gotta do. And frankly, oftentimes, a few misplaced jokes can flip a situation back into your favor."

I look over at him and nod in agreement. "It's actually happened quite a few times for me."

"You two are impossible," Jessica sighs.

I smile and respond, "As you have reminded me many times."

She smiles at me fondly and then sits on the side of the bed to tend to her own shoes, and I turn back to Seamus and ask, "Am I going to get any talking time, or is it going to be right to the fights?"

"I think some of them are intent on skipping any kind of discussion. Especially since those men are dead dead, and you obviously killed them."

"And Kaian?" I ask worriedly.

"They've accepted that he was working for me. And that if it hadn't been for your interference, none of that would have happened."

"Good," I reply with relief. "The last thing we need is two of us in trouble."

I turn to Jessica, now standing beside me, her hands fidgeting in front of her nervously. I hold my hand out to her and ask, "Are you ready?"

She eyes my hand warily before finally placing her hand in mine, and she whispers, "Yes. As ready as I'm going to be."

I step in closer to her, leaning in, pressing my lips softly against hers before pulling back and looking in her eyes. "Don't forget your promise."

She frowns, glaring at me, and for a moment, I think she's going to tell me to go fuck myself. But instead, she swallows and then answers, "I'll remember."

I walk toward the door, pulling her along with me, and then motion for Seamus to go ahead of us. He opens the door, exiting out into the hallway, and I push Jessica out in front of me as I shut the door behind me.

Seamus leads the way, and the closer we get to the great hall, the louder the ruckus becomes. There's shouting and some laughter, and general chaotic din of people intent on bloodshed.

Once we reach the doorway, the sound is almost deafening, but we only make it a few steps into the room before everything goes quiet, and then all we hear are whispers and the tittering of expectation.

I walk further into the room, but Seamus stops in front of me and says, "She should stay over here."

I nod and turn to Jessica, who is already shaking her head. When she opens her mouth to argue, I interrupt, "Yes, sugar. This is the safest place for you. If somehow things go to complete shit before my friends have come for you, find Kaian or Seamus."

She's still shaking her head, and I see the panic in her eyes as she glances around the crowded room. I grip her face between my palms, forcing her to look at me as I say fervently, "You're my answer. Don't forget."

She stares back at me, and I see that she's fighting the panic, so I yank her closer, pressing my lips against hers firmly and then pulling back and saying, "Forgive me."

Now, she frowns, continuing to shake her head as she processes my words, but I don't give her time to ask any questions.

I turn, walking into the crowd, ready to fight.

28

Revelations

Jessica

I'M STILL STANDING THERE, contemplating Matt's parting words, when I realize he has disappeared into the crowd.

Annoyed that I wasn't quicker to question him, I step after him only to be blocked by Kaian. My hands come up, and I shove against his chest as I say, "Get out of my way."

He raises his brows at me, shaking his head as he says calmly, "You know I can't do that."

I step back, crossing my arms over my chest as I scowl at him. "Yes, you can."

He laughs and then sighs as he replies, "I have my orders. You'll just have to deal with it."

I huff in annoyance, contemplating giving him a hard time but knowing it's pointless. I eye him, considering my next move, when finally, I say, "I just want to get closer so I can see."

He nods, motioning for me to step back toward the wall. Then, he slowly leads me around until we're standing off to the side of the stage. Poles and ropes have been added, so on three sides, it looks like a makeshift boxing ring, and I swallow down the bile in my throat at the implication of what's about to come.

I turn to Kaian, leaning in and whispering, "How many do you think he'll have to fight?"

He shrugs, his eyes on the stage as he replies, "Could be two. Could be two dozen. Hard to say."

I frown, my stomach rolling at the idea that Matt may have to fight dozens of men. Then I ask, "Matt told me to forgive him. Do you know what that means?"

He turns his attention to me, his eyes blank as he shakes his head and says, "No fucking idea. And knowing Matt, it could mean anything."

"Well, he's your friend," I reply exasperatedly. "Surely, you must have some clue."

"Define friend," Kaian retorts. "The only people who know Matt well are the men he's known his whole life. Sure, he probably trusts me not to stab him in the back, but that doesn't mean he's going to make a habit of turning his back on me. That man has enough secrets to fill a vault. So, whatever it is, I'm going to find out the same time you do."

I huff again, wishing there was a way for me to know what was going to happen. I step against the wall, leaning my back against the cold surface and turning my gaze back to the stage. Matt is just stepping up there, where he turns in the middle of the ring, staring down at everyone surrounding him.

The crowd is in an uproar; what appears to be dozens upon dozens of angry men, obviously spoiling for a fight. Matt doesn't seem bothered at all standing up there, looking relaxed with his hands in his fucking pockets.

I growl a little in my throat, and Kaian turns a questioning look on me, and I sputter, "You'd think that asshole was here as a spectator."

Kaian chuckles, glancing back at Matt and then back to me as he says, "That's called a lifetime of training his poker face."

I gape at him and whisper-shout, "This isn't fucking poker, Kaian."

He shrugs, obviously not bothered by any of this, which makes me want to punch him in the face. I must be looking a certain way, standing there staring at him with my fists clenched, because he leans in closer and says, "You can hit me if it will make you feel better."

I glare at him and then huff some more as I turn back to the stage, where some of the old men are joining Matt.

The old man, who always seems to be in charge, raises both of his hands over his head, and after a few moments, the room falls silent.

He looks back at Matt and says something incoherent, and then Matt steps forward and says loudly, "You all know that Matteo and his buddies were killed with cause. They attacked with plans to follow through with heinous crimes, so I intervened on behalf of Seamus and neutralized the threat. In order to prevent the Irish from seeking restitution for reneging on a marriage contract, I stepped up and married Seamus' daughter, Jessica. Since this changes my position considerably, anyone wishing to make her a widow and step into my place has the right to challenge me here and now."

Matt steps back, and the old man steps forward, saying, "Anyone wishing to challenge may step to the other side of the ring. Everyone else, remain where you are and know that this is your only chance. If you remain on the non-challenge side, you forfeit any future chance to interfere."

The old man turns back to Matt and once again says something incoherent, and Matt laughs. The old man frowns and says something else, and Matt laughs again, and Kaian shifts beside me, muttering under his breath, "What the fuck is he doing?"

I lean closer. "What do you mean?"

Kaian's focus remains on Matt, but he leans over to me and says, "He appears to be antagonizing him, and I have no fucking idea why."

"Who is he?"

"He's like the king of kings," Kaian replies. "The figurehead put into place when old man Ferro died with no obvious heir to take his place."

I frown, my heart racing in my chest at his words. Matt's laughter draws my attention back to him, and I see the old man's face reddening. He turns and looks behind him and spits something angrily, and then Matt steps into him, his hands grasping the front of his jacket, as he leans in and whispers into his ear. The old man's face pales, his eyes widening and his mouth gaping as he attempts to find words and obviously fails.

Matt steps back from him, a smug expression on his face. He lifts his chin defiantly as he scans over the crowd, and then his hand reaches for the old man. Matt grabs him by the throat, yanking him so his back is pressed to Matt's front.

The old man's shout of protest reverberates through the room, causing everyone to turn their attention to the stage. Matt grins, his eyes gleaming as he holds the old man with an arm across his throat, his free hand moving behind and then coming back in front with a blade gripped tightly.

The old man shouts again, struggling against Matt's hold, wild eyes focused on the knife as Matt holds him tighter. Matt doesn't say anything further, his grip on the knife handle tightening as he draws his arm back, quickly swinging forward and driving the knife into the old man's chest.

The king of kings struggles for another moment, then freezes, his eyes now focused on the knife sticking out of his heart. Slowly, his eyes lift, surprise and fright evident on his features. And then, nothing.

He sinks to the ground. Matt yanks the knife free as he allows the now-lifeless body to drop to his feet. Everyone remains frozen in place for a few moments, and then, like a light switch has gone off, many of them turn to search for an escape, scurrying for an exit.

A couple of dozen remain standing, staring up at Matt in horror and shock that quickly turns to rage, and then they move to step toward him when he holds the knife up, stopping them in their tracks.

A man appears on the stage behind Matt, slowly sidling closer, and I jump forward only to be held back by Kaian as I shout, "Matt, behind you."

I struggle, trying to break free from Kaian's hold, but he just holds me even tighter, bodily yanking me back and twisting me so I can no longer see the stage.

Then Marieka is in front of me, another woman by her side, and they grab me, taking me from Kaian's arms as he says, "Go with them. Now."

I struggle some more, twisting in the hopes I can turn back to at least keep an eye on anyone who could possibly sneak up on him.

Fingers dig painfully into my biceps, and I gasp in pain, turning to the person holding me and saying, "Let me go."

The grip tightens even more, and I look up into a stranger's face, but then Marieka is there, saying, "It's okay, Jess. We have to go."

I shake my head, still attempting to pull away, when she adds, "Don't forget your promise."

I scowl, shaking my head in denial, at the same time, knowing I have no choice.

I look back at the stranger and ask, "Who the fuck are you?"

She smiles, her grip on my arms easing slightly as she replies, "I'm the Fucklicker who's about to get you out of here."

My entire body relaxes instantaneously, that maniacal laughter bubbling in my chest, but I manage to hold it in.

They turn and start making their way through the room, pushing and shoving through the men, half of which are still panicking, and the other half infuriated and looking for blood.

"My name is Mathias Ferro," Matt's shout cuts across the din, and immediately, everyone stills, his words echoing through the hall ominously. He pauses, and what little chatter was left dies down completely as he continues loudly, "I am your fucking god. You kneel, or you die."

The strange woman leading me out of the room stops in her tracks, and I run into the back of her as she turns, her eyes focused on the stage. "What the fuck?"

She stands there frozen, her eyes locked on Matt, confusion on her face, but then Kaian comes up behind us shouting, "Get out. It's time to go."

His words jar her from her thoughts, and she shakes her head, immediately turning and pulling me behind her toward the exit, Marieka right on our tail.

There's another shout behind us, and I turn just in time to see the man behind him lifting his arm, a knife glinting in his hand as if he's going to throw it. I shout once again, struggling to get free.

Marieka and Kaian forcefully shove me from behind, the pull of the stranger jerking me away, and I glance back helplessly as the crowd surges forward, the man with the knife now standing there looking smug, the knife no longer in his hand.

Matt is no longer standing on the stage, and I scream incoherently, releasing the agony in my guts as I fight to get free, but now the three sets of hands hold me back, and then I'm lifted bodily off the ground and hustled out the door and down the hall.

Kaian grabs me more firmly around my torso, pinning my arms to my sides, and someone else holds my legs. I'm carried through the maze of hallways until finally, we burst out into the cool, dark night.

We're at the edge of the woods, a dirt path just wide enough for one vehicle, and I see a van parked there, waiting.

They hustle me to the back doors, which open immediately, and I blink in shock as Marieka appears.

I stop struggling, shaking my head as I ask, "What? What the fuck is going on?"

My legs are dropped down until my feet are on the ground, and then they release me. After a moment, Kaian eases his grip around me, his hands on my arms steadying me as I look at Marieka, confused as fuck. I turn back to the two women who helped me, seeing the stranger there but then also Marieka, and for a moment, I feel like I might pass out.

Marieka gets out of the van, stepping over beside the mirror image of herself. She leans in close, scanning the facial features, and she smiles and then laughs and says, "Isn't that fucking wild?"

I look at her and then stutter, "Wh-what is happening?"

She turns to me, smiles, and then points her thumb at the other Marieka and says, "Jessica, meet Camilla McDonough, master of illusion and deception."

The woman smiles, inclining her head good-naturedly, and I shake my head, waving a hand tiredly as I walk to the back of the van and sit on the edge.

I look at Kaian as I whisper, "You need to go back. I saw a man with a knife, and then he was gone. You need to go back."

He nods, then turns on his heel, and sprints away. I turn to the still unidentified woman who helped lug me out and ask, "And who are you?"

She smiles a wicked grin and replies, "Antoinette. Do you like my new look?" I groan, my head falling into my palms as I rub my face in an attempt to get my bearings, then I glance back up at her and ask, "Do you know anything about Matt being Mathias Ferro?"

She shakes her head and then motions for me to get into the van, and I don't bother standing. Instead, I turn my body and roll myself inside, where I lay down in the fetal position.

Antoinette steps in, Marieka and Camilla right behind her. The doors slam shut, and I'm surrounded by silence. Then Antoinette replies, "We're going to go find out."

I remain silent, lying there doing my best not to think the worst of what I saw, knowing that it's sometimes what you didn't see that matters.

But still, I pray.

29

A Heart-to-Heart

Antoinette

WHAT THE FUCK?

That's all that's been running through my head since that douchebag Mathias stood up on that stage and announced himself a motherfucking Ferro.

The mere idea that that asshole could possibly be my uncle is preposterous.

And, of course, Darius and Tony aren't even here to be my sounding boards. I'm stuck with a bunch of people who have no fucking clue who I am, who the Ferros are, or the fact that while placing the goddamn crown on his head, he also put up one giant fucking target.

This leads us to the other problem. Darius and Tony would have also been blindsided, and we had to leave them behind to face not only the people who would have wanted to take Matt's place as the head of the Irish but the hordes of people who would like nothing more than to end up at the top of the kingdom.

What the actual fucking fuck?

I pull my phone out and send more messages to Lilith, hoping maybe she can be bothered to reply to one. Of course, they're all delivered with no acknowledgment that I've asked anything, so I sit there in the passenger seat of the van, fuming.

We're almost to the outskirts of the city when I pull up Carolina's name and send her a message asking who all is about.

She answers almost immediately, listing off a laundry list of names, and I'm tickled to find one of them is Lilith.

It's about time my fucking mother gave us some answers.

The three other women are all silent, and I look back over my shoulder to see Jessica's still lying in the back of the van in the fetal position.

I sigh, and then, having been in that same position more times than I can count, I unbuckle my seatbelt and slowly make my way back there.

I kneel by her head, leaning over so I can glance at her face as I ask, "Are you all right?"

She doesn't look at me. She just remains lying there with her eyes squeezed shut as she shakes her head slightly.

I sigh, then inch my way around her until I can stretch out beside her. She tucks her knees up tighter into her body, and I'm able to move closer. I reach out and take both of her hands in mine and close the distance between us so it's close but still comfortable.

She doesn't attempt to pull away, and she also doesn't look at me or say anything, so after a few moments, I say, "I know exactly how it feels."

"How what feels?"

"To feel like you might die at the loss of someone else."

A sobbing laugh falls from her lips, and then she says bitterly, "I never wanted any of this."

She's still not looking at me, but I nod anyway and then say, "Me neither. I had every intention of killing the fucker, but look at me now."

Her eyes open, and she frowns at me. "You were going to kill him?"

I chuckle softly and then reply, "That was my job. Obviously, I fucking failed miserably."

She laughs for a second and then stops abruptly, as if she's afraid she was going to offend me, so I add, "Oh, it's funny. It wasn't funny at the time, but you know, hindsight is a fucking laugh and a half."

Jessica nods and then sighs. "Yeah, sometimes I'd like to go back and bash Bobby's head in again. And there was absolutely nothing funny about that at the time."

"See?" I chirp. "You spend enough time in this life, and you can find humor in anything."

"But at one point, you thought Darius was dead?" she asks quietly.

"Oh, yeah," I respond firmly. "Thought someone shot him dead almost right in front of me."

"That must have been terrible," she whispers sadly.

I shrug, bobbing my head around nonchalantly as I reply, "Well, it wasn't great. And over time, I learned to trust the process more."

She frowns and asks, "The process?"

"The process of kill or be killed," I explain. "It doesn't always come down to being the most powerful, smartest, or richest. Most of the time, it comes down to being willing to make the necessary sacrifices to come out on top. We've basically dedicated our lives to ensuring the future safety and well-being of those at risk. But in some circles, they still call us criminals."

Jessica snorts and rolls her eyes as she mutters, "And those are usually the fuckers you gotta watch out for."

"That's true. It's greed and the thirst for power that fuels most of the evil in the world. And some of the most ruthless criminal organizations in the world are considered to be aboveboard, legitimate businesses."

We fall into silence, watching each other as the van begins its stop-and-go pursuit through the city. Jessica sighs again, and then she asks, "How do we know what to do next?"

"I'm not entirely sure right now, but just as soon as we get back, I'm going to ask the person who probably knows."

We fall back into a comfortable silence, and I continue to hold her hands and just breathe the same air as her, until, finally, we pull to a stop. By the time they're opening the back doors, I've helped her sit up and adjust herself, wiping the drying tears from her face. I lean in and whisper, "He's okay, Jess. Just believe that."

Obviously, I don't know for sure this is true, but I do believe it in my heart. And if by chance I'm wrong, and my heart ends up crushed into a million pieces, at least I'll have that pain to fuel me for the reckoning.

We make our way into the building, going directly to the main communications area, where I know everyone is waiting.

Carolina meets us halfway across the room and immediately wraps an arm around Jessica's shoulders, leaning in and whispering to her softly. I don't waste any time with that; I walk directly over to my mother and stick my finger in her face and snarl, "Fucking explain yourself."

She doesn't blink or even flinch. She just raises a brow at me and asks, "You're going to have to be more specific."

I glare at her, pushing my finger a little closer as I say, "Don't fucking play with me, Mother."

Now, she flinches, her mouth falling open in shock. Then she glares back at me, slapping my hand away as she exclaims, "Don't you use that word with me."

I drop my hand, moving my hands to my hips as I lean in and ask, "And why not? Are you afraid I might know who my uncle is?"

Now, she frowns, a puzzled expression on her face as she parrots, "Uncle?"

I stomp my foot and exclaim, "Yes, uncle. Uncle Mathias, ring a bell?"

Her frown deepens, and after a moment, she laughs loudly. She continues to laugh while I stand there with my hands out, helplessly looking at Carolina for help. She shrugs, obviously uncertain what the hell is going on, and so I stand there and let Lilith laugh until she finally runs out of steam.

Eventually, she stands upright, wiping the tears from her eyes. She shakes her head at me and says, "You're funny."

"Funny or not," I reply. "Matt went in front of all those fucking people and declared himself a Ferro. So, you have some fucking explaining to do."

All humor falls from her face, and she cocks her head at me and says, "He what?"

I nod and reply, "That's right. Heard it with my own fucking ears."

She shakes her head and then says, "Well, that was kind of dumb."

"Dumb? How about maybe it's not true?"

She grimaces, and I immediately know that whatever the fuck is going on, the Ferro part is true and I sputter, "I can't believe you didn't fucking tell me."

"It's not my story to tell."

"I'm so fucking sick of hearing that."

"I understand that, Antoinette," she replies calmly. "But up until now, I didn't think it mattered."

"Well, apparently it does," I reply sharply. "Are you going to explain or not?" She pauses for a moment, giving me an assessing look, and finally, she nods and says, "I'll tell you."

I sigh in relief, then reply, "You may as well tell us all because I don't feel like repeating it."

"That's fine. I guess we're far beyond the need for story time. But I can assure you, he's not your uncle."

"How is he not my uncle if you have the same father?"

"We don't," she answers matter-of-factly. "I was never a Ferro."

I gape at her and then roll my eyes, muttering, "Of course you're not."

She smirks at me and then laughs a bit bitterly as she motions for the chairs in the corner. "Have a seat. This may take a minute."

30

A Very Lilith Story

Lilith

35-ISH YEARS AGO

To say there's no love lost between my mother and me would be an understatement.

And not just because she isn't my biological mother.

You see, when my father found a job for me, this meant, in her eyes, I was more useful than she was.

It was just happenstance that she fell pregnant a couple of months before I was sent out on my first mission.

Shockingly, her demeanor immediately changed, knowing that the child she carried would someday provide the Ferro family with even more power.

What she didn't count on was having that same child would be her end.

What *I* didn't count on is the fact that my father would be so overcome by the loss of her that he would get it into his head to dispose of the thing that killed her.

And this is when his habit of ignoring my existence became entirely convenient.

While he thought he was burying his wife and child together in a casket, I had worked to bribe people into placing the stillborn of a local in the casket and handing me the baby.

It was an impulsive move. I didn't think about how I was going to carry on with this ruse as this baby got bigger, never mind the fact I'd have to feed it and keep it away from the man who tried to kill it.

It was fun at first and certainly worked to pass the time as I waited to see if my first mission was a success.

Fortunately, some of my loyal staff assisted me in my duplicity. They took turns tending to the baby whenever I had to be out and about, and basically, intentionally, in the man's way. They brought formula, bottles, and diapers, and they also helped keep the evidence under control.

It became even more complicated once we had confirmation that my first mission was successful. And then, I had to learn, in real-time, the ill effects of first-trimester pregnancy.

Keep in mind that my thirteen-year-old body wasn't quite prepared for the job.

Weeks of sickness took its toll on me, and even with the help of the people around me, it became more and more evident that I wouldn't be able to keep up with the care of an infant under such strained circumstances.

And that's when I called Mickey.

Mickey had been assigned to me as a young child. He was tasked with keeping me out of trouble and also keeping me in line, both jobs which he took very seriously.

He knew I had taken the baby and made it look like it had died, and he didn't say anything. But that didn't mean he would be able to assist me indefinitely.

Every day that goes by, the more at risk all of these people are for helping me keep this secret.

And then, after a particularly bad night, I had to accept defeat and acknowledge we needed a new plan.

It was the cook who had the brilliant idea to find a suitable family and have them adopt the baby.

I was skeptical at first, but I knew Mickey would take the job seriously, and he would find not only a suitable home but perhaps even a loving one.

Or if nothing else, one that would provide protection to him through his formative years.

Now, here I am, enjoying my last few minutes of second-guessing the decision while knowing I have no other choice.

A knock at the door sounds, and after a moment of hesitation, I say, "Come in."

Mickey enters, shutting the door behind him and then walking toward me slowly. He stops in front of me and asks, "Are you ready?"

I shake my head, swallowing the painful lump in my throat as I try to fathom what it will be like to be alone again.

He gives me a soft smile and then inclines his head at me as he replies, "I know, Lils. But you're doing the right thing."

I nod, lifting a shoulder dismissively as I say, "Maybe. I guess only time will tell."

He raises his brows at me and responds, "Anything is better than the future he'll have if he stays here."

I scowl, knowing he's right but not wanting to admit it. So, he adds, "The only path he has here is one to death. And half of the people you trust here would go with him."

I wince, pain jackknifing through me at his words.

He's right. If I end up caught with this baby here, it will be obvious that many people must have helped me. And just for that, heads would roll.

I say nothing further, rising to my feet and holding the sleeping baby out in front of me. I kiss his forehead and then his eyelids and bring his little cheek right next to mine. I whisper in his ear, "I love you."

I pull back, knowing the tears are close to overflowing, so I clear my throat, and after one final kiss on his tiny little face, I hand him to Mickey and say, "You better go now."

He takes the baby almost gingerly, cradling him in his arms, and I wish I could take a picture of what a pair they make.

I smile fondly, sniffling and then laughing softly as I say, "Seems to me you're a little smitten, too."

Mickey glares at me and huffs, "You stop that, now. I don't get smitten."

I laugh, feeling a bit better about my decision, and watch silently as he turns and heads toward the door.

He reaches for the door handle, and suddenly, I take a step toward him and exclaim, "Wait."

Mickey stops, turns back toward me slightly, and raises his eyebrows in question. I don't move any closer to him; I just say, "Tell them his name is Mathias."

He looks down at the sleeping baby in the crook of his arm and then leans closer as he says, "Did you hear that, boy? Finally got yourself a name."

He looks back up at me and nods, and I manage a smile as he then turns and opens the door. He walks through the doorway, shutting the door behind him without a second glance. I just stand there, staring at the gleaming wood, fighting back tears.

I clear my throat, nodding to myself as I mutter, "This is the only way. You're doing the right thing."

But that fact doesn't stop me from walking to the door and pressing my face against it as I sob.

31

Explanations

Jessica

WE ALL SIT THERE in silence after Lilith finishes her story.

Carolina looks stunned, but Antoinette looks an odd mix between shocked and horrified, with an underlying glimmer of sadness.

Lilith glances at each of us and then focuses on Antoinette as she asks, "Do you have any questions?"

Antoinette frowns, shaking her head as she says quietly, "I don't know."

Lilith smiles, laughing humorlessly as she replies, "I totally get that."

"Have you known this whole time that Matt is the Mathias you named?"

Lilith frowns and shakes her head. "No, not the entire time."

"How long?" Antoinette asks with a frown.

"Mickey updated me after my initial resurrection."

"And Matt has known since then, too?"

She shakes her head, then answers, "No, I told him a bit later when the whole question of how best to save Carolina was circling. But then Tony grew into a man, and the problem resolved itself."

"By marrying me?" Carolina asks.

Lilith turns to her and nods. "Yes, that was a solid enough union to eliminate a lot of possible threats, so we ran with it."

Antoinette snorts and retorts, "As if Tony would've allowed someone else to marry Carolina."

"True," Lilith replies. "And he would've been even more infuriated by the idea that Matt outranked him."

Antoinette laughs. "Kind of sad I missed the opportunity to razz him."

Both women laugh, and I frown at what is obviously an inside joke. I wait for their laughter to die down and then ask, "So Matt being a Ferro means what exactly?"

Lilith and Antoinette look at me like I've suddenly sprouted two heads, and then Lilith turns to Antoinette and asks, "Is she for real?"

"She's been out of the game for a spell," Antoinette replies with a shrug. "And she's a bit younger than me, so she wouldn't know much about the old families."

Lilith raises a brow quizzically as she peers at me, and I'm just shy of starting to squirm when she beams a glowing smile at me and exclaims, "Well, the Ferros are the oldest and most powerful family in the organization. So being the head of the Ferro family puts a person firmly at the top of the entire empire."

"So, there's more of them?"

"Well, no."

"What?" I squawk. "What happened to them?"

Lilith's smile brightens even more as she responds, "Oh, I killed them."

I frown, squinting at her enthusiasm, completely lost for words. Then Antoinette adds, "They totally had it coming."

I rub my hands over my face tiredly as I mutter, "I'm sure they did."

Carolina sighs and moves closer to me, leaning in as she says, "You get used to it."

I turn raised brows to her and ask, "Get used to what?"

"The constant fuckery."

"Okay," I respond seriously. "Someone answer me one question." I glance around the room, and everyone stares at me expectantly, but no one says anything. So, after a beat, I ask, "Why would Matt announce this now? When everyone was already out for his head?"

"Oh, that's easy," Lilith answers with a smile. "Because he knows it'll spread like wildfire, and all the rats will come out of the sewers in the hopes of taking him out and getting themselves the whole lot."

"Surely there's a better way to go about it? Something more methodical and sinister. Less fucking crazy."

Lilith makes a face, tipping her head from side to side as she says, "Well, sure. But this way had far more impact given so many families were in attendance. And knowing he's a Ferro means they're less likely to kill him outright. Gotta stick with the rules and regs when you're trying to steal a throne." I nod but say nothing, too tired to think about it anymore tonight, and then Lilith asks, "Anything else?"

Antoinette presses her lips together, squinting her eyes, and then, after a beat, says, "Wait. How are you not related?"

"Oh," Lilith exclaims. "Old man Ferro stole me from my parents when I was a small child."

Antoinette's eyes widen as she says, "Stole how?"

"Well, he murdered them and took me."

"And no one tried to get you back?"

Lilith shakes her head and then shrugs. "He basically took out the majority of my family. The few who were left scattered into the wind, with the exception of my father's brother."

"And what did he do?" Antoinette asks cautiously as if unsure she wants to know.

"Oh, he stayed beside me my entire life. My most trusted confidante and colleague."

Antoinette frowns and looks around as she ponders the statement. Then, suddenly, her eyes light up, and she turns to Lilith and asks, "Mickey?"

"Yes," Lilith replies with a nod. "He snuck his way in there, and they were none the wiser."

"Why didn't he try to get you out?" Carolina asks.

"That would have been a death sentence," Lilith answers. "Unless he had a huge following for protection, there's no way either of us would have made it out alive. So, he figured the best thing he could do was to stick by my side and at least try to keep me from ending up dead in a ditch somewhere."

Antoinette's excited expression falls into sadness as she whispers, "Oh, the stuff that poor man had to witness."

We fall into silence again, each of us contemplating what Lilith has told us in our current situation. Which brings my focus back to Matt and the last scene I saw before our escape.

A choked whimper falls from my lips, and all the women turn to me. It's who Antoinette moves closer and rests her hand on my arm as she says, "It will be okay, Jess."

I shudder, shaking my head as I ask, "How can you know that?"

Antoinette sighs and then says, "Well, I guess I don't really, but I still believe it."

"Did you see it?"

Antoinette shakes her head, turns to Camilla, and asks, "Did you see it?"

She shakes her head. "I didn't see anything with us trying to get out."

Antoinette laughs, and I smile because she sure as fuck does look like Marieka. "It's fucking creepy how much you look like Marieka."

Camilla smiles proudly. "Stature aside, I can be pretty much anyone."

I shake my head, staring at her as I reply, "That is actually incredibly creepy and a little disturbing. And also empowering. I'm a little jealous."

Carolina and Antoinette nod in agreement, and Marieka steps closer to Camilla, staring at her in awe as she says, "I will never get used to it. Think about the pranks we could pull."

I sit there, enjoying a moment of calm. After a few minutes, I finally center myself and then say matter-of-factly, "So, what's next? I can't just keep sitting here wondering if Matt is alive or not. So how do we find out?"

Lilith walks over to me, her hands coming to my shoulders. She looks me in the eyes and says, "I know you haven't been around very long, Jess, but I think you already know the answer to that."

And I do.

I smile and nod my head, and then all of us collectively move to the other side of the room, gathering around a workstation.

Antoinette powers up the computer, then turns to me and says, "Let's get to work."

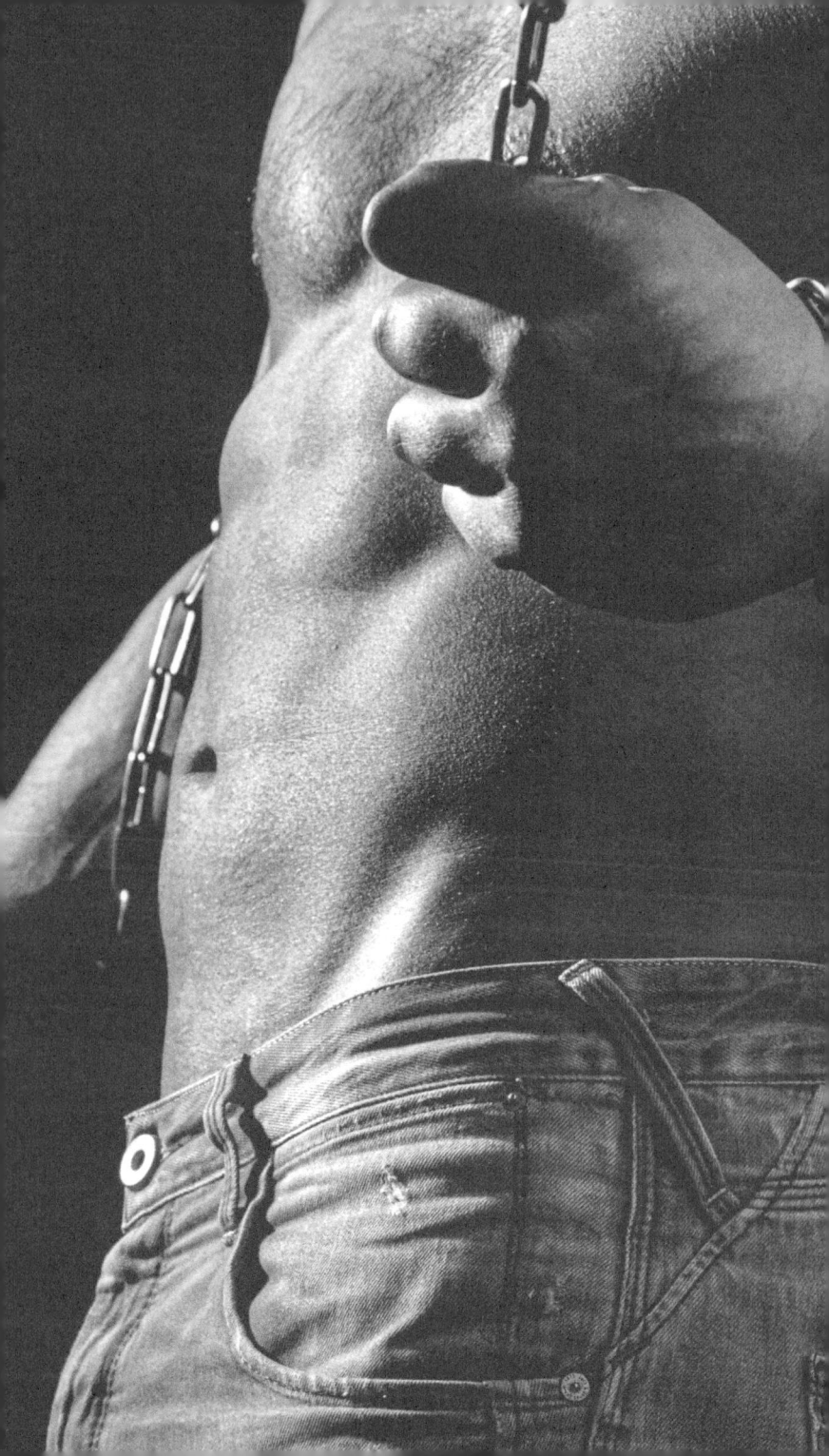

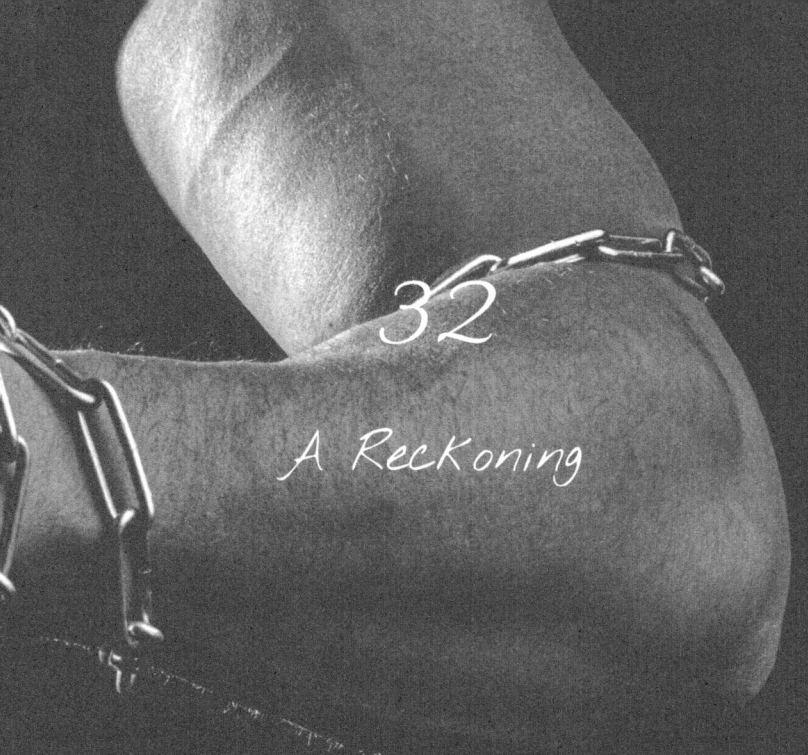

32

A Reckoning

Matt

WELL, THAT WENT TO HELL in a handbasket pretty fast.

I always wondered what it was like to say something excruciatingly dramatic in an over-the-top, theatric way.

And now I know.

While spontaneously stabbing that old man in the chest was entirely satisfying, strategically, it may not have been my best move.

But then, since I couldn't take it back, I figured my next best step was to cause a scene.

Hence, my decision to out myself as the head of the entire organization.

Of course, there's the problem where not everyone is just going to take my word for it, and I'll have to come up with some kind of proof. But frankly, my decision to kill every motherfucking one of them eliminates that problem.

It's not like that wasn't my endgame in the first place, so having to move the timeline up isn't that big of a hardship.

What I wasn't counting on is having Darius and Tony be there, so well made up that I have no fucking idea who they are.

My first instinct when I heard Jess screaming that someone was behind me was to defend myself. But then I hesitated because there has to be some way for me to figure out who's who.

If I ended up killing one of them by accident, it would be quite upsetting.

Never mind the fact Carolina and or Antoinette would string me up quicker than shit.

But it turns out that my moment of hesitation was the correct choice. No sooner did I pull back from stabbing that man in the chest did the knife he had been wielding go flying by me. I followed its path to see it embedded in another man creeping up on me from just outside my peripheral vision.

I turn back to the man I almost stabbed, taking a step closer and squinting at him as I say, "What's the password?"

The man smirks at me, a bit of a swagger in the step he takes toward me as he whispers, "Get your shit together, Fucklicker."

Motherfucking Tony Andersen.

I breathe a sigh of relief and then say, "You almost got yourself fucking killed, man."

He shrugs and replies, "You wouldn't kill me. You might try, but you won't succeed."

I roll my eyes, turning my body so our backs are pressed together. I take out a couple more people.

It's complete pandemonium in the hall, with most people attempting to escape, but several groups are coming together, most likely planning an attack. I wipe my knife off on my pants, craning my head over to Tony as I say, "Where's Dare?"

"Oh, he's here somewhere disguised as an Irish."

"Irish?"

Tony nods, pulling a new knife from inside his jacket as he says, "Oh, yes. He looks quite dashing, as well. Light hair and light eyes."

Tony remains at my back as I scan the room for Darius. I can't make him out in the crowd, but I see Kaian running through the doorway, where he stops.

He meets my eyes across the room and gives me a nod, and I'm flooded with relief at the knowledge Jessica escaped safely.

This also means that Antoinette and Marieka have escaped, so at least I can move forward with my plan without being concerned about their welfare.

I'm sure Jessica is quite unhappy leaving me behind, and I'm just hoping eventually she'll understand why it was necessary.

It's not that I don't feel she can hold her own; however, I don't want to put her in a position where she has to defend herself in a way that she may be forced to kill people again.

Antoinette is most likely annoyed she doesn't get to take part in it. Fortunately, she also takes it seriously when charged with keeping people safe.

Kaian moves, so he's blending in with a group of people who are obviously contemplating their next move. He melds right in, nodding his head, and I laugh. My moment of humor is cut off by someone shouting at me, "You seem awful amused for a dead man."

I turn to my right to see Franco standing there, an ugly snarl on his face, and I raise a brow at him and smirk, knowing it will infuriate him further. Then I reply, rather sarcastically, "You're awful bossy for a dead man."

He glares at me, and I laugh again, and his face reddens. He takes a step toward me only to have his friend hold him back with his arm. He turns back to his friend, muttering something incoherent, and after a quiet exchange, Franco turns back to me and says, "You may as well give up. You're significantly outnumbered."

I shrug, making sure my expression is as nonchalant as possible as I reply, "Maybe I am, maybe I'm not. Only one way to find out."

Obviously, I am seriously outnumbered. Even with having Tony, Darius, and Kaian on my side, there are a lot of men in this room. And likely, a lot of men who will help try to finish me off.

I see the groups of men shifting and flowing. Some leave the room entirely, but that doesn't mean they won't come back if they feel like the odds are turning in their favor.

I turn to Tony and ask, "What do you think?"

"I think we've seen worse odds," he replies calmly.

"This is true," I reply with a nod. "The real question is, do you think they'll kill us?"

"Nah," he replies. "They're too stupid. They're going to think they will have a big trophy that they can then sell to the highest bidder. Stupidity and greed."

I nod as I parrot, "Stupidity and greed. Gets them every time."

"And what are our chances of being located if they take us?"

"Well, Dare has his watch, so there's that. Then there's the fact that Antoinette and Carolina will go berserk and likely call in every person they can think of to find us."

"So good odds," I say. "Kaian also has instructions to retreat if necessary. He'll be a good asset for them."

"That's a good plan. And where does Seamus stand in all this?"

"Seamus is likely on the fence. I don't believe he'll do anything to hurt us, but it's unlikely he's going to help us either."

Tony sighs, shakes his head as he replies, "Well, that's a fucking shame."

"To be expected."

I look around the room again, still unable to locate Darius, and I see that Kaian has moved through a couple of groups now, likely trying to get an idea of where everyone stands. He turns and glances at me, shaking his head subtly, and I nod, acknowledging the sheer clusterfuck this is about to become.

I turn back to Tony and say, "So, I guess we just kill as many of them as we can until they overpower us?"

Tony nods and says nothing further. I look back around the room and see the groups are starting to move closer to us. Our biggest concern is somebody with a gun and a good shot, though it's a long-standing rule that no guns are allowed in the hall.

Of course, that doesn't mean that one of the people who left won't come back with one, given I killed a powerful man in front of an audience. So, I say, "We need to get the fuck off this stage. We're like sitting ducks up here."

Tony doesn't respond. He just walks over to the far side and ducks between the ropes, and I follow suit. The chatter increases, and I hear shouting. I stab two people who get in my way as I make my way to the wall.

A few other men trickle over and are instantly cut down, and then all movement stops. I turn to Tony and ask, "Are you ready?"

He grins at me, holding his hands up with a blade in each one, and I can't help but chuckle at the gleam in his eye. "You know I'm always ready to fuck around."

"Have I ever mentioned how glad I am I met you?"

He drops his hands, all humor falling from his face as he glares at me, "Don't fucking start that shit."

"What shit?"

"You know," he replies in disgust. "The end-of-days love fest. Don't do that shit."

I laugh, and I feel a little of that mania building up in my chest, so I squash it down. A shadow catches my eye, and I quickly turn, my knife raised, but then Tony grabs onto my hand as he says, "Not him."

I pull back, staring at the strange man in front of me, and then I laugh even louder when I recognize Darius. "Holy shit, man."

Dare pops up a bit, and I see he already has blood spatter all over him, and then he replies, "I could get used to it."

I shake my head, forcing myself not to continue with the inferred love fest. But I kind of want to.

It's not like I necessarily feel like this is the end, but I know the older I get, the more likely it is my luck will run out.

Dare's voice pulls me from my thoughts, and I glance at him and ask, "What?"

He looks at me thoughtfully for a moment and then says, "I can't believe you didn't tell me."

I frown. "Tell you what?"

"That you're a fucking Ferro."

I tilt my head at him, saying nothing because I know there's nothing to say. It's not like I want to be a Ferro.

After a moment, I look at Dare and reply, "Better the devil you know, right?"

He smiles, opening his mouth to reply, but Tony interjects, "Look alive, boys."

I immediately turn so my back is against the wall, Dare and Tony shifting around so we're in a more defensive position.

A wall of people inch toward us on both sides, a few more coming up over the staging, and as they press in closer, Tony says, "What do you think? Take down maybe half of them before they get us?"

I can't help but laugh, but I'm sure it comes out a bit nervous, and then Dare snorts and replies almost flippantly, "Only one way to find out."

Tony grins, and even with the new face, the mania is clear in his eyes. He faces off with the front row of men closing in on us, flipping the blades in each hand as he says calmly, "Fuck around time."

33

Preliminary Planning

Jessica

It feels like we've been waiting for days rather than hours.

Antoinette keeps fidgeting with some tracker she has since apparently having tabs on Darius is the norm.

I'm about to get my sixth or seventh espresso when a ruckus at the door draws my attention.

Lilith strides in, looking as disgruntled as ever as she says, "I found this asshole skulking around outside."

She steps to the side, revealing a disheveled and bloody Kaian, and I jump up, running toward him as I exclaim, "What the fuck, Kaian? Are you okay?"

He waves his hand dismissively as he replies, "I'm fine. It looks worse than it is."

Marieka appears at my side, concern on her face as she asks, "What happened? How did you get here?"

"Where's Matt?" I interject hurriedly.

Kaian shakes his head. "They got him and the others. Matt made me promise that I would bail when things started going to shit. I tried to talk him out of it, but he wouldn't have it. So here I am, fucking pissed."

Antoinette joins us. "Sounds like Matt. Did he say why?"

"He wanted me to be with you guys, so you'd have one more person who knew the ins and outs of the organization."

Lilith pipes up, "That makes sense. We all know quite a bit, but you can never know too much."

Camilla appears on the other side of Marieka, and she says, "How are their disguises holding up?"

Kaian looks over at her and then does a double-take, his eyes narrowing as he looks between Marieka and Camilla in horror. Then he looks back at Camilla and asks, "Why do you still look like my sister?"

Camilla laughs, and I smile. Marieka grins, eying Camilla proudly as she says, "Isn't it amazing?"

Kaian shakes his head and sighs. "The last thing I need is two of you."

Marieka punches him in the arm, narrowing her eyes. "You could only be so lucky."

We all twitter with laughter, and after a moment, Lilith interrupts, "I don't want to be the buzzkill here, but we probably should focus on what appears to be another Darius kidnapping."

Antoinette's eyes widen, and then she laughs again as she says, "You're right."

"Another?" I ask.

Antoinette turns to me and smiles as she responds, "Oh, yeah.

Darius is the king of getting kidnapped. We've had to save his ass so many times."

"You're kidding," I say in surprise.

"Totally not kidding," Carolina answers. "Actually, I think the only one who hasn't been kidnapped is Matt."

Now, Lilith laughs as she says, "There ends that streak."

Kaian's tired voice interjects, "I see they weren't fucking kidding about you people."

Antoinette gives him a suspicious look and then asks, "Did I not warn you?"

He raises his brows and nods. "You did. You sure did."

"Warn him about what?" I ask curiously.

Kaian goes to answer, but Antoinette puts her hand up and responds, "Our fondness for misplaced humor and ridiculous taglines."

I snort because I would have thought those two things would be obvious at this point.

"And big words that sometimes come off as unnecessary," Carolina adds proudly.

Then Lilith adds, "And the deep tendency to go off on tangents and completely overlook the seriousness of the situation."

Kaian and I look at each other, and he shrugs as I shake my head. Then Camilla says, "I'm going to go find my face while you guys figure it out, and I'll be right back."

She takes off in the direction of the bathrooms, and Kaian frowns after her, still shaking his head and muttering to himself.

I jab him with my elbow and say, "The bathrooms are that way if you want to get cleaned up. I don't think a few more minutes delay is going to make or break this whole mission."

He smiles gratefully and then slowly walks off in the direction Camilla just left.

The group of us return to the workstation, and Antoinette picks up her phone, glaring at the screen as she says, "Still no movement."

Lilith glances at the screen and then says, "It will take them a bit to move them anywhere. Then again, they may not need to, considering that facility is generally secure."

I frown and then ask, "What do you think they're doing to them?"

Lilith makes a dismissive motion with her hand as she says, "Probably nothing at this point. It always takes them a while to get their shit together. And most of the time, they call in someone else to do the dirty work."

"So, they don't just go right to hurting them?"

She shrugs and replies, "Well, they might smack them around a little bit, but nobody's going to do anything that would truly offend them or hurt their feelings or anything if that's what you're worried about."

"I'm not necessarily worried about their feelings so much as their physical person, but I get what you mean."

Carolina speaks up from my other side, resting her hand on my arm as she says, "Those guys are used to this shit. They can handle it."

I frown and ask, "But don't you worry about them?"

She laughs almost bitterly and then says, "Well, of course. Every fucking day."

"Then how do you stand it?"

Carolina gives me a closed-mouthed smile, but it's Antoinette who answers, "We don't have any other choice. This is the life we all signed up for."

Carolina adds, "Hence the inappropriate humor and completely ridiculous coping mechanisms."

I smile, knowing the truth behind those words.

But I didn't necessarily choose this life. I try not to think about this fact as I contemplate how I might handle the loss of the man I just got back.

"Stop that," Antoinette's voice breaks through. "Never think about how you might survive without them."

I meet her eyes briefly before returning my focus to the floor as I nod, swallowing the lump in my throat.

A door opens from across the room, and I glance over to see Kaian walking through the doorway. Camilla is a few paces behind him, and he looks over his shoulder, shaking his head and muttering something that has her grinning rather deviously.

I frown, glancing at Antoinette, whose expression mirrors mine. She looks at me, and we both raise our brows at each other and shrug.

At least that might be a story for another day.

The two of them join us at the workstation, and then Antoinette says, "There's still no movement, so I'm starting to wonder if they're just going to keep them in the facility they're at."

"It's likely they will," Lilith responds. "Any dirty work they want to do can easily be done from there. Moving them would actually cause more problems than anything else."

"They may be concerned about another breach, though," Camilla responds. "I'm sure they have no idea how we all ended up getting in there."

"Do you think they're going to question my father?" I ask.

Lilith speaks up, "Doubtful. Some of them may want to, but I don't think that's a hornet's nest they're willing to poke just yet."

"And all the boys will give them is trick answers and jokes and likely get themselves punched a few more times than necessary," Antoinette says.

I turn to Kaian and ask, "Do you think they've noticed you're gone?"

He shrugs, then replies, "Hard to say. It may take them a while to do a full headcount, given all the bullshit that's gone on recently."

"So, worst case, you might be able to sneak back in?"

He pauses, obviously contemplating my question before answering, "Probably. The difficulty will be me getting back out in order to relay any messages to you."

"What are the odds they'll be able to escape on their own?"

Kaian gives me an incredulous look, but it's Lilith who answers, "Nil. The boys are pretty wily, but the odds of them giving them even the tiniest chance to escape is none."

I sigh, worry twisting in my guts at the thought that they're locked up and being tortured. I may have been out of the life for quite a bit of time, but that doesn't mean I've forgotten how it works. I also know while my father might have done something to help me, it's highly unlikely he'll step up and help anyone else.

"So, we have to go get them then," I state. "We can't just leave them there."

"We're definitely going to have to go get them," Lilith says. "First, we need to take a moment to go over a game plan, decide if we're going to try to sneak in under the radar, incognito, or just go in as our true selves and blow shit up."

Kaian laughs and says, "Blowing shit up is probably the right thing to do."

Lilith smiles. "Abso-fucking-lutely. The key is timing all that blowing shit up to not blow ourselves up or anyone else we don't want dead."

Antoinette adds, "And not knowing exactly what we're going to run into when we get there means that timing could easily be fucked."

"So, you need to run on a timer instead of a detonator?" Kaian asks.

"Yes, timers are more foolproof in the sense that sometimes, detonators are faulty, or whoever holds the detonator ends up dead and can't push the button. A timer is a timer. You set it and eventually, it goes boom."

"So, you want to blow up the entire facility?" I ask.

Kaian and Lilith both nod emphatically. Antoinette says, "We'll try to send someone in ahead of time to give a heads up to the few people in there who we would prefer to escape."

"Are you sure that's a good idea?" Lilith asks. "Sometimes, a heads up means the wrong people live."

They all look at me, and after a moment, I ask, "What?"

Carolina answers, "You're the only one who might have someone in there to warn. So, really, it's up to you."

I frown, completely unsure of whether I give a shit if my father lives or dies.

And then I remember that if given a choice, he would most likely leave me to die.

"No warning," I reply firmly. "If we happen upon him while we're in there, he can be given a choice. Come with us, or die."

Antoinette frowns and says, "If that's what you want. But are you sure?"

I meet her gaze unflinching as I reply, "Yes. He hasn't been my family for the majority of my life. So, either he's with us, or he's against us. I expect you all to act accordingly."

She nods and turns back to the computer screen. Zooming in, she turns to Lilith and says, "You go get our supplies sorted. This place is fucking big, and it's going to take a lot to take it down. Also, reach out to Agatha and see where she and the other guys are."

Lilith says nothing. She just turns on her heel and takes off across the room.

Antoinette turns to Camilla and asks, "Do you feel like playing the decoy?"

Camilla's eyes light up, and she grins and says, "Always."

She takes a step back, running directly into Kaian, and from the coy expression on her face, it's obvious she did it on purpose. She turns back to him and rests her hand on his bicep as she says, "Oh, excuse me. I didn't see you there."

He glares down at her, and I cough back my laughter, pressing my hand against my lips to hide my smile. I glance at Antoinette to see that she's doing the same.

He doesn't say anything in response but backs away, putting some space between them, and her coy smile turns smug. She turns to Antoinette and asks, "Who do I get to be this time?"

Antoinette's smile broadens, and her eyes light up as she says, "Me."

34

Trapped

Matt

WELL, THAT FUCKING SUCKED.

Obviously, we were well aware that we were significantly outnumbered. And while we certainly held our own for longer than we figured we would, getting taken down and chained up is always a downer.

And they weren't even nice enough to put us all in the same cage, which is complete bullshit.

On the other side of that, though, they put us in cages next to each other, so I'm curious about the logic behind that move.

I'm sure it's just so each of us can witness the other one being beaten and tortured, but by now, they should be aware that we kind of think that's funny sometimes.

For example, Tony's response the first time one of these fuckers punched me in the face was some variation of, "Hit him again."

Not that I blame him. Tony has always been a rather straightforward guy, so the idea that he likely blames me for our current situation is not lost on me.

And then there's his first response to someone hitting him in the face, which is basically just a challenge to do it again because he doesn't have a fuck to give.

I never said any of us were smart.

I'm relatively certain Kaian managed to escape, which means he'll have reported back the current situation.

And since Darius still has his watch, it seems safe to assume that they're at least going to have eyes on us and most likely be storming the place at any moment.

There's also the slight chance that the ladies will leave us in here just a little while longer, thinking we might learn a lesson.

We will not.

Having gotten the first interrogation over with, we're now all lying around on the cold concrete floor, patting ourselves on the back for intentionally misleading those fuckers.

Because if nothing else, all of our lies will match.

All you have to do is play it up, delay, and then be a little morose, and they'll believe fucking anything.

"How long have we been here?" Tony asks.

"Oh, I don't know," Darius replies blandly. "Maybe a day, definitely not two."

I shrug, saying flippantly, "A day, two days, three. It all blends together."

"How many times have we done this now?" Tony says tiredly.

Now, Darius sighs and then mutters, "Like a billion."

I laugh, somewhat maniacally, and then respond, "Maybe a slight exaggeration. I would say more like a million."

Darius laughs and then adds, "How pissed do you think Antoinette is right now?"

"She's probably not even that pissed, mostly just laughing at you getting kidnapped again," I answer lightly.

"This isn't a kidnapping."

"She isn't going to fucking care. You were there, and then you vanished. Close enough."

He snorts, obviously offended, and Tony laughs and says, "Can't say I blame her. You do hold the world record of kidnappings."

"Yeah," Dare retorts. "I'm sure all the ladies are pretty annoyed that they're going to have to come rescue us menfolk again."

"Again?" I interject. "No one has ever had to save me from being kidnapped."

Tony scoffs, "And how did we even get here, then?"

"Hey," I reply. "I was never kidnapped. I came here intentionally, of my own free will."

"Well, maybe if you'd shared with the class, we wouldn't be here," Darius replies, slightly bitterly.

"Maybe, maybe not," I answer. "But regardless, here we are."

"What do you think they're going to do next?"

Dare says, "It's hard to say, really."

"What would you do?" I ask.

Darius is quiet for a moment, and then, after a few beats, he says, "I would definitely sell us off as a trifecta. They're going to go crazy."

"You think so? I would think that selling us off to the same person would be more of a liability," Tony replies.

"Yeah," Darius says. "And I suppose they might get more money doing it separately, but the same buyer could certainly buy all three. Right?"

Tony snorts now and says, "Could you imagine anyone wanting all three of us?"

"Hell, no," Darius says. "And if I was in charge of the whole situation, I would pay for us and then put a bullet in us one by one before even opening the cage."

Tony chuckles. "Well, good fucking thing you're not in charge, then. I'm happy that we're still surrounded by a bunch of dumb fucks."

The door creaks open, and we all crane our heads around to see who's coming.

Then I roll my eyes as I see Seamus walking into the room. He stops in front of the cage, puts his hands in his pockets and shakes his head as he says, "Was this really your plan, Matt?"

I give him a bland look and reply, "Well, not exactly, but sometimes, we gotta roll with the punches."

He looks down at me thoughtfully, and then he frowns and asks, "Were you serious about all this Ferro bullshit?"

I nod but say nothing, and after a moment, he continues, "Everyone was of the mind that Lilith was the only one left, and as fucking crazy as she is, no one ever wanted to get involved. But now here you are, a serious threat to everyone."

"I keep hearing that I'm a threat, which makes me even more confused on why they haven't just fucking killed me."

"Because there are still some rather big influences who give a shit about what happens to you. It has to go through the right chain, or it could backfire and blow up in their face."

I yawn and then say, "Well, isn't that all good and well."

"I don't think you're taking this seriously," Seamus replies sternly. "The likelihood you're going to live through this is nil."

I level him with a serious look and ask, "Did Jessica make it out?"

He nods. "Yes, your friends came and got her out."

"Then I don't fucking care."

"Then you're a stupid fucker. So basically, you piss off into the wind, worry her enough to come after you, so she ends up engaged to the enemy. Then you eliminate the enemy, marry her and go through all sorts of public displays, stand up on a stage, and make this big, dramatic statement only to then leave her as a widow?"

Darius and Tony both chuckle, and I glare up at him as I reply, "Well, when you put it like that."

He shakes his head, and then Darius interrupts, "Are you here for a reason, Seamus, or just to rub his nose in it?"

"I'm just here to see if he has another plan. Because so far, each plan he has had has just led to more fuckery."

"I don't see what the fuck you care, considering you're not going to do anything to help. You've made that clear."

"I was very clear in the first place that there was nothing I could do. I have too many fucking people depending on me to throw it all away on your dumbshit ass."

"Then get the fuck out of here."

He continues to stand over me, glaring intently, but then he sighs, his hands coming out of his pockets to rub over his face briskly before he says tiredly, "I have some correspondence going with the outside, so if I hear anything in particular, I'll try to sneak back over and give you a heads up. But there's not much else I can do."

I just roll my eyes, and then Darius says, "Well, we appreciate that. And don't let Matt fool you. No one understands your position more than he does."

I glare at him and show him my middle finger, and he blows me a kiss.

Seamus glances at Darius, then Tony, and back at me, and shakes his head as he says, "Fucking boys."

Without any further comment, Seamus turns and walks back out of the room, shutting the door behind him.

We sit there in silence for a while, all of us caught up in our own thoughts. The silence drags on, so finally, I ask, "What are you guys thinking about?"

Tony immediately answers, "I'm kinda fucking hungry."

Then Dare adds, "Sparkling water would be refreshing right now."

I bite back my own laughter and then say, "We really can't take anything seriously, can we?"

They both answer at once, "Nope."

I laugh again, and then Tony adds, "I figure if it does turn out that I end up dead, I'd like it to be a surprise and not something I figured would happen."

"Yeah," Dare says. "I want my last thought to be some variation of 'well, fuck'."

"I think no matter which way we cut it, that's pretty likely."

Tony says lightly, "But we had fun, didn't we?"

I smile. "We sure did."

35

A Criminal Strategy

Jessica

MATT IS GOING TO be pissed when he realizes I came back.

They all tried to dissuade me; for a moment, they even tried to forbid it, but when I used the argument that I have just as much right to be here as they do, they were kind of left without anything left to say.

It's slightly confusing to have most people looking like someone else, but then to have a new person looking like Antoinette is a mind-fuck. It is amazingly creepy how similar she managed to make herself. And then how easily she's picked up her mannerisms and speech pattern is just outright insane.

I also kind of want her to do me next, but that's a whole different story.

It's surprisingly easy to gain access to the facility. Given what's happened the last few days, I would think they would've doubled up on security. Since there's a small chance this oversight was intentional and we're walking into a trap, we have Camilla go in first, using Antoinette's face as a decoy to draw attention from our actual mission.

Kaian had returned to the facility the day before, and we managed to locate him per the instructions he had left with us.

This time, Antoinette, Carolina, and Lilith have all been given new faces. We decided to have me remain as myself since I can be a distraction if somebody comes upon us before we want them to.

Camilla goes in under the guise of Antoinette sheerly for the purpose of potentially fucking with people, which she truly enjoys.

And again, Matt is going to be pissed.

Lilith recruited Agatha, Anton, and their crew of miscreants to handle the explosives with strict instructions to eliminate anyone and everyone they come across in the process.

We have somewhat of a wide window between our entry into the building and when it's going to go up, but we know we have no time to waste.

Kaian leads us through the maze of hallways until we're standing outside a large door. He points at it with his thumb and says, "This is where they're being held. They're each being kept separately in a locked metal cage. One of the assholes in there will have the key on him, but I'm not sure who."

Antoinette presses her ear against the door, then turns back to Kaian and says, "It sounds like there's a lot of people in there?"

"Yes," he replies. "I had no way to figure out the exact timing, and our timing right now is not good."

A loud curse sounds through the door, and Antoinette frowns. Her hand comes out, and she rests her palm against it as she says, "That sounds like Tony."

"They're probably playing with them," Lilith replies blandly.

Kaian nods and says, "Yeah, I think Matt's next."

Carolina huffs, "I am not at all used to this fly-ing-by-the-seat-of-our-pants shit. Zero out of ten. Do not recommend."

Lilith shrugs and replies, "By the time you reach my age, you realize that you spend half your time making plans that are not going to work out and then the other half of the time figuring out how you're going to make flying by the seat of your pants work for you."

Antoinette smiles as she replies, "That's why we brought all these guns."

Footsteps sound on both ends of the hallway, and we freeze. A group of men comes around the corner, and Kaian steps into me, wrapping a hand around my throat and pushing me up against the wall, saying, "Where the fuck have you been?"

My first instinct is to attempt to knee him in the balls, but I do my best to control myself, knowing this was part of the plan if we were caught. A blond man who was leading the other group of men takes another step forward as he says, "That Killeen's daughter?"

Kaian turns his eyes to him and nods. "Sure the fuck is. Can't imagine what she thinks she's doing."

I show him my teeth, going up on my toes as he squeezes a little harder, and I snarl, "You can go fuck yourself."

There's a moment of silence, and then the group of men starts to laugh. The corners of Kaian's mouth turn up, so I shove my knee toward his balls. He easily deflects my attack with his leg as he says, "Watch yourself. Wouldn't want to accidentally kill you too soon."

My eyes widen, and I snap my mouth shut. I see Lilith out of the corner of my eye, reaching her hand into her jacket, and I shake my head, hoping to get her attention. Her hand relaxes back to her side, and I say, "Well, if you're gonna do it, get on with it. Wouldn't want you to bore me to fucking death."

The blond man steps forward, stopping a few inches from me as he leans in and says, "The fuckin' Irish got a mouth on her."

One of the men behind him retorts, "Well, that explains why Mathias would go rogue to get her."

The blond man points behind Kaian and asks, "Who are the bitches?"

The three ladies visibly bristle, but Kaian says, "They're with me. My father sent them over. I'm supposed to give them some education and then send them back unharmed."

The man eyes them suspiciously and then looks back at Kaian and shrugs as he asks, "What the fuck should we do with her?"

I know what's coming but knowing what's coming doesn't make me feel any less trepidation.

Kaian looks over at him and asks, "You want her?"

The man's eyes widen comically, and the group of men standing on the other side fidget nervously, and he laughs a little hollowly and replies, "Tempting. But one way or another, I don't see that ending well for me."

Kaian snorts and makes a face as he says, "What could possibly happen? Her husband's in a fucking cage. He ain't gettin' out of there."

"Maybe not," the man replies. "But we know he's not the only one that will be a problem."

Kaian scoffs, "You worried about her old man?"

The man nods. "Yes. Be a bloody fucking fool not to be worried about Seamus." I frown, wishing I felt as certain that the old man would defend me as this man is. And then the man adds, "And I don't care if Mathias is in a cage or not. It's safest to consider that guy a problem until you witness him dead and buried."

The guy who spoke previously speaks up again, "And both his buddies are in there. It's like a bad fucking omen."

"Is that why you're not in there watching the show?" Kaian asks.

They all nod and say, "I'm on enough hit lists without being added to theirs. And frankly, I get tired of beating up restrained people. It's fucking stupid."

Kaian nods, his grip on my throat easing so I'm no longer standing on my toes, and I relax a bit. After a moment, he releases me, and my hands come up, rubbing at my throat briefly as I scowl at him. I'm definitely going to kick him in the balls later.

Kaian turns back to the group of men and says, "Well, I guess I'll tend to this one, then. You guys can go about your bus—"

An angry voice shouts through from the other side of the hallway, and suddenly, I find myself bodily pushed back against the wall, vicious fingers pushing into my throat.

My hands come up, grabbing at the hand and clawing, but the grip doesn't ease, and then a face leans in so close that it's blurry, snarling into my ear, "You're fucking dead, you little bitch."

My eyes widen as my feet come up off the floor. I kick them out, connecting with nothing. Then, Kaian is there, his hands gripping the wrist connected to the hand around my throat. I attempt to pull my head away, but the back of my skull connects with the wall, so I turn my head away.

The girls are tense, obviously ready to make a move, and I open my eyes wide, shaking my head, knowing it's too soon.

Kaian shouts, but I can't make out his words through the ringing in my ears, and the edges of my vision start to dull. Just as suddenly as it appeared, the hand is gone from my throat, and I crumple to the ground, gasping for breath, coughing and choking.

A set of feet move toward me and then stops. When I glance up, Lilith has her hand on Antoinette's arm, keeping her back. Their typical poker faces are a mix of rage and worry.

They all quickly school their features, easing back slightly so as not to draw attention to themselves, and then Kaian is there. He kneels down, his hands on my upper arms, helping me to my feet. He then leans in and whispers, "Matteo's brother, Enzo.

I stand with Kaian's assistance, and after a moment, he releases me, and I lean heavily against the wall. Matteo's brother steps toward me and I do my best not to flinch back visibly, though internally, I want to wretch.

He leans in close to me and says, "When my brother was so ruthlessly murdered, you should have been mine."

I do recoil now, showing my teeth as I snarl, "Over my dead fucking body."

Kaian freezes. I see him roll his eyes a bit, but I know it's too late to play nice.

The man glares at me and replies, "You couldn't be so lucky. And once we make you a widow, you can just get married again."

Now I roll my eyes, the maniacal laughter building up inside of me as I say, "What the fuck is with you douchebags wanting to get in line for Mathias' sloppy seconds?"

Antoinette chokes, and Kaian groans loudly. Enzo snarls but says nothing, reaching out and grabbing me by the arm, his fingers digging in painfully. A bunch of other men rushes into the hallway from the same direction he came in, and he looks at the one in the lead and says, "Secure all these fucking assholes. I'm going to take care of her."

Kaian opens his mouth to protest, but Lilith reaches into her jacket again, and he immediately turns back to her, putting his arms out and forcing the three women backward as he says, "I got these ones under control. I'll get them secured and then report back to see what else needs to be done."

Enzo gives him a suspicious look, but then nods before turning his attention back to me. He leans his face close to mine, rubbing his nose on my cheek, and I shudder in disgust, turning my head so quickly that he doesn't have time to step back before I gnash at his nose with my teeth.

He jerks back cursing, and I laugh. "Don't fucking touch me."

And there's the maniacal laughter again.

I don't bother pushing it down this time. I let it erupt, spewing all over them until they're all standing there staring at me like the fucking lunatic I am.

Kaian doesn't wait. He uses the distraction to shoo the other women back down the hallway, and I continue my maniacal antics until they're out of sight, and then I stop.

I stop abruptly, standing at my full height, sticking my chin out obstinately as I say, "Are you just going to fucking stand there all day, or are you going to do something?"

Enzo raises his brows at me, but this time, his step toward me is a little hesitant and not nearly as aggressive. He grabs onto my arm and yanks me over, pulling me toward the door he pushes open roughly as he says, "Just for that, you get to watch."

I struggle, attempting to pull myself from his grip, but it's no use. So, I ask, "Watch what?"

He pauses halfway in the doorway, looking back at me as he replies, "You get to watch your husband die."

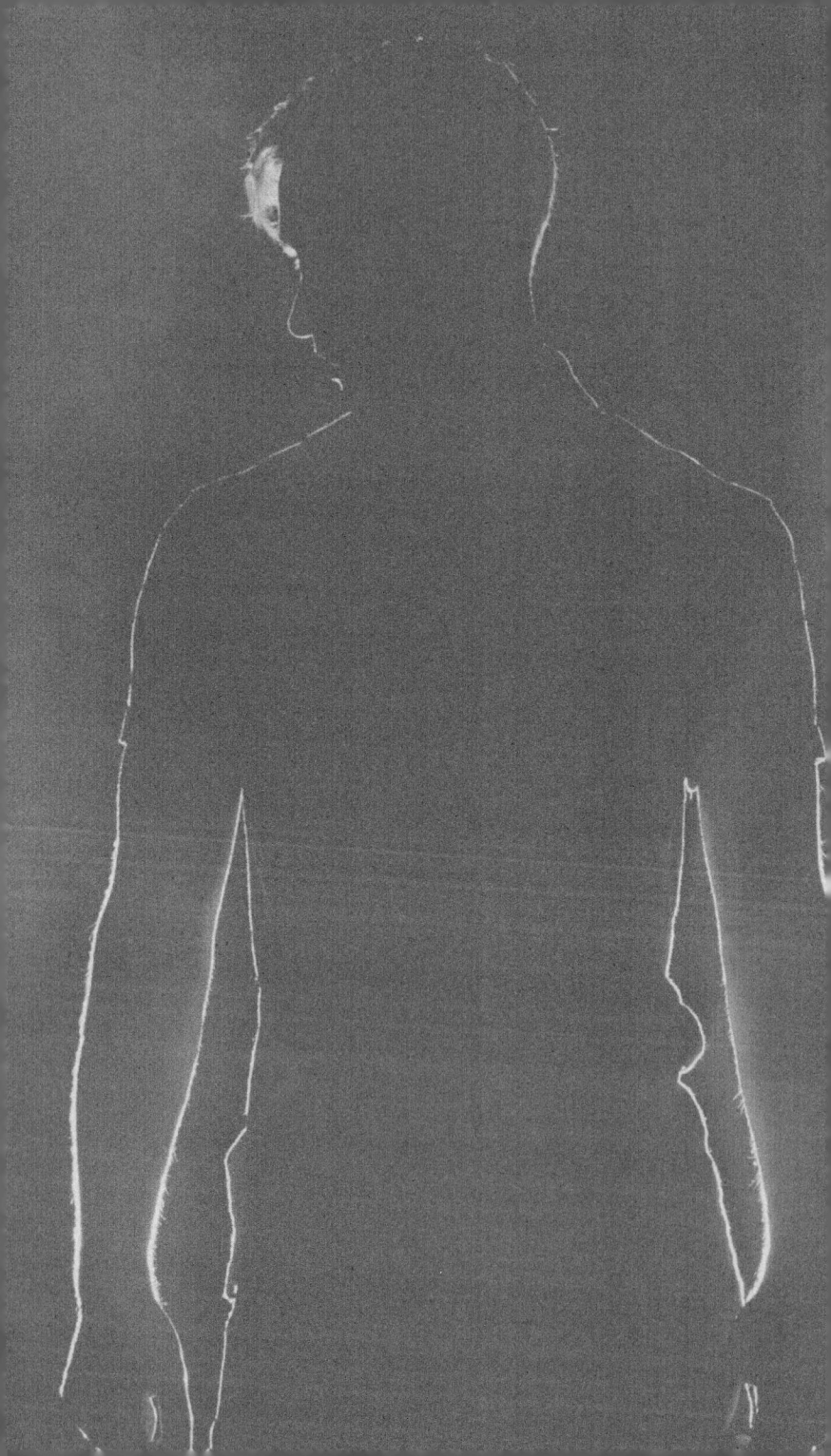

36

Fuck Around Time

Matt

THEY'D JUST DROPPED TONY on his ass on the floor and were in the process of opening my cage when the door bursts open.

No one pays it much mind, including myself, as they half-drag-half-carry me out into the open. Tony, long rid of his disguise, lies in a heap, and they kick him to the side so they can use the same hook to hang me up by my bound hands.

I'm too busy feigning being injured to bother looking up, but it's Darius' voice behind me that draws my attention.

I turn my head just enough so I can get a peek, and my blood runs cold to see Jessica standing there, being manhandled by none other than Matteo's brother, Enzo.

I twitch, fully intent on going berserk, when something cool touches my bare foot, and I glance down to see Tony with one eye open, giving me a hard stare.

I immediately go back to my former exhausted position, doing my best to keep the tremor of rage out of my limbs.

I can't even imagine why Jessica would enter this building after what she'd already been through, but I have a feeling I already know the reason.

Mainly me.

I take a few subtle calming breaths, Tony's hand on my foot, one of his fingers tap, tap, tapping rhythmically.

If Jessica is here, that means the others can't be too far behind, and most likely the reason that she's made it into this room without them is because the circumstances didn't allow for anything else.

I know this isn't my first rodeo, but it is definitely my first rodeo where someone I'm intimately connected to is at risk, and I totally understand Darius and Tony's previous inclinations towards chaos and psychotic behavior. Suddenly, my typical high functionality is moot, and I want to go berserker mode.

I chance another glance and see her staring at me intently. As soon as my eye meets hers, she shakes her head minutely.

I hang more heavily on the chain, intent on at least pretending well that I'm not operating on all cylinders.

Of course, Enzo's appearance doesn't mean anything good for me.

Last I heard, he was living his life perfectly fine outside of the spotlight, and with the demise of his brother, this means his life of leisure will have changed significantly.

So, I can imagine he's rather bitter and would like nothing more than to string me up by my toes and beat me to death.

Footsteps come closer, and two shiny shoes appear in my line of sight.

I pretend I don't see anything and continue to play possum, but then Enzo's voice is right in my ear as he says, "Playing dead won't work with me, you piece of shit."

I ignore him, mostly because I know it will annoy him even more, and then he adds, "I suggest you perk up, or else we'll be swapping places around here."

Nicolai, one of the men who's been in here with us for the duration and typically takes us in and out of our cages, speaks up, "What are you doing here, Enzo?"

Enzo steps back from me and replies, "It's none of your fucking business."

Nicolai snorts and responds, "It actually is my fucking business. So, watch your fucking mouth."

My heart rate picks up at the idea that they may fight amongst themselves, but that hope is quickly extinguished when Ivan interrupts, "Come now, Nicolai. We all knew he'd show up eventually. Just let him have his fun, and he'll go about his business."

There's a long moment of silence, and then Nicolai says, "You better watch yourself. If any of them turn up dead too soon, there will be hell to pay."

I'm not sure how I feel about this "too soon" bit, however I'll take that over should have been dead already.

Darius is muttering from his cage, but I can't make out anything he's saying, and then Nicolai goes over and yells, "Would you shut the fuck up?"

"Sure," Darius replies tersely. "Why don't you open this fucking cage and make me?"

Nicolai must have taken a step toward the cage because Ivan rushes over and says, "Now, don't you be listening to that guy."

"Why the fuck not?" Nicolai huffs.

"Because it's a fucking trap, that's why," Ivan replies firmly. "Just as soon as you nonchalantly open that cage, thinking you're going to make some fucking statement, the Beast is going to rip your throat out."

"Jesus fucking Christ, would you stop with that name," Darius replies bitterly.

I hear a muffled laugh at my feet, and I know Tony is once again gloating about the nickname he gave Darius many years ago. Nicolai mutters from behind me, and then his voice gets louder as he moves closer. He stops beside me and says to Enzo, "Just do what you're going to do and get the fuck out. We got business here."

"Make this motherfucker look at me," Enzo commands.

He steps back, and at the same time, a hand grabs me by the hair and yanks my head back violently. I open my eyes almost lazily, trying to keep my expression as bored as possible as I spit some blood on the floor. "What the fuck do you want?"

Enzo frowns at me, and Jessica's eyes narrow a bit. I'm hoping she'll remember all of our earlier conversations about me having to do and say bad shit in order to protect her. The last thing I want these guys to know right now is how much she means to me because that just gives them more leverage than they already have with me here, hanging by my wrists, not even wearing fucking shoes.

I glance around and see there are still a few people in the room, but not nearly as many as there were when Tony was getting his ass handed to him.

I know if we're going to attempt to make an escape, the timing has to be exact. The room can't be too full of people, but there also needs to be enough people to make it confusing for the enemy.

Given I'm working mostly on assumptions as to how much backup I have in the building, it could go to shit pretty easily.

"Since I finally have your attention," Enzo retorts as he walks over to Jessica and yanks her closer to him, pressing his body against hers. It's everything I can do to keep my expression neutral and my body relaxed as he adds, "I already explained the future to Jessica here."

I raise a brow at him as I ask, "And what might that be?"

"So glad you asked," he says with a smile. "About our impending nuptials once she becomes a widow."

He moves his hand from her upper arm to the back of her neck, and her expression becomes pained as he squeezes hard. He uses his free hand to stroke up her stomach, between her breasts, and then, with his hand pressed against the front of her throat, he leans in close, rubbing his nose on her cheek, following the same path with his tongue.

She grimaces and snaps her head forward, smashing her forehead against his nose, and he shrieks as his blood gushes. He jumps back, pushing her away as his hands come to his face, and he curses. She takes a step away, pulling a tissue or a handkerchief from her pocket and wiping the blood off her skin gingerly as she says, "Didn't anyone ever teach you the order of operations?"

I frown, and Tony's hand on my foot draws my attention down, and I see him frowning, as well. I look back up just as Enzo steps toward her and asks, "What the fuck are you talking about?"

She gives him an obstinate look and snarls, "The order of operations, you dimwit. If you're going to get lewd with a lady who obviously doesn't want your advances, you'd best properly restrain her first, or else you're going to get fucking hurt."

He lunges for her, and she only has a chance to take maybe half a step back before he has both hands wrapped around her neck, squeezing as he says, "Is this fucking hard enough for you?"

I can see she's still fighting him, and once again, I have to fight my urge to attempt to break free.

After a moment, she goes a bit lax in his grip, and I'm uncertain if it's intentional or it's because he's cutting off her airway. Regardless, I'm relieved some of the fight has gone out of her, so I might be able to draw his attention back to me.

"You might want to let her go," I reply blandly. "If you accidentally kill Seamus' daughter, there will be fucking hell to pay."

His grip eases on her slightly, and I see her take in a ragged breath as Enzo turns his attention back to me and says, "What the fuck do you know about it?"

I snort as I reply, "How the hell do you figure I ended up marrying the bitch?"

"Because you wanted to."

I laugh bitterly, and Jessica's look turns petulant, so I say hurriedly, "Your idiot fucking brother was going to pass her through his friends and then kill her, so your whole family should be thanking me for putting a stop to that."

"I don't fucking believe you."

"Believe whatever the fuck you want, but you should know by now that I'm not in the habit of exacting unsolicited bloodbaths without good fucking reason."

"I don't really fucking care what your reasons were at this point. I was living my life just fine, and then you went and fucked it all up."

"Wah, wah, wah," I reply flippantly. "If you're going to fucking do something, do it already. So far, you're just boring me to tears."

"Me, too," Darius pipes up from behind me. "I thought I was going to get my turn soon, and so far, this is taking way too fucking long."

"You shut your fucking mouth over there," Nicolai sputters.

But Ivan laughs and says, "Oh, leave him alone."

"Thank you, Ivan," Darius replies cordially. "I really appreciate that."

I glance over and see Ivan grinning at Darius like a goddamn fool, and I shake my head as I mutter, "Good fucking lord."

Pain blooms in my jaw, and my head jars around as a fist connects with my face. I slowly turn my head back around, spitting more blood on the ground as I say, "Do you feel better now?"

Enzo doesn't say anything. He just pulls his fist back and hits me again, and since I see where this is going, I close my eyes, go limp, and let him go to town.

I must say, I never did enjoy getting hit in the solar plexus, and this isn't any more enjoyable than I remember.

About the second time I lose my breath, I cough and sputter, taking my weight up onto my hands and bringing my legs up where I kick out with both feet and hit him square in the chest. He goes flying backward, and Jessica shrieks as she jumps out of the way. I place my feet back on the ground and use the few moments of reprieve I have to try to catch my breath.

It takes Enzo a minute to rise from where he was sprawled on the floor, and then he stands there, hunched over as he says, "Stupid fucker."

I feel one of my eyes swelling, and my lip stings where it's split open, but I say anyway, "I don't know what you hoped to gain from all this, but it seems kind of pointless. Why don't you just tell me what the fuck you want."

"I want your wife to watch me beat you to death."

"I don't see the point in that because she doesn't care."

Enzo laughs as he says, "I don't give a fuck if she cares. It makes me feel better."

"You didn't even like your fucking brother," Darius says calmly. "You should actually be happy that fucker's dead."

"No one fucking asked you, Darius," Enzo snarls. "Still a fucking know-it-all after all these years."

I raise a brow, craning my head around, trying to get a look at Darius as I ask, "You two fucking know each other?"

"Yeah, we go way back," Darius explains. "He's still salty over the last time I kicked his ass. Hindsight tells me I should have just fucking killed him."

I do another glance around and see that there are more people in the room now, which is less than ideal. I just wish Enzo would get on with it so that I could end up toppled on the ground next to Tony, and someone would open Darius' cage. But the likelihood that they'll leave us two out while letting him out is pretty slim. Occasionally, we have had a situation where some dumbshit didn't know any better. Which means Ivan needs to get the fuck out.

"If you're that bent out of shape, Enzo, maybe you should let Dare out of his cage, and the two of you can duke it out like men."

Enzo laughs and then says, "You really think I'm that stupid?"

"You seem kind of dumb to me," Jessica mutters.

Enzo turns his focus back to her and glares at her as he says, "You better shut your fucking mouth, or I'll shut it for you."

She curls her lip at him but says nothing further, and at this point, I kind of want to kick her ass myself.

I glance back at Enzo and do a double take as I see a subtle shadow behind him. I squint, attempting to focus on something along the wall in the darkness.

I clear my throat, covering it up with a cough as I almost smile.

The door opens, and Kaian appears, taking a step into the room and leaving the door ajar.

He looks around the room, finally focusing on me as he says, "Well, you look like shit."

I snort. "Well, fuck you very much."

Enzo turns to Kaian and asks, "What the fuck do you want?"

Kaian takes another step closer and shrugs as he says, "I just came to see if it was time yet or not?"

Enzo frowns, confusion on his features as he says, "Time for what?"

Kaian smiles and shrugs as he says, "Time to fuck around."

I laugh, and then Darius laughs, and then, like clockwork, Tony laughs at my feet. Enzo turns back to me with a concerned, puzzled look on his face as he says, "What the fuck is going on?"

The shadow behind him draws my attention again as it moves, and out of it conjures a woman, an unhinged look on her face, and I see that it's Antoinette, but at the same time, it's not Antoinette.

I frown, but I don't have time for much else, and the next thing we know, she's right behind Enzo, startling him as she says, "Time's up."

There's no hesitation on her part. She raises a hand, slicing through his throat in one smooth motion. He gurgles, his hands coming up as his blood gushes everywhere, and within seconds, he's crumpled to the ground, gasping like a dead fish out of water.

Ivan and Nicolai stand there shocked, and I sigh as Jessica says, "Cami, don't you think you could have been a tad more subtle?"

She grins, her resemblance to Antoinette uncanny, and once again, I shake my head at the thought of there being two of them.

Jessica rushes over at the same time Tony rises to his feet, and the two of them work to get me down from where I'm still hanging from the hook.

Nicolai yells, managing to put up quite a fuss before Tony makes it to him, drawing the attention of others in the room, who come running. Tony makes quick work of Nicolai, snapping his neck before the man even realizes what's happening, then manages to slash and dash the three men who attempted to intervene.

Ivan, on the other hand, stands there with his hands in his pockets, smiling, and it's Darius who says, "Well, Ivan. It looks like you're enjoying the show."

Ivan nods and says, "Oh, yeah. I've heard stories about this shit."

Tony frowns at him, then looks at me, and I shrug, so Tony turns back to Ivan and says, "Well, in that case, I won't kill you."

Ivan goes to speak but instead is met with Tony's fist directly in his face, and he drops to the ground, out-cold.

The door bursts open, and a bunch of women rush in. I figure it's safe to assume that they're with us, but the next thing I know, they're rushing toward us. One of them yells, "They're coming."

And then all hell breaks loose.

37

A Promise

Carolina

I ADMIT, BEING BACK in this type of shitty facility has been a shock to my system.

But having my appearance changed to look like a stranger has been helpful. It's almost as if Carolina isn't here, and it's just some new person looking in with a new perspective and new memories.

I had one instance where the flight option was coursing through my veins when all those men were looking at us and then that douchebag, Enzo, was telling them to secure us. It's the first time in a long time that it occurred to me that maybe I should turn on my heel and flee.

But then I remembered who I was with and who I am now, and I had to repress my urge to find my gun and shoot every fucking one of them.

Because I know what would happen if they attempted to secure us.

Luckily, Kaian was able to diffuse the situation and back us out of there so we could regroup. That left Jessica in a precarious situation, but she knew when she insisted she come along that would likely happen.

Kaian leads us to a small room that appears to be made for security. He flips some switches, and screens turn on, then he clicks through like he's flipping through channels until he reaches the one he wants.

I lean in closely and see Matt hanging from the ceiling, and upon closer look, I notice Tony sprawled at his feet.

I press my lips together and shake my head. Antoinette looks as well, and turns to me and says, "Do you think he's actually hurt?"

I shrug, my hand coming up and wiggling from side to side as I say, "Fifty-fifty."

Lilith comes up between us, shoving us away. She leans super close to the screen, pulls back, and says, "He's fine."

I reach out and give her a little shove, and then I turn to Kaian and ask, "Where's Darius?"

He points to the top of the screen, indicating further back in the room, and says, "There are some cages back there, so I assume he's in one of them."

"There's no way they're going to let the Beast out of the cage with the other two free," Lilith murmurs.

Kaian nods. "Yeah, usually they like to beat the crap out of the first two and incapacitate them a bit. But if they're smart, they'll put them back in the cage before taking Darius out."

Lilith smiles as she responds, "And we're always counting on them not being smart."

Kaian motions back to the screen and says, "There's Jessica."

Even knowing full well from half a lifetime of experience, I'm still shocked when Enzo puts his hands on her.

I flinch slightly, and then Lilith and Antoinette's crows of laughter draw my attention back to the screen. I see Enzo bent over with his hands covering his face, and Antoinette says, "That's right. Fucking give it to him."

I sigh and say, "Fighting back seems a little premature."

Lilith smiles at me, her hand going to my arm as she replies, "Sometimes we get in whatever shot we can. Oftentimes, it bites us in the ass, but it still feels good in the moment."

I roll my eyes a bit and then nod in agreement. The few times I managed to get a shot in in my younger years, it was usually worth the punishment.

And by the time I got out, I'd become so numb to the entire thing, it didn't fucking matter.

We stand there watching the screen, the people we care about appearing like actors in a movie.

Kaian says, "Did you see that?"

"See what?" Lilith asks.

He leans into the screen, pointing off into the back as he says, "There was a shadow."

Lilith leans in closely, scanning the screen, and then she says, "Yes. I see it."

They look at each other, their eyes alight, and finally, I ask, "What is it?"

Lilith turns to me and smiles. "Camilla. Right on time."

Kaian stares at the screen for a few more moments, a smile on his face, and then he turns to us and says, "It's time. Let's fucking go."

We head out the way we came in, rushing down the hallway, ignoring anyone we come across as if we're on official business, and for the most part, no one pays us any mind.

We get to the door and Kaian stops us as he says, "You know the drill, ladies?"

Lilith gives him a look and smirks as she says, "Yeah, I think we do, baby bear."

He scowls at her, and I attempt to hide my laughter behind my hand and fail miserably, and he turns his glare to me.

He turns back to Lilith and says, "Don't you fucking start."

She smiles and says nothing else, so he turns and opens the door, walking a few feet into the room, leaving the door ajar.

We hover around the doorway, staying out of sight, and I peek in, making out Jessica and Enzo with their backs to the door. Matt is strung up with Tony at his feet.

Kaian walks a few feet into the room, stopping beside Enzo as he says, "Well, you look like shit."

Matt snorts and replies, "Well, fuck you very much."

Enzo turns to Kaian and asks, "What the fuck do you want?"

"I just came to see if it was time yet or not?"

"Time for what?" Enzo frowns, confusion clear on his features.

Kaian smiles and shrugs as he says, "Time to fuck around."

Matt laughs, and then Darius laughs, and soon, Tony laughs as well. Enzo turns back to Matt with a concerned, puzzled look on his face as he asks, "What the fuck is going on?"

Matt frowns, and then a shadow passes in front of the door, and a body appears right behind Enzo, startling him. Then she says, "Time's up."

She doesn't hesitate. Her hand comes up in front of him and then jerks to the side. He gurgles, his hands coming up as his blood sprays, and within seconds, he's crumpled to the ground, gasping like a dead fish out of water.

Jessica asks nonchalantly, "Cami, don't you think you could have been a tad more subtle?"

I can't see her face, but she says nothing in response, and then Jessica rushes over as Tony rises to his feet.

The commotion behind me takes my attention away from what's going on in the room, and I turn to find Lilith stabbing someone in the throat. Antoinette rushes the next man to come around the corner, managing to take him out quickly, and then she leans her back against the wall, peeking around the corner down the hallway.

She immediately turns back, pushing off the wall and running back to where Lilith and I are still standing, and I ask, "What is it?"

"Lots of fucking men," she sputters. "A whole horde of fucking bad guys."

She wastes no more time explaining, shoving between us and pushing the door open forcefully. She runs through it, and we follow right on her heels as she yells, "They're coming."

We run directly toward where the boys are grouped, stopping in the middle of them and turning back toward the door.

The flood of men rushes in behind us and spread throughout the room. Lilith's shout draws my attention, and she points to the other side of the room, where another doorway shows more people running in.

Tony immediately starts in that direction, but then he turns and looks at me. I pull his gun from my jacket pocket and hand it to him and then two more rounds of ammo. He smiles at me, leaning in and giving me a quick kiss before rushing off.

Matt helps Jessica for a moment and then comes back to me, grabbing a gun and a knife that someone dropped as he says, "Get Darius."

I nod, immediately turning and rushing to where he's still caged further back in the room. He looks rather bored, and I can't help but laugh as I kneel, yanking on the lock.

"One of these fucking yahoos has the key," he replies calmly.

I pull out my gun, pointing it at the lock as I say, "Turn away."

He does as I ask, and I shoot the lock once, twice, three times, but it doesn't give.

Darius laughs as he says, "This newfangled shit is tough."

A bitter laugh falls from my lips as I glare at him and reply, "It might not be a good time for jokes, Dare."

"Always a good time for jokes." He shrugs.

I laugh hollowly this time, yanking on the lock, looking around for something I can smash it with while also knowing that it will be no use. I stop what I'm doing, my hands gripping the bar as I lean in and say, "This place is wired. The whole fucking place is going to go up."

He blinks at me for a moment and then laughs, and a small shriek of frustration comes out of me. He sighs and then asks, "How much time we got?"

I shake my head, my hands gripping the bars tightly. I attempt to shake it, but it doesn't even rattle. "I have no fucking idea. But I always assume we're on borrowed time."

"That's an accurate assumption."

He's silent for a moment and looks around, and then he asks, "I assume that Antoinette isn't actually Antoinette?"

I nod, glancing over at Camilla and then further over where I see the real Antoinette, happy in her murderous glory. I turn back to Dare and say, "Yeah, she's over to the right. She's really enjoying being a blonde."

He smiles fondly, and his complete lack of concern infuriates me.

I glance back over at Antoinette, hoping I can get her attention, but she's too caught up in her mission. I turn back to Dare, immediately startled to find that he's right there at the bars in front of me.

His hands cover mine where they grip the bars of the metal cage, squeezing tightly as he leans forward, forcing me to meet his eyes as he says, "You're gonna have to leave me here."

I blink at him in horror, shaking my head with such vigor I feel my brain rattle in my skull. "No. I can't. I won't."

The smile he gives me is calm, his eyes reassuring as he presses his face into the bars and whispers, "Yes, you can. And you will."

"No. No. I can't do it."

He laughs humorlessly, inclining his head as he says, "You will. You have no choice."

I glance back at Antoinette and shout, "Antoinette. I need you."

My shouts fall on deaf ears. She's too focused, and the room is too loud. I glance around for help elsewhere, just to find everyone focused on the people in front of them and the people coming up behind them.

I turn back to Darius, who's staring at me quietly. A sob catches in my throat, and then I whisper, "No. Please."

His hands tighten on mine again, and the smile he gives me is genuine. There's not even a glimmer of sadness as he says, "Promise me."

I grimace, my voice shaky as I say, "Promise you what?"

"Promise me you won't let her come back. You won't let any of them come back."

I know who he's referring to. I look over at Antoinette one more time to see she's moved even further away, everyone methodically moving closer to the exit plan, and I shake my head as I whisper, "I promise."

I look down at the ground, and one of his hands moves through the bars. He touches my chin, lifting his gaze to mine as he says, "And make sure you name that baby after me."

I laugh tearfully, shaking my head as I say, "Fuck you."

He chuckles almost wryly, but then his other hand moves away from mine, and he says good-naturedly, "Let's not forget, Car. I have a perfect track record of getting myself out of dumb situations."

I look at the steel lock on the steel cage and look back at him, shaking my head. "She's never going to forgive me."

"She will," he replies. "If anyone understands having to make difficult decisions in high-stress situations, it's Antoinette. Mostly, she's just going to be mad at me."

I hear shouting across the room, and I look up to see everyone in position. I turn back to Dare and ask, "Are you sure?"

He nods, moving back across the cage where he sits against the bars, his feet coming out in front of him and crossing at the ankle, looking relaxed as can be. "Tell her if she ever tries to fuck another man, I will haunt her."

I say nothing further and look up at him again, and he just nods and says, "Go."

I nod, incapable of words, as emotion overwhelms me. I shake it off, centering myself on the greater mission, knowing I have no other choice but to do as he asks.

I push away from the cage, rising and racing around the way I came, both guns at the ready to ensure I have a clear path. I push my despair aside, reaching deep for the rage, disgust, and tenacity that was forged over time. I push toward the exit, grateful that Kaian and Camilla are there and not Antoinette, Tony, or Matt.

We rush out the doorway down the hallway, Kaian leading our way through the labyrinth towards the exit.

I'm sure it's only minutes, but it feels like hours until we're finally bursting out into the darkness, cool air hitting me in the face.

We're running. I see Lilith on the far side yelling, and I run toward her, knowing that she's the only voice of reason to hear what I have to say.

I stop in front of her, and she grips my biceps, leaning in as she asks, "What is it?"

I shake my head, completely incapable of words, and after a moment, she frowns, glancing around.

She meets my eyes again as she whispers, "Dare?"

Once again, I shake my head, words stuck in the sob I'm holding deep in my chest.

She looks back at the building and then at Antoinette, who just now starts to look around. "Fuck."

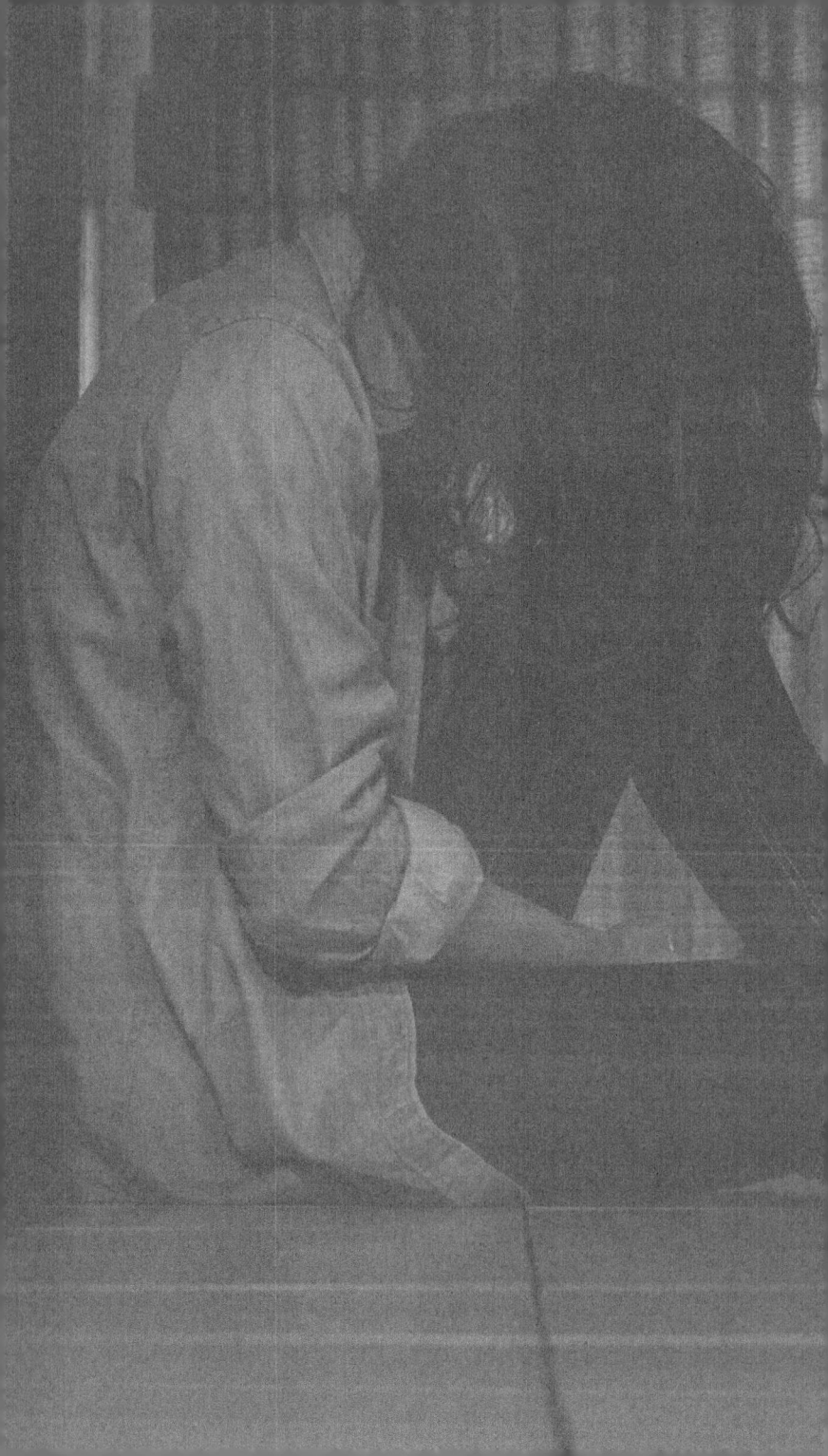

38

A Crack in the Armor

Antoinette

Where the fuck is he?

It would be just like that fucker to try to make a big exit when he finally gets out of the goddamn building.

I glance around again, taking count of all the familiar faces, even the ones that are made up not to be familiar.

I see Lilith and Carolina off to the side, and I do a double-take at the look on Lilith's face as she glances at me.

My heart sinks, and I turn my focus to Carolina, who looks grief-stricken as she stares at the ground. Pain jackknifes through me.

I'm already shaking my head as Lilith starts walking toward me, so by the time she gets to me, I'm muttering, "No. No, no, no."

She reaches for me, and I slip her hold, taking off back toward the building, but then Carolina, who had been still standing off to the side, is in front of me, blocking my way.

She grabs onto me, and I attempt to shake her off, but she tightens her grip and gets right in my face and says, "You can't."

"Get out of my fucking way," I seethe, once again attempting to shake her off, but her fingers dig into me painfully. She leans in closer, her nose touching mine as she whisper-shouts, "He made me promise."

"I don't fucking care about your promises," I shout.

I shove my knee into her leg, pushing her away violently, finally shaking her off and sprinting toward the building, only to have Lilith yanking on me from behind. Tony and Matt are suddenly standing in my way now, too.

Lilith releases me, and I fall into Tony and Matt, and it's not lost on me how I've come full circle once again.

Carolina speaks from behind me, even as I fight for them to release me, "The cage wouldn't budge. I tried to get someone's attention, but you guys couldn't hear me; then he made me promise to leave him and not to allow you guys to go back."

"Who's you guys?" Tony replies quietly, fighting to keep me in his hold as I still attempt to break free.

"Antoinette specifically," she replies. "But all of you."

A sob breaks free from my throat as I say, "Please. Please."

I pause my efforts to get through them, and they tighten their holds on me, pushing me backward as Matt asks, "How much time do we have, Lils?"

"There's no way to know," Lilith replies sadly. "So, you always assume your time is up."

"That's exactly what I said," Carolina replies. I stop fighting, allowing them to move me back a few more feet, and I focus on regulating my breathing and after a moment, they both ease their grip on me.

Matt takes a step back, and just as soon as Tony does the same, I turn around, kicking him forcefully in the gut and then turning back in the other direction, elbowing Matt in the face. He falls back, and then I'm running, sprinting so fast all I hear is the whistle of the wind in my ears, the sound of my pounding heart as I run to save him.

Thundering footsteps track me, quickly gaining on me, and then I run faster, the doorway getting larger and larger as I aim for it. I reach my hands out, ready to shove it open, and just as soon as my fingertips touch it, two sets of hands grab hold of me, and I'm yanked bodily right off my feet.

I'm airborne momentarily, and falling backward onto my back, hitting the ground so hard the wind is knocked out of me.

I immediately roll onto my front, coughing and choking for air, while at the same time, I attempt to gain my feet, turning back toward the door, but hands are on me, pulling and yanking, and I scream, "Let me go. Let me go."

My voice is broken, gasping, almost drowned out by the shouting of people who know that, if nothing else, they have to save me from myself.

I make one last ditch effort to move through the door, then I'm being dragged away, my hands outstretched as I scream, "Darius."

And then time stops momentarily. As if all movement and sound are being sucked into an abyss, and then a split second later, it releases, and that door I was reaching for bursts open one second before the boom hits.

My scream is yanked from within me and shoved outward. We're all airborne, landing in a heap and rolling briefly before coming to a stop in the dirt.

And I stop fighting.

I lie there, face-down, feeling the scrape of the rocks against my cheek, grateful for the numbness that washes over me.

After a moment, hands are gripping me again, lifting me into the air, and I'm weightless.

My ears ring, and I hear murmuring in the periphery of my psyche. And then there's coolness beneath me, the smell of rubber, and the slamming of doors.

Warmth presses against my back, and fingers slide along my cheek, and then arms wrap around me. Lilith's voice is in my ear whispering incoherently.

Warmth settles in front of me, and I'm cocooned, and then there are more fingers stroking my cheek and moving down my shoulder and arms, and I hear Carolina in front of me, "Antoinette."

I squeeze my eyes shut, shaking my head slightly, but then she pleads, "Please look at me."

I frown, not wanting to, but the pain in her voice cues me. I open my eyes, meeting her soft brown ones full of sadness and pain as she whispers, "Can you ever forgive me?"

I laugh bitterly, a choked sob escaping, and I manage to swallow down the mania and the misplaced anger. I nod and whisper, "Already forgiven."

She stares at me through watery eyes, my own watering in response, and then I shake my head, not ready to give in to anguish.

I clear my throat, searching for some kind of misplaced humor to bridge the gap, and so I ask, "Did he say anything?"

She clears her throat and says, "Other than all the reasons why I had to leave him?"

I nod, "Yes, other than that."

"He said he loved you."

Now, I frown and snort. "Try again. There's no fucking way he said that."

She giggles and then replies, "You're right. He never fucking said that."

I laugh again, grateful for the reprieve. "Go ahead. Tell me what he said."

She pauses for a moment, rolling her eyes a little, and then she whispers, "He said if you ever fuck another man, he'll haunt you."

I laugh, and Lilith laughs behind me, her arms tightening on me, and then Carolina laughs as well, and I hear Tony and Matt and their low chuckles on the other side of the van. We all laugh for one single moment in time.

And then we stop.

I'm enveloped by the echoing silence, the subtle ringing in my ears, and the crack of my heart in my chest.

I take a shuddering breath in, releasing it as I mutter, "Fuck."

And then I let it all go.

And I cry.

39

A Jagged Landscape

Matt

By the time we make it back to the city, Antoinette's sobs have quieted to whimpers, the equivalent of a wounded animal.

Jessica crawled into my lap, curling into me like a child, and I did my best to console her while also keeping my own emotions in line.

But all it took was a glance from Tony for me to recognize the futility of it all.

On the other side of that, I keep reminding myself of our old motto about no one being dead until you yourself have removed their head and set their body on fire.

Of course, in this situation, I hate to give myself any hope at all.

Upon arrival at the warehouse, we stagger from the van, slowly making our way inside.

We're all slow to enter, none of us wanting to leave Antoinette behind, and all of us completely unsure what to do.

It isn't until we're in our main communication room that she finally stops, turns to us, and says, "You all should get some rest. We'll make some plans first thing in the morning."

Tony and I look at each other and then back at Antoinette, and then Tony shakes his head, stepping forward as he says, "We're not going to leave you."

She laughs bitterly and raises her brows at him as she replies, "And staying with me is going to accomplish what?"

Tony shrugs, his eyes moving to mine as he motions to her, obviously looking for my assistance. So, I step forward, resting my hand on her arm as I say, "The same thing we've always done for each other, just be there."

Her features soften, and she smiles slightly, and then steps in closer to me, motioning for Tony to come near. Then she leans in, her eyes moving from mine to Tony's and back again as she says, "The best thing you can do right now is to take care of your wives." She pauses, taking in a shaky breath and turning to Tony, adding, "Especially you. It's not her fault. We know Darius, and he never would have allowed her to risk her own life to save him. If he had thought there'd be even a tiny chance she would have succeeded, he would be standing here with us. She needs to hear that."

Tony nods, and she turns to me. I nod in acknowledgement, and then we both step back and move to walk away. Then, I turn back and ask, "What are you going to do?"

She looks across the room where Lilith is speaking with Agatha, and then she turns back to me. Her smile is a little brighter as she says, "I'm going to find him."

I frown, and Tony stops, a matching frown on his face as he asks,

"What are you talking about?"

She looks over at him and then shrugs as she replies, "You of all people aren't allowed to lecture me on reality—not yet."

He looks at me and shrugs, too, so I sigh. "Reality's got fuck all on us. Come get us if you need us."

Antoinette takes off toward her mother and her sister, and Tony and I head off in the direction of our private rooms. Tony speaks softly to Carolina, who shakes her head in response, but he ignores whatever she's saying, stooping down and hefting her over his shoulder and taking off through the doorway, the slap of her palms on his back reverberating through the room.

I stop beside Jessica and ask, "Are you going to come willingly?"

She glances back at the other woman, then turns to me and says, "Yes. The last thing they need is to feel like they're babysitting me."

I take her hand, leading her out of the room and down the hallway through the maze of corridors until we reach the door to my room. I turn to her with a sheepish look as I say, "Obviously, the last time I was here, I was not expecting to bring company back with me."

She frowns and then asks, "Are you saying it's likely a pigsty?"

I laugh and shake my head. "No, they would have made sure it was cleaned regularly on the off-chance I was going to be back without notice."

She raises her brows at me questioningly. "Then why the explanation?"

"Tony likes to leave me gag gifts. I'm preemptively assuming he has done so liberally while I've been gone."

She giggles, looking intently over my shoulder as I turn and open the door. I flip the light on, bracing myself for some crazy scene, and then laugh as I enter the room.

Jessica enters right on my heels and then laughs as she sees the gift that Tony left for me on the bed—an intricate and life-sized blow-up doll.

She walks toward it, leaning over the bed and squinting as she says, "This thing must have cost a fortune."

I sigh heavily, closing the door and leaning against it as I reply, "Tony would spare no expense."

We both laugh, and the short reprieve makes me feel a tiny bit lighter.

I motion to the doorway on the other side of the room and say, "There's a bathroom over there if you want to freshen up a bit. I'll take care of our friend here in the meantime."

Still laughing, she walks in the direction I indicated, glancing over her shoulder as she jokes, "Do I dare leave you two alone?"

I laugh again, shaking my head as she disappears. The smile drops from my face, and I frown down at the lifelike doll in front of me. Sighing, I heft it over my shoulder, turning and walking to the doors across from the bathroom. I swing one open, careful to make sure the other remains shut, as I lean in and toss the doll on the pile of other objects that Tony has been leaving me over the years.

"What else is in there?" Jessica's voice behind me startles me.

I whirl around, shutting the door and leaning back against it as I say, "Nothing."

She squints at me with a knowing expression as she says, "Liar, liar."

I laugh nervously, shaking my head as I step into her, my hands going to her wrists when she attempts to go around me. I pull her in close, wrapping my arms around her, pinning her arms to her sides, and pressing my face into her neck. "Plenty of time for all that nonsense later."

She pulls back just enough to look me in the face as she says, "You mean plenty of time for you to get rid of the evidence."

I walk her backward until the backs of her legs hit the bed. She topples over, and I follow her, my body pinning her to the mattress. "Would I do that?"

She nods enthusiastically and says, "You absolutely would."

I raise my hand as I reply, "Scout's honor."

She giggles and then sputters, "As if you were actually a fucking boy scout."

I laugh and shake my head, but I say nothing as I allow myself to sink into her while focusing on not crushing her.

We fall silent, and her hands are on my back, rubbing soothingly. Then her face is in my neck, her breath warm against my ear as she says, "I'm sorry."

Pain jackknifes through me, and I clear my throat as I whisper, "Let's not talk about that."

She wraps her arms around me more tightly but says nothing. She just nods, her only response an incoherent cooing.

I sigh deeply, willing the agony in my chest to ease, and then she's pushing against my chest. I sit back and ask, "What is it?"

She slaps at me until I move back more, and she sits up, pushing me backward so I'm standing, and she says, "You're disgusting."

I look down at myself, frowning at the fact I didn't immediately head for the showers. I look down at her and frown again, shaking my head as I reach for her, yanking her to her feet.

I attempt to lead the way toward the bathroom, but she steps in front of me, grabbing my hand in hers and leading the way.

She stops abruptly in the middle of the room, and I practically run into the back of her, barely managing to stop up short. She whirls on me, her hands making quick work of my shirt, and soon, it's lying on the floor in a heap. She kneels, and I'm looking at the top of her head as I ask, "What are you doing, sugar?"

"Taking care of you."

I smile, the agony in my chest mixing with sheer emotion. I attempt to speak but choke instead. I clear my throat, looking up at the ceiling, praying she'll see what I'm working so hard to deny.

I'm still not wearing shoes, so I easily step out of my pants and underwear, and then she's pushing me toward the shower, which somehow is already running.

She pushes me under the spray and then turns, quickly removing her own clothes and leaving them piled on top of mine before turning and entering the shower, closing the door behind her.

I'm still standing there, frozen and numb. She says nothing. She just moves in close to me, the press of the front of her body against mine urging me to step backward until the hot water runs down my back and then along the back of my head.

I continue to stand there, willing my arms and legs to move but deeply paralyzed, every ounce of my energy being expended into pushing down that fierce agony still boiling inside me.

Jessica remains quiet, but her hands are firm as she meticulously cleans me up, first washing my hair and rinsing it clean. She then grabs the washcloth, soaping it up and scrubbing every inch of my body until finally, she's satisfied.

She cleans herself much faster, and before I know it, she's wringing the washcloth out and hanging it on the rack. She turns back to me, pulling me into her, one of her arms going around my back and the other hand along the back of my neck. She hugs me to her, urging me to hold on.

A guttural sob falls from my lips, my arms come up and around her of their own volition, and she whispers to me soothingly.

And I stop fighting.

I let that wall inside me crumble, unleashing decades' worth of pain in one fell swoop.

And Jessica, she stands there and holds me up.

40

Brotherly Sentiment

Declan

Antoinette: We need you

Declan: What?

Antoinette: It's Dare.

Declan: What happened?

Antoinette: Nothing good.

Tony: Not a drill, man.

Declan: How bad?

Antoinette: BAD.

Declan: Is he alive?

Antoinette: Yes?

Tony: Maybe.

Declan: Well, that was clear.

Tony: Just get here, you fucking asshole.

Declan: Already on my way.

"Has that chat changed at all since the last time you looked at it?"

I turn my gaze to Issa, smiling slightly as I shake my head. "I keep thinking if I stare at it long enough that maybe he'll pop up."

Her smile is tinged with sadness as she nods and replies, "Given the circumstances, the likelihood of that happening is beyond nil."

"Obviously, this was fueled by wishful thinking and incredible delusion."

She sighs, leaning in close to me and resting her head against my arm. "Wishful thinking and incredible delusion are two things I can get behind."

I lean close to her, placing a kiss on the top of her head as I once again turn back to the phone and stare at it.

After a few minutes of silence, I ask, "I would know, right?"

Issa straightens in her chair, giving me a speculative look. "You'd know what?"

"If he was really gone."

She raises her brows at me, her lips pursing briefly, and then she says, "Well, you're not twins, right?"

I frown at her and sputter, "Do I look old enough to be Darius' twin?"

She smirks at me and then shrugs. My frown turns into a glare. "Take it back." She laughs and shakes her head, and after another glare, her lips twitch, a sparkle in her eye making me narrow my eyes even more. "I see what you're doing here." Her look turns innocent, increasing my suspicions, and when she says nothing, I add, "Trying to distract me with misplaced humor."

She smiles rather smugly. "Is it working?"

I sigh deeply, giving her a disapproving look. "Maybe."

She smiles and pets me on the arm. "Obviously, I can't predict the future, but you know that I'm a cup-half-full kind of girl."

"So, you're saying you think he's fine?"

She raises her brows at me and then laughs a bit hollowly. "I'm not sure I'd go that far, but you know I'll believe that until proven otherwise."

"I'm inclined to feel the same way." I nod.

"How's Antoinette holding up?"

"As only Antoinette could," I reply. "She isn't really the glass-half-full kind of girl, but she's definitely the not-going-to-believe-anything-until-she-sees-concrete-evidence kind of girl."

My phone pings as a new message comes through the group chat.

Antoinette: Dec, what's your ETA?

Declan: Should be in the building within a couple of hours.

Antoinette: Okay, we'll be ready.

Declan: Just out of curiosity, what are the odds for him?

Antoinette: 80/20 against

Tony: 20/80 for

Matt: 50/50

Carolina: I don't dare speculate.

Declan: Well, that was clear.

Antoinette: Yeah, just get here.

I send a token thumbs up and close out of my app.

I know asking was probably stupid, but for some reason, getting three completely different answers makes me feel better.

We manage to make it to the warehouse in just over an hour, which is exceedingly good, given the time it takes to taxi an aircraft and maneuver through traffic.

It's the wee hours of the morning, but everyone is congregated in the communication room, our version of the family room.

I walk directly to Antoinette, pulling her into my arms and hugging her. I open my mouth to speak, but she interrupts, "I swear to fucking

Christ, Declan, if you try to give me condolences, I will kick you in the balls."

I flinch and then laugh. "I was just going to ask who we get to kill first."

She relaxes in my embrace, patting me on the back awkwardly in her prisoner-hug position. I step back, my hands squeezing her biceps. She gives me a small, grateful smile, tension around her eyes and in the set of her jaw evident. "We've got a list going."

I step back with a nod, then walk over to greet Matt and Tony, taking a mental headcount of everyone in the room.

I look around for Issa and find her standing with Jessica and two women I don't recognize. One of the women hands something to Issa, and I take a closer look, noting a handgun. I walk over to them, stopping beside Issa as I say, "Come on now, dollface. Put that down."

She glances at me with her eyebrows raised. "Excuse me?"

I wince, immediately realizing my error, but then I say, "That's not a toy."

Her eyes narrow further. I wince again, and Jessica laughs. "By all means, Dec, keep going."

I grit my teeth, searching for words that won't escalate the situation. I glance at Jessica and then back at Issa, who's staring at me, and when I remain silent, she smirks knowingly. "Was there anything else?"

I bite the inside of my cheek and shake my head, realizing there's nothing else I really can say so I turn back to Antoinette, who's smiling at me teasingly. I glare at her. "Don't fucking start with me."

"What could I possibly say?"

"I just don't like seeing her with weapons," I reply grumpily. "It just doesn't fit for her."

"I get it," she replies. "She hasn't had to be part of this world, and I totally understand you wanting to keep her away from it."

"I tried to get her to stay home, but she wasn't having it."

"I don't blame her. She knows if you're coming over here to fuck around, anything could happen."

I laugh and nod. "And that's exactly what she said."

Antoinette levels me with a serious look as she says, "You do realize if she decides to come with us, there's nothing you can do, right?"

I bristle, frowning as I sputter, "Don't remind me."

"I'm not saying she'll want to," she replies with a laugh. "Just making sure you know what'll happen if you try to interfere."

I look back at Issa, who's now holding a bigger gun and talking animatedly to Jessica, and I sigh. Antoinette rests her hand on my arm, drawing my focus back to her, and she says, "We won't let anything happen to her."

"If only it was that simple."

She snorts. "Ain't that the fucking truth."

"Any buzz on the streets?" I ask hopefully.

She shakes her head and says, "No one's saying anything at this point. We don't want to divulge any possibilities, so we're waiting for chatter to come up on its own."

"And nothing on his watch?"

"No," she answers. "But Matt and Tony said they took his watch, so that being out of commission doesn't actually confirm anything."

I glance around the room again, settling on Carolina, who's sitting on a chair in the corner, looking morose. "What's up with her?"

Antoinette looks over at her, her lips pressing together, and then she turns to me and responds, "She blames herself."

"For Darius?" I frown.

Antoinette nods. "Yes, she was trying to get him out, and he made her leave. Made her promise she wouldn't let anyone come back."

I grimace, glancing back at Carolina briefly before turning to Antoinette and saying, "Well, it's not her fault. Lord knows when Darius makes up his mind, there'd be no changing it."

"That's for fucking sure."

"Should I go talk to her?"

"Yes," Antoinette replies firmly. "Some reassurance would probably be good."

I walk across the room, stopping in front of Carolina, who's still sitting in the chair. She stares off blankly, apparently not even noticing I'm there. I reach out with my foot and tap her on the ankle until she starts, her gaze flying to mine. "What's up?"

Her eyes immediately water, becoming glassy but not overflowing. I immediately kneel in front of her, saying soothingly, "None of that, now."

A short hiccupping sob escapes, along with a tear that she wipes away hurriedly. "It's my fault."

I shake my head. "No. It's no one's fault, but it's certainly not yours."

She shakes her head slowly as she whispers, "I shouldn't have left him."

I laugh bitterly and raise my brows. "We all know you didn't have a choice in that."

"Of course I did. I should have just told him to fuck off and got him out."

Her hands clutch together in her lap, and I rest one of my hands on top of both of hers as I say patiently, "You know it's not that simple."

"No. I should have stayed the course. I should have done my job."

Now, I glare at her, my hands moving to her upper arms. I yank her to her feet as I rise, then I lean down so I'm right in her face as I hiss, "You know for a fact that wouldn't have done you any good."

She shakes her head some more, and I give her a tiny shake and then add, "If Darius thought for one second you could have gotten him out, he would have helped you try. The fact that he gave up and made you leave and promise to keep everyone out means in his eyes, he was doomed."

She meets my eyes head-on, searching intently, and then she deflates a bit as she says, "But maybe he's alive?"

It's hard to tell if it's actually a statement or a question, but still, I pull her into a hug. "Maybe."

Her arms come up around me, and she clutches me briefly before pulling back and giving me a watery smile. She clears her throat and then says, "I never thought a maybe would make me feel better, but here we are."

I grin at her, tilting my head in agreement. "We're going to find out one way or another. And until then, let's not speculate too much on the end."

She nods and then pats me on the chest as she says quietly, "Thank you."

I frown down at her and ask, "Thanks for what?"

"Giving me a little shake. You always know how to bring me back down to reality."

"One of the many services I offer."

I turn back and look across the room, noting more people have arrived, and then I look back at Carolina. "Are you ready for it?"

A sudden coldness goes over her features, and my eyes widen at the glint in her eye. She steps back from me and it's like she's grown a foot taller as she lifts her chin and replies, "I'm ready."

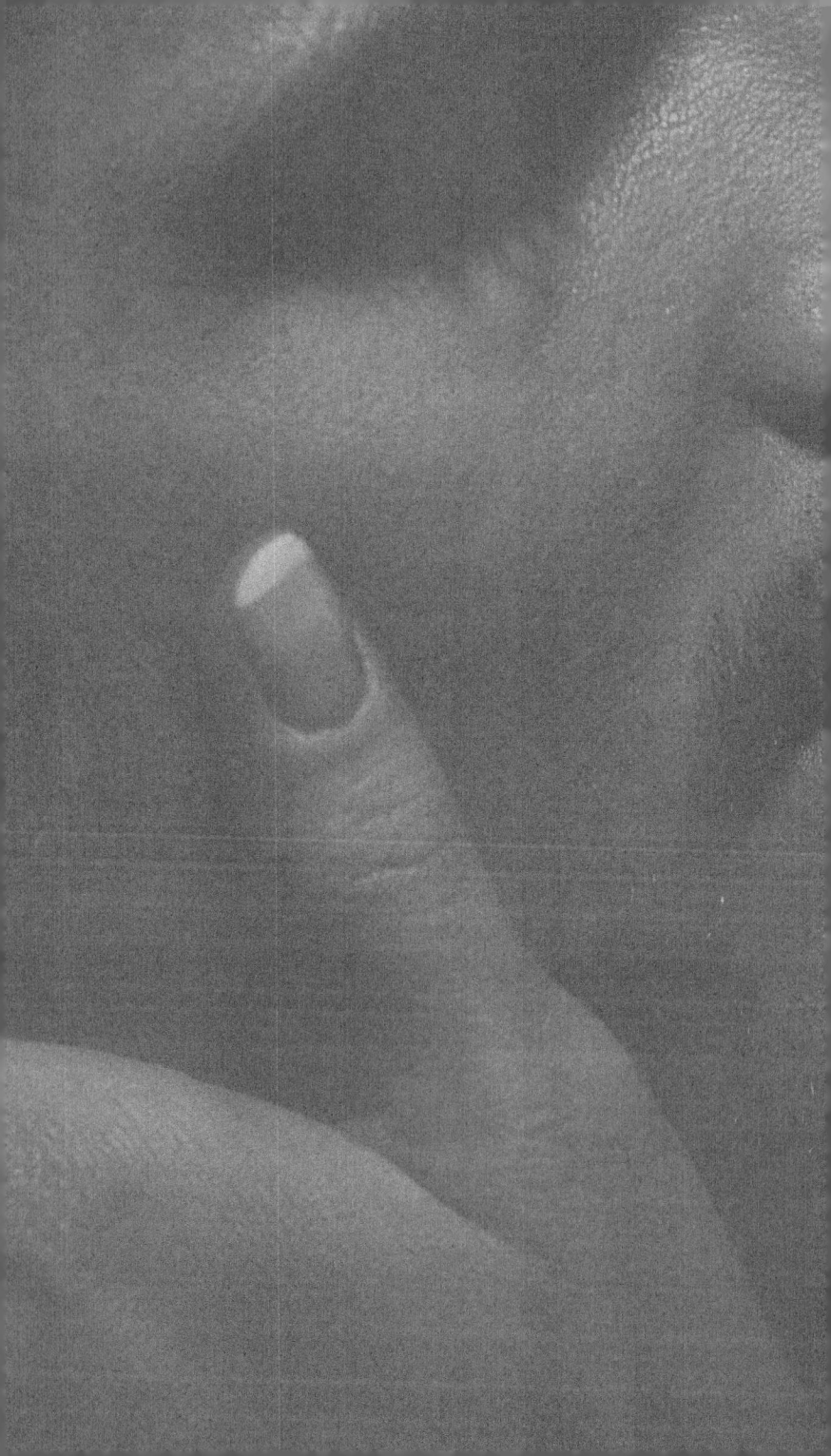

41

A Devil's Distraction

Matt

I COME AWAKE IN stages.

The pre-dawn light casts an eerie glow through the room, my name a familiar hushed whisper cutting through the silence.

I glance toward the sound, fully expecting Darius to be standing there, telling me to get my lazy fucking ass moving, only to be met by the sharp sting of nothing.

I inhale sharply through my nose, once again looking up at the ceiling as I shove the pain aside, burying it beneath false hope and wishful thinking.

I roll to my right, directly into a warm body.

She's here.

I reach out for her, forcing my arm beneath her, the other reaching around and gripping the back of her thigh, pulling her over on top of me.

At first, she's dead weight, but within moments, she comes awake, the tension in her body almost thwarting my mission to move her.

"Matt," she mutters sleepily. "What are you doing?"

I ignore her question, instead continuing to manhandle her until she's lying on top of me, exactly where I want her.

I wrap my arms tightly around her back, one hand pressing against the back of her head as I lift my face into her neck and breathe her in.

Peace.

She mutters to herself but doesn't attempt to break free, so I relax my hold, reveling in her comforting weight on top of me.

I press my hips up, rubbing my dick between her legs, earning a soft moan from her. She presses her hands into the mattress on either side of my head, some of her weight shifting back as she looks down at me with a knowing smile on her face.

"Touch my neck," I whisper, feeling desperate to be lost in her.

She shakes her head, replying quietly, "Not this time," then laughs as I glare up at her.

"Why not?"

She shrugs, sitting up fully and then turning and falling back on the mattress where she was before.

I sit up, leaning toward her, as I ask, "What are you doing?"

"Waiting for you."

I frown again, confused about what's going on. "Waiting for what?"

"For you to take what you need."

Anxiety bubbles up in my chest, and words immediately stick in my throat. She reaches up and grips the edge of her sleep dress, wiggling and yanking it up over her head, and then tosses it on the floor.

She turns toward me slightly, getting her elbow up underneath her so she's resting her head on her hand, and then she says, "Do it."

I swallow the lump in my throat, pushing down the anxiety that I can't even explain. She waits a long minute and then another, staring me down. When I still don't move, she says, "I'm serious, Matt. It's okay. Just take what you need."

Trust shines in her eyes, the relaxed position of her nude body proving she means what she's saying.

Yet still, anxiety jackknifes through me, releasing with a guttural growl as I search her gaze for any type of hesitancy. Finding none, I slide closer to her. "Fuck it."

The smile on her lips is challenging, self-satisfied, so I reach out, grabbing her by the hair at the back of her head, yanking her head back sharply.

She gasps but also laughs breathlessly. "That's right. Fucking take it."

"Oh, I'll fucking take. I'm gonna take until you beg me for more."

She opens her mouth to speak, but I cut her off by pressing my lips against hers, shoving my tongue inside, and basically mauling her.

She squeaks, so I attempt to pull back, but her hands move to the back of my head. She pulls me closer, opening her mouth wider, her tongue seeking mine.

I moan into her mouth, suddenly frantic to be closer, to be inside her.

I pull away, moving into the middle of the bed, grasping her by her legs and yanking her down. Crawling up the bed, I straddle her head, then lean forward, bracing my weight on one hand. I slide the other between her thighs, spreading her legs for me.

She gasps beneath me, her breath warm on my inner thigh as she turns her head and licks me. Taking more of my weight on my hand, I lean closer, licking a path down her stomach, up over her pubic bone.

I latch onto her clit without preamble. Her breath catches, and then she moans, her hips pressing up as I eat her. My lips and tongue are firm against her flesh, my teeth nipping as I shake my head, sucking her clit into my mouth.

I move my free hand between us, grabbing my dick and holding it for her. "Suck me, sugar."

Her tongue is hot and wet on my throbbing flesh, and I groan loudly. "Don't play with me. Put it in your mouth. I want to fuck that throat."

Enveloped in the wet heat of her mouth, I moan, reveling in the feel of her tongue stroking, her lips a tight band, sliding down me.

I latch back onto her, easing down onto my forearm so I can loop my arm around, sliding a finger inside her. She moans around me, and I press in deeper, sliding in and out of her mouth in time with my finger in her cunt.

I slide out of her mouth, immediately shoving back in, the sudden tension in her body making me immediately pull back, still worried I might hurt her.

Cool air hits my dick, and then her hands are circling the back of my thighs as she gasps, "Don't stop. Fucking use me, you asshole. All of me. Take what you need."

With my mouth still pressed between her legs, I shake my head, but then she closes her legs around me, her thighs pressing against the sides of my head as she bucks her hips up and says loudly, "Don't be a fucking pussy."

Startled by her words, I freeze, but then, after a moment, I attempt to twist my head out of her grip as she laughs. "If I wanted to fuck a pussy, I'd go find me a woman. Is that what you want?"

I frown at her question, my head locked between her legs, her hands pressing against the back of my thighs. She lifts her head, her hot breath and wet tongue on my balls, and then she licks the underside of my dick. "Or would you rather I find another man—"

I cut off her words by lying flat against her body, pressing my full weight into her as my hands yank her thighs apart. Then I'm off the bed, one hand gripping her hair, yanking her across the mattress until she's sprawled with her head off the edge.

I grab her face, squeezing her cheeks with my index finger and thumb, and she pants, excitement in her eyes and vibrating through her entire body as I lean in close. "The first thing you're going to do is shut your fucking mouth."

She laughs again, and I shake my head, once again turning my body so I'm facing her feet. Then I place my dick at her lips and say, "Open up."

She glares at me, her words rather garbled as she says, "But you told me to shut my fucking mouth."

I growl, gripping her head more firmly in my hands, tilting her head down, and forcing her mouth open. She makes an exclamation of pleasured surprise, and I shake my head as I force her mouth open, shoving my cock inside. "Don't fucking bite me."

She smiles around my dick, and I shake my head. "You fucking like that? You like choking on my cock, sugar?"

She bobs her head slightly as she nods, and I slide my dick in deeper until the very end of me is pressing against the back of her throat.

I slide in and out slowly, constantly pushing right to the back of her throat. I scan down her body, taking great pleasure in seeing her lying there, her knees bent and her feet flat on the bed.

Leaning forward, I brace myself on the mattress with one hand, slapping at her legs with the other. "Spread your fucking legs. Let me see my pussy."

She hesitates for a moment, so I slap her thigh again and then again until her legs fall open. I hunch over so my face is directly in front of her cunt, running my nose along the outside until she's squirming.

I thrust deep into her mouth, a thrill going up in my spine at the sound of her choking. I lick her clit, moving my hand down so I can push two fingers inside her pussy.

She moans around my cock, the vibration coming up her throat and straight into my balls. I lick her faster, my fingers spearing her in time with my fluttering tongue and thrusting cock.

I pull my hips back, allowing her to draw in a ragged breath before shoving deep again, sucking on her clit, shoving my fingers deep, and pulsing rhythmically.

Now, she sobs, her feet flat on the mattress, and she presses her hips up, pushing her cunt against my face as she moans her pleasure.

I pull back slightly, breathing heavily as I gasp out, "That's right, sugar. You fucking come for me. You fucking come for me while I fuck your throat."

I ease off her, allowing her air for a few beats before I dive back in, sucking on her clit, using my tongue and lips as I finger fuck her.

I drive my cock into her mouth, this time shallower, wanting her to focus on her own pleasure.

And then she comes. Her pussy tightens around my fingers, her inside walls quivering, pulsing. I push my cock into her throat, blocking her air as she shrieks and sobs.

I wait until she starts to quiet, then I pull out, allowing her to drag in a ragged breath as I focus on fucking her with my fingers, my mouth working feverishly on her clit.

She comes again, cursing and shrieking, and a zap of pure ecstasy runs up my spine as I push her and push her and push her over the edge.

I don't stop until she's lying there limply, one of her hands slapping at my leg tiredly.

I step away, wiping the proof of her release off of my chin with my fingers. I kneel by her head, shoving those same fingers in her mouth as I ask, "Don't you taste delicious, sugar?"

She doesn't say anything, but she does close her lips around my fingers, nodding, and when I remove my fingers from her mouth, she giggles.

I lean down, pressing my lips against hers, making sure she can taste herself on me before I pull back, gripping her hair again, using one hand on her back to shift her upward until she's sitting.

I wrap an arm around her waist, yanking her backward, and she yelps as I swing her around so she's kneeling on the floor, her torso stretched out across the bed. She turns, looking at me with soft eyes as she asks, "What are you doing?"

I kneel behind her, using my knees to spread her legs wide. I rub my dick against her pussy as I reply, "Taking what I need."

I shove inside, hissing at the stretch of her around me. I lean forward, pressing my forehead against her back, allowing pleasure to enrobe me in peace.

She adjusts her stance, leaning the front of her body into the mattress as she shoves her ass back against me. I slide in deeper, my balls slapping against her clit, and she gasps. "Yes. Fuck. Just like that."

I straighten, bracing a foot on the floor, using my leverage to boost her up as I grip behind her knee. I yank her leg up, spreading her wide open for me as I push inside sharply, burying myself balls deep inside her slick pussy.

I lean forward, blanketing her with my body. Pressing my face into her neck, I say gruffly, "This won't take long."

I rotate my hips, pulling out slightly and then shoving in deep, and she moans again, pressing back against me, begging for more.

I slide my hand between her and the mattress, pressing my fingers against her clit firmly. I don't bother with gentleness. Instead, I thrust into her hard and fast, my fingers on her clit rubbing in cadence with the rut of my body into hers.

She eggs me on with whispered curses and words of affirmation, begging me to take what I need while giving her everything.

And then she comes again, a whimpering sob that grabs me by the balls and yanks me over the edge with her.

I groan against her neck, my teeth sinking in, leaving a wet trail of saliva on her skin. "That's fucking right, make me come. Fuck. Fuck. Oh, fuck, I'm gonna come."

My hand moves to the back of her head again, and I grip the hair at the nape of her neck, yanking her head to the side. I scrape my teeth up her neck, fire running through me as my dick throbs inside her, my hot cum painting her insides. "You're fucking mine. Mine for me to take, mine for me to have. All mine."

After a moment, I collapse on top of her, my cheek wet with my own saliva. I move to lift myself off her, but her hand comes up, hooking around so her palm is on the back of my head, and then she whispers, "Stay. Not yet."

So, I relax back on top of her, bringing my forearms in so they're pressed against her, protecting her from my weight.

And then I just breathe.

42

A Trope Interrogation

Matt

WE'VE BEEN SITTING HERE for hours waiting for God only knows what.

Or, in this case, only Antoinette knows what.

I spent the last hour or so sitting in the corner, conversing quietly with whomever swings by while Jessica naps in my lap.

I'm attempting to have a serious conversation with Kaian, but a lingering presence to my right finally draws my attention.

Antoinette.

I give her a bored look and ask, "Can I help you?"

She grins at me, and then Carolina shifts from behind her, giving me the same grin. I sigh, already knowing where this is going.

Neither of them says anything; they just continue to stare at me with that same knowing grin on their faces. Finally, I huff, "Just get it over with."

Antoinette's grin breaks into a beaming smile. "This friends-to-lovers thing is super cute."

I groan, and Jessica squirms in my lap, so I wrap my arms around her a bit more snugly. She presses her face into my neck, breathing a soft sigh against my skin as she settles back in. I narrow my eyes at Antoinette. "Seriously? That's what you want to talk about right now?"

Her smile brightens, and Carolina takes a step toward me as she adds, "We've never had any variation of friends to lovers before."

Antoinette nods enthusiastically. "I know, right?"

"Really?"

They both nod. And then Carolina says, "Definitely not. We've had enemies, dislike, and even some hate, but no friends."

"But would this even be friends to lovers?" Antoinette asks, more to herself than any of us in the room. "Like when did the lovers part happen?"

"Yeah," Carolina asks. "Did you even take the time to become friends first or was it more strangers to lovers?"

Antoinette frowns. "Is that a thing?"

"I don't fucking know, but it is now," Carolina responds with a shrug.

I glance between the two of them, certain my eyebrows must be in my hairline, but they both look so happy and eager that I give in. "What else?"

Part of me doesn't want to humor them, but the bigger part of me understands that, if anything, Antoinette needs to lean on her many inappropriate coping mechanisms right now.

She laughs gleefully, clapping her hands with such pure excitement that I don't bother trying to hide my smile.

She walks over to Kaian, shooing him until he shifts down to the end of the sofa, making room for both women. They perch on the edge of the seat as if they're about to conduct some super fancy interview.

Antoinette turns her focus to me, her hands rubbing over the tops of her thighs as she says, "First, you have to answer a question for me."

I groan, immediately wishing I hadn't opened myself up for this interrogation. But being the good sport I am, I incline my head for her to proceed. "Was this insta-love?"

I quirk a brow at her. "Insta-love?"

Carolina gapes at me as she squawks, "Yes, insta-love. You know, love at first sight."

"Well, our first interaction was a phone call that I intercepted," I reply dryly.

Antoinette leans closer. "But was that the moment?"

I laugh, shaking my head. "Certainly not."

Antoinette squints at me and then murmurs, "But it must've been pretty quick."

"Why would you think that?"

Antoinette smirks at me, tossing her head side to side as she sings-songs, "Because I saw you and how you were with her after that whole thing with Declan."

Carolina giggles next to her, reaching out and patting Antoinette on the leg. "You told me all about that. It was so cute."

"For the love of fuck, would you quit calling it cute," I sputter. "I can assure you there was nothing cute about any of it."

Antoinette bristles, and Carolina purses her lips at me.

Once again, I groan, knowing I'm going to be in the shit if I don't get in line. I wait a moment and then say, "You really want to know?"

Antoinette and Carolina both nod vigorously, excitement back in their eyes. So, I sigh and reply, "It was the first time she wrapped her fingers around my neck and squeezed."

Their jaws drop simultaneously. They both sit there, gawking at me, and I have to repress the laughter bubbling up in my chest because I know for a fact that was not what they were expecting.

After a beat, Antoinette manages to recover. "Choking?"

And then Carolina recovers. "Wait. *She* chokes *you*?"

I nod, squirming around in my seat as my cock pays heed to the conversation and the memory. "She sure does."

"And you like that?" Antoinette asks. "Like, that's what you want?"

"Yes," I reply seriously. "She wouldn't do it otherwise."

"Don't even think about it," Tony interjects from behind me.

He walks around my chair, coming to a stop in front of Carolina, who's looking up at him innocently, a less-than-innocent glimmer in her eye. "You even think about choking me, and you're going to find yourself back in the box."

Her eyes widen, and I can tell from her expression that she's not too worried about the threat, an assumption confirmed when she smiles saucily. "Promise?"

Tony sighs, looks over at me, and says, "Would you quit giving them ideas."

I raise a hand defensively as I retort, "I think my ideas are the least of your problems."

He snorts and turns his focus to Antoinette. "Don't forget the possibility of a love triangle."

Antoinette makes face. "But is it a love triangle?"

Carolina presses her lips together, her brow furrowing in concentration as she makes air quotes and says, "Love triangle? Maybe?"

"But does there have to be love to make that triangle?" Antoinette asks seriously.

Tony takes the chair opposite us, sprawling back and getting comfortable. "I don't know. I don't think there's any such thing as a coercion triangle, but maybe there should be."

Antoinette laughs. "Let's not go making up a bunch of new tropes. That'll get you in trouble."

Tony snorts and says flippantly, "I do what I want. You should fucking know that by now."

"I'm pretty sure all of y'all do what you want," Jessica pipes up from my lap. She squirms around, half turning her body so she can look at Tony as she adds, "Some people might think you have a fuck-around-and-find-out problem."

Antoinette laughs and says, "Well, what do you expect when that's the only fuck we have left."

"Good point," Jessica answers affably. She's quiet for a moment, and then she giggles and says, "Don't knock the choking until you try it, Tony."

She slides her hand up my chest, bracketing my throat just the way I like it. I lean my head back, a quiet moan falling from my lips before I can stop it. She squeezes just a touch, and my arms tighten around her involuntarily as I press my hips up into her ass, my head coming forward so I'm pressing my face against her neck. I bite down gently, eliciting a laugh from her, and that familiar warmth rushes over me as I nuzzle her ear.

"Oh, Jesus fucking Christ. Cut it out," Tony grumbles.

"I'm pretty sure he owes us all a few at this point," Antoinette says.

Everyone falls silent for a moment, and I hug Jessica to me, just breathing her in and enjoying the moment of calm.

Eventually, I'm forced to release her. She turns, sits up, and places her feet on the floor, immediately jumping away as I make a grab to pull her back. She tsks at me, putting some space between us by moving across the sitting area and squishing in between Carolina and Kaian.

She leans into him comfortably, and I glare at him, earning a smirk in return. Then Antoinette says, "So, shall we speak of the elephant in the room, Mr. Ferro?"

I groan, knowing I wouldn't get out of it but still wishing I didn't have to talk about it. "Must we?"

She gives me a serious look. I sigh, straightening in my chair as I prepare myself for the onslaught. "Lilith gave us the short story version already, so we get the gist of it. If there's any pertinent information you feel would be helpful, now is the time."

I shrug and shake my head as I reply, "There isn't much to tell."

"Why didn't you say something sooner?"

"I never planned on saying anything at all. It was supposed to be my dumb little secret to take to my grave."

"Why?" Antoinette asks incredulously.

"Because no good could come of it."

"But by birthright, you're one of the most powerful men in the world."

"So fucking what?" I growl. "That entire," I pause, making air quotes, "'dynasty' should have died with this generation."

Antoinette rolls her eyes, and I bristle. Then she retorts, "If it's being run by people who can do good in the world, then it shouldn't have to die."

"Maybe I don't want to be responsible for doing good in the world for the rest of my fucking life."

She frowns, looking at me and then over at Tony with a dumb-founded expression, and Tony sighs. "What does that even mean?"

"Maybe I just want to kill all the fucking bad guys once and for all and then go about my life as a regular goddamn person."

Everyone falls silent, and I give myself an internal eye roll at what a drama queen I am probably coming off as. But when I say I didn't sign up for this, I absolutely mean it.

The silence drags out, and I'm just to the point of starting to squirm when Tony says, "You can have that, you know."

"What?"

"A regular life like a regular person."

I snort with a shake of my head. "How?"

Tony raises his eyebrows at me, and the expression on his face makes it clear that he thinks I'm the stupidest person he has ever seen. And then he says, a little more slowly than necessary, "You're only the smartest fucking person any of us know. Just go. Cover your tracks. No one will know."

Antoinette snickers, and I turn my gaze to her, glaring. "What's so fucking funny?"

Humor immediately falls from her features, and she shrugs. "Nothing."

My lips twist, but I don't bother calling her out on her obvious lie. Instead, I turn back to Tony and respond, "It's not that simple."

He laughs hollowly. "It *is* that fucking simple. You're the one making it more complicated than it needs to be."

"I can't just fucking leave you all."

"Why the fuck not?" Antoinette asks. "We're grown-ass adults. We'll figure it out."

Lost for words, I frown in her direction then back to Tony, who's nodding in agreement. I glance at Jessica, who's looking on with a neutral expression on her face, and then to Carolina, who, other than the small smile on her lips, isn't giving anything away.

I switch my focus to Kaian, meeting his gaze. He gives me a little shrug and then he responds, "It could be done. If you really wanted to."

I curse under my breath, sitting forward in my seat and dropping my head in my hands as I think over my response.

"Whatcha guys talking about?" Declan asks when he drops down beside me.

I turn to look at him but say nothing, so Tony answers, "Just discussing the possibility of Matt being a regular guy with a regular life."

"Why the fuck would you want to do that?" Declan asks with a tinge of disgust in his voice. "You weren't born to be boring, man."

"Being a regular guy with a regular life wouldn't be boring."

"Like fuck it wouldn't be," he scoffs.

"Then I guess being boring wouldn't be so bad," I retort pissily.

Declan peers down at me, squinting slightly, and then he says, "For a smart fella, you're really fucking dumb, aren't you?"

"What?"

"Seriously," Declan persists. "If you think you're the type of guy who can live a regular life, you're really fucking stupid."

I grit my teeth, saying nothing, knowing full well that now I'm just acting like a petulant child. But I feel like a goddamn petulant child.

Declan squats down beside me, looking me right in the face as he murmurs, "I'm sure this asshole," he pauses, pointing his thumb over at Tony, "said that you being a regular guy with a regular life was possible and that everyone here would be fine if you decided to choose that path, but let me assure you, he's fucking lying."

I glance at Tony, who now has his poker face on, but he doesn't argue. So, I turn back to Declan as he continues, "Most people always assume that Darius is in charge around here. And sure, Darius makes a good figurehead, and having The Beast at the top of a roster is a great strategy. But anyone who has even an inkling of what goes on here knows that that's bullshit."

"What are you talking about? Everyone knows that Darius is the big man on campus."

Declan laughs, shaking his head as he waves a hand dismissively. "Yes, Darius, the big and scary. We all get it. But being big and scary isn't what gets shit done."

"I think you're crazy. Being big and scary has certainly gotten a lot of shit done."

Declan inclines his head in acknowledgment but then replies, "Sure, but that isn't what has gotten your team where it is. You guys wouldn't even be here if it wasn't for you."

"I'm not sure if Darius would agree with you at this point," I mutter.

Declan's fist snaps out, connecting sharply with my thigh. "I'm being fucking serious, fuckface. It's your constant oversight and guidance that has kept everyone alive this long. It's your dedication and devotion to not only the mission but to the entire family that you all have built for yourselves."

He gives me a slight smile, then pats me on the leg where he previously had punched me, and rises to his feet. I stare up at him, saying nothing, mostly because I don't know what to say, and then he nods almost to himself, looking completely self-satisfied. "And let's not fucking forget that none of us believe in that whole, 'If you love someone, let them go' shit. So, be warned."

I chuckle, shaking my head. "Can't forget that."

We all fall silent again, and I look over at Jessica, who gives me a little wink, and I revel in that now-familiar warmth that settles over me.

I glance at everyone sitting around me to see each one of them is still looking at me, and I sigh and then groan, shaking my head as I rush to my feet, knowing this tail end of our whole conversation was completely pointless because where would I even fucking go.

I turn to Declan, who was still standing by my chair. "What did you even come over here for?"

"Oh," he replies, "Lilith told me to come over here and let you guys know our visitors are here."

Antoinette's eyes widen, and she jumps to her feet. "It's fucking showtime."

Everyone else follows suit, taking off across the room behind her, and then it's just Tony, Declan, and I standing there watching after them.

Declan pats me on the shoulder, giving me a smug look, before he, too, walks off, leaving me with Tony.

Tony rests his arm over my shoulder, maneuvering me with him as he starts to walk across the room, and I fall into step beside him. And then he murmurs near my ear, "Shields or Ferro, makes no fucking difference to me."

I choke on a low laugh, emotion churning in my chest as I loop my arm under his. I squeeze his shoulder, letting him pull me into his side like we did back when we were kids, and he'd razz me for being a boy scout.

With a final squeeze, he pulls away, shoving me to the side and stalking off without further comment.

But I know what he's leaving unsaid.

Brothers in life, brothers in death.

43

Finding Hope

Matt

It turns out Antoinette's surprise guest happens to be her father, Antonio Rossi, along with an entourage of what appears to be European kingpins.

It's hard to say if they're here under duress or of their own free will, but from what I understand, Antonio Rossi wouldn't give a fuck either way.

I use his arrival as an excuse to hang back, needing a moment to get my bearings and my emotions under control. I'm just walking up to the group when Antoinette says, "If you fucking call me that again, I will shoot you in the face."

Having zero context, I raise an eyebrow and ask, "And who are you talking to?"

She glances at me and then points at her father, who puts both hands up in surrender. "My apologies. I had no idea you were so sensitive."

Within a split second, she's got a knife in her hand, pointing it at him. "Call me sensitive one more time."

"Antonio," Lilith intercedes. "If you really want to see something happen, tell her to calm down."

Antonio turns his attention to Lilith cocking his head at her, as he says sarcastically, "Obviously, I'm not the smartest man in the room, but I'm not that stupid, either."

Lilith opens her mouth to respond, but Antoinette puts her hand up and interrupts, "Don't you two fucking start."

Lilith rolls her eyes and mutters under her breath, and Antonio does a rather decent job of swatting away an invisible fly.

Antoinette sighs and then continues more calmly, "We don't have the time to even begin to unpack the bullshit that's between you two. And you both already know that's not why we're here."

They both remain quiet but nod in acknowledgment of her words. Then she turns back to Antonio and asks, "Have you found out anything?"

"Just what you already know."

Antoinette squints at him, her body visibly tensing. "And that would be?"

He crosses his arms over his chest and tilts his head at her as he considers his next words. And then he explains, "That the entire warehouse exploded, and there are no known survivors."

Her jaw clenches as do her fists, and she slams the knife she was still holding down on the table, "Try again."

Antonio's features soften, and he makes a move to step toward her but then stops short, dropping his hands and looking at her helplessly.

"Do you want me to lie?"

She turns away, heavily resting her hands on the bench in front of her, and then she turns and looks at him over her shoulder as she whispers, "I won't believe it until I see proof."

His eyes widen, and he shakes his head as he replies, "The entire building was practically vaporized. What kind of proof are you hoping for?"

Her jaw clenches, and then she slams her fist down on the workbench viciously. Once. Twice. "He is not dead until I see it with my own fucking eyes."

No one says anything, and silence echoes throughout the room. With a shout of frustration, she lunges for a computer monitor, yanking it up and bodily throwing it across the room. I turn my eyes to Tony, who's staring at her in amusement as she stands there, trembling with rage and anguish.

Slowly, she turns to face us, but now her shoulders droop. She hangs her head as she whispers half-brokenly, "You know the rules."

Her statement hangs out there in the universe. I scan the usual suspects, who are all standing around, and this time, everyone just looks helpless.

I start forward but stop short when Jessica beats me to it. She steps in front of Antoinette and grips her by her upper arm, giving her a shake. Antoinette raises her head slowly, her eyes slightly glassy as she looks at Jessica. And then Jessica replies firmly, "They're not dead unless you've removed their head and set their body on fire yourself."

Antonio opens his mouth to speak, but I do first. "That's right. That's the rule."

Antonio gives me an impatient look, and I lift a shoulder, shaking my head slightly. Carolina joins Antoinette and Jessica, putting an arm around each of them as she leans in and speaks softly. Jessica laughs, and Antoinette gives her a somewhat watery smile as she nods. Carolina turns to me and says, "We've done enough waiting around. Let's go fuck shit up."

Tony laughs, and Antonio mutters, "Finally, something I can get behind."

I nod, turning to Antonio. "I take it you have some actual leads?"

He inclines his head to his entourage and replies, "These fuckers do."

"How do we know they won't just lead us to our own slaughter?"

Antonio shrugs, looking unfazed. "Well, I guess we don't really. But most of them have families they'd rather not see tortured and murdered. So, the odds are in our favor."

"How many countries are we talking about?"

"Just the usuals: Russia, France, Italy. That should probably cover it."

"And Boston," a voice responds from across the room.

I step away from the group and look around Antonio to see Camilla striding closer, a disgruntled look on her face.

She stops next to me, anger burning in her eyes as I ask, "What the fuck is in Boston?"

"Seamus," she growls. "He barely made it out of that fucking building before it went up. Got knocked senseless for his trouble."

"Then how did he end up in Boston?" Jessica asks.

"One of the rival families took him. I'm getting some conflicting information, but the common correlation is that they have him."

Jessica snorts and mutters, "Well, they can fucking keep him."

Camilla laughs bitterly, and she turns her gaze on Jessica. "I'd be inclined to agree. However, I'm also hearing chatter that he's not alone."

"Is it just some of his men with him?"

Camilla shakes her head. "No one is saying who they are. Which means either they don't know or have good reason not to say."

I look at Antoinette, who's already wide-eyed and staring at me. A slight chill goes down my spine as she whispers, "Could it be him?"

I shake my head and shrug helplessly. "I don't know—"

"Fucking right it's him," Tony chirps.

I raise a hand as I say, "Let's not get ahead of ourselves here. We can hope for the best as long as we're prepared for the worst." I turn back to Camilla, leveling her with a serious look, as I say, "Have they given any real information about the men they have?"

She smiles and replies, "Oh, yeah. An old Irish who's half-dead. Some young fucking nobody who doesn't say much." She pauses, looking over at Tony, then Antoinette, and then back at me as she adds, "And one big fucking belligerent asshole who threatened to rip out a spine and ass-fuck someone with it."

An audible gasp rushes out of Antoinette, and she exclaims, "That's fucking got to be him. He's the only guy I know who talks about fucking people with spines."

"But how?" Carolina exclaims.

Lilith turns to her, placing her hands on her hips as she sputters, "You're seriously going to fucking knock it now? After all of your dramatics?"

Antoinette opens her mouth to speak, but all that comes out is a choked-up sob of excitement. She bends at the waist, resting her hands on the tops of her thighs as she expels several days' worth of frustration and fear. Jessica pats her on the back, and Carolina does the same; both sets of eyes are a bit glassy at the news.

Then Tony steps up, clapping his hands together as he bellows, "Enough with this crybaby bullshit. We got fucking work to do."

I nod in agreement, finding myself giving a clap of my own before

I can stop myself. Then I frown and turn to Camilla. "So, who would you like to be this time?"

Her smile broadens, a mischievous glint in her eyes, and she replies, "I'm so glad you asked."

44

Not a Moment Too Soon

Darius

A FEW DAYS AGO.

Well, that sucked.

I mean, sitting here trapped in this metal cage, knowing that at any moment, I will literally be blown to kingdom come isn't ideal.

But having to force Carolina to abandon me here was not on my list of last shitty deeds I needed to cross off.

I sigh, leaning my back against the metal bars as I listen to the fading footfalls and shouts mixed with intermittent groaning, coughing, grunting, and generally people dying.

I chuckle, somewhat relieved to learn that moments before your imminent demise, your life does not flash before your eyes.

"What the fuck are you laughing at?"

I start, then crawl to the cage door to see Ivan has come around. He's lying on his back, rubbing his temples, and I say, "If you want to live, I suggest you get the fuck out of here."

He groans and mutters, "Not so loud, man."

I laugh humorlessly. "Seriously. This place is going to literally explode at any moment. I suggest you run."

He peeks an eye open at me, slowly sitting up and rolling onto all fours. He shakes his head slightly, likely attempting to clear his thoughts through the ringing in his ears from Tony punching him in the face.

He heaves himself to his feet and stands there momentarily, weaving back and forth. Bracing his hands on the top of the cage, he takes a deep breath in and expels it quickly as he forces himself to straighten. He stands there, looking around rather aimlessly, so I add, "I'm not kidding. Don't just fucking stand there like a moron."

He waves a hand at me as he replies, "I'm just looking for the dickhead who has the fucking key."

He glances around again, and then his eyes light up, and he rushes over to one of the bodies near where we all had been strung up at one point or another.

He rolls the body over, quickly digging through pockets and pulling out a key ring that he holds up in victory, and I reply dryly, "That's great. But use it or lose it."

He rushes over to me, falling to his knees in front of the cage door, grabbing onto the lock as he fumbles with a key ring. "Which one is it? What the fuck?"

"I still think you should just get the fuck out."

He gives me an incredulous look and shakes his head. "I can't just fucking leave you here."

"Yes, you fucking can. Who the fuck would know?"

"I would fucking know."

He attempts one key after another in quick succession, cursing to himself when none of them fit. Once again, I find myself peering through the bars as I say, "You're going to have to leave me here."

Ivan makes a face, but he makes no move to run out of the room. The door slams behind me, and Ivan looks up, his eyes widening as he says, "What the fuck are you doing here?"

I turn to see Seamus running toward us, not slowing until he grabs the corner of the cage. Using his grip, he abruptly turns himself so he is kneeling in front of it next to Ivan, a key ring in his hand.

He shoves the key into the lock, and it turns. Then I'm staring at an open door.

Seamus is already up, running back across the room, yelling over his shoulder, "Get your finger out. We gotta go."

That gets my attention.

I quickly crawl out of the cage, immediately gaining my feet and pulling Ivan to his. We both race after Seamus as I shout to Ivan, "You're going to have to lead the way. I have no fucking idea where I am."

Seamus is right in the doorway, and Ivan runs through, the two of us directly behind him. He sprints down corridors, briefly slowing to manage corners. I swear I can hear the tick-tock, tick-tock of a clock in my brain.

We're sprinting toward a doorway at the end of the corridor, and Ivan stops short before barreling into it head-on. He hits the bar, and it doesn't budge. He hits it again and again. I stand there, gasping for breath as I say, "My people probably barricaded this one."

Seamus glares at me, and Ivan immediately pushes off the door and takes off again. "I know a better way."

Seamus and I sprint after him, Seamus muttering lowly, "We're out of time. We're out of fucking time."

We increase our speed, sprinting blindly now as another door comes into view. We barrel toward it, all three of us together, knowing that if this one is locked, we're completely fucked.

I pull up abreast to Ivan, the two of us zeroing in on the door as we run full out. At the last second, we each turn a shoulder, our hands out, bracing to push the bar.

I grip the cold metal a split second before my shoulder smashes into the door. At first, it doesn't give, and then Seamus comes up behind us, slamming into us full force. The door bursts open, and we fall through it, our forward momentum rolling us out onto the ground, just in time to feel the inferno at our back.

I'm shoved further by the force, bodily thrown through the air, the impact from the explosion behind us scorching and vibrating. I hit the dirt face-first, my chest driving into the gravel, forcing the air from my lungs, but I manage to get up on my hands and knees, my palms digging into the dirt as I choke and cough.

Then I fall forward, rolling onto my back, my arms coming over my face as dirt and debris rain down on me.

With my ears ringing, my arms fall to my sides, then I blink up into the inferno-tinged sky.

Yeah, that fucking sucked.

I manage a small choking laugh, and then I sink into the darkness.

45

A Case of the Darius'

Matt

"THIS ISN'T GOING TO WORK," Antoinette sputters.

I try to hide my smile and fail. I look over at Tony, who has the same amused expression, and then he meets my gaze with a shrug, laughing loudly. "This is fucking wild."

"Do you feel different?" I ask seriously. "Because I think I feel different."

"Yeah," Tony replies. "It's like just pretending to be him makes me feel invincible."

"You two fucking cut that out," Antoinette exclaims.

We both attempt to put on a serious face, though I see Tony's lips twitching in time with mine. Then Kaian says from behind me, "I always knew it must feel good to be The Beast. And this just proves it."

He shoves something in front of my face, and then I'm staring at my own reflection.

Or rather, Darius' reflection.

I smile broadly and then laugh loudly. I turn to Kaian, laughing again, to find I'm just staring at another version of Darius.

"I don't know," Declan replies from my other side. "I was definitely better looking before."

Camilla laughs as she says, "Well, you look pretty similar to the old man. I certainly had to put in less work changing you over."

"This is fucking crazy," Carolina murmurs.

Jessica walks over, stops directly in front of me, and leans in as she peers into my eyes. "Obviously you're not built the same, and you don't sound the same, but this is amazing."

And she is absolutely correct.

None of us are built like Darius, but Camilla managed to make all four of us look like him at a glance. Even given a hard stare in the face, most people wouldn't be the wiser.

"You do good work, Cami."

She smiles at me. "Why thank you."

"Who are you going to be today?" Tony asks.

She shakes her head, a serious expression on her face. "I'm going to be me today."

Antoinette frowns and asks, "Why is that?"

"I want them to see which Irish lass is sending them to hell."

She walks over to Tony, glancing at his face briefly, and then to Kaian, where she pauses and leans in close with a grin. "I see you in there."

Kaian glares at her and steps back. "Fucking cut it out, Cami."

Her smile broadens, and she laughs. "Make me."

Declan jabs me with his elbow, and when I meet his gaze, he wags his eyebrows at me and whispers, "What's going on over there?"

I whisper back, "I don't know, but it looks entertaining."

Cami moves closer to Kaian, her lips moving, but I can't make out her words. Kaian's glare sharpens, and he leans in so his face is directly in hers as he says clearly, "Not if you were the last fucking woman on Earth."

A gasp from near the workstation draws my attention, and I turn to Carolina and Antoinette, who are leaning against the workbench. Antoinette presses her hand over her chest, shock and awe on her features, as she mutters, "Enemy to lovers."

Carolina rests her hand on Antoinette's arm as she leans in and says, "Maybe another hate with benefits to lovers."

"You two fucking cut that out," Kaian snarls. "Your romancey trope shit has no business here."

"Oh, we've heard that one before," Antoinette quips. "And even though it does feel weird seeing Darius angry flirting with another woman, I'm fucking here for it."

"I'm not flirting," Kaian snarls.

Antoinette's smile only broadens, and Carolina does an excited little jig as she sing-songs, "Heard that one before, too."

Kaian turns bewildered eyes on me. "Are they for fucking real?"

I smile and nod. "Yes. And I hate to break it to you, but they're usually spot-on."

Camilla doesn't say anything. She just stands there, smiling up at him. He glances down at her, baring his teeth, a little growl of frustration brewing in his chest, and I sigh, moving to step between them.

I put my hand on his shoulder, turning him around as we walk a few feet away. He glares over his shoulder in her direction, and I slap him on the back. "Is there a reason you have a problem with her?"

He throws one last glare in her direction and then turns his focus to me as he replies, "Just that she has the ability to literally be anyone at any time."

"So? Why does that bother you?"

He gives me an incredulous look, shaking his head. "She's basically a walking, talking weapon, Matt. Look what she's done to us. She's created four new Beasts."

I laugh. "Isn't it great?"

He shakes his head, his eyebrows raising as he exclaims, "No. It's fucking crazy."

"So, what are you afraid of?"

"What isn't there to be afraid of?"

I pause for a moment, and then I say, "Well, if she's on your side, it's perfect. So maybe you should try to be a little more friendly with her."

"I want nothing to do with her."

"I hate to break it to you, but this intense reaction is usually indicative of something else going on."

He puts his finger right in my face as he says, "Don't you fucking say it."

I laugh again and then say, "Obviously, I don't have to say it." I pat him on the shoulder, giving him a sympathetic look as I refrain from saying all the things I want to say. Because any one of us here knows that regardless of how we may feel about a situation, by the time we even realize it's happening, it's out of our hands.

The door at the other end of the room opens, and I look over to see a whole mess of people filing into the room.

Lilith is the first one to reach us, Issa and Marieka following closely behind. "Everything's in place."

Any humor that was left in the room immediately vanishes.

Antoinette steps forward. "Good. Will it be a synchronous assault?"

Nodding, Lilith replies, "Yes. It means some of the European assaults will take place in daylight, but it was more important that we're in the dark here. Issa and Marieka will stay here and run communications, so we'll have tabs on all locations."

She looks at me and blinks, then does the same with Kaian, Declan, and Tony, and then she frowns. "Well, that's fucking wild."

Antoinette chuckles. "Right? I don't know what I was expecting, but for some reason, this was not it."

"They're going to shit their pants."

"I kind of feel like the boogeyman," Kaian says. "I just don't want to go around scaring people all day."

"If that's the case, I can take Dare's face off of you," Camilla replies flippantly.

He glares at her again and opens his mouth to reply, but I hit him with my elbow, turning his attention back to me. "No flirting, right?"

He rolls his eyes but manages to remain silent, and then Antoinette, Carolina, and Jessica all move closer to us. We naturally shift, so our circle narrows, with a group of extras hanging out in the wings.

"Does everyone understand the mission?" I ask seriously.

"Save Dare," Antoinette replies.

I sigh and shake my head. "No. Finding and freeing Dare is obviously a part of the mission, but that is not the actual mission."

Antoinette gives me a sulky look but, after a beat, manages to nod. I take a minute to look at each person in the room, earning a nod from each of them before nodding myself. "Good. Let's go in there and finish this."

Antoinette looks at Kaian, and then at me, quickly moving to Declan before zeroing in on Tony. "You wanna do the honors for old time's sake?"

He smiles wickedly, pulling two blades from where he has them hidden on his person. He spins them on his palms before gripping the handles. "Are we ready for this?"

We all reply in the affirmative, and the tension in the air sizzles, the ominous buzz of excitement like an old friend.

He waits for everyone to quiet, that wicked grin turning menacing as he says clearly, "It's fuck around time."

46

Out of the Darkness

Darius

I AM RELATIVELY CERTAIN I'm not dead.

I've lost count of the number of times I've blinked, yet I remain in the darkness. I open my mouth to speak, then grit my teeth, forcing myself to swallow a few times as I do my best to peel my tongue from the roof of my mouth.

It takes a few attempts, but I manage to clear my throat and then croak out, "What the fuck?"

And then I chuckle to myself, that odd feeling of déjà vu wrestling with my bones.

"What could possibly be funny?" a voice comes out through the darkness.

"Who the fuck are you?" My words are rough, but they travel well in the silence.

The voice retorts, "Who the fuck are you?"

I groan, shaking my head and then laughing again at the ridiculousness that this could be happening a second time.

Trapped in the fucking dark.

I don't say anything for a few moments, mostly because I'm stubborn and I don't want to. And then the voice comes back, "Beast, is that you?"

"Oh, for the love of fuck, don't call me that."

"It's me, Ivan," he replies. "And you should be embracing that name at this point. Who knows how many times it's gotten you out of hot water."

"Well, apparently, this wasn't one of them," I reply dryly.

"I don't know. You had one big moment of threatening to rip out a spine before you passed out. I think it helped."

"Would you two yahoos shut the fuck up," an old Irish voice says from the other side of me.

"Seamus. So good of you to join us."

"Yeah, that's what I fucking get for bothering to save your dumb ass."

"Just let me get my bearings, and I'll try to poke around and see where we're at," I say tiredly.

I move to sit up, cracking my forehead on something hard, just as Seamus says, "I wouldn't do that if I were you."

I raise my hand to my face and end up driving it into the same hard surface I bashed my head off of. Slowly, this time, I manage to rub my fingers on my forehead as I mutter, "Well, this is getting better and better."

"Just be glad you were knocked out-cold when you got put in here. I got shoved in this thing wide awake," Ivan answers.

I shrug and then chuckle again at the ridiculousness of my nonverbal cues. "Lucky for you, this isn't my first time trapped in the dark, nor is it my first time stuck in a box."

"Do you have any brilliant ideas on how to get us out of here?" Ivan asks sarcastically.

"Not hardly. Seamus, what are the odds of someone leaking our location?"

"Well, it depends," he replies. "Going by Ivan's descriptions, I think it's safe to assume they've moved us east."

"East? Why east?"

"He said they had us in the back of a van for around four-ish hours. From our previous location, I think around four hours' distance from there, in any direction, the most reasonable explanation would be the Boston area. That's also the only place I would consider being enemy territory."

"That makes sense. Dare I ask what fun awaits us in Boston?"

"Nothing super fun, that's for sure. I assume they'll try to ransom me. They may try to do the same with you, but that's less likely, given you're worth more being sold off to the less savory."

I snort. "You know they've tried that a few times and failed. At some point, you'd think they'd smarten up."

"Well, if the only thing keeping us alive is stupid people, then God bless them."

"I would cheers to that if I had a drink," Ivan interjects.

"I could go for a drink."

"Yup. Me, too."

"And at least you can rest assured that since they've moved us a couple of times within sight of other people, that at least one of them would spill the beans. There's always somebody out there looking for a cash payout. And they would know that this would be a big one."

"Good," I answer. "Then that means my people will be coming."

"They won't think just you're dead?" Ivan asks.

"I'm sure for a fair amount of time there they did. But my people aren't the type to just assume someone is dead."

"The giant explosion wouldn't be enough for them?"

I laugh, and, for a moment, I feel bad because, for at least a small amount of time, they would've grieved. "First rule. Never assume anyone's dead without real proof."

Ivan snorts and mutters, "You'd think a kaboom would suffice."

"And see, that's where you'd be wrong because look at us now. Not dead."

"You have a fair point," Seamus replies. "There was certainly a time in my life I would've believed the explosion. Now, I'm way too old to assume anything."

"The only good thing about dehydration and my previous stay in a cage is I'm less likely to have a need for the facilities anytime soon."

Ivan snorts and retorts, "And speak for yourself."

"If nothing else, piss away from me. Okay?"

"Hopefully, we'll get rescued before I have to worry about that."

"Do you think that'll be soon? Do we know how long we've been here?"

Seamus answers, "Last time we tried to assess, we figured it'd been a day or two. I figure it would take them a couple of days to get word that you're possibly not dead and then maybe another one to determine where you're being held, so we're probably still looking at another day or three."

"For fuck's sake, man," Ivan exclaims. "When you word it like that, it may as well be years."

"Not really. They're going to have to come tend to us at some point. If they let us die of dehydration, heads are going to roll."

"And shockingly," I respond blandly. "This is not the first time that I had to consider the possibility that I get snuffed out in the dark. Nothing more than rat food."

Both men are silent, and as time drags on, I finally ask, "What? Is it something I said?"

"I don't know," Seamus retorts. "You're just a regular ball of sunshine."

"That's quite funny given our current circumstances."

"I think I liked it better when he was knocked out," Ivan mutters.

"Me, too," I say with a laugh.

"Do you hear that?" Ivan asks.

I hold my breath, straining to hear anything in the distance but coming up with nothing but that echo of silence. "No. Hear what?"

"Ssh," he shushes me, so I go back to holding my breath and listening.

Then I hear a thud—a running cadence—and swiftly, it gets louder and louder until there's a crash from what feels like behind us.

And a new voice cuts urgently through the darkness. "I'm fucking telling you. I saw it clear as day with my own eyes."

"You're fucking crazy," another voice pipes in. "I put that fucker in the box myself."

"Did you even know what the guy looks like? Or did you just put a guy in the box, and they said that's who he is?"

There's a long stretch of silence as the steps get closer, and then, suddenly, a few pinpricks of light shine through minuscule cracks in what is definitely a concrete box. My heart rate picks up, and my curiosity is piqued to find out what the hell they're talking about.

Metal clanks, and then there's a soft whir of a motor, followed by the scrape of concrete against concrete. The top of the box shifts and groans, and then I'm squeezing my eyes shut tightly against the glare of light in the room.

Before I have even a moment to collect myself, hands are grabbing onto my shirt front, and I'm being yanked from the box, the two men heaving me up. They drag me a few feet and toss me on the ground, where I land in a heap.

I groan, attempting to open my eyes and, once again, immediately squeezing them shut against the pain of the light.

I catch a boot to the gut, and I choke, rolling over onto my front and wheezing to catch my breath as one of the men says, "Is that the guy you saw?"

"Yes, it fucking is," he exclaims. "How can there be two of them?"

This time, the boot hits me in the thigh, and when I open my eyes, I manage to squint enough to see my surroundings clearly. I sneak a glance over my shoulder, getting a glimpse of the two men who should be old enough to know better. The older, dark-haired one asks, "What's your fucking name?"

I don't reply for a moment. I just look between him and his friend with what I'm sure must be a predatory grin.

Then the lighter-haired one stutters, "I do-don't know, man. We should just put him back in the box and let someone else worry about it."

The dark-haired one scowls at his friend, then turns to me, bringing his foot back like he's going to kick me again, but just as he moves to slam his foot forward, I twist around and grab it. I don't wait for the man to get his bearings. I twist that fucker around with enough force that he comes right off his foot, the crack of the bone punctuated by his scream of pain.

As soon as he's down, I leap on him, grabbing his head between both my hands and slamming it against the concrete floor without mercy. Once he stops screaming, I jump up, and I'm on the light-haired man before he can reach the doorway, snagging him by the back of the hair and yanking him off his feet.

He flies through the air a few feet, landing on his back, and I turn, shutting the door before strolling back to stand over him.

He stares up at me wide-eyed, fear etched into his features, and I tilt my head at him as I squat down, staring him dead in the eyes as I say, "It's the easy way or the hard way. You choose."

47

From the Shadows

Matt

So far, pretending to be Darius has been quite fun.

We decided our best course of action would be to split us up. It would be far more impactful to think there was a Darius at every corner rather than a pack of us in front of you.

Unfortunately, that meant the girls would be on their own, which was only problematic to us guys.

It only took a few minutes before people started obviously noticing me. At first, it was some passing glances and a few whispers, but after a while, I ran head-on into a man who jumped back from me as if he'd seen a ghost.

He took off with such haste that I figured it's safe to assume he had seen Darius recently.

We're all in the general vicinity of each other, so I report my suspicions, knowing everyone will start heading toward my general direction. The spooked man heads down a side street, and I sneak behind him as close as I dare without the risk of being spotted.

I peek around the corner just in time to see him disappear into the side entrance of an old pub near the docks we'd been keeping an eye on, which is perfect given our end-game plans.

Knowing old buildings as well as I do, I recognize the likelihood that this building doesn't end at ground level, so I step back and send an update to the group on how to proceed.

Antoinette confirms a front entrance, with Jessica and Carolina confirming alternate doors on either side of the building. Kaian, Tony, and Declan report that they're a few steps behind.

Cautiously, I make my way over to the door the man disappeared through. It appears to be secure; however, it has an old, rudimentary lock. I pull out my lock-picking kit, making short work of it, and then I ease the door open, torn between shoving it open and attempting to slide inside inconspicuously.

I stop with the door opened a few inches, listening intently, but I can't make out anything of interest with the general street noise at my back.

Cursing softly, I push the door open and step inside with all the swagger The Beast would muster. Then I deflate a bit when I find an empty room, slightly annoyed that I wasted time being cautious.

I shut the door behind me, making sure to check that it's unlocked, and then I proceed further into the room until I stop at the far doorway. I lean out, glancing in both directions, listening for any type of ruckus.

Thinking of the general blueprints of these buildings, I take a right, doing my best not to be deterred by the fact the light becomes dimmer with every subsequent room I walk through.

I stop beside what appears to be an exterior door. I open it and peek outside, confirming that it's the street, which means it's likely one of the doors the girls came in, so I'm not far behind them.

I continue forward, moving more swiftly now, less concerned about remaining quiet, knowing my people are also in the building.

I stop at the top of a stairwell, glancing down suspiciously. A loud clang followed by a shout sounds from below, and I throw what little caution I had left to the wind, carefully walking down the stairs.

I exit the stairwell into a large room that reeks of damp and stale beer. I'm surrounded by old brewery machinery that blocks the light, leaving this side of the room dim, so I hurry over to hide behind one of the large metal drums. Sliding around the cool metal, I peer across the room, noting a small group of men standing there, and I can just make out the low murmur of another voice on the far side outside my view.

Then, a ginger-looking man in the middle of the group steps forward and says, "Don't try to bullshit me, Jessica."

My heart stops in my chest at the same time fury erupts inside me. I clench my jaw, forcing myself to remain in this spot, ignoring my innate urge to charge and destroy.

And then I see her.

The group of men disperses some, leaving the ginger-looking man and Jessica standing in plain view.

She walks up and stops a couple of feet in front of him, her expression furious as she says, "Let's not pretend that you have a proclivity for discretion."

"What the fuck is that supposed to mean?"

She steps in closer, pointing her finger in his face as she says, "You gave that disgusting fucking video to Bobby. And in doing so, you managed to hurt a lot of people."

His hand shoots out and grabs onto her wrist. "I didn't give Bobby shit."

"So, he was bluffing?" she asks incredulously.

"No," he answers. "He managed to steal it, and before I could get it back from him, he was dead."

Jessica glares at him, shaking her head as she retorts, "I don't buy it. He had that video for a long fucking time before he was dead."

He shoves her away and scowls. "What good would it be to me if that thing got out?"

"Oh, I don't know. Maybe you could just rub it in a lot of people's faces. Get me permanently erased from the world."

He raises his brows at her. "And incriminate myself."

Now, she frowns, shaking her head at him and saying, "What are you talking about?"

He smirks at her, puffing at his chest a little bit as he says, "Oh, you never figured that out?"

"Figured what out?"

He laughs, the malicious undertones sending a chill down my spine, "The fact that you didn't *give* me anything."

Shock falls over her features, and she slowly shakes her head in denial. "What do you mean?"

"Quit fucking around," one of the other men says hurriedly.

The ginger-looking man turns to him and retorts, "Shut the fuck up. I finally get to tell this bitch how I pulled one over on her, and I'm not going to miss my only chance."

"You had ample chances to explain whatever you're talking about, so why bother now?"

"Because if you're here, that means you're going to be dead soon, which means it can't fall back and kick me in the ass later."

"Well, go on then. What are you waiting for?"

His smile turns evil, and he squints at her, a pleased expression on his face. "You didn't give me your virginity. I took it."

Once again, she shakes her head, confusion on her face and her whisper barely audible to me as she replies, "No. No, that's not what happened. That's not what you said."

He inclines his head at her, rolling his eyes as he retorts sarcastically, "Because I'm always the epitome of honesty."

"But why?"

"Because I can. Because I could. And I wanted to."

She looks down at the ground, a kaleidoscope of emotions shadowing her features, and then suddenly, she smiles, her eyes raising to meet his, as she says calmly, "Well, that'll make this a lot easier."

He frowns and asks, "Make what easier?"

"Fucking killing you, that's what."

He pauses briefly, and everyone is silent for a moment, and then he laughs and the men with him laugh. "And how the fuck do you expect to do that?"

"Swiftly and methodically."

"You don't actually think you can take us all?"

Her smile broadens as she shakes her head. "Of course not, silly."

The men fall silent again, all of them looking at her like she's completely insane, and I have to say, I'm probably looking at her in the same way.

But then, a more sinister-yet-playful voice pops up from the far side of the men. "She's got a little help from her friends."

Carolina lunges from the shadows, grabbing the man closest to her by the hair and yanking back viciously, immediately dropping her body down to add to the momentum of his falling backward.

Two of the men move like they're going to help him, but it's too late. As soon as his body hits the concrete, he has a knife sticking out of his throat.

Carolina is on her feet again, pulling the knife out and stabbing him several more times to ensure he won't be getting up to defend any of his friends.

Then she stands there, an Antoinette-worthy grin on her face as she asks, "Who's next?"

The group of men lunges for her when a shriek from behind me draws their attention. Startled, I turn, pressing my back against the metal drum just in time to see Camilla streak by, her battle cry almost more intimidating than the large knives she's brandishing in each hand.

Camilla makes short work of the remaining men, and then it's just ginger-looking guy standing there, looking like he's going to shit his pants.

Camilla and Carolina circle him, but they make no move toward him as they each stop beside Jessica, flanking her. Carolina turns to Jessica and asks, "Did I hear this fucker correctly?"

"Depends on what you think you heard."

"Did he say that he's a no-good piece of shit rapist?"

"Well, he may have implied some form of coercion and exploitation, but I do think that the gist of it was definitely rapist."

He frowns, shaking his head and attempting to take a few steps backward, but then Camilla points at him and says, "Don't fucking move."

He stops moving and says nothing, likely realizing that anything he says won't do him any good.

Then Camilla asks, "Do you know where Darius is?"

The man swallows and then nods, and Jessica says, "Then you can either lead us to him, or you can fucking die here."

"I'll take you," he replies quickly.

Camilla puts her weapons away and then pulls zip ties out of her jacket pocket. She yanks his arms behind him, none too gently, securing the zip ties with such vigor that I'm sure she's cutting off all blood supply to his hands.

Not that any of us give a fuck.

She leans in over him and says, "Don't be a fucking asshole."

He looks back at her wide-eyed, shakes his head, and says, "I know the drill."

She steps away from him, and he raises his head to indicate a door to the left. "It's this way."

"Well, let's go then," Camilla replies.

The man turns, walking off in that direction with the three women close behind him.

They disappear through the doorway, and I give up my hiding space, following behind them slowly, knowing they can totally handle themselves in any situation, I'm happy going in as a beast in the shadows.

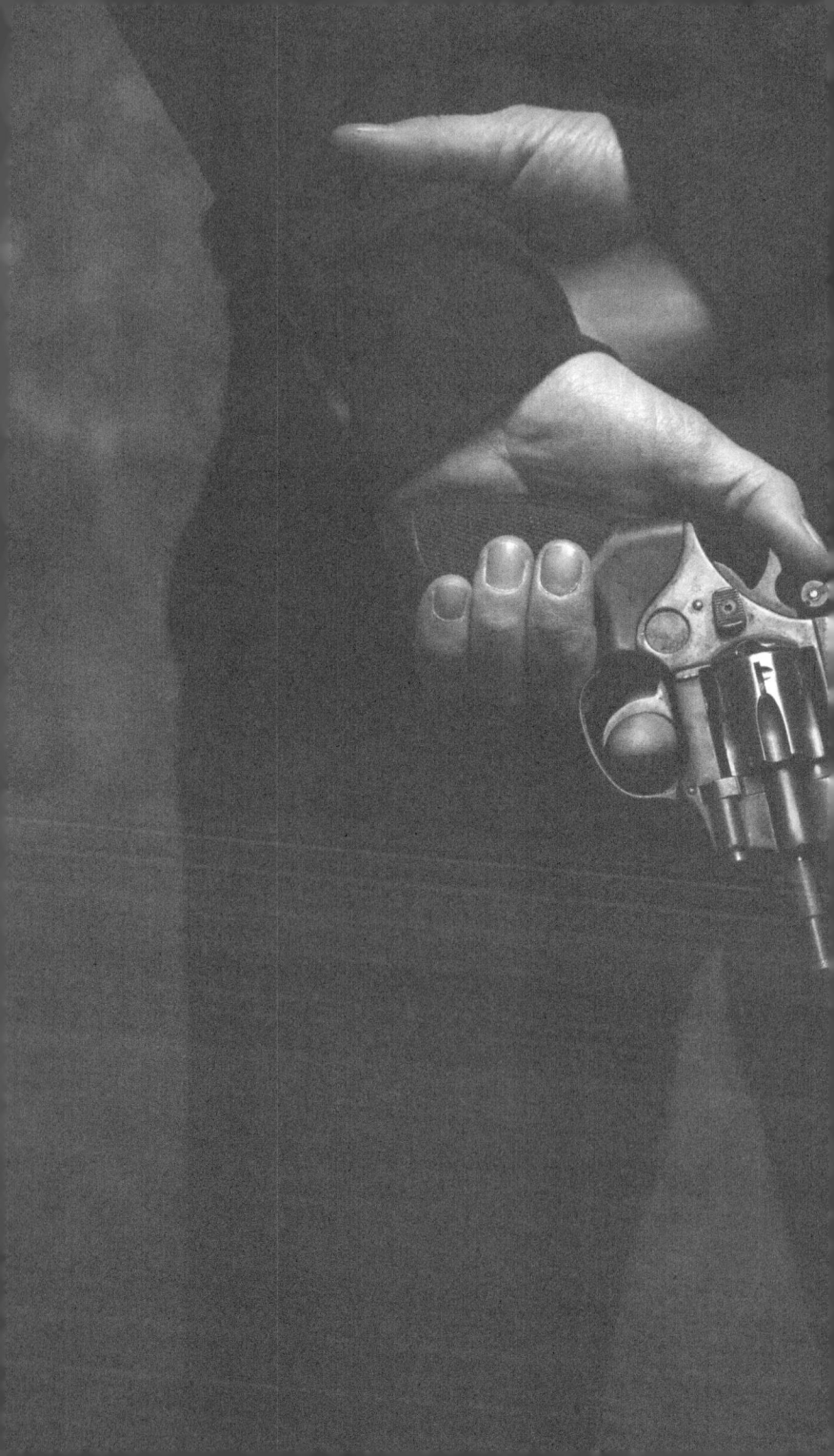

48

A Sliver of Revenge

Jessica

WHEN I FIRST SAW that ginger-looking dude, I did a double-take. It was my own immature idiocy that had me cursing out loud when I realized who it was. And then, of course, they spotted me, and it was too late for me to make a break for it.

So, I did the only thing I could think of.

I played nice and friendly.

Which, given my current reputation, was a mistake because, if nothing else, the likes of Finn McDonald knows who I am, the type of industry I now work in, and the reputation I have at this point in my life.

And that would be someone not to be trifled with.

Unfortunately, I was correct in the assumption he would have an inkling who I am now, and he immediately called me out on my bullshit.

Now, I can't say that I was totally surprised by his big revelation about that one time we fucked.

The fact that I didn't remember it was a good indication that something was amiss, but by then, it was too late to do anything about it, and if nothing else, it gave me options I wouldn't have had otherwise, given he connected me with my first Hollywood manager. Without his connections, I still would've been at the mercy of my father until I eventually managed to make a life of my own. Taking the Hollywood route set me on a fast track, even if some methods were less than above board.

But still, for him to so callously want to give me a detailed explanation of his obviously premeditated assault of me.

Fuck that.

I had spotted Carolina lurking in the shadows while he was running his mouth. Knowing her opinion of his type of people, I figured it was safe to give her an opening to get a jab in.

I was mildly surprised that she so joyfully stabbed his friend in the throat, but I suppose I shouldn't be shocked by anything at this point.

Camilla screeching in when she did was a nice bonus.

Since she knows most of the people in this building, she has been most gleefully making her way through it. I never thought I'd meet anyone who could out-crazy Antoinette and Lilith, but Camilla just may do that.

I'm a little disgruntled having to follow this shitbag rather than stab him in the throat, but knowing there's a method to the madness, I follow along as necessary.

I'm sure I'll be given the chance just as soon as we have everything secure, but the urge to say fuck this entire mission and end his miserable life right now is strong.

"You better not be leading us in a fucking circle," I sputter.

Camilla pulls him up by yanking on his arms with a touch more force than is probably necessary, then he turns toward us, glowering as he says, "And what fucking good would that do me?"

I step into him, incapable of keeping my mouth shut as I ask, "So, how did you do it anyway?"

He squints and asks, "Do what?"

"Manage to coerce me into you fucking me?"

He snorts, smirks at me, and retorts, "Drugs, sugar. How else?"

A scream forms in my chest, and I grit my teeth as rage surges inside me. I yank a knife out of Camilla's belt, burying it into his shoulder without hesitation. "Don't fucking call me sugar."

He shouts in pain, fighting to get away from me as I twist the blade. Carolina grabs me from behind, yanking me back as I attempt to pull the knife out of him, wanting nothing more than to stick it somewhere fatal.

Carolina holds me tighter, and after a brief fight, I settle, raising my hands in surrender. "I'm alright. It's fine."

Carolina slowly releases me, stepping back but keeping her hands on my arms as she looks me over. "I'm alright. Seriously."

Carolina nods, and then Camilla laughs behind me. "You got a little fire in you. I like it."

I frown, shoving my shaking hands in my pockets as I shrug. "He pissed me off."

Camilla throws her head back and laughs. "For some reason, I don't think it'll be the last time."

I sigh, motioning for them to continue on. Finn takes a step down the hallway, muttering to himself, and Camilla retorts, "Keep running your mouth, and I'll finish it for her."

He stops muttering, but his gait is slightly slower now that he's injured. We walk down a flight of stairs. Then another. And another. Trepidation runs over me as we sink further and further underground.

We continue walking, and then he stops aside a large metal doorway. Finn throws the huge deadbolt back and shoves the heavy door open, wincing at the pain in his shoulder. He walks into the room, and we follow, and then he flips on a dim light, and I blink at what appears to be a row of large concrete boxes. Or in their current shape, caskets.

"What the fuck is this?" Camilla asks.

"Prisoner storage."

He grabs a box hanging from the wall and pushes buttons. A motor whirs, the chains creaking as they tighten, and the heavy lid starts to rise.

Carolina stoops over, peering into the box, and then she straightens, glaring at him. "Is this a fucking joke?"

He raises his brows and asks, "What do you mean a joke?"

"That's not him," she replies as she points at the box. "I don't fucking know who that is, but it's not Darius."

The cover continues to rise as Camilla looks closer and then adds, "And also, this man is dead."

He drops the controls, walks over to the edge of the box, and looks down as he whispers, "Oh, fuck."

I stare at him with raised brows. "What do you mean 'oh, fuck'?"

"This is the one he was in."

"What do you mean 'this is the one he was in'?"

"This is the fucking box he was in, so if he's not in it, that can only mean one thing."

Camilla, Carolina, and I all glance at each other and then look back at him as he mutters, "That must mean he got out. That means The

Beast is free."

I frown, then laugh. Then Carolina and Camilla laugh with me.

"That sounds like a fucking you problem, then."

Carolina nods, then walks over to me, pulling a knife out of her belt and handing it to me handle first. "You wanna do the honors?"

Finn's eyes widen, and he puts both his hands up in front of him. "Wait, wait. What are you doing?"

Camilla laughs. "If The Beast is free, we have no more use for you."

He gapes at her and stands there shaking his head, looking scared.

I take the knife from Carolina, feeling the weight of it in my hand as I look between it and him, contemplating what I want to do.

I want to. I'd like nothing more than to stab him repeatedly until I appease the fury that swirls inside me.

I look down at the knife again, gripping the handle tightly, imagining how satisfied I'd feel bringing an end to someone who so obviously has no conscience or decency.

A hand on my arm startles me from my thoughts. I look up, meeting Camilla's eyes as she smiles at me. "It's okay if you don't want to."

I press my lips together, a short, pained sob escaping as I nod and hand her the blade. She takes it from me easily, understanding in her eyes as she leans in close. "Don't worry. I got you."

I return her smile, nodding as I blink back tears. She looks to Carolina, nodding toward the door. "You two go on. I'll tend to this and meet you outside."

Then Carolina is beside me, her hand extended.

I look back at that fucking asshole, my lip curling in disgust before I turn away, taking Carolina's hand and allowing her to lead me away.

Camilla's laughter echoes behind us, and I smile to myself as the first plea falls from his lips.

But I keep walking, and I don't look back.

49

A Divide

Matt

I REMAIN IN THE shadows as the girls walk by me.

Watching them until they disappear around a corner, I then turn into the doorway, leaning against the doorjamb and watching Camilla take a moment longer than absolutely necessary to eliminate that ginger-haired dude.

Part of me wanted to intercede and have a little fun with him myself, but knowing time is of the essence at this point, I refrained. She turns away from his crumpled body, a smile on her face, and her eyes connect with mine.

She doesn't even flinch, as if she knew I was there the entire time.

Which she probably did.

I return her smile and ask, "Was that as satisfying as it looked?"

She nods shortly and says, "Would rather have taken my time with him, but we get what we get."

I laugh, knowing exactly what she means but still slightly surprised, given I'm not talking to Tony. I raise a brow at her and then ask, "Are you really this certifiable, or is part of it an act?"

The smile falls from her face, her expression turning pensive, and then she answers, "This is 100% who I am. I've tried to fake it, but that usually just makes it worse."

"I never thought I'd meet another woman who is equally or more certifiable than Antoinette and Lilith, but here I am. Intrigued."

She smiles at me almost saucily and winks. "Just think. Under different circumstances, you could have had me."

Now, I laugh outright, shaking my head. "Oh. You would not be happy with someone like me."

She frowns and asks, "And why not?"

"Because deep down, I'm far too submissive for you. You need a man who will meet you head-on and never back down."

"And do you maybe have a recommendation?"

I squint at her, thinking over my response for a moment, before replying, "I think you already have someone in your sights."

The smile falls from her face, turning somewhat coy as she shrugs again. "Maybe I do, maybe I don't."

Part of me wants to razz Kaian about his impending future, but the other part prefers to watch it unfold in real-time. It's not like I'm not an old hand at that, given my experience with Dare, Tony, and Declan. Watching the mighty fall to their woman is one of my favorite pastimes, after all.

I smile at her knowingly. "Don't worry. I won't tell."

She rolls her eyes and snorts as I walk further into the room, looking over the array of concrete boxes. A shiver goes down my spine, having spent some time in similar places and remembering it as being an unenjoyable experience.

"Do you think these other ones are empty?"

Camilla looks over the boxes and then says, "If anything, the two on either side of the open one might contain something, but you'd think they would be yelling?"

We both stop speaking, walk closer to the boxes, and bend forward, and then I smile. "I hear something."

Camilla moves to the end of one box, and I move to the end of the other one, and we both use the control to slowly open the lids.

I drop the controller, moving over to the side of the open box and peering in to see Ivan's relieved face. I smile, kneeling as I say, "Well, how did you get here?"

He blinks up at me, intermittently squeezing his eyes shut until, finally, he squints at me. "Just lucky, I guess?"

I laugh. "Pretty lucky you didn't get blown up."

He cocks his head at me and is silent, but then he says, "Good point."

I look over at Camilla and ask, "Who's in that one?"

She looks over at me but says nothing, a look of concern on her face. So, I rise and walk over, kneeling next to her and looking into the box. "Do you think he's dead?"

Dread settles over me as I look at the still form of Seamus. Dread at the fact that it seems likely the man died saving one of mine. And also dread at what his death will mean for Jessica and me.

Camilla reaches her hand in, pressing it against his neck for not even a second before yanking it back. She looks at me, resignation in her eyes as she says, "Yeah, that seems dead dead."

I reach a hand out, resting my fingers on the top of his hand, feeling how cold he is and that waxy, unworldly feeling that comes on when you're just shy of too late.

Ivan slowly climbs out of the box, rolling onto the floor and getting his bearings before finally rising to his feet. He limps over toward us, stopping beside me as he whispers, "He saved us."

I look up at him in surprise because, given everything Seamus has said, the idea that he risked his own life, never mind the lives of his people, to save Darius is shocking.

Ivan laughs almost bitterly as he adds, "Well, he saved Darius. I just got to tag along."

Camilla and I both stand, and I rest my hand on Ivan's arm as I ask, "Did you not have a chance to run?"

He smiles almost sheepishly. "Run to what?"

"Maybe run for your life?" Camilla interjects blandly.

He shakes his head and then answers, "Run for my life, knowing I willfully left someone behind?"

I smile, and Camilla snorts, "If saving that life would've been completely fruitless, yes."

"Well, I guess in this case, it worked out," he replies seriously. "If I had escaped initially when I had the chance, then I wouldn't have been there to lead the two of them to safety."

His gaze moves back to Seamus, and then he says, almost sadly, "Well, at least I saved him from being blown to smithereens."

"No one wants to be smithereens," Camilla jokes.

Ivan frowns at her but says nothing, and so I add, "And you've also gained something to run to in the future."

"What do you mean?" he asks.

"You risk your own life to save someone you had no personal relationship with. We won't be forgetting that."

He gives me a closed-mouth smile and then nods.

Camilla sighs as she turns to me. "How do you think Jessica's going to take it?"

"It's hard to say. At first, she probably won't be too bothered, but it's likely the more time goes on, the more affected she'll be by it."

"If you don't need me for whatever you're doing," Ivans says and sighs. "I'd like to get him out of here."

"Please do. It's best if we have a body. And since the majority of people won't know who you are, it's safer if you exit the building as well."

"Quickest, likely safest route is to head straight down the hallway and then keep to the right up the stairs. Once you're at ground level, the back exit is right there." Camilla hands him a set of keys, which he pockets, and then she steps in close, her expression serious as she whispers, "There's a windward blue '69 GTO parked in the alleyway to the left of that door. If you hurt my car, I will hurt you."

Ivan's eyes widen comically, but before he can reply, she smacks him on the arm and laughs. He looks at me, and I shrug, not having the first clue how to explain her and not really caring to try.

It doesn't take long for Camilla to locate some large garbage bags, and then we help Ivan remove Seamus from the box, no easy task given his state. Once we secure him properly, Ivan hefts him into a fireman's carry and walks toward the door. He stops in the doorway, turning back to me with a sad look. "I'll make sure he's tended to properly until you can come for him."

"Thank you," I answer honestly. "We appreciate you."

He frowns slightly, opening his mouth as if he's going to say something further, but then he closes it. He gives me a curt nod, turning and heading back through the door, disappearing into the darkness.

Camilla walks over to me, stopping beside me and looking down the hallway. "I suppose we should get back to it."

I nod, motioning for her to proceed me. We hustle down the hallway, continuing downward, since typically, that's where all the bad shit goes down, and soon, we end up in another cavernous room.

Camilla stops short, raising her hand to indicate that I should wait. She cocks her head, obviously listening for something, so I do the same. At first, there's nothing but silence. But then, voices and heavy footfalls get increasingly closer.

Camilla grabs me, swinging me around and pushing me off to the side, just as a man flies by, quickly followed by a horde of men running by, obviously intent on the hunt.

I step back from the wall, moving so she's standing in front me. "For fuck's sake, Cami. Do you have to be so rough?"

She doesn't say a word. She just stands there, staring wide-eyed at something over my shoulder. A shiver runs down my spine, and I whisper, "Someone's behind me?"

She nods minutely. "Run."

I don't bother looking behind me to see what she's talking about. I grab onto her wrist, yanking her through the doorway, and we take off at a sprint, the ominous thunder of shoes on concrete driving us blindly.

Camilla looks over at me as we run, shouting, "We need to get to the dock exit."

I don't reply. Instead, I change gears as we slow, intent on them following us. Needing them to take the bait.

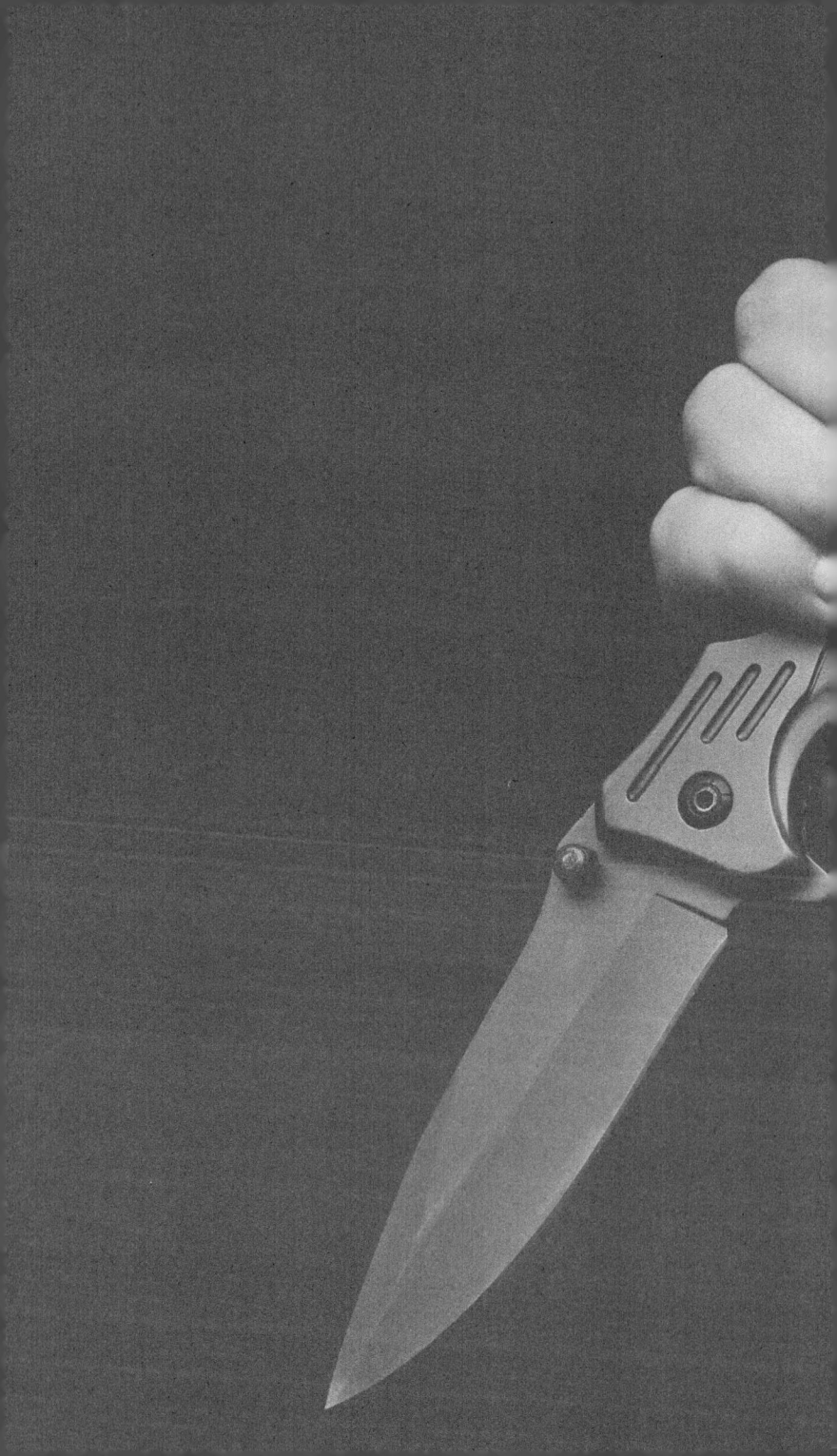

50

We All Fall Down

Jessica

"FUCKING STOP IT."

Startled, I stop moving down the hallway, turning to face Carolina as I say, "Excuse me?"

"She's talking to me," Antoinette retorts, having met up with us a ways back. She crosses her arms over her chest, a petulant expression on her face as she glares at Carolina.

Carolina steps into her, glaring right back as she says through gritted teeth, "Your inability to focus is going to get someone killed."

"Fuck you," Antoinette snarls. "There's nothing wrong with my focus."

"Don't try to pretend you're not on the lookout for Dare."

Antoinette frowns and presses her lips together as she glances away.

Carolina's expression softens as she adds, "I get it. I would totally do the same thing. But we have to focus on the mission, and the mission isn't to find him."

"And let's not forget," I add. "There are four other men out here who look like Darius."

Both women turn their focus to me, the coolness of their gaze making me squirm a bit as I smile awkwardly. Then Antoinette giggles and replies, "Can you imagine four Dares for real?"

"Sounds like an epic why choose," Carolina retorts. They both laugh, and then we're all headed down the hallway again, them focused on the task at hand and me suffering from whiplash at how quickly they change gears.

We creep through the building, listening for any sign of people in our way, but we manage to make it down a floor into another large room without incident.

Antoinette stops in the doorway, raising her hand to indicate we're to wait, and then she peers around the corner. She listens intently for a beat, her brow furrowed as she squints off into the distance. Carolina makes an impatient noise and pokes her in the side, making Antoinette slap at her hand blindly in retaliation.

I shake my head, not quite accustomed to their foolery in high-stress situations, though I suppose I best get used to it, considering this is my life now—no takebacks.

Shouting behind us draws our attention away from the room, and we all turn, slowly backing into the room and moving to the side as we await what's headed our way at a quick speed.

I blink, straining to see in the dim light, and then Darius appears, sprinting down the hallway at top speed. Antoinette steps out, her eyes wide with excitement, a smile blooming on her lips that's quickly extinguished when he shouts, "Run."

None of us wait to find out what the rush is. We turn heel and take off into the room, and I move into position behind Antoinette, following her lead.

Darius quickly overtakes us, rushing ahead and taking the lead as we all race away from what sounds like a mob of people. We run faster, my lungs screaming for air and my legs burning from exertion, the sound of a murderous crowd pushing us up, up, up from the deep belly of the building until we burst out a doorway.

We stop running a few yards from the exit, all of us turning to see who will follow. Antoinette speaks incoherently to Darius, and I look over as she frowns and then shakes her head. I take a closer look, immediately recognizing the small mark on his neck, indicating this Darius is actually a decoy.

Tony.

The door bursts open again, revealing another Darius coming out at a sprint, quickly followed by Camilla. The two of them run to us, and I see this Darius is Matt, as Camilla yells, "Fucking move it. They're coming," as they run by us without slowing.

We wait a beat until the door explodes, and two more Dariuses run through, immediately followed by Lilith and then a whole mess of angry men. These new Dariuses bolt toward us, the look on their faces enough to have us all turn tail and run.

Tony and Matt take the lead, and we all follow, knowing exactly where we're headed and needing the swarm of bad guys to follow us.

Because we can't very well blow up a building in downtown, so the next best option was leading them to an outside location where they can be corralled and dealt with accordingly.

We make it to the ship in record time, barely managing to find the balance between wanting to be followed and not wanting to be caught just yet. A walkway leading onto the ship has been left in place, and I run up it between Matt and Tony.

Antoinette and Camilla are right on my heels as we race up the middle of the ship, but then Matt stops short, and I run into the back of him.

"What the fuck are you doing?" I mutter as I give him a shove.

A gasp behind me gives me pause, and I turn to find Antoinette behind me, her eyes staring beyond Matt in shock. "What the actual fuck?"

I whirl around and peer around Matt, my eyes widening as two more Dariuses stand there, staring back at us. One looks thunderous, and the other looks smug, and then, in a blink, they're gone, one giving chase to the other.

"How the fuck is there an extra Darius?" Antoinette sputters.

Camilla raises both hands in the air. "I have no fucking idea. But if I can get close enough, I'll know which one isn't our Darius."

Antoinette nods, then shakes her head briefly as if she's trying to clear her thoughts. She turns to who we assume are our Darius decoys and says, "Get rid of the disguise."

She doesn't wait for a reply. Instead, she takes off with Camilla, running in the direction of the other two Dariuses, knowing if there's anything shady with these four, it will be handled.

Within seconds, the masks are peeled off, revealing Matt, Tony, Declan, and Kaian. All four appear relieved to be themselves again.

I meet Matt's gaze, my half-smile matching his for only a brief moment, and then we all turn and race after Antoinette and Camilla.

Kaian and Declan take off in one direction as I follow Matt and Tony along the large freighter, completely awed by how massive it is, even while scurrying like a fool. Matt motions between a stack of containers, and I take off down it, locating the ladder that's rigged there and hurrying up it.

The containers are stacked six high, and though I'm not opposed to heights, running from bad people on top of stacks of metal has my nerves on edge.

The others join me as I carefully run across the tops of the containers, but then I slow as two people come into view on the stack across from us.

"Motherfuck," Matt snarls from beside me, and I turn to him, my heart jackhammering in my chest. He frowns, cursing under his breath as he looks around, only to once again focus on the stack of containers across from us as two more bodies pop up.

Tony appears on my other side, cursing the same as Matt, and then he spits out, "This was not part of the fucking plan."

"Everyone else set?" Matt asks, his eyes still watching the scene play out across the way.

"Yes," Lilith answers from behind me. "Locked and loaded and ready for shipment. We just have to go in and get the stragglers."

"We have to get over there."

Tony shakes his head, a helpless expression on his face. "There's no quick way. Can you get a shot?"

Matt shakes his head, then moves to the very edge of the container, looking down for a moment, and then back up to the edge of the other containers.

"Don't even fucking think about it," I mutter.

He raises his brows at me, shrugging as he goes to speak, but a shriek cuts him off.

I look back across the aisle. Camilla is now in hand-to-hand combat with someone we're assuming is not our Darius. The man manages to shove her off, stepping in and kicking her square in the chest, sending her to the ground. She rolls onto her front as the man moves in on her, obviously intent on causing more harm, but then Antoinette is there.

He gives Camilla another solid kick, effectively knocking her out of the way where she lays there, stunned, then he turns on Antoinette.

The other Darius appears, drawing Antoinette's attention away just long enough for the man to grab her, and he spins her so her back is pressed against his front.

She reaches back with both hands, scraping her nails down the man's face without mercy, and within seconds, the intricate Darius mask gives way, revealing a haggard face twisted with fury.

Bloody welts rise on his cheeks and over his eyes as Antoinette continues to assault him, going completely wild in his hold. He manages to snag her wrist with one hand, but she hits him again with her free one, oblivious to the man reaching behind him.

He pulls a gun out, whirling it viciously, catching her in the side of the head, and she stops fighting. Blinking dazedly, she sways on her feet, and then she's staring vacantly out half-closed eyes.

Darius shouts incoherently, his pained words taken by the wind, but I don't have to hear him to know what he's saying.

No. No. No.

Then he's running, blindly racing toward the edge, where the man is standing next to Antoinette who is weaving precariously, an evil grin on his distorted face as he turns the gun toward Darius.

But Darius doesn't slow.

He doesn't pivot, parry, or even attempt to dodge the inevitable bullet that erupts from the barrel of the gun he's staring down. He races straight as an arrow, taking the shortest path possible in the hopes of saving her.

Even knowing it's coming, the crack of the shot still startles me. We're all standing there in a row, too far away to intervene, the angle of our view too sharp to attempt to take him out as Darius bears down on him.

He lets off a couple more shots, but Darius keeps coming, a bellow of rage emitting from within him, echoing through the dock and sending a vibration of energy through all of us. I shiver in response.

The man smiles wider, dropping his empty weapon as he uses both hands to shove an almost limp Antoinette to the side. She teeters there, right on the edge of the containers, like a slow-motion ballet of gravity.

And then, she's gone.

Darius doesn't slow as he runs into the man head-on, his low rumble of rage a vibrato of fear that surrounds us as he sweeps him up, driving him over the edge with a scream.

Then, they both disappear, followed by a succession of splashes.

And then all there is is silence.

51

Toward the Light

Darius

I CAN SAY WITH certainty that in the many instances where I thought I was going to die, my life did not flash before my eyes.

Hindsight being what it is, it would appear that the reason behind this was simply because my life, as it was, just wasn't of any great consequence.

And it's not lost on me the complete ridiculousness of this entire scenario, but here I am, once again, watching her fall.

Just as before, agony and rage cut through me, but this time, Tony isn't here to keep me back, to be the voice of reason, to stand between me and the edge.

And then that bright light settles around me, a sweet vibration of rage that I can taste in the back of my throat. I'm completely blind to caution, blind to the imminent danger directly in front of me.

The man now has half my face so twisted with anger and malice that I can't even fathom what I possibly could have done to him, given the fact that he still breathes. He stares me down, a twinge of recognition settling over me, followed by a coldness I have to shove aside as I focus on the here and now.

Maybe I would've got the jump on him if I'd kept my fucking mouth shut, but all the rage bubbled up inside me, erupting from my mouth as I started toward him. Antoinette offered a bit more distraction, but once he throttled her, she stood there dazed, standing on the brink of unconsciousness.

She steps back, weaving and teetering on the very edge of the container, one wrong move short of toppling over the edge and plummeting the equivalent of six stories into the harbor.

I'm not even fifteen feet from them, but I know I'm not going to make it. Desperation builds and boils over when his hand moves and the revolver is aimed at me.

I don't flinch, I don't waver, I keep barreling forward. And then, for the second time in my life, I watch my heart, my very own breath, disappear off an edge, plummeting into the unknown.

The bang of the gun cuts through the silence, but it doesn't deter me. He continues to shoot, and I continue to come until he's standing there, frozen in time with an empty weapon that falls to the ground as he braces himself for impact.

I don't slow at all. I ram into him full throttle, putting my shoulder down in the last second and jamming it up into his solar plexus as I lift him off the ground, the intensity of my forward momentum, launching us off the side of the container into space.

And it's in this moment that I completely understand Antoinette's previous inclination. Take them to hell with you.

There is no moment of being suspended in air or time. We're instantly falling, gravity taking hold of us and yanking us straight down into the water.

I lose my grip on him, but I immediately reach out, searching with my arms and legs until I make contact. He fights me, and I shove him down, wrapping my arm around the front of his throat, attempting to lock in the hold.

He twists, shoving me away as he kicks out, catching me in the chest. The force of his foot in my sternum jars me, and I release him. He quickly becomes a dark shadow, suspended in a current that's pulling him God only knows where.

I can't see much, dark saltwater distorting my vision as I swim toward one shadow and then another, desperate to have one of them be Antoinette.

And then she's there, clear as day.

Maybe it's the lack of oxygen, maybe it's the loss of blood, but I chuckle, shaking my head at the impossibility of it all.

Or maybe this is my life flashing before my eyes.

Maybe this clear vision of her in the murky depths of the ocean is a sign that my time is up. Maybe she's also gone, and she's come back for me with my ticket to paradise.

I'm not even mad.

Because at the end of the day, knowing I will never have to live one single day without her brings me peace.

I reach my hand out, stretching my entire body toward her as pain explodes in my torso. I force myself not to retract, to not fold into myself to ward off the agony. Her eyes widen as they lock with mine, fear and resignation mingled with love radiating from her gaze, and I reach harder, determined to grab her, to save her, to keep her.

Somehow, the water darkens further, dusky clouds floating along the periphery of my vision, and I'm suspended there, arm out-stretched, as our fingertips just touch.

I smile.

Light explodes in my vision.

And I let go.

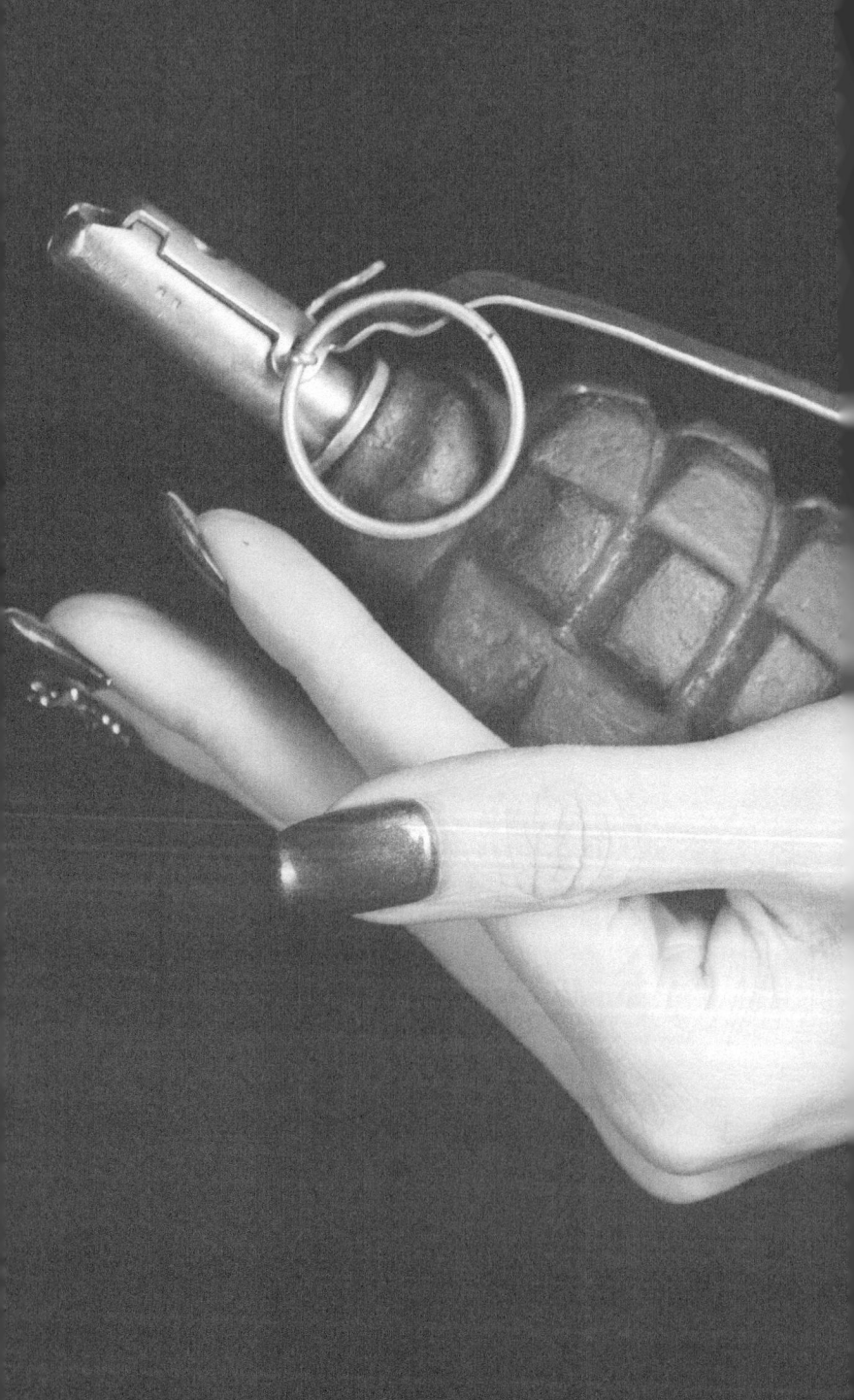

52

The Devil May Come

Jessica

DECLAN, MATT, AND TONY take off at a sprint, running recklessly across the giant tower of containers toward the ladder.

They all but fall down it, their feet running before they've fully touched the deck, and they're racing toward the side of the ship where Darius and Antoinette fell.

It takes the rest of us a minute longer to get down the ladder, and by the time I'm maneuvering through the narrow gap between container stacks, the three of them are leaned over the rail, shouting.

But no one's there.

No one answers.

I scan the dark water, stepping right out onto the edge and bending down as far as I dare, but there's nothing. No air bubbles, no agitated water indicating something is beneath, struggling to break to the surface.

Declan is already in the water, having left a trail of clothing in his wake. Tony has his shirt off; his boots half-kicked off, and his phone and weapons in a pile at his feet. He dives into the frigid water without hesitation, disappearing beneath the surface as we look on helplessly.

Matt pulls his shirt over his head, bending and unlacing his boots as he turns to Kaian and says, "Call in for help and then take the girls and make sure this is fucking done. Make sure every fucking last one of those motherfuckers is dead, and if they're not dead, then make them fucking dead."

Kaian nods, looking at me and Camilla expectantly as he pulls his phone from his jacket pocket. We both step toward him, ready to make good on the mission. He types out a message, pocketing the phone before turning to Lilith and Carolina. "You coming?"

They turn distraught faces to him, and my breath catches in my throat, sadness and anger boiling in my guts at the thought that Darius and Antoinette won't be found.

I take a shuddering breath in, intent on controlling myself as Matt dives into the bay, but all I want to do is throw myself in after him. To protect him. To shield him from whatever pain might find him.

"Focus."

Kaian's sharply spoken word draws my attention back to him.

He gives each of us a sympathetic look, then scowls. "I know not thinking about what's going on in the water is difficult, but right now, you all need to keep your head in the game. We're going back in there, not knowing how many people we're up against, which means we all need to be on guard and ready. Do you understand?"

I swallow the lump in my throat and nod. Everyone else nods as well, and Kaian pulls the backpack off his back, dropping it on the ground in front of him and unzipping it. He pulls out a weapon, checking that it's loaded, and then hands the bag to me. "You know how to use any of that?"

I roll my eyes at him and snort. I don't bother replying; instead, I fish around inside the bag until I find a standard nine-millimeter. I pull it out, hand the bag over to Lilith, and then go through my own checks without any comment. Kaian squints at me and then nods.

Once everyone has refreshed their weapons and ammo, the bag makes it back to him, though now it looks rather empty. He zips it up, places it on his back again, and then turns and walks in the direction of the building. "Let's go get this shit over with."

I fall into step beside him, more than ready to get it over with. "How do we know who to shoot?"

"If they're not standing in this group right now, shoot them."

"That's not a problem," Lilith replies.

Kaian laughs and shakes his head. "This is not surprising coming from you."

"Who was that other man disguised as Darius?"

Kaian shrugs, his pace slowing as we come up on the building. "I have no fucking idea. Hopefully, we'll find him, so we'll know."

"Maybe Dare knows," Carolina interjects. "And he'll tell us when we find him."

I grit my teeth, sudden pain echoing in my chest, and I squash it down. Clearing my throat again, I align myself against the wall by the door right next to Kaian. "I'd sure like to know how he had such a good disguise."

Camilla barks out a bitter laugh. "Me fucking, too. Because whoever did that's also going to fucking die."

Kaian gives her a strange, almost hostile look. "You worried you're going to have a little competition in the old illusion business?"

She glares at him but says nothing, so Kaian turns, putting his hand on the door, waiting for us all to line up with him.

He pulls the door open, and Lilith immediately steps through it, gun drawn. She does a quick side-to-side and then motions for us to follow. "We'll have to split up. Some of us can go right, the others can go left, so if nothing else, be careful not to shoot each other."

Camilla, Lilith, and Carolina head off to the right while Kaian and I break off to the left. For the first few minutes, the place is quiet, but then we hear far-off gunshots, indicating the others have engaged somewhere in the building. We take turns scoping around corners and being back up. After a few long minutes, I peek around a corner at a T-intersection, immediately falling back when met with a bullet into the wall.

Kaian motions that he'll go straight across, using his fingers to count down. Three. Two. One. Then he takes off, and I immediately drop down, bringing my upper body along the floor in such a way my gun is pointed down the intersecting hallway.

Sure enough, someone sticks their head out, taking a shot at Kaian. Luckily, they miss. I do not.

I remain in this position, my gun still pointed at potential targets. Kaian peeks around the corner and then quickly steps out, keeping his body pressed against the wall, as I quickly rise to my feet and get in position with him.

There's no great way to walk down the hallway. Regardless of how careful we are, someone could easily come up behind us or jump out in front of us, so all we can do is attempt to remain as aware as possible in the hopes that we'll get them before they get us.

Kaian stops when he gets to the man I shot. He pushes him with his foot until he rolls on his back, and then Kaian smirks at me. "Good shot."

I shrug dismissively, knowing full well what an excellent markswoman I am, even under extreme pressure. He doesn't wait for me to reply; he simply kneels, pulling the radio from where it had fallen under the man's body. He grins at it, then turns his smile on me before motioning ahead of him for us to continue.

One thing we found from our research and cross-referencing what Kaian and Matt knew is that this place is an intricate web of hallways and tunnels that all lead back to the same place.

A great fucking hall, much like the one where all the fucking bull-shit happened.

I grimace, not at all looking forward to going to that place but knowing I have little choice in the matter, considering our goal is for all of us to be there without any potential threats.

Because all the potential threats will be dead.

Somehow, we manage not to run into anyone else on our journey, but each new hallway we encounter is met with the far-off sounds of gunshots elsewhere.

This means, according to Kaian, everyone else is getting to have all the fun.

I'm feeling more relieved than let down, most likely because I'm not accustomed to being surrounded by people who deserve to die.

After a short amount of time, which feels like hours, we make it to the doorway leading into the hall. I start to walk through but then hesitate, and Kaian walks into the back of me. "What the fuck, Jess?"

I step back, turning to him as I frown. "This place gives me the ick."

He raises his brows at me, giving me an obviously befuddled look. "The ick? Really?"

I sigh, suddenly having difficulty meeting his gaze for how completely ridiculous I sound. "Yes, the ick."

His expression softens, and he takes a step toward me, resting his hand on my arm as he whispers, "Nothing like that will ever happen to you again."

I wince, embarrassment and horror washing over me at the reminder he was there for that. I allow myself a moment to live there, and then I shake it off. I lift my head and straighten my spine, taking a deep breath and then replying firmly, "Fucking right."

"You good?"

"Yes. Let's fucking do this."

He moves to go ahead of me, but I stop him, not wanting anyone to think I'm not at least capable of faking it until I make it.

I walk in silently, keeping myself to the far recesses of the room, where it's still dim. I inch around, keeping some of the larger pillars between me and the voices on the far side.

We creep to the far corner from where we came in, and I get a clearer view of the scene that's unfolding.

A group of men stand there all looking rather smug. It appears as if Camilla, Carolina, and Lilith got ambushed, each of them being held by two men. Camilla and Lilith look outraged enough that they're practically frothing at the mouth; however, Carolina stands there calmly, looking almost bored, which is a testament to her history.

One of the men holding Camilla releases his grip on her neck, and he leans close, stroking his hand down her chest as he says something close to her face. She reacts by attempting to bite him, getting a tiny nip in that has the man jumping back in order to avoid serious injury.

He pulls his hand from her chest, giving her a good slap across the face, and for a moment, I'm confused by a soft growling that seems to be happening near me.

I glance over at Kaian, raising my brows in amusement, but then an escalated ruckus across the room draws my attention back to the group of people.

I recognize some of these men from being around before I left. One of them, in particular, was good friends with Finn, and the likelihood that he stood by and watched as I was drugged and assaulted is high.

I turn to Kaian and whisper, "How many rounds do you have left?"

I quickly check my own weapon while he does the same, and then he pulls his backpack off again, pulling out the extra rounds and handing two to me, keeping two for himself. He drops the bag on the ground, immediately changing the magazine for a full one and pocketing the other as a reserve. I follow suit, and then he leans in closely. "Accuracy is key here. Don't stop until they're all dead."

I nod as he steps back, motioning that he's going to circle around and for me to wait. I track him silently while keeping an eye on how things are escalating across the room.

It doesn't take him long to get in position, and though I can't see him clearly, when his first shot goes off, I quickly follow suit.

Half the men are down before the other half has time to react. In the ruckus, Carolina and Lilith escape the men holding them.

Those four men turn their attention to us, attempting to locate and eliminate us, but all this does is open themselves up for our bullets.

The men holding Camilla double down as she fights them. I manage to take one of them out before I start clicking empty. I pull out my last reserve magazine, quickly exchanging it for the empty one and returning my sights to where they were.

The man is now dragging Camilla away. I race around the pillars, bringing my gun up and taking aim again just as a body flies in front of me, obstructing my view. Kaian comes out of nowhere, grabbing Camilla's attacker by the head and bodily pulling him away from her.

He tosses him on the floor, driving the butt of his gun into his face over and over again before he loses his grip on it, and it tumbles to the ground. The man's hands are still trying to push Kaian away, so

Kaian reaches behind him, pulling a blade from its sheath on his back, flipping it in his grip, and swinging it around in one smooth motion.

The man twitches a few more times before his body goes lax. Kaian stands, his chest heaving, with blood splattered all over him. He looks at Camilla, saying something I can't make out. She glares at him, and I quite clearly hear her words. "You can fuck all the way off with that hero bullshit. I was fine."

I close the distance between me and them, completely understanding both sides of the impeding pissing contest, even if neither of them wants to admit it. "Let's get the fuck out of here."

They both snap their mouths shut, but continue to glare at each other, and I slowly turn away. Carolina and Lilith are standing nearby, watching on curiously, and I shrug as I join them, the corners of my mouth twitching as I do my best not to smile.

Kaian and Cami walk over, both of them outwardly disgruntled, but then Kaian looks at Lilith. "Everything secure?"

She nods. "As far as I can tell."

Kaian removes his phone from his pocket, sending off a quick message before pocketing it. "Clean-up crew will be here in thirty minutes."

"They gonna fumigate?"

"Nah, just a thorough extermination for now. Make sure we don't have an infestation hidden somewhere."

"Good plan."

Kaian motions toward the door. "I know the shortest way out back."

We follow him out of the room with less excitement than we normally would under typical circumstances. While I'm relieved to be done in this building, my anxiety and nervousness over the fate of Darius and Antoinette has my guts churning.

It only takes a fraction of the time for us to exit the building, once again on the harbor side. We hurry toward where we last left Matt and Tony, but now, the entire area is illuminated, guiding our way.

My heart sinks at the number of people who are obviously actively searching, and my eyes scan the crowd for Matt.

I locate him further down the terminal, where the massive ship is tethered. They've set up a temporary base, equipment dotting the dock. Men race around, boats slowly maneuvering through the water, and spotlights shining brightly.

I manage to catch his gaze from about twenty feet away. I raise my brows in question, and he shakes his head, the pain on his face cutting and deep. I frown, wanting nothing more than to go to him, to comfort him, but I know now is not the time.

So, I turn to Kaian and rest my hand on his arm. "What next?"

The look he gives me is surprised, but then Lilith, Carolina, and Camilla all gather around, waiting to find out what's next on the list to complete a mission that has otherwise gone to hell.

Kaian sighs then raises a hand, motioning for us to follow him as he turns on his heel and walks away from the dock. "Let's go."

53

Futility

Matt

THIS CAN'T BE FUCKING happening.

"Keep fucking looking," Tony shouts. "There's still time."

I sigh heavily, looking out over the many boats and personnel searching the vicinity for any sign of Antoinette and Darius.

It's been several hours and still, there's no sign of either of them.

I've called in every favor anyone ever owed me, but even with every resource available in on the search, the futility behind it feels imminently inevitable.

A hand on my shoulder startles me. "Matt, how much longer do you want us to look?"

I stare at my Coast Guard contact blankly, unsure how to answer since my most immediate thought is any variation of forever.

He gives me a sympathetic look, his lips pressing together as he contemplates his words. Finally, he nods, then turns without saying anything, barking orders at everyone in his way.

I know he'll do all he can for however long as he can, but at some point, they'll have no choice but to abandon the search for more pressing official business, and it will all be over.

Annoyed, I pull out my phone, scrolling to the number I want and hitting connect. It rings a few times, and then a voice answers, "Shields?"

"Hey, Mark. How's it going?"

He's silent for a moment, likely infinitely confused about why I would be calling, but not so confused that he had deleted my number from his contacts. "What's up?"

I clear my throat, uncertain what exactly I called him for, and after a moment, he says impatiently, "Spit it out, dickhead."

"A five-mile-per-hour current isn't fast, right?"

Again, I'm met with silence, and for a moment, I wonder if he hung up on me. I glance at my phone screen, confirming the call is still ticking on, then put the phone back to my ear just in time for him to reply, "Why are you asking?"

I sigh, not wanting to explain but knowing I have to if I want his professional opinion. "A couple of my people fell into the water. We starting searching for them immediately, but so far, no sign of them."

"From what height?"

"About six containers."

"Which body of water?"

"Boston Harbor."

He snorts, and I'm sure he's rolling his eyes at me through the phone. "From that height, they could end up submerged fifteen feet or so. Current down there may sound slow, but it would be different when viewed from the surface and certainly feel different if you were down there fighting against it."

"But a strong swimmer could get to the surface pretty quickly?"

"Matt," Mark sputters. "People fall off fishing boats in the middle of the day in a busy fishing harbor and are most often found weeks later or never."

I frown. "What does that have to do with this?"

"Everything. It's the middle of the fucking night. They fell the equivalent of more than eight stories, so if they weren't already injured, which, given your track record, I will assume they were, they would most likely have been injured upon impact with the water. Assuming they weren't knocked senseless, the depth they'd have reached by the time they got their bearings enough to attempt to swim to the surface would be nearly impossible to recover from. And just to complicate matters, it would be pitch-black down there, and they'd be dragged down by their clothing. Assuming they were clothed, of course, which could go either way with you."

"So, you're saying what exactly?"

"I'm saying, good fucking luck ever finding them."

Tony catches my attention, and I wave him over. I point to my phone and mouth, "Mark."

Tony's eyes widen, and he makes a face likely because the last thing he wants is scientific information, stats, and facts. Nonetheless, he sighs and asks, "And what does Mark have to say?"

I move the phone from my ear, hitting the speakerphone. "Mark, Tony's here asking what you have to say."

Again, I'm met with silence. Tony looks at the phone, then looks at me questioningly. I shrug, motioning to the phone, and after a beat, Tony takes it from me. "Just fucking spit out."

"Hi, Tony."

"Mark."

I hide my smile behind my hand, not wanting to rile Tony by laughing at his awkwardness. Mark clears his throat and sighs. "Look. I know you all want me to fill your heads with all sorts of rose-colored goodness, but I also know you called specifically because you trust I won't do that."

Tony looks at me, his expression grim, but still, he shakes his head. "No way. No fucking way."

Tony's hand tightens on my phone, and I snatch it back before he can smash it or throw it, as he's known to do. I shove him back when he tries to snatch it from me, turning my back on him as I say, "Thanks for the info, Mark. I appreciate your candidness, as always."

"Anytime. And let me know how it turns out."

"I will. Once we know."

We don't bother with an official goodbye. The call ends as quickly as it began. Then I stand there, staring helplessly out at the water.

"We have to find them," Tony whispers, his voice hoarse.

"I know."

Tony goes silent, his stillness so finite I glance over to see if he's still standing next to me.

He is.

He's staring out at the water, his jaw clenched just like his fists. Then he whirls on me, his hands fisted in my shirt as he leans close and grits out, "Maybe they got out."

I frown, wishing this to be true more than I could ever explain. But I don't. I grab his hands, still fisted in my shirt, holding them tightly as I stare back at him. "If only."

His jaw tightens further, and for a moment, I think he may take a swing at me. I don't even care, but a second later, he eases his grip, then releases me, pushing my back slightly as he steps back.

Then, without another word, he walks away.

And I watch him go.

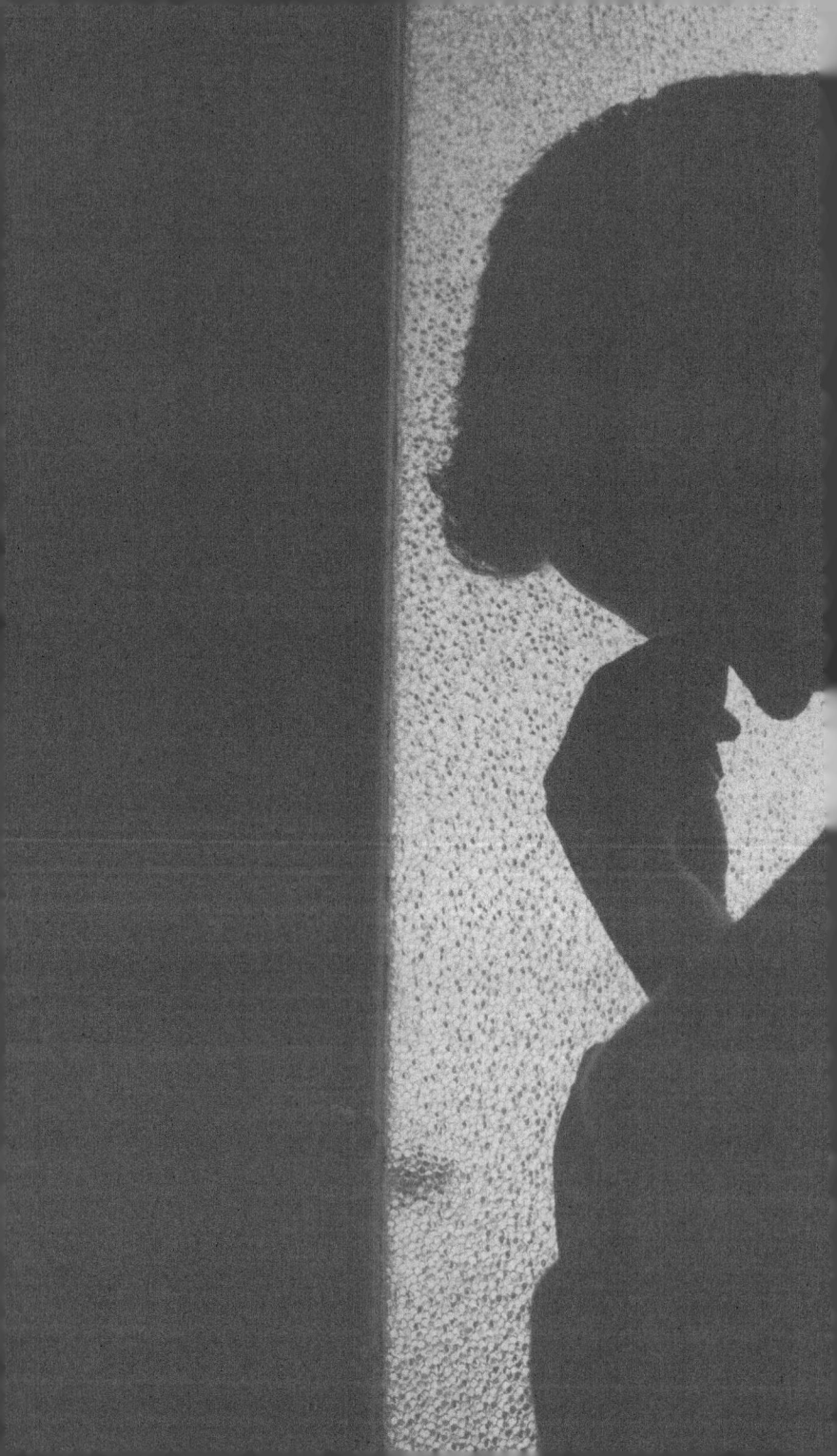

54

Grief and Hope Collide

Matt

THE OVERALL TONE OF the room can easily be described as somber.

At a time when we would otherwise be celebrating a great victory, we're instead bogged down by what can only be described as a crushing loss.

Whenever we prepare for a mission, we always go over our list of pros and cons, doing simple math to establish whether the victory is worth the cost.

In this case, I believe Darius and Antoinette would still consider the victory well worth the loss, even if that loss was at the expense of their own lives.

I'm not so convinced. Lilith, even Tony, a man who is well-known for being able to rationalize necessity, a sacrifice for the betterment of mankind, is battling the sacrifice that feels too great to comprehend.

By the time we were forced to abandon the search, Kaian had received word that all of the individual missions were successful.

This means a huge chunk of the criminal underworld was officially handicapped, some of them even completely out of business.

Any excitement I may have had over this achievement feels muted by the gaping void of our personal loss that's too painful for us to even begin to celebrate.

A crash on the other side of the room draws my attention. I rise from the chair I've been sprawled in for the last hour, walking across the room to Tony as he rage-smashes another computer.

Normally, I would be upset by this, but my own urge to indiscriminately smash inanimate objects tempers my annoyance.

I stop a few feet from Tony, watching the various emotions run through him, taking note of each one and how it feels within me.

Rage is the simplest emotion to manage. It runs hot and thick through your veins, an electric current keeping at bay the sticky emotions you prefer to avoid.

Sadness. Bitterness. Grief.

Carolina's standing off to the side, looking as grief-stricken as the next person, but she's not stunted by the life-long conditioning of burying your feelings.

Her eyes are glassy, and tears stream freely down her cheeks as she looks on helplessly. Her eyes meet mine, and I mouth silently, "I've got him."

Her small smile is grateful, though close-lipped and sad. Then she turns silently, making her way to where Lilith, Issa, and Jessica are sitting.

Another crash drives my attention back to Tony. He's now standing there, wild-eyed, having run out of things to smash. He outright bellows in fury, the outer limits of the sound tinged with anguish.

He twists around, obviously looking for something else to grab. When he comes up with nothing but air, he spins back, losing his balance and toppling to the floor.

He catches himself on his hands and knees, suddenly becoming still and quiet. I close the distance between us, dropping to my knees beside him, resting both of my palms on the top of my thighs as I await his next move.

"It wasn't supposed to be like this," he whispers harshly.

"You're right. It wasn't."

"Part of me doesn't wanna believe it. Part of me feels the mere idea that this is our new reality is completely preposterous and impossible."

"Same."

He pushes his upper body back and swings his legs around so he's sitting on the floor with his knees bent. He leans forward, crossing his forearms across the top of his bent knees as he hangs his head. "This fucking hurts, man."

"Fucking right, it hurts," Declan interjects as he seats himself next to Tony, throwing an arm over his shoulder and yanking him closer.

Tony stares at him with watery eyes, snorting as he attempts to shake him off. "Get the fuck off of me, Dec."

"No."

I laugh, a bit envious of Declan's ability to manage his emotions given any situation. Complete transparency has always been his baseline, and today will be no different.

He looks at me, and the distinct lack of hope in his eyes cuts me like a knife. Pain rockets through me; my attempt to choke it back down only makes it more shocking. Tony shakes his head as he says, "I'm scared letting myself grieve is like giving up hope."

Declan's arm around his shoulders tightens as he gives him a little shake and says softly, "Grief and hope go hand-in-hand, Tony. Sometimes, the only way to survive the pain is to let it rip you open."

I can count on one hand the number of times I've ever witnessed Tony shed a tear. And even with those times, I likely have a few fingers to spare.

Now, I likely won't have enough fingers to keep count.

Tony inhales a ragged breath, immediately expelling it as tears begin to fall with such ferocity they don't even have a chance to touch his skin. I watch them fall into his lap, giving up my idiotic idea that I'm capable of holding the tears back.

It's quiet; there are no wailing sobs or anguished screams.

Carolina appears on Tony's other side. She sits beside him, scooting in close, wrapping one arm around his shoulder and her other gripping his front.

Issa kneels behind Declan, her hand resting on his shoulder. He reaches back, snagging her wrist and pulling her until she squeezes between him and Tony.

Jessica sits quietly on my other side, her upper body pressed close to mine. She rests one hand on my back, the other gripping the front of my shirt, and I wrap my arm around her shoulders, pulling her more firmly against me.

Lilith sits in front of Carolina, turning so her side is pressed into Carolina's front, her legs beneath Tony's raised ones. A hand squeezes my forearm, and then he grips me by my elbow, yanking so sharply that I fall forward into Declan. "For fuck's sake, Dec."

"Shut up."

I don't bother trying to escape; instead, I scoot in closer, taking Jessica with me, leaning partially on Declan and partially on Tony as grief envelops us.

More people arrive, silently settling in the middle of the room with us. Kaian is there on my other side next to Jessica, Marieka with him, and Camilla leaning into Lilith.

We remain like that, a group of shattered humans piled beneath crushing grief.

Declan chuckles randomly, and I turn my head to look at him. "What is it?"

He swallows, then clears his throat. "I was just thinking what Dare would say right now if he could see us here like this."

Tony chokes on a laugh and says, "Likely some infinitely clever piece of wisdom that would make us wanna punch him in the face."

"And then there's Toni," Lilith retorts. "She'd be throwing words of encouragement to get it all out."

"With a prisoner hug for every last one of us," Carolina adds sadly.

We all laugh for a moment, that one tiny anecdote managing to dull the pain just enough that I can take a deep breath without feeling like I'm going to choke on it.

But none of us move.

We remain here, suspended in this place where grief and hope collide.

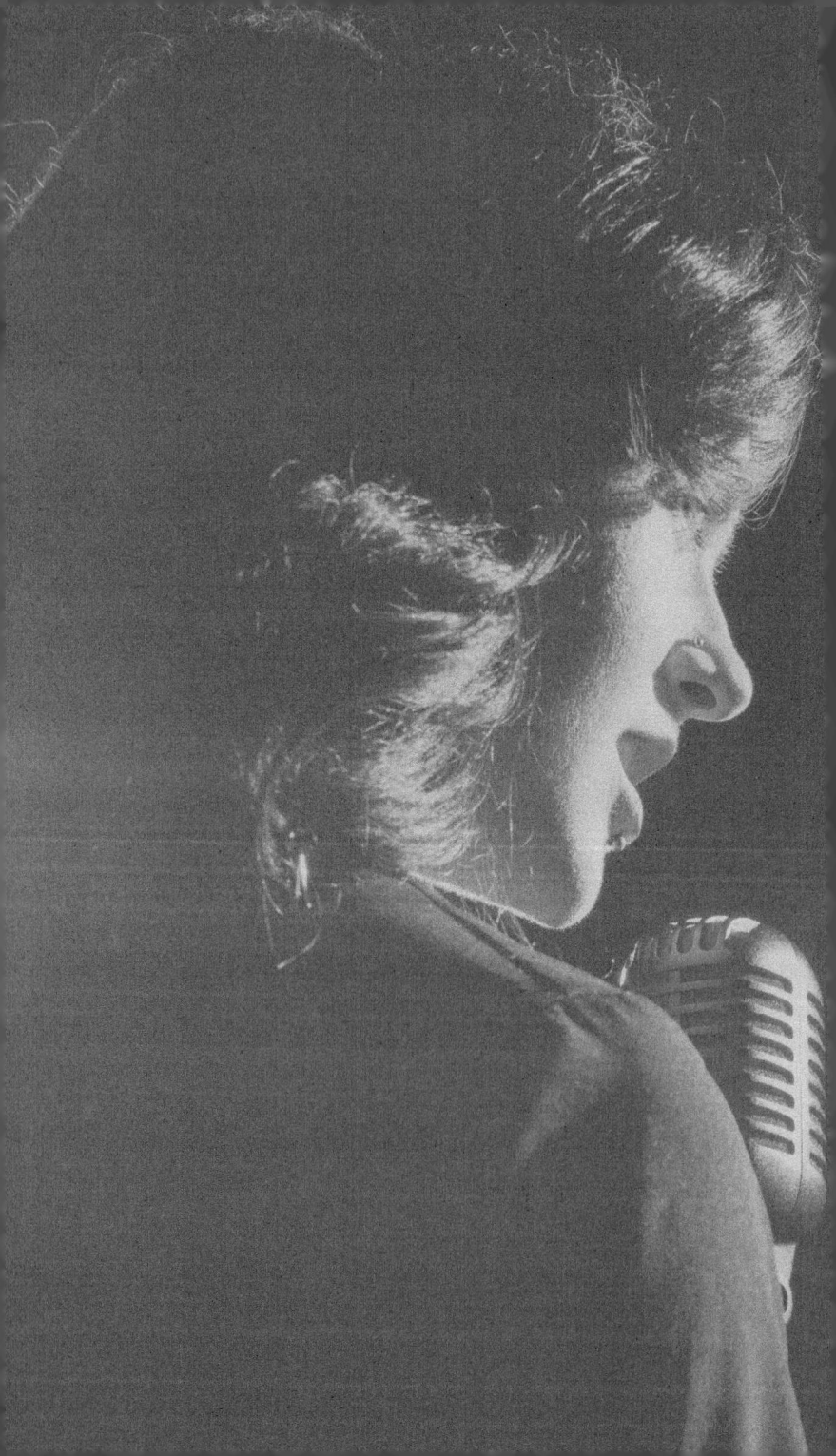

55

The Final Curtain

Issa

It's been a fucked-up month.

The sudden loss of Darius and Antoinette immediately threw everyone into a tailspin.

As one of the newer family members, my interactions with the beloved couple had been minimal. But that doesn't mean I'm not finding the shock cutting and painful. And the worst part is watching Declan suffer one of the greatest losses he is ever likely to live through.

I've been in constant communication with Carolina and Jessica. They, too, have been jockeying between their own grief and the grief of the men they love. Matt and Tony have known Darius for most of their lives, and the bond of the found family oftentimes is stronger than blood.

Each of them has handled it in their own way. Tony tends to resort to violence. He's been making his merry rounds, hunting down those he feels will cause trouble in the future.

Matt is a bit more subtle, though certainly not lacking in vindictiveness.

And then there's Declan.

As with any strong emotion, Declan always takes the same path.

He works himself to death.

We had just entered the last leg of our American tour when Declan was first called back. He ended up canceling a large portion of dates and then tacking them back onto the end. He only gave himself a few days before throwing himself back into the process. This time, leaning heavily on music to give him the strength to keep moving forward.

And that's how we end up here—at the very last tour date on a tour that can only be described as insane.

Initially, this was supposed to be one of our smaller venues, but after canceling two dates in this city, he decided to make it one over-the-top finale in the stadium.

One can't imagine what it's like to hear the roar of a hundred thousand people until you're actually faced with it.

He'd already announced that he would make a big announcement at the show, and he also warned everyone that his sassy-pants wife would be in attendance and joining him on stage at his leisure. His words, not mine.

And then there's the new song that he has been working on for the better part of a month. The song that fought back tooth and nail until he finally reached down into the very guts of himself and ripped it out. It was painful to watch but also fascinating.

And even at sound check, he was saying it wasn't ready, but when I told him he didn't have to sing it, he scoffed at me. Because yes, he did, and yes, he would.

He started the show as he always does, working the crowd up into a frenzy, holding them in the palm of his hands.

And then intermittently, he would call me out, basically having us do a reenactment of our previous live performances. Starting with Stevie Nicks and eventually ending with a new rendition of our rock-opera rap battle. We've done that on a few occasions, always changing the lyrics to suit our current moods and relationship. It's a crowd favorite and quite entertaining for us as well.

Now, the show is over, and he's backstage, preparing for his encore. I'm not entirely sure what he plans on doing, though I know if he's going to sing his new song, this will be the time.

I walk over to him, giving him a nudge with my elbow. "You okay?"

His eyes meet mine, and he sighs loudly as he shrugs. "I'm fine. No problem."

I snort and shake my head at him. "You really going to do this?"

He nods, yanking his sweat-soaked shirt off and quickly replacing it with a fresh one. He picks up his acoustic guitar, strapping it on. Then he looks at me again and asks, "You going to be okay for this?"

I nod, holding up the microphone in my hand. "I got you. No fucking idea what I'm going to say, considering you've given me no heads-up like usual, but I'll manage."

He grins at me, and for the first time in a while, his grin meets his eyes as he steps in close to me, bending down to steal a quick kiss that I don't have time to return. Then he walks around me, heading out onto the stage without further comment.

He's lucky I already know what's going to happen as far as him calling me out there, likely with some kind of joke that only he finds funny.

I move to the edge of the stage, peeking through the curtain so I can see him, but no one will be able to see me in the darkness.

The crowd has been going bonkers, but as soon as he seats himself in the middle of the stage with the spotlight shining on him, everyone goes silent.

He adjusts his microphone in front of him until it's exactly where he wants it, strums a few chords to ensure the sound is ideal, and then pulls his microphone closer, clearing his throat before saying, "Well, hasn't this been a night?"

The audience immediately screams their approval. The bright smile he shows them is genuine, though sadness still twinges his features.

He waits for the noise to die down. When they're all once again silent, he continues, "I know I said I had some news, and I guess this is a good time to say it. No one's going to be very happy about it, but let me assure you, it's not forever."

There are a few negative shouts in the audience, some laughter and random shouts, and he sighs and shakes his head. "Now, let's not pretend it's a big surprise. But I'm not getting any younger, and I've dedicated practically my entire life to my career, and as much as it pains me to do so, I've accepted that I need a break."

There's some clapping and hooting, but for the most part, the tone of the crowd remains excited. He pauses for a few moments longer than he probably anticipated, his jaw clenching as he works to keep himself collected. "My wife and I have plans. We want to expand her entertainment management business. We want to ensure everyone has a safe space as they work to begin or even maintain their career. This expansion will take considerable time, and given how hard we've been working, this seems to be the best time for us to shift our focus."

My eyes burn, a wall of emotion churning in my chest at his first official statement of our immediate future. He glances over at me, a small smile on his lips, and he winks. Then, he turns back to the crowd with a sheepish expression. "And then there's the fact that other than our short honeymoon, we haven't had time to truly sit back and enjoy being married. As time has gone by, and each of us has put considerable time and effort into maintaining our own careers, we've had to spend more and more time apart. Frankly, we don't want to be apart at all—ever."

He waggles his brows, his expression playful, and the crowd cheers, hooting and stomping their feet in reaction. I shake my head, entirely accustomed to his antics, but still, my cheeks burn.

He lets them have their bit of fun and then raises a hand, urging them to calm down. They do almost instantly, and he stares out at them, that tinge of sadness back in his eyes. "As you all know, from the sudden cancellations in my tour schedule, we suffered a great loss to our family. I've been fortunate so far in my life, where though I had known loss, I had never truly known grief. That visceral, soul-altering feeling of anguish. It's easy to sit on the outskirts of such untenable emotion if it isn't actually touching you. But when it comes for you, when someone you truly love is ripped away from you, you find yourself yanked down into an absolute sea of pain. And no matter how much you fight it, regardless of how much you pretend, deny, and put on a front of strength and perseverance, it will get you."

The typical screaming, clapping, and stomping has dulled, his words now echoing sniffles and words of encouragement. He sighs again, shaking his head before continuing, "The only plus, well, I don't really want to call it a pro, but for lack of better words..." He pauses, laughing at himself, and everyone laughs with him. "Listen, y'all know that I'm an over-the-top melodramatic pain in the ass. So, for me, this great loss added fuel to the fire. With great sorrow comes greater creativity, and though I have no idea if this new song is going to be complete shit or not, I feel inclined to sing it anyway."

The crowd roars their approval, knowing, if nothing else, Declan Hughes throwing a brand-new acoustic song at them is something for the ages. He raises his hands again, and the crowd quickly quiets. "First, I need you to once again welcome my wife to the stage."

The crowd immediately starts chanting my name, and I roll my eyes, though I'm happy for the short reprieve from sadness. He looks over at me, and I step through the curtain, turning my mic on and saying into it, "Really?"

He smiles, rising from his seat and meeting me halfway across the stage. He takes my hand, leading me to where one of his stage crew has put another stool out, assisting me to get comfortable before sitting back on his own stool. He adjusts his guitar and microphone again and then looks over at me, the despair in his eyes reflecting the sad smile on his face.

"Fair warning, my wife hasn't actually heard this song." He smirks and shrugs, and the crowd at first gasps and then joins him in his humorous moment. "And it's not just because I like to put her on the spot. In this case, I need her knack for improvisation to fill in the gaps, where either I fuck up or I just need a moment."

I frown, glaring at him. "Well, thanks a fucking lot."

His smile is affectionate, and again, he winks. "You know you love me."

I make a face, bringing my hand up and wiggling it back and forth as I reply, "50/50, sliding scale." I give everyone a few moments to laugh at our little joke, but then I ask, "So just to be clear, you're going to sing your parts, but then if you look like you're fucking up or just need a moment to collect yourself, you want me to jump in and just throw out whatever I feel like?"

"Yes," he replies seriously. "That's exactly what I'm saying."

I raise my eyebrows, grimacing theatrically as I mutter, "Well, this won't be awkward at all."

"What do you all think?" he asks the audience. "Do you think she can handle it?"

The crowd's response is a whole new decibel level. I'm sure quite a few people here have seen our previous concerts, whether live or on streaming, as they're always a crowd favorite. And though this one certainly has a less excitable tone, they likely all think it'll be amazing.

I'm not quite convinced, but if nothing else, it will be something someone writes about tomorrow—good or bad.

Declan shifts on his stool, adjusting his microphone one last time before sitting back, his hands going to his guitar. He looks over at me questioningly, and when I nod, he turns back to the crowd, waiting for complete silence.

Then, his voice rings out in a rough musical whisper. "You dirty, rotten, no-good motherfuckerrrrrr."

I frown. But then he pulls back from the microphone and laughs, almost like he's laughing at his own inside joke.

He clears his throat again, looking out of the crowd as he says, "You know the drill, folks. Just bear with me. I'll get my shit together eventually."

The audience has their laugh and then quiets down, waiting in anticipation for Declan to get his shit together.

His expression turns serious, that sadness morphing and shifting until it's tinged in anger, love, and despair. As if this kaleidoscope of emotions is coalescing inside of his brain in order for him to properly articulate in such a manner that even the most untouched might feel it.

You didn't get my permission

You didn't stop to think about
The rest of us, lost here now without you
One minute, the world spins
And in the very next instant, it stops
Because you're just...gone

I want to pretend it didn't happen
That maybe your existence was a
Figment of my imagination
That faking this new life is feasible
A moment of peace attainable
Where I forget you, even for a moment,
But then, the pain dulls
And the visceral fear of
Never having known you
Rips my guts out
Because who am I without you?

All these complicated emotions
Fire and ice in my veins
When at the end of the day
Everything I have to say
Comes down to
The simplest of sentiments
I miss you
Come back

He stops abruptly, his head turning, eyes shut. I don't hesitate or wait for him to cue me. I pick up my mic and go with it.

Permission, it's amusing, really
This mere idea of control, lunacy

I pause for a moment, allowing Declan's band to kick in some rhythm. Then I close my eyes, picturing Declan in his studio, kicking and fighting to find the words to truly convey his own brokenness.

You're here, then you're not
A heart so unstable that I think we forgot
Forever is a dream, a myth
A romantic's notion of misfits
And heaven forbid, you find yourself
Not suited to the tenacity it takes
To get through it
On days when the pain's too great
And you have to stop fighting
Stop pretending, stop faking
The it's okay, I'm fine bullshit
Where you're forced to dig deep
To let go, to embrace that searing agony
Your fear will drive you over a cliff
Into oblivion, so you say enough's enough
And you give yourself permission
To scream into the void...
I miss you
Come back

I barely manage to choke out the last word, emotion rushing over me like a suffocating blanket attempting to snuff out creativity.

Declan grabs my stool, yanking me closer to him so our legs are touching. His hand moves to mine, and he squeezes, pulling my hand over and placing it on his thigh. I scoot as close as I can get with the guitar in the way, but then his lead guitarist, Connor, appears on his other side, his hand extended.

Declan smiles gratefully, removing his guitar and handing it over without hesitation, decades of trust illuminated in that one exchange.

Connor sits on the stool that has magically appeared on the other side of Declan, then sits quietly, waiting for the cue to continue.

Declan takes a shuddering breath and then nods. Connor picks up the melody, knowing exactly how to play it as Declan collects himself.

Then Declan opens his mouth and sings,

> *We went a decade without a word*
> *years gone by sitting on the sidelines*
> *of our own individual reality,*
> *too stubborn to take the first step*
> *Reconciliation, a foreign concept*
> *Not realizing the clock is ticking*
> *A veritable time bomb, just waiting to*
> *Explode our initial expectations of*
> *All the years we thought we had plans for*

> *Now, all time is lost to us,*
> *Time to refocus and rebuild*
> *A future in stone now turned to glass*
> *And the knowledge that just like you*
> *Time and space and the fucking*
> *Landscape of our future...*
> *It's all...gone*

Gone, never to be made up
No amount of pretending
will resurrect the impossibility
That I will ever get on with it
That there will come a time
Where I wake up and don't think
About what is missing

All these fucked-up emotions
Fire and ice in my veins
When at the end of the day
Everything I have to say
Comes down to
The simplest of sentiments...
I miss you
Come back

Declan's final words come out a broken whisper, and then Connor immediately stops playing, his band picking up a tempo without even needing to be cued. I swallow the lump in my throat, wanting nothing more than to curl up around Declan and soak up every second of his pain, but knowing that will never be possible.

So, I do what we do best. I lift my mic and let the words out.

Time, what a messed-up notion
As if it gives a fuck about you
Or me or how much we depend on
Such things as hope and infinity
How we lie to ourselves habitually
Leading our lives with the arrogant notion

That it won't run out
That we won't be left standing here
With our ass in our hands
As we wax on poetically about love
Lost, while wallowing in deep misery

Some people will say we reap what we sow
That we're weak-willed, willfully
Incapable of moving on from the bad thing
That didn't even happen to us
As we still live and breathe

But fuck that and fuck them
The unsolicited judgment of those
Fortunate enough to never have
Had loss touch them or
Even worse, those who feel they
beat it, they fought grief and despair
And came out the victor, as if any amount
Of time will erase the impact they still have
On your everyday existence
Past, present and future

And so, you continue to dig deep
To let go, to embrace that searing agony
You fear will force you into a purgatory
Of despair, so you say enough's enough,
And you take my fucking hand
As you scream into the dark...
I miss you

Come back

Declan stares at me, all the love and light shining in his eyes, and the tears I've been holding back for the entire night immediately overflow. I don't bother trying to hide them or wipe them away, I allow them to coast down my cheeks, a cleansing balm meant to ease the soul one teardrop at a time.

He leans over, grasping my cheeks between his hands and pressing his lips to mine, not bothering with subtle or finesse. He opens his mouth, his tongue swiping against my lips, demanding entrance. I give in freely, meeting his lips, teeth, and tongue urgently, needing to convey the sheer depth of my emotion where words will now fail me.

And then, just as quickly as he was there, he's gone.

Straightening on his stool, his hand gripping mine tightly, he leans into his mic, his voice soaring over the stadium, pure and guttural.

All these fucked-up emotions
Fire and ice in my veins
When at the end of the day
Everything I have to say
Comes down to
The simplest of sentiments...

I miss you
Come back

I miss you
Come back

Come back

The music fades away, quickly replaced by the buzzing of a crowd overwhelmed by emotion.

He stands, pulling the microphone from the stand as he steps to the edge of the stage, right in front of where Matt, Jessica, Tony, and Carolina have been watching the show.

He reaches down to each of them, speaking quietly to them before stepping back. He looks out over the audience, taking it all in one last time, the smile on his face sad yet also content.

He raises a hand to the crowd, and they settle, allowing him to speak. "I'm truly blessed to have had this career, to have all of you and so many more supporting me, regardless of my antics or how I may handle life in general. I will never forget all that you've given me."

Choking up, he lowers the mic, his eyes looking to the heavens as he takes a deep breath. Then he continues, "I won't say this isn't goodbye because, well, we all know we have no fucking idea what will happen in the future. Be kind, take care of those you love, and never forget that time truly waits for no one. So, grab it by the balls and make it your bitch. I love you."

With those parting words, Declan turns away from the chanting crowd, setting the mic on the stool as he walks by.

Snagging my hand, he leads me off the stage.

And he doesn't look back.

56

You've Got Mail

Matt

I KNEW GOING INTO it that Declan's farewell concert would be an emotional rollercoaster. But even knowing this didn't properly prepare me for how much it would affect me.

By the time we make it backstage, I've managed to get control of myself to the point that I no longer fear I'm going to lose it at any second.

I've spent the last month keeping myself busy, tying up the loose ends of the criminal organizations we managed to dismantle. Once that was complete, I began implementing plans to prevent them from ever rising to power again. Having this daunting task to focus on kept most of the gut-wrenching emotion at bay, but I knew at some point, I wouldn't be able to hide from it anymore.

We've all worked tirelessly to ensure there's no chance that our life's work and the death of Darius and Antoinette won't have been for nothing. This means I've had to come up with an intricate and detailed accounting, which consists of one of the wealthiest people in the world being fictional, with an entire conglomerate of shell companies that have to look real beneath him.

Or, in this case, her.

I have created and utilized every LLC, foundation, corporation—if it could possibly be a moneymaker, I've brought it into the mix.

Luckily, I understand what it takes to keep the government off your back, and I sleep easily at night, knowing my less-than-scrupulous activities are being done for the greater good.

It also helps that the considerable fortunes that we have managed to reap from our work can easily be funneled back into this new business venture.

Along with this came a flurry of interested parties wanting to get in on expanding our initial plan to build and maintain housing and other life-building services for those less fortunate and disadvantaged.

One such man, Albert Power, from the Power PR Management Firm, reached out specifically because one of his employees had had a violent run-in with a sports figure they manage.

While our first instinct is to go out there and rid the world of such men, working out some subtleties to remove the woman from the situation while also not having to completely change her current life was a challenge we happily took on.

Though I got the impression Albert was hoping we would stick with our typical Plan A procedure, he accepted that the best plan was to make this woman unattainable to the player and set up appropriate roadblocks to keep it that way.

With that being the first mission we'd taken on, we're just now feeling comfortable letting loose of the reins we've been holding so tightly to for so long and handing them over to the people we trust most.

So, this concert wasn't just a big announcement for Declan; it was a big announcement for all of us.

I enter Declan's dressing area, mildly surprised by how spacious it is, given this was an impromptu event.

I stick to the wall, watching everyone mill around, taking a few final moments to feel the impact of Declan's words spoken only a few short minutes ago.

Slowly, everyone begins to breathe more easily, smiles shine more brightly, and laughter echoes freely.

I wait until Declan is alone and then make my way over there.

"Great show, Dec." I extend my hand, which he grasps firmly, immediately yanking me in for a hug, and I laugh, going willingly and slapping him on the back.

"It was a little touch-and-go there for a moment. I wasn't sure I'd get through it."

"I'd say you more than got through it."

"It was Issa," he answers seriously. "She got me through it."

I smile, knowing exactly what he means. "She really freestyles her parts on the spot?"

"Oh, yeah. She does it all the time, though it's not as impressive when she does it during an argument."

I laugh, finding this tidbit entirely entertaining while also being relieved Jessica doesn't have a penchant for freestyle rap.

Declan steps close to me, his arm coming around my shoulder as he leans down. I attempt to inch away from him, but his mischievous smile stops me. "What are you doing?"

"Did you get it?" Declan asks eagerly.

I frown, quirking a brow at him as I reply, "Get what?"

He frowns at me, an impatient noise brewing in his throat as he leans in even closer. "Don't play with me, Mathias."

I return his frown, straightening my spine as I bristle. "Honestly, Declan. I have no fucking idea what you're talking about."

He squints at me, then drops his arm and motions for Tony to come over. Tony gives me a questioning look as he strolls across the room, stopping beside Declan, who gets right in his face as he asks, "How about you?"

Tony raises a brow at him and snorts. "What about me?"

"Did you get it?"

"Did I fucking get what?"

Declan scowls, his fingertips tapping on his thigh nervously. He looks from me to Tony and back again.

"What is Declan muttering about now?" Jessica asks from behind me, having just walked over with Carolina.

"I have no idea. He asked me if I got something and then went all weirdo when I said I had no idea what he was talking about."

Jessica frowns, her eyes immediately going to Carolina's, whose eyebrows raise into her hairline, her eyes widening almost comically.

I turn back to Jessica, who's now looking at me with that same wide-eyed expression, and I groan, my eyes going to the ceiling as I say, "What? What did you do?"

She smiles at me humorlessly, her hands coming up as she responds, "Well, I didn't do anything, per se."

"They fucking around again, Matt?" Tony asks from my other side, and I turn to face him, nodding. "Apparently."

Tony steps closer to Carolina, only stopping when his front is pressed right against hers. She doesn't flinch or pull back, but her eyes are wary as she watches him.

He leans in, his eyes on her lips as he says, "Somethin' you wanna tell me, sweetheart?"

She swallows, then shrugs and feigns innocence. Tony's eyes narrow even further. He tsks her, then shakes his head before looking at me. "They're definitely hiding something."

Jessica fidgets, her hands twisting together, and sigh. "You may as well just confess. There's no getting out of it now."

"Yes," Declan chirps. "Fucking confess so I won't look like a complete fucking lunatic for once in my goddamn life."

"We may as well just give it to them," Jessica mutters, nudging Carolina with her elbow. Carolina sighs, then digs into her inside jacket pocket, and pulls out a small piece of card stock.

Jessica slaps her hand on my chest, startling me, and my hand comes up automatically, gripping her wrist firmly. I pull her hand back, a similar piece of card held between her thumb and index finger. I take it from her gingerly, realizing immediately that it's a postcard.

I turn it over and over in my hand, unsure which side I want to focus on first, but finally settle on the front, where typically a picture would be. In this case, it's not a picture at all. Instead, the front is pitch-black with a foiling that's such a deep red it almost blends in.

I move it up and down, allowing the foiling to catch the light, revealing a rose, dripping blood, with two revolvers crossed over beneath it.

I glance at Tony, who's doing the same with his postcard, his brows pinched together in concentration. I close the distance between us, holding my postcard next to his, confirming they're the same exact thing, and then I turn mine over, and he does the same.

The text is different on each card and makes no sense.

ATL AV

2 AM

Suddenly, my postcard is yanked out of my hand, and I yelp in protest as Declan also makes a grab for Tony's, who spits out, "What the fuck, Dec?"

Declan flips both around, eagerly scanning each side before holding them both in one hand. He uses his free hand to dig inside his own jacket pocket, walking across the room to a table where he sets the two postcards down, text side up.

We crowd around him, leaning close as he sets a third card down, which shows tomorrow's date.

Declan is grinning like a fucking lunatic, and I frown in confusion, my heart pounding in my chest at the many implications of what this could mean. "What the fuck does it mean?"

Declan stops grinning, giving me an impatiently grumpy look as he sputters, "Atlantic Aviation, 2 am, tonight."

Tony laughs hollowly and then retorts, "Absolutely not."

"No fucking way, man," I spit out angrily. "There's no fucking way I'm going to a private airstrip at 2 am with no information on why, how, or for whom."

"Come on. It'll be fun."

"No, it's not gonna happen."

Declan turns to Tony, his lips pursed, and I already know he's gonna say something shitty. "Looks like the boy scout is back."

I grit my teeth, annoyed that he knows how to push my fucking buttons so easily. "Nice try, Declan. I don't give a shit what you call me. I'm not stupid enough to get on that plane."

"Tony, help me, man."

Rolling my eyes, I turn my focus to Tony and then immediately groan at the expression on his face. "Oh my god, please don't do this."

Tony shrugs, his trademark smug smile on his face as he crosses his arms over his chest. "I mean, he's not wrong. It could be fun."

"It also could be a death trap."

"If we die, we die," Tony drawls. "It'll be like a final adventure."

"Yeah," Declan adds. "Just think 'what would Darius do'."

"Not a great example, considering the circumstances," I mutter.

They both give me closed-mouth smiles, eagerness shining in their eyes like a pair of puppies. I look to Jessica, hoping she'll throw down some form of defense and insist I not go on this stupid adventure.

But she doesn't, the fucking traitor.

"Fine," I sputter. "But don't go blaming me when we end up blown to kingdom come over the fucking Pacific. Or worse."

Declan shouts excitedly, swooping in and wrapping his arms around me. He lifts me right off the ground, bouncing me up and down excitedly, then sets me on my feet, turning and walking briskly toward the door. "The car's waiting. We better hurry."

I groan, looking up at the ceiling as I curse my entire life up to this point. Tony scoots in close to Carolina, pressing a kiss on her lips. She giggles, kissing him back enthusiastically.

Jessica steps in front of me, placing her hands on my shoulders and rising up on her toes in an attempt to kiss me. I glare down at her, wanting to give her a good spanking for keeping that postcard from me.

She eyes me a bit warily, but then her hand moves from my shoulder to my neck, her thumb stroking down my throat firmly. I try not to respond, but the low growl that forms in my chest is an automatic response I can't seem to control.

The corner of her mouth curves up knowingly, and I sigh, grabbing her by her upper arms and yanking her closer so my breath paints her lips as I whisper, "Don't think just because I'm leaving that I won't punish you later."

She smiles brightly, kissing me lightly and then pulling back to stare up at me mischievously. "I'm counting on it."

I shake my head, bending down to kiss her once more before releasing her.

Tony is waiting by the door, anticipation in his eyes and his demeanor as he shifts from one foot to the other. "Let's go, asshole."

"Shut your hole, fucklicker."

He smiles brightly, putting an arm around my shoulder as he maneuvers me down the hallway toward the open door, where Declan's car awaits. "Aww, fucklicker. That one never gets old."

We exit the building to find Declan waiting impatiently by the car door, which is standing open. He motions for us to hurry, which we don't, and then we stop outside the car door. "Is this a giant fucking mistake?"

"Maybe. Maybe not."

"Only one way to find out," Tony adds helpfully.

Declan climbs into the back of the car, quickly followed by Tony. I pause with one hand on the top of the car door and the other braced on the car's roof.

I look back at the door we just exited to find Jessica, Carolina, and Issa standing there. They smile and wave, and I shake my head, entirely certain the expression on my face is pained coercion.

I take a deep breath. "Fuck it."

Then I get in the car, slamming the door behind me.

57

A Final Adventure

Matt

WE MADE IT TO the airstrip just in time.

While the jet that was waiting for us appeared luxurious, the staff on board was less than congenial. Which under normal circumstances may be alarming, but at this point, for us, we didn't bat an eye in response.

They insisted we keep the shutters drawn the entire flight. And I'm relatively certain that while it felt like the longest flight of my entire fucking life, they spent considerable time flying in circles just to throw us off.

And then, just to add insult to injury, we land in a field in the middle of fucking nowhere.

But at least it's daylight.

We stand there, watching the jet fly off, and I shake my head, annoyed that I let myself be talked into this. "I swear to fucking Christ, Declan. If this is one big trap and we all die in the middle of fucking nowhere, I'm going to haunt you for the rest of your life."

"How can you haunt me if I'm dead?"

I glare at him, poking my finger into his chest as I grit out, "Believe me, I will find a fucking way."

Tony huffs out a breath, his arms crossing over his chest. "So, do you think we literally just got left in the middle of nowhere on purpose?"

"Who fucking knows?" I retort grumpily. "For all we know, the girls got sick of our moping around and came up with this giant ruse just to fuck with us."

Tony's eyes widen, and Declan barks out a laugh. "Oh, shit. That's highly possible."

Tony's lip curls, his hands dropping to his sides. "Carolina likes the box, but I don't know if she likes it so much that she would pull this kind of stunt."

Declan gives Tony some side eye and shakes his head. "Issa doesn't care for the cage, so if this is true, I can't believe she had anything to do with it."

I sigh, rubbing my hands over my face tiredly. "Jessica is highly capable, and I have no doubt in my mind that if she thought the three of us needed a little lesson, she would do it."

Realization settles over all of us, and Tony groans. "Well, aren't we a bunch of fucking daisies?"

"So, do we just wait here? Do you think they're going to come?"

I shake my head, kicking the dirt as if it's going to help. "Not a fucking chance. They won't come for us until we learn some fucking lesson we didn't even know about."

"What lesson do we need to learn at this point?"

"I don't fucking know. But it's in our best interest if we find some sort of path and follow it."

Declan snorts. "So, you think there's some yellow brick road around here or something?"

"No way," Tony sneers. "It would be some bougie color like toasted-teal or crispy-caramel."

Declan jumps toward Tony, slapping his hand over his mouth. "You just shut the fuck up. They're going to hear you, and then we're really going to be in deep shit."

Tony grips him by his wrist, ripping his hand away as he steps away from him. "Hear us how? There's nobody fucking here."

I glance around suspiciously, looking for any indication that we may be being watched. "I'm with Dec on this one. I don't know how, but they would know."

Tony frowns and then groans. "Fucking women."

Declan shushes him again, and Tony rolls his eyes and then walks away. "Well, let's get fucking looking, then. The sooner we find something, maybe the sooner we get the hell out of here."

We spread out, keeping a few feet between us to expand our reach for clues. Declan is on Tony's far side when he suddenly stops. "What in the actual fuck?"

Tony and I walk over to see what he's talking about, then I frown and laugh. "What is that?"

Declan kneels, examining what appears to be a polyurethane slab. Tony and I kneel next to him, and I brace my hands on the ground, bringing my face closer, as I whisper, "Are those actual breadcrumbs?"

"I think they are."

"How fucking peculiar."

I get to my feet, stepping to the end of the slab and peering down at it lengthwise. "Oh, you guys gotta check this out."

They both join me, staring incredulously, and after a moment, Tony mutters, "It's a fucking arrow."

"An arrow pointing in the opposite direction in which we were going."

"Do you think this is for the pilot?"

Tony glares at Declan. "And how would the fucking pilot see this from the air?"

Declan shrugs. "I don't fucking know. Maybe it's illuminated. Maybe you can see this super special product from space."

"Are you listening to yourself, man?"

Declan sighs. "I'm just drawing straws like the rest of you, all right?"

I don't bother responding; instead, I turn tail, heading in the opposite direction. They quickly follow along, and we spread out once again in the hopes we won't miss another clue.

Sure enough, at the far end of the runway, hidden in the shadows, is a rather fancy golf cart with the keys in it.

I eye it suspiciously and then turn to Declan and Tony who are giving it the same suspicious look. "But where do we take it?"

We ignore the golf cart for now, each of us scurrying off, hoping to find a clear answer on where we're going.

It takes a bit of time, but eventually, Tony yells, "Think I got something."

Declan and I run over there, and at first, it appears as if he's standing in front of just another line of trees and underbrush. But then he steps back, pulling a few branches with him, and clear as day, there's a path. "It's not color-coded, but I think it'll do."

Declan takes off toward the golf cart while Tony and I stand here and wait. I don't know about Tony, but there's no fucking way I'm turning my back on this newfound path for fear it will vanish into thin air.

It doesn't take long for Declan to drive the cart back to us, and he immediately vacates the driver's seat, sitting in the back bench seat, giving us an impatient look.

Tony gets behind the wheel, and I maneuver the tree branches out his way and then take shotgun, bracing myself for what I know will be a wild ride because Tony drives a golf cart like he drives any vehicle—as if he has nine lives and hasn't already used up eight of them.

I hold on for my life, but Declan sits in the back, allowing himself to slide back and forth and be jostled around haphazardly.

We come to a steep incline. Tony slows considerably, and about halfway up the hill, Declan exclaims, "There's a fucking cooler back here."

I twist around, frowning at his statement, but sure enough, he starts pulling beverages from beneath the seat. He hands me a bottle of water, which is so cold that it immediately starts to sweat, and my incredible thirst squashes any hesitation I have about drinking this magical cold water.

Tony also grabs a bottle, immediately cracking it open and holding it in the air. "Fuck it."

If nothing else, I don't believe the girls would be intent on poisoning us at this point in the game, but there's always that tiny sliver of not really understanding what's happening that has me swallowing it with a cringe.

The three of us finish the water and then relax some when we hit the crest of the hill with no ill effects. We follow the winding path along a flat area, circling a large rock embankment, which is obviously in the middle of a landscaping project.

Tony stops the cart so abruptly that I'm thrown forward, barely managing to put my hands out in front of me to prevent my face from colliding with the dash.

"What the fuck, Tony?" I sputter.

He doesn't reply, and I glance over him to see him staring wide-eyed straight ahead. Slowly, I turn my head to see what the fuck the problem is, only to be met with what looks like a giant construction project.

There's a finished building farther back in the corner, moderate in size compared to what some of us are used to but certainly big enough for the pickiest person to be happy with.

There are other large buildings scattered across the property, each at a different stage of construction.

After another moment, Tony starts the cart and heads to the finished building. Tony's speed is much slower than it had been previously, allowing us to take in some of the surroundings, and that's when I notice something along the perimeter, which I point out as I ask, "Do you see that?"

Tony and Declan turn in the direction I'm pointing, and Tony nods. "Perimeter fencing. Big time, too, if that barbed wire is any indication."

"Do you think it's a cult?" Declan asks quietly.

I shake my head, my hands coming up in front of me helplessly. "I have no fucking clue, but this seems a stretch, coming from three women who have basically spent every waking minute with us."

Once Tony stops the cart directly in front of the finished building, I hesitate to move. Tony and Declan have no such hesitation, and they both leap from the cart, running halfway up the stairs before Tony turns and gives me a dirty look, motioning for me to hurry.

Begrudgingly, I remove myself from the cart, trotting over and catching up with them just as they hit the door.

Tony grasps the two large handles and pulls them back. "Watch out."

Declan and I step back, allowing him room to open the doors fully, and then the three of us stand there, staring into a large room that is obviously a centerpiece of the building. The entire back wall is glass windows, and the large room sparkles with natural sunlight.

Large sliding doors open out into the back, and the three of us walk there, standing in the open doorway, staring off into the impeccably landscaped backyard.

Movement in the distance catches my eye, and a man appears on the horizon, walking toward us, but I don't recognize him from here. I elbow Tony, motioning in that direction, and he looks over there, at first squinting and then frowning. "Is that Ryan Gray?"

I cock my head, the name being kind of familiar, but at first, not placing it. Then it dawns on me that Ryan Gray was the man who treated Carolina way back in California when she was injured.

Unease bubbles up inside me, and I feel that sharp pain where grief and hope collide.

I take off down the stairs, booking it up the hill, not quite running but on the verge. Ryan doesn't slow when he sees me; he just keeps on walking at the same slow pace, but then he stops, turning and looking behind him as he speaks to someone still on the other side of the hill.

Slowly, a seemingly familiar head appears in my line of vision but then, just as quickly, dips down out of sight. Two loud gasps behind me tell me I wasn't seeing things, that it wasn't a mirage or a figment of my imagination.

I take off at a sprint, not even realizing the sheer distance between us and them. Sure enough, after a few feet, that figment takes shape, and I stop so abruptly that Tony and Declan run into the back of me, almost knocking me flat.

We three stand there, standing abreast, looking on in shock as it all coalesces, a month's worth of agony and despair boiling inside me.

I don't dare move, open my mouth, or blink for fear that time and space will crash, and when I open my eyes, none of this will have been real.

Tony's hand on my arm draws my attention to him, and when I turn to face him, he's staring back at me, wild-eyed. "Is that who I think it is?"

"I think so," Declan replies breathlessly. He reaches a hand out for me, but instead of grabbing me, his hand slides down my arm as he falls to his knees, his eyes squeezed shut in such a manner it's as if he doesn't dare look.

I squeeze my own eyes shut, taking in a few long breaths before forcing myself to open them, and sure enough, the two figures are still there, yet closer now.

Yanking Declan to his feet, we hurry toward them, my heart pounding in my chest, every tear and bellow of agony merging into this one moment.

But then, I stop again. Only this time, Declan and Tony stop with me, both of them realizing at the same moment that things are not as they seem.

"What the fuck are you doing here?" Tony growls.

I grind my teeth, and Declan's hand squeezes my arm as he turns away, his pained expression focused on the back of the house. I know without asking, we all thought the same thing and felt the same moment of relief when hope tried to overtake grief, which makes it hurt all the more.

Bright blue eyes meet mine, matching pain reflected back at me as Agatha says, "I'm sorry. I meant to have you speak to Ryan first."

I deflate. We all deflate.

Whether we want to admit it or not, even before we saw the top of that dark head in the distance, we all thought the same thing.

We were being called home.

58

Split Decisions

Matt

WE ALL REMAIN QUIET as we slowly make our way inside.

Well, except for Tony.

Tony mutters, curses, and kicks the dirt as only Tony can do. But this time, it makes me feel a bit better.

Once we're inside, Ryan and Agatha walk to a sitting area on the far side of the room. They motion for us to sit, and even though I'd rather do anything other than sit, I do so anyway—manners and all.

Sometimes, I wish I was Tony.

At first, no one says a word. Each of us sits there staring at the floor or the ceiling or just off into space, seemingly incapable of coming up with words to explain how we're feeling.

Numb.

Finally, after a long spell of silence, Declan speaks up, his voice strained. "What is all this? Why are we here?"

Agatha lifts her hands in front of her. "This is Dare's dream."

I frown. I look to Tony and Declan, who are both frowning. Turning my gaze back on Agatha, I sigh heavily and then reply, "A dream we never knew anything about."

"Apparently, he'd been planning this for a long time," Agatha replies, her voice devoid of emotion. "He purchased this property like a decade ago and only just started building in the past year or so."

Tony squints, his lips pressing together in irritation for a moment before he opens his mouth and asks, "And where is here?"

"Montana."

Tony grunts in response, hurt evident on his features, though he won't come out and say it. So, I do. "And why the fuck would he keep this from us?"

Agatha sighs. "I don't think he was intentionally keeping it from you. He was just waiting for the perfect moment to unveil it."

"This seems like the worst fucking moment to me," Declan mutters sullenly.

I nod in agreement but then ask, "But why, exactly, did he build this place? Is that explained?"

"According to the documents, it's for all the people out there who've lost hope. For the countless souls who've been saved from one evil bastard or another who need help moving forward."

"We can't hold their hands forever," Tony responds bitterly.

"No, but Dare always thought we could do more," Declan interjects. "He believed that if we had the ability to provide other services, like medical care, mental health programs, proper education, etcetera, it could help people truly overcome their past."

"So, this is a cult," Tony deadpans.

"Oh my fucking Christ, Tony," Agatha sputters. "It's not a cult."

Tony laughs loudly. "Sounds like a cult to me."

Agatha glares at him and shakes her head. "Well, I see you haven't changed at all."

Tony grins at her words, lifting a shoulder nonchalantly. "Why change perfection?"

Agatha's glare intensifies, but the corners of her lips twitch. A laugh catches me off-guard, and I suddenly feel lighter. As if the weight of the world has been lifted from my shoulders, and I can finally take a deep breath.

"I guess it makes sense, but why tell you and not us?"

"According to the documents, I'm the least likely to be affected by his loss, hence I'm the most appropriate to be able to manage the completion of the project without distraction."

I groan, looking up at the ceiling as I process this new information. Then Agatha adds, "I don't know if I was the right person to hand this over to, but it is true that I'm less likely to be swayed by sentiment. Sure, I love Toni and Dare, but my connection to them is different than yours. And frankly, I'm just a different breed entirely due to a lifetime of conditioning to not give a fuck about anything beyond immediate survival."

I nod, knowing this is true. Agatha's upbringing within the organization has shaped her in ways most people wouldn't survive. It's not that she doesn't love or feel pain; she feels it differently. But when she says she loves you, she will quite literally lay down and die for you.

"How long have you been here?" Declan asks.

"A couple of days. Once I'd gone through all the documents and had a decent understanding of what I was looking at, I came directly here."

She stops speaking, her lips pressing together as her breath catches in her throat. She swallows a few times, obviously attempting to get control of her emotions, then, after a deep breath, she continues, "A stupid part of me thought maybe it was all a rouse, that I would get here, and they would be waiting for me."

The room falls silent once more, Agatha likely reliving her disappointment and all of us reliving our own. Finally, I say, "That must've been difficult. I wish we could've been here to support you."

She gives me a small smile. "Probably best that no one actually witnessed any of my ridiculously human behavior."

There's a long pause, and then Declan asks, "And Ryan? How the fuck did he get involved with us?"

"That's a bit of a long story."

"I think we've got fucking time," Tony retorts.

"Oh, I can answer that," Ryan replies. "Not long after I treated Carolina in California, Antoinette reached out to me. She had an inkling I wasn't too excited working for the people I worked for, so she offered me a job. A job with a real mission and a purpose."

I looked to Tony, who seemed less puzzled. "Did you know about this?"

He nods and then tosses his head side to side a bit. "Well, yes and no. Antoinette mentioned that she wanted to see if he'd come to work with us. But I never followed up to see if it actually happened—"

"That's all good and well," Declan interrupts impatiently. "But how the fuck did this guy end up here before us?"

Agatha's lips twitch, her eyes moving to Ryan, who is now looking at the floor. I raise my brows as understanding dawns on me, and I briefly consider not pressing the issue. But then the decision is taken out of my hands when Tony cackles knowingly.

Ryan glares at Tony, which only makes Tony laugh even louder. "So, I take it you were together when this all came to light."

Rubbing his hands over his face, Ryan sighs, then gives Tony a bland look. "Yes, I guess you could say that."

Tony looks at Agatha, a particularly smug look on his face. "And what abo—"

She puts her hand up, her face twisting angrily as she snarls, "Don't even fucking start with me, Tony. I can fuck anyone I want whenever I want, and there's no one on this fucking planet who can tell me any different."

Tony starts to say something further but then snaps his mouth shut and nods. Declan laughs, reaching out and punching him on the arm. "I guess she told you."

Tony scowls and then shrugs. He is not one to take much personally, and most certainly not hard facts from someone he actually respects. "She made a good point, Dec. I'm not foolish enough to argue with that."

Agatha continues to glare at Tony, but then her features relax, and she almost smiles. Tony sighs, relaxing back in his chair. "In all seriousness, Aggie, who brought you the documents?"

She shakes her head, her shoulders lifting slightly as she responds, "I have no idea. They were delivered by courier, and I was unable to locate their absolute origin."

"What do you mean you can't locate where they came from?"

"I've searched, snooped, and even gotten outright belligerent, and there's no trail at all."

"And you're sure they're legal? You're absolutely certain this is the brainchild and property of Darius?"

"Yes," she replies firmly. "I checked and tripled checked. It's all legit."

Declan nudges me with his knee, drawing my attention to him. He's staring at me hard, his eyes gleaming a bit madly, and I shake my head. "No, Declan. Just fucking no."

"Come on, Matt," Declan croons. "Don't be like that."

"Absolutely not. I'm not playing this 'might be' bullshit again."

Declan's eyes move to Tony, the look on his face pleading. "What about you, Tony? I know you're game."

Tony gives Declan an assessing look as he thinks over his response. Then, after a few beats, he says, "Sure, I'll bite."

"So, you think it could be him?"

Tony sighs, his head moving side to side. "Never say never is a motto that has always served me well."

I roll my eyes, annoyance bubbling up inside me at the implication that these two buffoons feel Darius may still be alive and is just hiding from us.

Thankfully, Agatha changes the subject, "How'd Jessica take losing her father?"

I make a face, unsure how to answer the question. Finally, I respond, "That is yet to be determined. I feel it will be something that comes up over time rather than the initial reaction. They had a very complicated relationship, and at the end of the day, he stepped up in a big way. And paid the ultimate price."

"And where does that leave the Irish?"

"Also, yet to be determined."

Her eyes widen almost comically. "So, it's just in limbo? Out in the wild for anyone to steal?"

"No," I reply with a laugh. "On paper, it belongs to Jessica and me, but the idea that we will take it over is absurd. We're taking our time vetting people and will make sure the right person is put in charge before we piss off into the wind."

Declan snorts. "You mean before you piss off to LA to take on an even bigger, uglier endeavor."

"Well, yes. Basically."

"I heard about your sudden change in job description from Jayme. You have this big PR management move that's going to cripple some big names in the industry?"

"That's about right."

"What brought that on?"

"Albert Power had an incident with one of his female employees. He reached out to Declan, who put him in contact with me."

"You take him out?"

"No," I answer honestly. "We relocated her and made it impossible for him to find her."

"And what if he manages to find her? You know how clever those bastards can be."

"Then we deal with him the old-fashioned way," I reply patientl y."Why not just do that in the first place rather than potentially leave her at risk?"

"Because in this industry, we can't just off every person who steps out of line. People are going to notice."

Agatha stares at me for a moment, then sits forward in her chair. "We want to help."

"We?"

"Me and Lils," she responds. "Since we're using The Dead as a front for cleansing the world of human trafficking scum, it would be beneficial to join forces."

"I'm not sure exactly how that would work, but you know we'll always take the support, no questions asked."

She smiles happily, looking exceedingly pleased with herself, but then her eyes narrow, and she frowns as she mutters, "It still doesn't make sense."

Tony and I look at each other, and then I look over at Declan, who's staring at Agatha with the same look of confusion as I'm feeling. Then he asks, "What doesn't make sense?"

"I think I agree with you, Dec," she says quietly, indecision on her face. "I don't want to, and I tried to pretend I don't, but the more I think about it and talk about it, the more inclined I am to agree with you."

My eyebrows raise into my hairline. "What? Why?"

"I have a letter for you guys," she confesses. "I assume from Darius."

"Really?" Declan asks eagerly.

I give him a dirty look and then turn back to Agatha. "And what does that have to do with Declan's delusions?"

"I wasn't going to say anything until after you read the letter because it all seems preposterous, but something just doesn't add up."

"Which something?"

"For example, there's no letter for Antoinette."

"I don't get it," I reply dryly.

"If Darius drafted a letter for you guys just in case he died, there sure as shit would've been a letter for Antoinette, too."

Tony sits up, sliding to the edge of his chair, his expression now as eager as Declan's. "I'm listening."

"And managing to deliver shit to me that I can't trace?"

She's looking at me accusingly, and I hold up both hands defensively. "Don't look at me. I swear on everything I've ever loved that I have nothing to do with anything that may or may not be going on."

She narrows her eyes, her lips pursed as she stares me down. Then, she nods and stands abruptly. "I'll go get it, and we can goddamn well find out."

She heads toward the door, but when she's about halfway across the room, I shout, "Hey, Agatha."

She stops and turns back to me with a questioning expression.

"Did he happen to mention what he wanted to call this place?"

Agatha gives me a questioning look, so I add, "You know. When people are gonna be sent here, where would they say they're going?"

Agatha smiles the first real smile I've seen from her in an age.

Then she replies, "The End."

59

A Parting Word

Matt

It DOESN'T TAKE LONG for Agatha to return with a standard legal-size envelope. She hands it over, and I snort at the *assholes* written on the outside of it, showing it to Declan and Tony, who both chuckle appreciatively because that was just Darius.

Clearing my throat, I read out loud:

> *Hey assholes,*
> *Well, if you're reading this, there's a high probability*
> *I'm dead.*

That being the only sentence on the page, I frown, and then my frown turns into a scowl when I turn the page over, only to find the back is also blank. I open the envelope, finding it empty, and then groan, my urge to throw a very Tony tantrum on the brink of overriding my typically unflappable persona.

I look at Agatha, who's looking greatly amused, and my frown turns suspicious. "What is this?"

She grins and then hands me another envelope. I snatch it from her, this time glowering at the front that reads, *hand this over after they look mad.*

I give her a disgruntled look. "Yeah, well, you didn't have to actually do it, you know."

She shrugs, not looking even the tiniest bit guilty. "Just following instructions to a tee."

I sigh heavily as I rip the envelope open, this time pulling out a page that has writing on both sides. Then I clear my throat and continue.

> *I'm sorry. Writing that and then leaving you hanging totally made me laugh.*

I snort, rolling my eyes at his dickish sense of humor, wishing I could throttle him for messing with me at a time like this. Tony snickers, and I throw him another dirty look, and he at least pretends not to be amused, covering his smirk with one hand as he nods for me to continue.

> *Anyway, I know you have loads of questions, such as, how is this possible? And why haven't I contacted you sooner? Unfortunately, you're just going to have to be content without answers right now because I don't have*

the time or patience to write it all down. I also take great pleasure in knowing it's gonna make you crazy, so that's a nice bonus for me.

For the record, I wasn't going to say anything, but with all the changes going on with you all, it seems to be the ideal time to get my project officially up and running.

Now, I know some of you will think it's crazy and may even consider it to be rather cult-like, but after the sweat, tears, and bloodshed we've put into eradicating the Earth of monsters, it would be a complete disservice to those we've saved for us to stop there.

For those who have been scarred by the atrocities of humankind, the trauma inflicted doesn't end just because their monster has been eliminated. The monsters live on in the shadows, lingering in the deep recesses of the injured mind. For the broken and the aggrieved, the lost and the wounded, the nightmare of their past is a chronic companion in their present-day existence. The only way to not let the monsters win is to provide help for those who are still fighting until they reach a point where they're strong enough to venture out into the wild as a newly rejuvenated version of their true self. To do this, they must always know one thing—they are not alone.

I wish I could divulge more about where I am and what I'm doing, but I don't dare put anything in writing. Keep an eye on your mailboxes as I will do my best to include you in my continued plans to seek and destroy those who want to bring harm to others.

With all that being said, I'm relieved I don't have to waste any time on sentiment and lovey-dovey bullshit,

*but one thing I will say is that I'm entrusting you all
with what is currently known as my legacy, so you better
not fuck it up.*

Take care of each other, as well as those we love.

Dare

P.S. I'll be back.

*P.P.S. If you didn't say that in the Terminator voice,
you're an asshole.*

*P.P.P.S. Don't forget to "Mission Impossible" this note
once you've read it.*

"Yup," Tony retorts. "You're an asshole, Matt."

I glare at him. "No one fucking asked you."

He grins back but says nothing further as we sit there in shocked silence for long moments. After a few sighs, Agatha says softly, "So Declan was right."

Declan is sitting in his chair looking even more morose than he was previously and I reach my foot out, kicking him in the leg. "Why the long face? You were right."

"Yes, and now I'm just pissed."

"Me, too," Tony responds. "That motherfucker sat back and let us mourn his ass for months only to randomly turn up with this 'hey guys, it's me' bullshit."

"Yeah. It does seem kind of dickish," I add. "But Dare doesn't do severely dickish things like this without good reason. And he doesn't mention Antoinette, which is greatly concerning."

Agatha frowns, nodding as she says, "I thought the same. Do you think maybe she's dead dead, and he just didn't want to tell us in a letter?"

I shrug, taking a deep breath through my nose and expelling it out my mouth in a huff. "Could be any number of reasons. We won't know anything until Dare decides it's time."

Tony curses. "God, he's fucking annoying."

I laugh, shaking my head at what a fucked-up turn of events we've walked into.

"What do we do now?" Agatha asks.

Declan, Tony, and I look at each other briefly, each of us nodding because we know there's only one thing we can do. Tony stands, stepping close to me and taking the letter from my hands. He stares down at it for a moment and then pulls a lighter from his pocket before looking over at Agatha with a smirk. "We continue to do what we do best."

She quirks a brow at him. "And that would be?"

I laugh, watching Tony flick the lighter, holding the flame to the corner of the paper, which immediately ignites. We all watch the flames for a moment, and then Tony's smirk blooms into a smile as he looks over at me, flames reflected in his eyes.

"We fuck around."

60

Let's Make a Deal

Matt

THREE MONTHS LATER

It's been a rough few months.

While we found great relief in learning that Darius wasn't actually dead dead, the gaping hole left by his continued absence is still felt every day. And then there's Antoinette and her still unknown fate.

Then there's the fact that this is the first downtime I've had since losing my job. A job I loved—a job I would still love to have if not for my habit of skirting the law basically all the time.

And then, there's Jessica and me. It's safe to say that our fledgling marriage hasn't gone to plan, though that's definitely not for lack of caring for each other. It's just our current circumstances have thrown curveballs that I'm constantly fouling, and she doesn't always take it well—not that she should.

While I understand that no two people are going to get along all the time, the amount of unnecessary bickering we tend to do on a daily basis is bordering on unreasonable.

Don't get me wrong, I know she wants to be there for me wherever she can, and it frustrates her because this isn't a situation where any amount of being there for me is going to help. I also recognize that my tendency to be a closed-off, emotionless bastard is becoming a bigger problem.

And the whole "It's not you, it's me" bullshit only makes it worse.

So, after months of all of us being on top of each other, everyone finally decided to go about their business. Tony and Carolina decided to go on an extended honeymoon. Declan and Issa dove head-first into their new business venture with Power PR Management. I'm relieved that things with Power PR are falling into place, so I'll be able to take a bigger role in the near future, but in the meantime, I know I need to focus on salvaging my relationship.

Even Kaian pissed off into the wind, having to go back home to tend to the family business. Camilla decided to take some private contract in the middle of God knows where.

So, basically everyone has abandoned us. And I know they did it on purpose, considering every single one of them told me specifically to get my shit together or else.

Jessica went upstairs a while ago with the idea she would be taking a bath and relaxing before bed. And me, well, I've been sitting here the entire time, contemplating absolutely fucking nothing.

I call this my deadhead portion of depression. The moment when I have a lull in all the things I can hyper-focus on, and I come crashing down into what can only be described as the pits of despair.

Dramatic, I know, but here I sit.

Glancing at my watch, I shake my head, snorting at my own idiocy. A previous version of me would have immediately followed my wife upstairs to help her in the bath. Yet, here I sit like an asshole, trying to work up the energy to even walk up the stairs.

Don't get me wrong, managing to overcome a mental fog daily in order to go about your business is difficult on a good day. And I know that being sad and angry over the loss of a loved one or a job or whatever may ail me doesn't necessarily make me an asshole, but some days, such as this moment, I feel I could be making a better attempt at not ostracizing my wife.

I grit my teeth, cursing under my breath as I force myself to stand. I plod upstairs on heavy feet, using the banister to half-drag myself upward. I methodically put one foot in front of the other, only managing to trip over the top stair, where I fall face-first.

Immediately rolling onto my back, I lie there with my feet placed on the stairs, my torso across the landing. Then I laugh, having a good chuckle at my own expense.

"Get up, asshole," comes a whisper off to my left. I turn my head toward the sound, frowning to find no one is standing there.

My breath catches in my throat, and for a moment, I choke and then cough. Then I curse some more, once again staring up at the ceiling as I work up the energy to keep moving.

"What the fuck are you doing?" Jessica asks from my right-hand side.

I turn my head toward her, shrugging as I reply, "I was coming to ravage you."

She gives me a completely incredulous look and shakes her head. "Well, I see you're making as much progress as normal. Carry on."

I open my mouth to reply, but she turns and walks back down the hallway, disappearing into the bedroom. I scowl, annoyed that she so frankly called me out, mostly because it's true.

My scowl deepens, as anger bubbles up inside me because true or not, it was kind of a dickish thing to say.

Suddenly rejuvenated, I roll onto my front, get on my hands and knees, and then rise to my feet. I stride down the hallway and into the bedroom like a man on a mission, walking up behind Jessica, who's sitting at her vanity, combing her hair.

She doesn't look at me or acknowledge that I've entered the room. So, finally, I clear my throat and ask, "Is that really how you're going to talk to me?"

Her eyes meet mine in the mirror, her hand holding the comb stopping mid-stroke through her long hair. Slowly, she pulls the comb free from her hair, dropping it on the vanity with a thwack. She visibly bristles, her jaw clenching a few times before she cocks her head at me and says, "You want to rephrase that?"

I glare at her. "No, I don't think I will."

"Are you sure?"

"Yes, I'm fucking sure. Just because I'm going through some stuff—"

"Don't you even fucking start," she interrupts angrily, standing so abruptly the stool she was sitting on topples over. She steps right in front of me, her finger poking me in the chest as she adds, "I'm well aware that you're going through some stuff. I'm right here. I am always right here, ready to support you, to listen to you, to just be there for you."

Her lips press together as she pauses, anger and sadness marring her features, but then she pokes me in the chest again. "You know what, if you want to fucking wallow, you go fucking wallow. But why don't you stay the fuck out of my way while you do it so I don't have to watch you."

My glare intensifies, and this time, I swat her hand away before she can poke me again. "And where do you suggest I do my wallowing, then?"

"I don't fucking care. How about I just leave so then you can wallow at will wherever you want, whenever you want."

"Leave and go where?"

"Who fucking cares?"

"You can't leave, Jess," I retort. "We're stuck together, so just get used to it."

Her eyes widen, and she laughs bitterly. "I can assure you, I'm not stuck anywhere, ever."

"We're married. That means we're entirely stuck with each other."

She shakes her head, brushing by me and walking toward the bed as she replies, "I don't think so. I didn't work this long and hard to end up stuck anywhere I don't want to be."

I turn toward her, taking a few steps in her direction before I stop, the deep ache in my chest intensifying at her words. "What do you mean?"

She turns to me, eyebrows raised as she says, "I'm not stuck anywhere, Mathias. I am not a fucking tree."

"So, you'd leave me?"

She raises her hands in front of her and shakes her head. "Well, I don't see any point in being here. It's not like you're here."

"But I love you," I reply helplessly, having no idea what else to say.

She rolls her eyes and snorts. "And I love you, but I also love myself, and I'll be damned if I sacrifice everything I've worked for to spend the rest of my life feeling like I'm alone with someone else in the room."

We fall silent, and she busies herself, continuing her typical bedtime routine. I stand there frozen to the spot, clearly unsure of how to proceed.

Finally, I whisper, "I don't know what to do."

She says nothing in response. She just pulls the comforter and sheet back and slides into bed without comment.

I stand there for a few more moments, staring at the back of her head, and then I turn and walk into the bathroom. I go about my own sparse bathroom routine, methodically washing my hands and face, stripping out of my clothes. Then I stand there at the sink, staring at my own reflection in the mirror, hardly recognizing myself.

I place both palms on the counter, leaning closer and closer to the mirror until all I see is one giant eyeball staring back at me.

I inhale through my nose, expelling the breath out through my mouth, the one-eyed version of me fogging over until it's nothing but a shadow.

A shadow of my broken self.

Startled, I shove away from the counter, stepping back until I give myself a hard look in the mirror. "What have you done?" I whisper to my reflection, and a sudden twinge of unease zaps through me.

For me, the most difficult stage of grief is my tendency to bury myself in work, to push those painful, gritty emotions down and keep them walled up behind anger, ambivalence, and the deep need to separate myself from that which might hurt me again.

But here I am, hurting myself.

Whirling around, I hurry out of the bathroom into the bedroom, over to the side of the bed where Jessica is still lying with her back to the doorway.

I grab the comforter in my hand, yanking it back, and Jessica rolls toward me, staring up at me, wide-eyed as she exclaims, "Matt, what are you doing?"

I stoop over, gripping her by her arms as I half-drag-half-yank her out of the bed. She manages to get her feet under her, and I use the added leverage to boost her up, my arms snaking around her torso, pinning her arms to her sides as I squeeze.

She's now at eye level with me, and I'm sure I must look like a crazed lunatic as I say, "You can't leave me."

She looks taken aback, and then she frowns and shakes her head. "What? What are you talking about?"

"You can't fucking leave me. I won't have it."

She laughs almost hollowly. "Well, you're not the one who has the final say on that."

My arms tighten further, right to the point where it becomes visibly uncomfortable for her, and her eyes widen further as she squirms in my grip. I lean in close, my nose touching hers as I grit out, "Over my dead fucking body."

She goes to speak, but she can't draw in any air, and only a squeak comes out, so I add, "Let me be crystal fucking clear with you, sugar. If you leave me, I'll make my friends look like docile little lambs."

She narrows her eyes, her squirming turning into an outright struggle. Her knee connects with my thigh once, twice, a little harder each time, so I step closer to the bed, tossing her down on it, and then quickly follow, using the weight of my body to pin her down so she can't escape.

She manages to punch me once in the chest before I snag both of her wrists and pin her arms over her head. She attempts to knee me again, so I straddle her thighs, effectively stretching my torso out over the top of her.

My eyes scan down her body from her angry fiery green eyes to her heaving tits, and my dick immediately hardens against her hip.

I lean over her, licking a path up her stomach, between her breasts to her neck, until I have my face pressed into her hair by her ear.

I settle some of my weight over her, my chest pressing against her tits, so with every inhalation, her hard nipples rub against my skin.

I groan, adjusting my grip so I'm holding both her wrists with one hand. I slide my free hand over her shoulder, along her collarbone to her sternum, and down to her waist, quickly circling back around. Cupping her breast, I pinch her nipple with my thumb and forefinger until she gasps, pushing herself more firmly into my hand.

I groan, intent on moving between her legs, when she suddenly jerks her wrist from my grip, and her hands come up and cup my face. I blink, shaking my head so I can meet her gaze head-on, as she whispers, "Everything will be okay."

I frown, a hot jolt of pained rage zipping through me at her words. I shake my head again, intent on ignoring her, but her grip on my face tightens, and she gives me a little shake as she lifts her upper body off the bed, bringing her face mere inches from mine. "I've got you. It's okay."

At first, her words confuse me because my coming to her in this moment wasn't supposed to have anything to do with me or my bullshit stuff.

I try to pull back, pushing my hands into the mattress in an attempt to extricate myself from her grip, but she doesn't relent. If anything, her grip tightens further, and she uses the distance I put between us to move so she can wrap her legs around my waist, effectively attaching herself to me. I stop moving for a moment, and she hangs off of me, and I laugh then shake my head unsure of what to do at this point.

She uses my moment of confusion to her favor, dropping one of her legs and using the leverage of her foot on the mattress to flip us so I'm on my back.

I lose my breath for a moment, and then I'm staring up at her, the smile on her face nothing less than smug. Her hands go back to gripping my face, a small smile on her lips that sends a rush of warmth through me.

She straddles me, placing a knee on each side of my torso so her pussy is pressing into my stomach instead of my cock. I wiggle around, intent on fixing this, and she tsks at me with her hands on my face, squeezing to get my attention.

My eyes meet hers, and she sighs as she says, "I've given you all the space I'm going to give you."

I frown and shake my head, but when I go to speak, she moves one of her hands from my cheek to my lips. "I don't want to hear any more of your bullshit. I'm going to help you, or I'm going to kick your ass."

I smile against her hand, my tongue flicking out and wetting her palm, but she doesn't flinch or even attempt to remove her hand. So, I nod, hoping I'm relaying what I feel with my eyes since she won't let me have my words.

After a moment, she removes her hand, and then she removes her body from on top of mine, moving to the side so she's lying there facing me with her head cradled on my arm. She grips my far arm with her hand, yanking until I take the hint and roll toward her, and then we lie there facing each other, staring silently.

"How are we going to fix this?" I finally ask, having no other option but to dig in.

"I don't fucking know," she replies a bit breathlessly. "But we will. Slowly and with great care. But we will."

We fall into silence once again, and it's there in that moment while I'm staring into her eyes that I remember.

My answer.

"I had forgotten," I whisper.

She frowns and shakes her head. "Forgotten what?"

I laugh, suddenly feeling weightless, and she raises her brows at me, likely because I sound like a crazy person once again. "You're my answer."

She sighs and laughs, continuing to shake her head, but she doesn't argue or try to move away. I inch in closer so our faces are directly in front of each other, and I say, "Use me."

"Use you for what?"

"Anything you want. Whenever you want."

She gives me an assessing look and then asks, "You mean anything? Like anything, anything?"

"Obviously, I meant sexually. But whatever works."

"So, you're saying you're giving me 100% free use of your body? No rules, no regs, no questions asked?"

I nod, entirely committed. "I'll do anything you want."

She smiles at me wickedly. "So, you're saying pegging is on the table?"

I wince, and she laughs loudly, but I nod. "If that's what you want."

"Why?"

I shrug and then sigh. "Because I need you to take from me what I'm having difficulty giving to you. Everything I have, everything I am is yours, so it's only fair."

She lies there beside me, searching my eyes for a few long moments. And then, after a beat, she nods. "Okay."

I smile, allowing more of that warmth to sneak in as I pull her close, wrapping my arms around her.

I press my face into the crook of her neck and whisper, "Thank you."

Epilogue: Full Circle

Matt

WHEN JESSICA ACCEPTED MY free-use deal, I foolishly figured she would ease her way into it. Instead, she has thrown herself so eagerly into the situation that I fear I may have to put some rules and regs in place.

I can't tell if she's just insatiable or trying to prove a point, though, honestly, I have no idea what that point might be other than I have the stamina of someone a decade younger than me.

I'm not sure how long I can keep that up, but for the most part, I'm willing to accept the challenge.

One thing I can say is that she's certainly doing her best to take my mind off my problems.

We haven't heard anything further from Darius, and we still have no idea on the fate of Antoinette. I know these questions weigh heavily on everyone, and there are some days I'd just rather not do anything.

Luckily, things are already beginning to pick up with Power PR Management, and I know that once it's up and running completely, I'll be busier than ever. That also means that I will likely be doing a fair amount of travel, and with Jessica based in the Los Angeles area, this may prove to be a problem for her.

Not that I want to be separated from her for long, but a lot of her business is still hands-on and requires her to be in the building. Maybe it's her knowing this that has her so amped up to have me on every surface of her office and our home.

Recently, she ended up moving her office to a different part of the building. She hadn't planned on it, but one day, when I was visiting her there, she seemed out of sorts, so I mentioned it.

Most of the time she wasn't consciously aware that she was having any type of reaction to being back in that room. But I could see, looking from the outside, the nuances she had blocked from her own mind.

She had her things moved that same day, and by the end of the week, she seemed to be a different person.

Her new office is bigger and on the top floor. It has an en-suite bathroom and a nice sitting area, and I'm a bit confused about why she didn't move sooner.

And today, our standing weekly plan to meet for lunch, I walk into her office completely unprepared for what I'm going to find.

It takes me a moment to truly comprehend what I'm seeing, and then I immediately turn, closing the door and locking it. Turning back to face her desk, I cock my head, my eyebrows raise, and my eyes open wide. "Did you need something, sugar?"

She smiles as I close the distance between us, stopping beside her and peering down. "I take it that you are to be my lunch?"

She nods, her smile widening as she says, "This is fun, right?"

I chuckle and shake my head. "While I didn't expect to come in here and find you in this position, I'm not unhappy about it."

I step back a few feet, taking in the picture she makes. She's bent over her desk, arms out in front of her with her wrists tied to the corners. I walk behind the desk taking in the sight of her ass in the air, her feet forced apart with a spreader bar that appears to be slightly uncomfortable. I walk behind her, pressing my front against her ass. "Dare I ask who helped put you in this position?"

She giggles, pressing herself back against me. "I think you know the answer to that."

"Do I?" I ask playfully. "It appears you've become rather close to everyone I know."

She giggles again, her breath picking up as she continues to rub herself against me. "Sure, but I wouldn't let anyone see me in this position who hasn't already seen me naked."

"So, you're saying if any of them ever see you naked, then it's fair game?"

"Oh, does this fair use game extend to group stuff?"

I move my hands to her hips, pulling her back against my hard cock, thrusting rhythmically. "Maybe. I mean, technically, that's up to you. I am just here to serve at your will."

I step back a pace, putting some distance between us. She groans in frustration. "I take it you want me to be in charge for lunch?"

She nods emphatically, her ass wagging in front of me as she pants. "Yes. I need it."

I place a hand on her lower back, my other hand stroking and kneading her ass cheek before placing a swift slap on it. She gasps, then moans again, and I repeat the process, this time the crack of my palm on her soft skin sounding through the room.

"I do think you've earned some punishment. You've certainly been going out of your way to test me."

"Test you?"

"Yes. All this jumping on my dick at every turn. It's almost like you're trying to get me to refuse."

"Why would I want you to do that?"

"So, you can gloat. Maybe that's like winning?"

"Hell, no. I've been winning every time I get to have you."

I smile, kneeling behind her and massaging both ass cheeks with my hands. I rub my nose along each side, slowly working my way into the middle, where I blow little puffs of air on her clit. Her legs tremble, her breath catching as she tries to shove herself back onto my face. I quickly pull away, tsking her. "Patience, sugar, or I'll make you wait."

"You wouldn't dare."

I laugh, flicking her clit a couple of times with my tongue before responding, "Oh, I sure as fuck would."

She moans again, muttering under her breath, and I inch closer, stopping a hair's breadth from where I know she wants me. She freezes and holds her breath, and I wait a handful of seconds before asking, "Tell me what you want, sugar."

"Please. Please."

"Please, what? Tell me what you want."

"Eat me. Lick me. Suck me."

I bump her clit with my nose. Then, I press my lips against it, chuckling so she'll feel the vibrations.

She moans wildly, undulating her hips in an attempt to get more friction. I let her have her way for a moment, helping her out by laying the flat of my tongue against her. I remain firm against her, letting her rub against me at will until she's panting and moaning, begging me to stay there and not to move.

And then I move.

She shrieks in frustration, fisted hands banging on the desk, even with what little leeway the restraints provide.

Excitement builds in my chest, my cock hardening even further in my pants at the thrill of torturing her. I may enjoy the time I spend being a good boy, but that doesn't mean I don't also enjoy flipping the tables, making her curse and scream.

I rise to my feet, moving to the lower right-hand drawer of her desk and sliding it open. She cranes her head around, trying to see what I'm doing, and I slap her ass again. "Mind your business, sugar."

At first, she ignores me, trying harder to see, so I slap her again. "Do as you're told, or I'll make you wait longer."

She chokes out a curse but eventually faces forward again, her feet shifting back and forth anxiously. I turn my focus back to the drawer, reaching all the way in the back, beneath a bunch of papers, I pull out the small bag I have hidden there.

I move back behind her, opening the bag and dumping its contents in my hand. She attempts to look again, and I give her one more slap. She glares at me before turning forward again.

I open my hand, looking down at the small bottle of lube and the butt plug, smiling proudly. We haven't done a lot of anal play, so the plug I got is small, just a little tease to spice things up. I pocket the butt plug, open the lube, and dribble it down between her ass cheeks. She tenses, a gasp falling from her lips as I smear the warming liquid around, focusing on her asshole.

I smear the liquid around, adding a little more as I probe her asshole, slowly sinking my finger in further and further. Once she's prepped appropriately, I remove the plug from my pocket, adding more lube to the end of it before pressing it against her back hole.

At first, she tenses up, then I use my free hand to rub her lower back and massage her hip, moving over to her ass cheek and pulling it aside, squeezing rhythmically.

After a while, she relaxes, her breath and gasps increasing rapidly as she begins to push back. She forces the toy to slowly penetrate and then slides easily up to the base, the bulbous end staying in place.

"Holy shit," she moans. Her body is trembling. She looks back at me, blatant want on her face, and I look between her eyes and the toy in her ass, one hand stroking her hip while the other goes to my belt. "Do you like that, sugar?"

She replies breathlessly, "Yes. I love it."

"You want more?"

"Yes. Yes."

"Tell me what you want, sugar."

"I want your cock."

"Want it where?"

"In my pussy. In my mouth. Anywhere. Everywhere."

I smile, unbuttoning and unzipping my pants, pushing my boxers down enough to free my cock. I consider moving around the front, shoving my cock down her throat. But one glance at her glistening pussy changes my mind.

I dribble lube along my cock, cap the bottle, then toss it on the desk. I rub the tip of my dick along her pussy, tapping her clit a few times before shoving inside a few inches. I slide in a little more, pushing against the toy in her ass, enjoying her choked sounds of pleasure.

I slide in all the way until my pelvis is pushed up against her ass cheeks, then I pull out, shoving in sharply and enjoying the slap of my balls against her clit.

Reaching my hand around her front, I press my slick fingers against her swollen clit, thrusting in and out of her slowly, methodically, as my fingers stroke and pinch her sensitive flesh.

I work her up to a frenzy and then immediately withdraw, taking great pleasure in her frustration. I do it again and again until she's a sweating, drooling mess bent over her desk.

And then I stand there stroking my dick, watching her as she curses me.

She's on a roll, calling me every name in the book, a rather vicious verbal attack if I do say so. Nonchalantly, I stroll up to the front of the desk, pulling the quick release on one of her wrists before grabbing her by the hair at the nape of her neck, my other hand gripping her chin. "I think that's just about enough of that."

She opens her mouth, likely to send another volley of insults at me, but I take this for the opportunity it is, pushing the tip of my dick between her lips.

I shove in all the way to the back of her throat, cutting off her air and her words, knowing that with one of her hands free, she can stop me at any time.

Her hand touches my hip, and I pause, waiting to see what she'll do. When she doesn't pinch me, I continue.

I don't go easy on her. I shove into her throat over and over, intermittently remaining pushed inside until she chokes and gags around me. Then I pull out, allowing her to take one gasping inhalation, drool flying everywhere, before thrusting back in, over and over again.

Tears and mascara streak her face, and the warmth in my chest explodes. Knowing I'm the only one she'll take it from. Knowing she becomes this needy, desperate version of herself only for me.

Just like she's the only one who gets the good boy in me.

I slide back into her throat, pushing deep until I feel her hand on my hip again. I consider waiting, consider forcing her to give up. But then, at the last second, I pull out and step away from her.

Her head hangs down, drool, snot, and tears falling on the floor, and I smile in satisfaction. Then I move to the wrist that's still bound, pulling the quick release.

I walk around the desk, bending and releasing her ankles from the restraints and bar. Then I stroke my hands up her back, moving to her shoulders as I urge her to sit up. She does so slowly, using her hands on the desk to push herself upward until she's standing precariously.

I scoop her up into my arms and walk around the desk. She says, "What are you doing?"

"Taking care of you."

She stiffens in my arms, pushing against my chest halfheartedly. "But I want—"

"Don't worry, sugar," I interrupt in a soothing tone. "You will."

She smiles tiredly, relaxing into my arms as I walk across the room to the sitting area.

I move to set her on the sofa, but she wraps her arms around my neck and shakes her head. Smiling fondly, knowing exactly what she wants, I instead bypass the sofa, moving to the chair in the corner where I fall back into it with her in my lap.

She lies there for a moment, cuddled close, and I wish I had taken the time to remove my shirt.

As if she can read my mind, she moves back, yanking at my dress shirt, so I sit up, unbuttoning the top two buttons, pulling it over my head and tossing it to the side.

She comes back close, rubbing her cheek against the skin of my pectoral muscle, and I wrap my arms around her, my hand resting on the curve of her ass. I give her a moment to relax and then slide my hand over, my middle finger tap, tap, tapping the toy still in her ass.

She moans a quiet gasp of pleasure and then squirms.

I move both my hands to her hips, nudging her until she sits up, shifting around so she's straddling me. She moves off enough to yank my clothes out of the way and grips my dick in one hand, lining herself up and sinking down slowly.

I inhale sharply, pressing my hips up, enjoying her clinging walls gripping me tightly. She sits fully, rocking her hips so she's rubbing her clit against my pubic bone. I move both of my hands to her ass, playing with the butt plug as she rocks over me.

Her hands move to my shoulders, and she straightens, expanding her range of motion to slide and down a few inches. One of her hands starts to slide down my chest, but knowing what she's going to do, I move one of my hands between us, my fingers stroking her clit, pinching and teasing as she rides me.

She smiles, her head falling back on a moan, and I rest my head on the back of the chair, my eyes closing as I focus on the feel of her, the sounds she's making, and the smell of her.

"Look at me."

My eyes open immediately at her words, meeting hers, normally a soft green, now darkened by desire. Her hands move to the hair at the back of my head, tugging gently before moving around to cup my cheeks. She leans in, feathering a kiss on my lips, then kissing a line down along my jaw to my neck, where she sinks her teeth in.

I shudder, my hips bucking up erratically, and she leans in closer, trapping my hand between us. She grinds against me, my dick pushed all the way inside her, her clit rubbing against my knuckles.

She works her way back up until she's at my lips again, and her hands move down to my neck, feathering lightly and then stroking more firmly. Pleasure overflows in me, and I know I'm done for, so I grit out, "Do it. Fucking choke me already."

Her lips curve up. Her eyes are feral as her hands slide back so her fingertips grip the back of my neck, her thumbs squeezing the sides and along my throat. She leans in, the grip strength exercises she's been doing obviously paying off as she immediately restricts my breath and blood flow.

I choke and gasp on a broken sob, my hips pumping up into her rapidly, my hands gripping her, pulling her into me as I shove up inside. She grinds against me, losing all rhythm as she presses her lips against mine, eating the choked noises falling from my lips.

She pulls back slightly. "Look at me. Fucking look at me."

My eyes open halfway, and I stare up at her, a half-choked sob falling from my mouth into hers. She tilts her head back briefly then her head rolls forward and her eyes meet mine again, "That's right. Come for me. Give me my prize."

My grip on her ass tightens, and I shift so my foot is braced on the floor, using the leverage to rut up inside her like a fucking animal. She sobs with pleasure, her body shaking as she starts to come apart.

White hot euphoria shoots down my spine, right into my balls. My dick throbs and pulses in her pussy, erupting inside her as the pressure reaches a peak and shatters, just as her hands suddenly release my neck. I take in a loud, ragged breath, and pleasure boomerangs inside me. I can't tell if I come again or I'm just still coming.

I thrust up into her until her sobs ebb, and she's a boneless, quivering mess in my lap. She leans heavily against my chest, her hands tucked between us. I stop moving, relaxing into the chair, my arms coming up and wrapping around her snugly. I press my head against the back of the chair, craning around to look at her face, and then I mirror the small smile on her lips, the sigh that falls between us.

We remain like that, pressed tightly against each other, as that gentle silence echoes around us.

After a while, she stirs in my arms, and they tighten, my head falling forward so I can press a kiss against her forehead. "Not yet. Just stay."

She settles immediately and then giggles quietly as the mess between us increases. I ignore it completely, unconcerned while also grateful for the shower in her en-suite bathroom.

More time passes, both of us quietly lost in our own thoughts, but then she shifts again, rolling back so she can look up at me. "What do we do now?"

It's a question we've both asked many times over the last few weeks. While things have started to change, I have come to accept that none of this will ever be easy. And I don't mean our relationship; I mean this whole new dynamic within our extended family.

In the beginning, we all attempted to pretend that things weren't different, that the void in the room had no bearing on our everyday existence. But it didn't take us long to realize this exact mentality was what was destroying us all.

So, we've been working to change our mindset, adjusting our goals, putting in place new processes and procedures in the hopes that we'll be better prepared in the future for whatever may be thrown our way.

Jessica pushes her finger into my chest, getting my attention, and when I meet her gaze, she says, "Have you heard from Kaian lately?"

I laugh and nod. "Yeah. Apparently, Cami is giving him a hard time."

Her eyes widen comically, and she giggles. "Well, that sounds like a good time."

I laugh and nod because I would love to be a fly on the wall for when those two are forced into facing their real feelings for each other.

"I'm sure when she gets back from whatever weird assignment she's on, we'll find out exactly how entertaining it's going to be."

She laughs again and then falls silent, cuddling back into me, and then her breath catches, and I squeeze her even more tightly. "What is it?"

She presses her hand against my chest, her fingers flexing rhythmically. "Do you feel that?"

"Feel what?"

"That magnetic pull. The tangle of electricity."

I smile, the warmth like an inferno in my chest. "What does it mean?"

"I have no fucking idea."

"Should we be worried?"

Her lips curve up, her eyes glowing with emotion. "Probably."

"Will that stop us?"

"Fuck, no."

I smile, allowing myself this brief reprieve from the chaos that usually chases us. She leans into me once more, her hands tucking in, and I wrap my arms around her snugly, pressing my face into her neck.

And then, for the first time in a very long time, I breathe.

THE END

Well, I did it. I wrote five books. And this one legit traumatized me, I am not even exaggerating. I wrote the ending like four times and each time it was more painful. I'm not sure what I thought I was getting into when I decided I was going to write a book, but I know it was not this tendency to bleed all over the page while praying it comes out even remotely coherent.

I have a lot of people to thank from one book to the next, but for the sake of space I'm going to narrow this down to THIS book.

To you, the readers: thank you for taking the time to read this book. Some of you already know I sometimes poke fun at negative reviews, but you should also know I appreciate everyone who takes a chance on my books regardless of the star review they may leave. Continue to read what you love, and love what you read.

My family: I think the whole schedule is easier with this new process, even with my soul-crushing self-imposed deadlines. But thank you for continuing to humor me.

Jess: How is it October and we've not gone on one trip? ILY.

Heather and Sara: Thank you for dragging me out of my hole for some old school friend time. Even if I did spend an entire day of our trip finishing this dumbshit book. ILY. A3S4E.

Layla Towers: It's been two years since I asked you if you'd like to take a look at a book I was writing. Can you believe it? ILY4E.

Still Censored: Carolina Jax & VR Tennent — Still saying what I say with my whole chest. Keep going. ILY.

Issa: I will forever be thankful for Declan and forever grateful for your friendship. ILY.

Kayla: This thing needs GIFs to explain our lives together. ILY.

Sam/April: Y'all are nuts for doing what you do, but I appreciate you. ILY.

Smutty Author Resources: Thank you for continuing to promote Indie authors!

Manda: I truly appreciate the time you put in to transcribing this book. I wish I could afford hazard pay because listening to the sound of my voice for hours is hard. ILY.

My ARC Team: You're the best. Lots of bad jokes and ridiculous polls to come.

My Street Team: I appreciate every post you make, even the ones the apps doesn't tell me about.

Extra special shoutout for sweeping up behind me when this book attempted to take me down. **Anne, Annette, Cami, Christina, Jacklyn, Stacey.**

Kirsty McQuarrie with **Let's Get Proofed:** We got it down to the wire. I mean, it's still fine...everything is fine...

M. Losinski: For taking the time to send me an email explaining how and why my work is valued. It's shocking how easily we get swept up in the negative, and this particular email came in exactly when I needed confirmation that what I'm attempting to do has not been overlooked. Always appreciate your insight and kindness.

An Open Letter To My Brother:

Dear A-Hole,

On release day of this book, you'll have been gone two days short of 27 years.

So that's means (yes, I'm going to count again) that you've been gone for 9860 days, or 236,640 hours, which shockingly is still around 14 million minutes.

300 million breaths.

1 billion heartbeats.

You've been gone so long that somedays I can't decide if I remember us as we once were or if I'm daydreaming what we will be, come the end.

There were moments while writing this book where I had to take a step back and tell myself "no, you can't do that" because the story of this found family isn't dictated by the losses of its scribe. I don't get to fashion a pretty little ending for them just because I didn't get the pretty little ending I wanted.

And still, it hurt me.

Never in my short writing career have I ever been so conflicted by a story written by my own minds eye. Many times, I was utterly flayed open, my guts splashed all over the pages, on the very cusp of quitting because as I already said, it hurt me.

And I know you're to blame.

Every time one of my fictional characters feels pain, it hurts me. My writing process doesn't allow me to see the future, so everything occurs in real time as I have no vision beyond what has happened in that moment. I cackle with every laugh; I curse every curse. I feel every cut, I cry every tear, and I scream every scream.

It's as cathartic as it is traumatizing and most days, I wear my tattered cape like a hard-earned badge of honor because I know my ability to convey great emotion is a direct reflection of the great losses I've endured.

Many people will appreciate what I've attempted to do with my books. Some people will fall down into the abyss of my creativity and wallow there with me before eventually coming up for air, ready to fight their own demons in whatever capacity they reasonably can.

Obviously, we can't throw grenades or do any of the incredibly illegal shit my characters do, but we can love and protect and support each other. We can learn to forgive and heal and move on at whatever pace we're capable of.

We can reassure and show people that they're not alone. We can remind ourselves that we are not alone.

This doesn't mean that we no longer feel the pain, that some days the pain isn't just as agonizing as that very first cut. This doesn't mean we forget those we grieve, or we pretend to no longer be touched by that which previously destroyed us. This doesn't mean we carry on our everyday existence completely free of our past sufferings, free of the monsters who may haunt us, free of the constraints of time and space and the inevitable counting of breaths and heartbeats.

This simply means we allow ourselves the freedom to grow. We allow ourselves grace to fail. We forgive our many mistakes while still looking ahead to a future that is not already written for us. We look ahead to a future we're still actively writing because we alone have the power to forge a new path in our own personal redemption story.

We accept all this while carrying you with us. Whether "you" is a lost sibling or loved one, or "you" is yourself—the "you" who has been lost for far too long.

Because in the words of Declan Hughes—at the end of the day, everything I have to say, comes down to the simplest of sentiments...

I miss you
Come back

I love you.
Your a-hole sister,
(no)Mercy

Also by

Want to see more of Kaian and Camilla? You can find their story in the
All Shades of Romance Anthology!

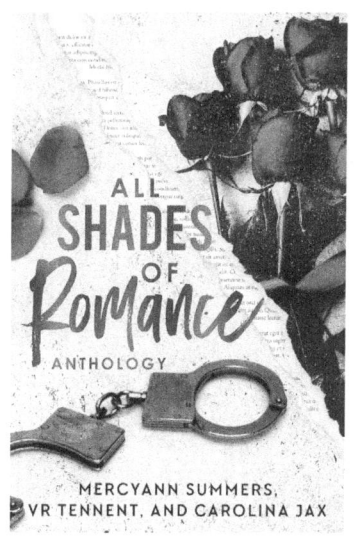

Have you missed the rest of the ends series? Make sure to grab them
to get the full story!

Made in the USA
Columbia, SC
16 September 2025

62194374R00300